TRANS TASMAN WARS

SCROLL 1

THE GREAT COMPETITION

Meadehampstead Publishing

Copyright © Shaun Clements 2018.

All Rights Reserved

ISBN: 978-0-6482265-2-9 Paperback
ISBN: 978-0-6482265-0-5 Paperback
ISBN: 978-0-6482265-1-2 Kindle

**MEADEHAMPSTEAD
PUBLISHING**

TRANS TASMAN WARS

SCROLL 1

THE GREAT COMPETITION

NEVILLE NAZZARI

CHAPTER 1

The information from this translation of Scroll 1 is not intended to amuse politically correct do-gooders, and it may be offensive to feminists. It touches on subjects that some might prefer to sweep under the carpet or ignore completely.

It was bloody hard working out where to start all this, but I think I'd better kick off with Merl Malloy, and hopefully things will pick up from there. If you continue reading this all the way to the end, you'll never – ever – be the same again.

Anyhow, Merl Malloy's a Kiwi sheila who goes around telling everyone she's an 'Irish Colleen', and when she tells people that, there are those – supposed experts on the Irish – who reckon her fake Irish accent's seriously crappy.

She first came to just about everyone's attention in the West Aussie outback some years ago because she was a barmaid and was said to be fairly slack. With regard to the latter, she has a reputation for being a nympho! Just about every driller and drill offsider I bumped into, from the Eastern Goldfields – the seaside town of Esperance – all the way to the Pilbara – reluctantly confessed to having know her intimately! She also must have a penchant for uniforms since nearly every single cop serving in the bush – plus some married ones – has been overwhelmed by her rather dubious charms.

She certainly isn't all that much to look at; nevertheless a member of the fairer sex in the outback with just a hint of lipstick or makeup on – and when you get a lonely, randy bloke who's had a gutsful of either

Swan Draught or Emu Export – any example of the female gender can honestly be a treasure to behold! Especially if you've been in the bush after a couple of months with no female company other than the odd roo or emu. A barmaid in an outback pub can take on almost celestial proportions! Even such a woman as Merl!

While one of the police sergeants in charge of the Laverton cop shop reckoned she has eyes like two piss holes in a salt lake, my younger brother Trev, who's not well known for his charity, insists that they look identical to those of a pig that's just been stabbed in the arse with a pitch fork! It's this same little brother who first started calling her 'Jabba the Hutt'; a nickname that has stuck with Merl throughout Western Australia.

It's a fairly accurate label, too, as her puffy cheeks do kind of resemble those of a bull frog. She's short – maybe five feet nothing. Chubby arms and legs with a backside turning to serious fat. She has boobs like rock melons, plus a bit of a pot gut. When I first saw her, she was well and truly teetering on obesity. Her face is fat, and her hair varies on occasions from blonde to black. Like take for instance when she was a barmaid at the White House Hotel in Leonora she was a blonde, then while working at the Menzies pub she'd dyed her hair black.

It was from a short stop at the old gold mining town of Menzies that I first got to talk to her when she was on her own. My brothers and I were drilling for gold on Riverina Station at the time when my elder brother Kev sent me into Menzies to wait for a courier to come past with a couple of new drill bits. Kev also warned me that he'd bite my scrotum off if I went into the Menzies pub and got on the piss, but, what the hell, it was bloody almost forty-two degrees Celsius in the water bag! A couple of middies were hardly going to touch the sides – were they? Besides, a barmaid, who was presumed to be a nympho, was actually toiling at the Menzies Hotel!

Merl had just put down an icy cold middy of Emu Bitter in front of me, when she insisted on knowing my name. When I told her that it was Neville Nazzari – or 'Nev' for short – she said she knew another bloke by the name of Nazzari, and then muttered something about wanting to remove his nuts with a blunt pair of scissors; regardless if the law of the land outlawed such behaviour! A kind of sixth sense alerted me that it might've been Trev who'd been up to no good, but I wasn't going to go out of my way to tell her that we were related. Trev has a habit of pissing off any number of sheilas.

Then she started working on me. After pouring me another middy and refusing payment, she asked if I could run her down to Kalgoorlie. When I hastily declined, she wasn't going to take no for an answer: "Ah, come on, Nev – Kal's only an hour or so from here if you put your foot down. Just drop me off at the Tower Hotel. It'll only take a couple of hours max'."

"Bullshit!" I disagreed with her. "Kal's over a hundred and thirty K's from here. With the cops swarming all over the place, I'll get done like a dinner. If my older brother finds out, he'll rip my bloody arms and legs off."

She still wasn't about to be put off that easy. "Is Kev Nazzari your elder brother?"

"Yeah, where do you know him from?"

"I bumped in to him and Trev in the Conglomerate Hotel up at Nullagine. How come you weren't with 'em?"

"Stuffed if I know. I must've been on another rig."

She demonstrated that she knew a fair bit about the drilling game, when she pointed out the front door of the pub. "That your Land Cruiser ute? You only got that, the drilling rig and a support truck?"

"Yeah."

"How the fuck's Kev gunna find out? He's hardly gunna come and look for you with the drill or the support trucks. The courier can drop the drill bits off at the pub here, and you'll be back before you know it. . . Go on, Nev – I'll really make it worth your while."

The glint in her eye immediately caught my attention. "How you gunna do that?" I demanded.

"Let's get down the road a bit and you'll see."

She was staring at my crutch!

It was when we were driving past Lake Goongarrie on the way to Kalgoorlie when she put her right hand on my left leg! Now, I won't go into the sordid details as I'm a fairly shy sort of a bloke, and I doubt if people are interested in others getting blowjobs. If there was one item that I found most extraordinary, it was when Merl took her false teeth out to do the job, and she had a full set – both top and bottom! What was different about them was that they seemed to have three horizontal layers of different colours. First there was the pink, gummy layer. Next came a layer of dark-olivey-mustard, and the bottom layer was orangey-yellow! Trapped between the front teeth looked to be grey, cheesy material and black, wiry hair. Possibly pubic hair!

Let it suffice to say that the only sex I'd had up till then was in Kalgoorlie's brothels; all of which had been paid for in advance. Except one time when the boss and owner of our drilling outfit shouted a couple of drillers and offsiders, plus me a free jump one Christmas at the Pink House in Hay Street; an establishment that's been going nearly a hundred years or more. Hay Street's brothel's are under financial duress ever since the Asian prostitutes moved in with their mobile phones; however I've been told you have less chance of getting the clap in an established brothel, and, if you look for sex elsewhere, you can pick up anything.

Nevertheless, I wasn't going to allow the state of Merl's false teeth to trespass on such an auspicious event! I used my best endeavours to ignore them.

I'd often fantasised about getting a blowjob, and had thought about offering extra money to a prostitute to give me one, but I'd never had the guts to come out and ask for it. As a matter of fact there's this one mate of mine, Jeremy Johnson, who offered an extra fifty bucks to a Hay Street hooker for a blowjob; however he was soon told 'don't be fuckin' stupid!' Not long after I was informed by another driller that only Asian prostitutes gave blowjobs if you paid them a bit extra; even so I've never been game to go down that route, either.

With all that aside, it can get bloody hot in the Eastern Goldfields! On the day that I carted Merl down to Kalgoorlie it was well over forty degrees Celsius. In order to combat the searing heat outside, the windows in the Land Cruiser were wound up tightly shut and the vehicle's air conditioner was going full blast. The Broad Arrow pub was just coming into view when suddenly there was an overpowering stench in the cab! Bloody hell – it was as if someone had just shit themself!

I was at a total loss of what to do, but Merl had her window down in a flash. "Fucksakes – Nev!" She yelled out with a grin from ear to ear. "I'd have to crap myself to beat that one!"

I was both embarrassed and confused! There was no way that I was responsible for the stink, yet I couldn't come to terms that it might've been *her!*

All doubts were soon expelled when I pulled up in the drive-through bottle shop at the Tower Hotel in Kalgoorlie. Merl reached over, kissed me on the cheek, and then she disappeared into the pub. Her breath was identical to the stench that had filled the Land Cruiser's cab! There was no mistaking it!

I managed to get back to Menzies no problem, and much to my relief the courier still hadn't dropped off the drill bits at the pub. It was getting late afternoon, so Kev could hardly object if I had a couple more middies. The temperature was still in the forties, and it looked like we were in for a bloody hot night as well. Our caravan out on the drill site had no air conditioning, so I purchased a couple of bags of ice and packed them around a carton of Emu Export stubbies in an esky that was sitting in the tray of the Land Cruiser. Finally the bits arrived and I headed out to Riverina Station.

"Where the fuck you been?" Kev was still standing by the controls of the rig when I got out to the drill site.

I wasn't having a bar of that kind of attitude. "What the fuck do you mean – where've I been?"

He tapped his watch. "Look at the fuckin' time – you've been away for nearly eight hours! The bit I'm using is just about fucked."

"The courier only pitched up after four," I protested. "It wasn't my fault I had to fuckin' hang around."

Kev cheered up no end when I showed him the esky full of ice and Emu Export stubbies. We normally drilled till it was almost too dark to see, but not on that particular shift.

I suppose when a bloke's been given the first free sex in his life, and a blowjob at that, it's not extraordinary if he should want to skite about it. I waited till we got back to town before I mentioned it to Trev.

"Ah fuck – not Jabba!" He certainly wasn't impressed. "I hope you washed your dick after? Don't you bloody come near me – you never know what I might catch off you."

That's fairly typical of Trev; however I took a poke back at him. "When I told her my name, she reckoned she knew some other bloke by the name of Nazzari. Reckoned she'd like to cut his balls out. I doubt if it was Kev, so it had to be you – Trev. You shag her or something?"

His look of shock and horror was clearly exaggerated. "I wouldn't touch her even with yours. I wouldn't be able to hack her breath. She fart in the vehicle when she was with you? She'd kill a fuckin' brown dog with those farts of hers!"

Another two principal characters in my story have to be my brothers Kev and Trev. Now I know it sounds really corny – three brothers – Kev, Nev and Trev. Especially when you consider that we come from a dinky di Italian family with the surname of Nazzari. My old man Roberto Nazzari's folks came over from Italy just before the Second World War when he was still in nappies, while my Mum, Lena Battaglia's grandparents arrived from northern Italy just after the First World War. My brothers and I are all Boulder born and bred. We also have three sisters: Louisa, Bella and Sophia.

And how did we brothers end up with such names? You might have to blame it on Mum. Although we come from Italian stock, she wanted her sons to be more 'Aussie' than the Aussies themselves. Her granddad had told her about the race riots in Kalgoorlie and Boulder on Australia Day back in 1934. Her old man's shop in Boulder's Dingbat Flat was burned to the ground by the outraged and rioting Aussies who'd taken a set on all Italians and Slavs because they reckoned that the mines on the Golden Mile were giving the Europeans or 'New Australians' much higher pay than what the ordinary Aussies were getting . Also that the 'dings' and 'wogs' were doing lines for Aussie women, and that was considered a most outrageous taboo back in those days!

It certainly wasn't Dad's idea giving us such names. Dad scarcely went to school and he was brought up speaking both English and Italian; although he can hardly read or write a word of either language. The first and last job he ever got on the Eastern Goldfields was wood cutting for the gold mines' steam engines and power stations. Cutting wood when he was a young bloke must've been bloody hard yakka. They certainly didn't have chainsaws in those days, and you only got paid for the wood you cut with an axe. Nevertheless, his career on the wood line was pretty short-lived, for he was riding pillion passenger on his mate's motor bike when they came a gutser out on the Mount Monger Road. Dad's leg was seriously buggered up and he's been on an invalid pension ever since. Being unemployed has never really sat well with him, and he has more or less become a hermit. He doesn't want people down the street seeing him as a bludger, which some of the bastards around Boulder tend to do. He doesn't drink, smoke or drive a car; unlike his three sons.

Dad being a sort of recluse has had quite an impact on Mum. She's also fairly shy and sticks close to home. The only time she goes up the street is on her three-wheeler pushbike when she needs groceries. It's a real treat for her when one of us kids takes her in a car to the big shops like Woolies and Coles in Kalgoorlie.

I'm prepared to bet big bucks it's my Uncle Mario on Mum's side of the family who came up with the names Kevin, Neville and Trevor. He's a smart-arsed old wanker, and if he wasn't our uncle and Mum's favourite brother, either I or both of my male siblings would've given him a smack around the ear on more than one occasion.

Then again, I'm prepared to wager quids that Dad had a hand in choosing our middle names. Kev has the middle name Giuseppe after Dad's grandfather who died back in Italy. My middle name's Giacomo; however both Mum and Dad have cousins with that name back in the home country; both also having karked it some years ago. Or perhaps my middle name was given to me in order to honour Giacomo Puccini?

7

My dad loves his wonderful operas! Trev's middle name is Carlo. Mum might've contributed to that, what with Carlo Ponti being her idol, plus the fact that he was a famous film producer and husband of Sophia Loren. Maybe also since Dad believes that all blokes involved in the movie industry are mostly gay, anyway. He's a bit old fashioned like most goldfields blokes – in the outback homosexuals are by and large regarded as being blokes to stay away from.

So, getting back to Kev and Trev. Although they're much more outgoing than Mum and Dad, these two blokes are absolute – total – opposites! In every way whatsoever! For starters, Kev's a big man like Dad. Not big – huge! Gigantic even! With his leg being mangled, Dad hasn't been able to get around too good, so he's piled on the weight; whereas Kev's absolutely massive and he's all muscle. Not like those body builder freaks – he's just hugely big and muscley! He may be only five feet eleven inches tall, but he's built like a brick shithouse! And he's bloody strong to go with it! I've met some horribly tough jokers in the drilling game, but I've never come across someone who can lift a full forty-four-gallon drum of diesel onto the tray of a Land Cruiser. Kev does it on a regular basis without giving it a second thought! He's got nondescript brown eyes like Dad, plus the same shaggy, brown hair. Kev and Dad are similar in that neither of them ever had any time for school and they both loath school teachers with a passion.

They also have an obsession for the past. Kev's pride and joy is a 1969 model Holden Belmont HT utility that's almost in mint condition. You get him going, and he'll spend hours extolling the virtues of the red motor, and then he'll go into great detail of why all modern Holdens are a heap of shit after they started making them out of plastic and putting 'foreign made' engines in them.

Dad's infatuation for the past goes even further back. What gives him the most joy are the kitchen utensils he inherited from his parents – the bone-handled cutlery – the crockery – the stainless steel pots and pans – soup ladles, tongs, frying pan etceteras. All manufactured before the Second World War! If you really want to fire him up, you just have to mention the 'Chinese crap' that's on sale in a good many Australian department stores. Supposedly stainless steel cutlery that rusts after spending one night in the dishwasher that Kev and I bought Mum for Christmas. Cooking pots where the copper bottoms peel off once heat's applied to them, plus the plastic 'toxic shit' that's bought as toys for grand kids. The latter riles him the most! At Christmas time there are always mountains of toys and clothes donated by loving uncles and grandparents to my sisters' kids, then Boxing Day hardly comes by before the toys are mostly stuffed, plus after a couple of washes the clothes fall apart at the seams.

Kev's of a like mind to Dad; still he blames the Aussie shops or department stores that sell the Chinese shit in the first place. It's these stores that actually inspect and buy the crap. He's gone shopping in Perth with rellies of ours, and they came across whole shopping centres peddling Chinese garbage!

Although Kev's recognised as being one of the best drillers on the Eastern Goldfields, he's fairly thick when it comes to everyday life, and it's not too hard to put one over him.

Trev takes after Mum. Although any son would say this, my mother – and she's getting on in years now – is one of the most beautiful women to ever grace the amalgamated gold mining cities of Kalgoorlie and Boulder. When she was in her late teens there were blokes who'd be prepared to jump down a mine shaft just to see her smile. It had the entire male population of both Kalgoorlie and Boulder completely stuffed how she could've picked Roberto Nazzari out of the mob! Especially with his buggered leg and so on.

Trev's got Mum's black, curly hair. He's also got her brains. You'd never put one over him in a hurry. No bloody way! That might be why he keeps breaking Mum's heart. He bolted it through school and passed every exam put in front of him with flying colours. He even won a scholarship of some sort to go to a uni in Perth, but no – he decided to come drilling with his two dopey, elder brothers. Mum wanted him to do so much more with his life. With his grey cells and spontaneous but rather malicious sense of humour, he has the capacity to achieve anything. He could've become a lawyer, politician; the prime minister of Australia even!

That's where, in the brains department, I come somewhere between Kev and Trev. I'm not as thick as Kev, but I'm certainly not as clever as Trev.

My younger brother also has my mother's good looks to go with his razor-sharp mind. Like Dad, Kev and me, his complexion has been tanned dark by the hot and lethal goldfields sun. He's different in that he's got Mum's crystal blue eyes. Those blue eyes that she got from her Swiss mother who was born in the Italian/Switzerland border region. Mum also likens Trev's physique to that of a Roman god, or perhaps an early Greek Olympian. He's the absolute apple of her eye, and the family favourite in most instances.

So there you have it. Kev's a big, boring and lovable boofhead. Trev's handsome and quick off the mark.

There's another massive difference between my two brothers. Kev, despite his huge size and strength, is as gentle as a butterfly and wouldn't dare hurt a flea. He views the world and life through rose coloured glasses, and I doubt if I've ever heard him bad mouth anyone or anything. He's an eternal optimist and exudes an almost fuzzy glow. Yes, life and the universe to him is a bed of roses, and when you're in his company his happy outlook's almost contagious. With his all-round, rather plain features and generally dopey nature, I haven't seen him have much luck with sheilas; whereby I've never come across a female that Trev couldn't wrap around his little finger.

I'm not kidding you! In the outback I know of blokes who've travelled hundreds of miles on some of the roughest roads – through the driest deserts – in temperatures that would boil your blood – just to visit a pub that has a new barmaid! And then, with men outnumbering sheilas the way they do in the outback, the chances of ever doing any good with that barmaid are about a million to one!

All the same I've personally witnessed where barmaids – once three in number at the same time – who'd been more than happy to travel the same distances – with the same conditions to put up with – just to visit a pub where Trev was known to have a beer!

But bowling sheilas over isn't where the main difference lies. You could almost swear that Trev hates the planet and everything on it; humans, animals, plants – you name it! He can't see good in *anything!* If you take too much notice of his bullshit, the bloody world's going to end at any second with no chance of a single survivor! The Doomsday Clock's gone well past midnight by a couple of decades! His sense of humour's both cruel and vicious; in fact there are times when he's downright depressing to be around. If Kev says something good or kind; Trev's lightning brain will come up with something vindictive or nasty in order to cancel it out. That's where I find myself firmly wedged between my two brothers. I don't necessarily walk around with Kev's optimistic outlook and cheerful disposition, but, by the same token, I certainly don't harbour the dark and sinister beliefs of my younger brother. I'm somewhere in the middle – I'm not as trusting of life as Kev is, but I don't search for its faults like Trev does.

The latter's lethal outlook on life, and possibly the entire universe, most likely upsets Mum the most. If anyone ever needs or deserves a smile, compliment or some encouragement – it's most definitely her! All in all fate hasn't been all that generous to such a wonderful person. With Dad's stuffed leg, she's had to work just about all of her adult life; either as a cleaner of other women's houses or as a checkout operator or shelf stacker in one of the Italian owned supermarkets in Burt Street; Boulder's main thoroughfare. Sure, she's got a bunch of healthy kids who she simply adores; still I'm certain there's much more that she might've done with her life. With her obvious intelligence she could've really gone places. She's certainly capable of having been a doctor or uni professor and so on. Perhaps that's why Trev being so slack disappoints her? She's a prolific reader, which is a trait that's been passed on to him.

Mum's also very religious, and such a quality has most certainly *not* been passed on to her youngest son. If it has, you wouldn't've spotted it in a year of Sundays. Mum's a Catholic and she goes for mass twice a week. Dad accompanies her on most occasions.

My bloody oath, but *there certainly is* male sibling rivalry in our family! Mainly between Trev and me. Because Kev's a bit slow, Trev's forever taking the piss out of him. On the other hand, Trev sees that as a special privilege that's his alone, and if there's one thing he simply can't hack – it's someone else having a go at our elder brother. You say something bad about Kev, or try and put one over him, and you'll have Trev in your face real quick smart! And Trev can handle himself. I suppose we all can – Kev – Trev and me. Perhaps you can relate our pugilistic prowess to Johnny Cash's '*Boy named Sue*' for we were always copping it at school, in pubs and at work because of the rhyming abbreviations of our first names. As for Kev, I haven't seen him in a blue for as long as I can remember. Or at least since he nearly killed a bloke in Kalgoorlie's Star and Garter Hotel in Hannan Street. If I can remember correctly, the blue was over what this dickhead said about our sister Louisa, and Kev just lifted the bloke up by his neck in one hand. It took the combined strength of Trev and me, plus a couple of other punters to prevent Kev from suffocating the stupid bastard! When he sobered up the next morning and realised what could've happened, he more or less gave up drinking in hotels. He'll have a couple of jars in the odd outback pub, but does most of his drinking either at home, mates' places, or in our various drilling camps.

Having lived all my life with Kev, I know when the time's come to give him a *very wide* berth! As I said previously – he views life with rose coloured glasses, but certain things really piss him right off. When that happens, his eyes seem to take on a queer kind of green colour – like the Incredible Hulk – and it pays to stop what you're doing if you're truly bugging him!

Another thing that has added to our talent at fisticuffs, or aptitude for outright brawling, is the fact that we've worked for Wally Growford's drilling outfit in Hay Street for quite a few years now. The same Hay Street where Kalgoorlie's brothels are! Wal doesn't mind his drillers or offsiders getting stuck into one another, and he learned his knuckle dancing and eye gouging skills back in the Nickel Boom days of the 60's and early 70's when head stomping, biting and eye gouging were the favourite pastimes of most drillers and offsiders back then. That and trying to roger barmaids. We've had some fairly pugnacious, Neanderthal-like specimens who've signed on with our drilling company, but Wal seems to have no problems keeping them in line. He's fairly cluey when it comes to picking out fair dinkum jokers from the mob. Most of the guys that we work with are bonzer blokes in general. Take for instance the drill crews who were actually sent to Africa by the boss when the Aboriginal Wik and Mabo bullshit stopped exploration and drilling dead in its tracks in Western Australia. One of the drillers, a blackfellah who was actually born somewhere in Africa – Joe Schultz – is the bloke who gave me the idea of writing all this in the first place. He's written a couple of books himself, which even the boss reckons is quite amazing, when you consider Joe being a humble driller and blackfellah to go with it. Joe's books are as rough as guts! There's stacks of swearing in them, but they're as accurate as anything. He's captured how drillers talk, or how most Aussie blue collar workers or labourers express themselves. To tell it any other way just wouldn't be '*bona fide*', or so Dave Wheeler pointed out. Dave's another driller who went with Joe Schultz to Africa – I think it was a place called Namibia – and he helped Joe with writing his books. He's been helping me with this, and has given me a list of long words to use. Yes, Dave Wheeler's one the smartest blokes I've ever met, and that's not discounting the fact that the piss has got him by the balls.

Also the reason why I mention that Joe has written a couple of books is very important, as you'll find me referring to what he's written down in the chapters to come. My style of writing's different to Joe's. He's totally refused to be PC or politically correct. Joe calls a spade a spade in his books. He tells the absolute truth, and that doesn't go down too well with certain do-gooder people. Not that you'd find such a creature in Wally Growford's drilling outfit! My book's got some swearing in it, but leaving it out altogether would make everything I'm trying to tell you a complete sham.

Although I wouldn't dare let them know, Joe and Dave are a couple of heroes of mine. Them and Wal Growford my boss.

Joe Schulz's drill crew are very similar to our crew. He has an offsider, Jeff Panizza, who's probably as big as Kev, although mostly fat. But that's where any similarities end abruptly! While Kev wouldn't hurt a flea, Jeff – the big fat bastard – would happily kick the crap out of his own shadow, and that's always getting him into strife; with his missus, the cops, the boss – you name it! Blokes in the company, plus plenty throughout the outback, reckon they'd like to see Jeff and Kev in a blue, but I know for certain that that'll never happen. They're both huge men, but don't carry around egos whereby they need to be seen as better than the other. They have a kind of mutual respect for one another, and enjoy a beer or two when our drilling rigs are working on the same client's prospect.

I'm pretty good cobbers with Joe's other offsider, Nick Lovadina, but we're also kind of opposites of a sort. Nick's got blonde hair and blue eyes, plus a physique like Trev's. He wears real thick lensed glasses which doesn't stop him being a real hit with the ladies. He's just like my younger brother when it comes to that; whereas I've never really raised an eyebrow of any sheila, no matter how ugly or fat. The only thing that Nick and I have in common actually bugs the crap out of Trev. We can both fart like masters! Look, I know this sounds pathetically immature for a twenty-eight-year-old to be mentioning this, but it's probably the only *real* talent I can lay claim to. I've already told you that I'm the middle of three brothers, and – using Dave Wheeler's words – as mediocre as they come. Furthermore, and like Joe admitted to in one of his books, I find farts and farting quite funny. Same do most of the jokers in the drilling game that I've ever come across. Also, like Nick Lovadina says, it proves that God's alive and well and *has indeed* got a sense of humour. After all, as he's pointed out on countless occasions, farts didn't necessarily have to make funny noises or stink, but *the majority* of them did. And that's what made them such great levellers. According to him there's no difference between a drunken driller, who's spent a month in the broiling Simpson Desert without having a shave or shower, or a beautiful blonde secretary like the boss has, and who spends the majority of her working hours in an air-conditioned office. Both their farts are made up of special chemicals that will make them stink. The only difference is that a driller will fart as loudly as possible, especially if in the company of his workmates or crew; whereas a beautiful secretary will only fart out loud if she's on her own and nobody else can hear! As Dave Wheeler also said – 'depressing logic, but authentic in its entirety!'

Yes indeed, Nick and I have always derived a great deal of pleasure from our capacity for breaking wind. Him much more so than me. He's studied just about everything to be found on the internet about farting, and knows the best tucker and things for creating the loudest and most foul smelling of farts! Some of that expert knowledge he's passed onto me. My situation's quite straightforward, really. A mixture of beer, cabbage, baked beans and salami make me fart long, loud and rank – with Coopers Best Extra Stout and vitamin B tablets I can fart quietly but *outrageously* foul! Nick's also much braver when it comes to letting go. He'll fart in supermarket queues, aeroplanes, brothels, lifts, plus even the boss's office, and keep his face as expressionless as stone. I've never had the guts to do that, if you'll forgive the expression or pun, and I still find it a battle when it comes to not laughing at other people's discomfort, surprise or embarrassment. I'm getting pretty good at it all the same. Especially when I'm trying to embarrass or humiliate Trev!

Nick's also good at coming up with sayings that even the boss quite admires him for. Take for instance when we had two rigs working on the same contract just outside of Southern Cross, an old goldmining and wheat belt town. As usual Nick, with his blonde hair, good physique and blue eyes, had a barmaid in one of the pubs literally eating out of his hand. So much so he camped in town while Wal Growford, me and Joe Schultz headed out to our caravans on the drill site. When Nick fronted up at the camp the following morning, the boss asked him if he'd had any luck with the barmaid. "Nah," Nick told him. "Her pussy's got the Dolmio Grin!"

While most of our crew and Joe Schultz and his offsiders didn't have a clue of what Nick was talking about, our employer picked up on it straight away. The barmaid was having her period!

The following night was a special treat for some of those in the drilling camp, and a nightmare for others! As usual Nick was one of the main movers and shakers. He was sharing a caravan with Wal, Jeff Panizza and Trev, while I shared another one with Kev, Dave Wheeler and Joe Schultz. The evening had started out not too bad. The country around Southern Cross can get bloody cold in Winter; still, with a roaring camp fire going, each of us managed to swallow down half a dozen King Brown bottles of Emu Export before we got stuck into the Bundy Rum which had been supplied by Archie Styles the geologist in charge of the drilling programme. If Archie's running a programme, it's compulsory that all those taking part have to drink gallons of Bundaberg Rum!

It was Jeff Panizza's turn to cook, and he put on superb spaghetti bolognaise with lashings of mince, garlic, Pecorino cheese and homemade tomato sauce.

After dinner I was sitting next to Nick as we gathered around the camp fire to have a last Bundy, and I saw him empty a handful of something into his mouth while pretending to cough at the same time.

I knew he was up to no good, so I whispered to him when the others were fully focused on a yarn that Archie was recounting to the boss: "What the fuck's that you got there, Nick?"

Making sure that no one else was watching, he muttered out of the side of his mouth. "Some vitamin Bs and stuff called fenugreek. You wait till later on and I'm gunna start a fuckin' riot! If you reckon my guts stunk before – you wait till you see what the boss, Trev and Jeff reckon once they climb into their fart sacks. Vitamin B and fenugreek seeds – plus Jeff's bolognaise – fuckin' lethal, mate!"

There was no chance of anyone hearing Nick's and my clandestine conversation, for Archie's yarn had everyone riveted! Little wonder there, as he was voicing his disquiet about the possibility of same-sex marriages being made legal in Australia. He was telling the boss how his nephew Peter Jermyn – a total poof who Joe, Jeff and Nick had come across on a previous drilling contract for Archie – had married some sheila in order to try and cure his homosexuality. Apparently the worst outcome imaginable arrived shortly after! Jermyn was in the process of divorcing his wife so that he could marry his father-in-law – who was more than happy to dump his own missus – when and if the same-sex marriage law was introduced by the Labour Party and the Greens!

It must've been perhaps a quarter of an hour after our employer turned off the overhead gas light in their caravan, when he roared at the top of his lungs. "Who's the – dirty – rotten – bastard – who done that? Who fuckin' dropped his fuckin' guts?"

Then it was Nick's turn: "Trev – you dirty – filthy – fuckin' animal!"

Jeff Panizza followed straight after: "Fucksakes – I can't fuckin' breathe! Hey – what the fuck?"

Seconds after Jeff's bellow of alarm, I heard the sound of bodies going in all directions! Jeff was still yelling out, "What the fuck ya doing?" while the boss was still bull roaring, "Where's a fuckin' torch?"

Following that there was what sounded like a cooking pot breaking glass, and then the same pot hitting something fairly solid but softer! That was pursued by the sound of a bunk collapsing or perhaps the caravan table?

"You do that again and I'll fuckin' kill you – you bastard!" the boss was still in fine tune.

"Get off me – you fuckin' dickhead!" Jeff wasn't very happy at all!

"Where the fuck are you – Nick?" that was Trev.

"It wasn't me – you arsehole!" Nick sounded distinctly aggrieved.

"Where's the fuckin' door?" Wal's' voice drowned them out. "Who's got a fuckin' lighter?"

"Fuckin' let go of me!" Jeff's voice sounded like thunder. "I'm not kidding – I'll break ya fuckin' neck!"

There was the crash of empty King Brown bottles smashing, and the boss yelled out in pain!

It was Dave Wheeler who restored some sort of order. He managed to get his hands on a Dolphin torch which he shone through the doorway of the caravan where all the action was taking place. A moment later four grown men were standing outside it; three of them shivering in their jocks. Nick wasn't too badly off because he was clad in pyjamas that had prints of pink rabbits all over them, plus a pair of Fremantle Dockers footy socks. He was also in far better shape than the others! The boss had blood dripping from his right nostril and he'd trodden on broken glass. Jeff was nursing a massive egg on his forehead plus a swollen lower lip, and Trev was displaying what was going to be a marvellous black eye!

"What the fuck's been going on?" Joe Schultz – also shivering in his jocks – demanded. Being the owner of his dusky features, it was only his teeth that were displaying that he was grinning like a Cheshire cat!

Actually the whole farce turned out to be quite hilarious! The caravan that Nick and them were in had a set of double bunks on each side of it approximately a metre apart; the boss and Trev on the top ones and Nick and Jeff on the bottom ones. When Wal turned out the gas light, Nick waited a while before letting go a silent, but really putrid fart! The same fart immediately made its way upwards, thus causing the boss to bitterly complain as loud as he could. Nick then accused Trev of committing the atrocity, and my younger brother wasn't going to have a bar of that. So much so that he jumped down from his bunk to give Nick a biffing, but he'd forgotten that Nick had swapped bunks with Jeff, for the latter preferred a bunk that wasn't abutting the caravan's shower and shithouse. Naturally Jeff objected to being punched in the throat, so he retaliated by taking a massive swing and his fist connected with Trev's right eye! By that time the boss, too, decided to bail out of his bunk and he landed on top of Trev. Seconds after Jeff most likely decided to vacate his swag as well, and his head butted into Wal's crutch, so he then received a smack in the mouth from our employer!

Feeling his way around in the dark, Trev was obviously still determined to exact his revenge on Nick, and to this day he can't explain how he managed to get his hand on a cooking pot in the pitch dark. Swinging the pot wildly he managed to shatter the mirror on one of the van's wardrobes, while a further blow managed to connect the brow of Jeff's head just before the boss got the big fat bastard in a headlock.

The ensuing struggle between them caused a top bunk to collapse, thus forcing Wal to let go of Jeff, and Jeff managed to elbow him in the face. Wal then desperately tried to find the caravan door, and that's how he managed to barge into a row of empty King Brown bottles and thus trod on the broken glass!

While that was going on, Nick had kept quiet as a mouse in his swag, while the remainder of the van's occupants tried their best to kill each other!

What had also contributed to the mayhem were the van's curtains. They were heavy and made of black velvet material on account that that particular van was decked out to cater for night shift workers. The black drapes were excellent for keeping out the sunlight during the day, so at night its occupants wouldn't've been able to see a thing!

Although his caravan had been wrecked, Wal soon saw the funny side of things, and a couple of further slugs of Bundy in steaming coffee soon calmed everyone down. When he offered to trade bunks with Dave Wheeler, Dave politely told him to go away and make love to his hand!

That's why Nick's such a great mate! With only the slightest of effort, and with the most rudimentary of materials, he can cause a holocaust! Or so Dave Wheeler reckoned at the time.

There was another phrase of his that also charms the boss. When Nick wants to emphasise great speed, he grins and says: "As fast as Chinese stainless steel rusts, mate!"

Yes, there's mostly rivalry between me and Trev, and, with his three-speed brain, he usually comes out on top. It's not that I don't win the odd skirmish or two. It's his nasty, sneaky, vicious streak that gives him the advantage, and he doesn't hesitate to put the boot in if he's got the upper hand. He's a treacherous little prick to go with it! I could be drinking grog and playing pool all day with him in the Shamrock Hotel in Boulder, or the Criterion in Kalgoorlie, and we'd be getting on as peaceful as anything. In would walk somebody that we knew and Trev would tell him that I was gay and would be coming out of the closet! He's always telling barmaids how embarrassed he is because I'm his brother, and how I'd told him that I wanted to root Justin Bieber! What really bugs me about that carry on is that nothing could be further from the truth. Okay, so nowadays people are far more tolerant when it comes to homosexuality, but I find homosexuals and lesbians repulsive. Although I would never wish a poof or lezzie any harm, and there's obviously some pretty decent ones getting around, I would rather not have *anything* to do with them. I wish to leave them alone and want them to stay well away from me. While they may want to enjoy the freedom to indulge in their choice of sexuality, and good on them, I would much rather have nothing to do with them. Surely that's my freedom of choice? I don't even like seeing queer blokes and sheilas on the TV and films, either. That's also surely my prerogative?

While on the subject of homosexuality and this new political correctness whereby people are talking about homosexuals being able to marry and actually foster kids, I expect my bleak attitude towards them comes from being raised by a pretty straight-laced father, plus I've grown up in one of your typical goldfields, blue collar families.

Dad and Kev are not only cast from the same mould, so to speak, they also harbour very similar beliefs. Dad has come from a long line of Italian farmers and reckons that if animals were into same-sex fornication, they'd soon be put down. If you mention queers to Kev, he has a stock standard policy: "They'd better fuckin' not come near me!" Although I very much doubt that there's any likelihood of that.

In the drilling company I work for, both the bloke who owns the outfit, plus his employees in their entirety struggle to come to terms with this 'newfangled political correctness' that seems to have – in the boss' terms – 'grabbed all Australians by the nuts'. Take for instance when the Australian federal cops lumbered some Muslim blokes planning to blow Aussies up. It appeared that most of these Muslim jokers were recent immigrants who were hell bent on trying to stuff up our Australian way of life and trying to force their brand of religion on us. Okay, so if you were to say out loud in a public place that Muslim fanatics shouldn't've been allowed into the country in the first place – and those that were whinging and complaining about Aussie should be kicked out – you'd have every chance of being called a racist or an islamaphobe, plus you could be covered in a shower of shit by a bunch of do-gooders in Canberra who reckon they know what's good and necessary for all Australians. People like those simpering do-gooders in the Green Party who're barracking for same-sex marriages, and allowing anyone who pitches up in a boat to be given instant Australian citizenship; regardless of the poor bastards elsewhere in the world who're trying to come to Australia using legitimate methods.

I haven't come across anyone in the Eastern Goldfields, or anywhere in Western Australia that I've been to, where a person has been too happy with people from places like Iran, Iraq, Sri Lanka and Afghanistan pitching up in boats. All we seem to see of these people on the TV is them massacring and blowing each other up, plus firing AK47s into the air. Most of the people I've spoken to reckon that if they carry on like child murderers and dickheads in their own countries, what's going to make them change now that they've come to Aussie? Especially after that Taliban arsehole publicly executed a woman for alleged adultery, and he was surrounded by a crowd of similar wankers who were clapping their hands and cheering. Plus we'd witnessed the Cronulla riots in New South Wales, and the blood on the faces of cops in Sydney – Aussie cops – who'd been injured by rioting Muslims after some scumbag lowlife in America had made a movie scorning the Prophet Muhammad. And the placards calling for people to be beheaded! Like Dave Wheeler said – how long will it take for Australia's Muslims to start firing AK47's in the air and burning Australia's flag?

And then, of course, there's the unease of most of the people I know when it comes to the 1,700 foreign workers they're talking about bringing into Western Australia to work on one of the iron ore mines. There's some debate about where these workers are coming from.

If Dad and us brothers really have a united opinion in life – Mum and our sisters need to be protected from this political correctness or 'PC' as the trendy people on the TV and in the newspapers call it. All in all we've become almost paranoid about what Mum sees on the telly.

As we were growing up Kev, Trev and I have always been quite excited when the rare glimpse of a woman's boob can be seen on the telly, but now it seems anything goes – blokes rogering women dog-fashion – pussy – dongers – blokes kissing blokes – you name it! And that's not mentioning the swearing that's now common on the TV. Especially on 'poofter' channels like the ABC as the boss calls it.

While Mum's certainly a lot brighter than Dad, she hopelessly outclasses him in the naivety stakes. She finds men and women kissing and shagging people of the same sex totally unnatural and degrading. Also she reckons that such a carry on is illegal for Christians or a mortal sin, for it says so in her Bible. She often mentions Sodom and Gomorrah that were destroyed by fire in the Book of Genesis, plus she's not so sure about Muslims. She's read a magazine article on Afghanistan where sodomising boys is a popular pastime for a good many Afghan blokes, and she reckoned that she hoped that all the refugee men from Afghanistan aren't going to do the same sort of thing to Aussie boys now that they've come to Australia.

It's the bastardry of some of the clergy in the Catholic Church that Dad really wants to shield Mum from. As I pointed out, her naivety has left her with some of the most vulnerable beliefs in life. She's positive that the Pope's infallible, and that the local parish priest's the pillar of our community; despite that he's Irish and dribbles a load of shit because he's half senile. From the news that's coming in from all over the planet, it appears that just about every second member of the Catholic clergy's into buggering, raping and brutalising kids in orphanages, private schools, plus even those within their congregations! It seems that every day some new outrage has been committed! It's obvious that this has been going on for years, but the bigwigs in the Vatican – plus the bishops in charge of Catholic churches around the world – appear to have done a bloody good job at covering everything up. Naturally, with the news of Catholic clergy atrocities pouring in via all avenues of the media, it's been impossible to keep Mum in the dark totally. Especially when she reads anything she can get her hands on; the newspapers, second hand magazines, plus the countless books she draws out from the public library in Kalgoorlie. As far as she's concerned, the reports coming in about the Catholic Church are the work of the devil, and that gay blokes and lezzies can possibly be dissuaded from rogering each other, and be led away from this kind of behaviour. For, and after all, to her homosexuality's an affront to Mother Nature's laws, and that no decent or respectable society should tolerate it. When someone in the supermarket in Boulder told her that some American blokes and sheilas in the US and elsewhere were *actually allowed* to marry people of the same sex, she just refused point blank to believe it. I think it was Louisa, the eldest of my three sisters, who suggested that Ellen DeGeneres from the TV show '*ELLEN*' was most probably partial to a length or two of vibrating dildo or rubber strap-on donger since her spouse didn't have a dick, and Mum took at least a week to get over it. How could a beautiful and famous woman such as Ellen be sick like that, she argued; nevertheless we never saw that same TV show in our house again.

No, there's never been room for homosexuality in my family, so Trev telling people that I'm a queer really rankles!

I did try to get my own back on him, though. To this day I still reckon it was quite simple and ingenious the way I went about it. Using a black permanent marker pen, I wrote on the shithouse wall in the Palace Hotel on Hannans Street: 'IF YOUR'E LOOKING FOR SOME TIGHT ARSE FOR FREE – JUST PHONE TREV. And I put Trev's mobile phone number on the wall!

And did that cause a stir! Especially as Trev has a habit of answering his phone: "Trev Nazzari here!" For weeks after he was getting calls from all sorts. Some blokes wanting to meet him in a public Gents craphouse somewhere, and others abusing him for a being a poof and calling him all kinds of filthy names! Even the boss and Jeff Panizza got in on the act, plus most of the blokes in the yard, until he finally dropped his mobile down a drill hole and bought another one with a different number.

Okay, so I come from a typical blue collar, Eastern Goldfields family, and perhaps my brothers and I've been case-hardened because we've worked for Wally Growford's drilling company for the bulk of our adult lives. Wal has zero tolerance for gay men and will never employ one, and I've *never ever* met another driller in the entire state of Western Australia who's admitted to being fond of another bloke's bum.

Although we brothers, especially Trev and me, manage to get on each other's tits from time to time, we are known to support each other and our family in times of adversity. I suppose one could put it down to our deep respect for Mum, plus coming from an ancient and conservative Italian family on our father's side of things, that Kev and I never swear while we're in our family home. Trev has been known to let the odd 'fuck me dead!' slip out from time to time, and he has on occasion been known to call a Labour or Green Party politician a 'fuckwit!', but a glare from Dad and Kev generally dissuades him from doing that again for at least a couple of hours.

If there's one particular occasion when Trev swears even if Kev and Dad are in the kitchen, it's when people from India or the Philippines call our phone number just as we're about to have dinner. Mum never picks up the phone, and Dad's just as hesitant to. After having been trapped by these same Indian and Filipino callers, Kev generally leaves the phone alone as well. He makes outgoing calls, but never picks up the receiver if there's someone else around to do it. Trev's more than content to answer any call. After hearing that nearly every second call from Indians and Filipinos is some sort of a scam, and after one outfit managed to put a 'worm' in his computer, he's always delighted when he hears an Indian of Filipino voice at the other end of the line, and he uses words that would burn holes in this page when he tells the caller what to do with himself or herself! Still, the stupid dickheads keep calling!

Generally my brothers and I don't swear in front of females, and we don't like hearing women or girls use foul language; another legacy of our Italian upbringing, I presume. I – and particularly Kev – are uncomfortable when other blokes swear in front of females. Especially in front of our sisters; Louisa, Bella and Sophia. The kind of people who come round to visit Mum and Dad are generally of Italian lineage, therefore bad language is very rarely brought by outsiders into our house. Louisa and Bella are married and live in their own homes, while

Sophia's shacked up with a bloke in Geraldton. Although Dad's dead set against our youngest sister living in sin, we've all been able to keep Mum in the dark about it. Sophia's had all sorts of strife when it comes to blokes, and it was necessary for Trev and I to panel beat a couple of the more dickheaded ones. There was one joker from Perth who was actually smacking her around, so Trev and I fixed him by breaking his right arm and left leg in the car park at the back of the Broken Hill pub. That took place with Kev and Jeff Panizza keeping an eye out for the Boulder cops, and the bloke was quick to head back to West Aussie's capital after that. Sophia's also stuffed around with drugs, but there's not one drug pusher in the Eastern Goldfields who'd be game to supply her, for they'd have all three of the Nazzari brothers come after him or her! From what I can gather, the bloke she's living with keeps her on the straight and narrow.

As far as swearing goes, it's a completely different matter for us Nazzari boys in the Hay Street drill yard, on a drill site, in a pub playing pool, or in a drilling camp. Having a boss who's a master at adding his own particular brand of magic to the crudest of expletives – who's invented some of the foulest of terminology possible – the filthiest of innuendos – his employees, too, generally have become similar legends throughout the length and breadth of Western Australia. And that's not saying that drillers from other yards can't also be talented. No, the boss must spend a lot of his time both at home and in his office perfecting his profanity, and heaven help any bastard who falls into his 'P' portfolio. It seems that everything he loathes in life starts with a 'P'; pushers as in drug pushers – poofs – paedophile priests – payday lenders and pawnbrokers – pederasts and perverts. It appears that the drilling fraternity in general shares the same contempt for these kind of people; however with the political correctness and do-gooders that are taking over Aussie these days – it appears that these same types are perfectly acceptable to quite a lot of the community.

While we might hassle each other constantly, Trev and I've have had only one dinkum blue since we've been over twenty-one, and it's one of the worst experiences I've ever suffered in my life! True, we'd came to blows stacks of times when we were kids, but being adults it's a very different story altogether! As I've said before – Trev can handle himself. Actually, he can go like a thrashing machine, and the last time we'd got stuck into one another was at the drill yard in Hay Street. The day had been a typically broiling hot, Kalgoorlie summer's day, and Trev had been niggling me incessantly for hours while totally ignoring Kev's warning to pull his head in. Trev was in one of those moods where he was determined that someone's blood was going to be spilt. And it didn't matter if it was his, mine or anybody's that got between us.

To be totally honest, I was most likely the one who really started the actual blue itself. We were working on our Edson 2000 drill rig's multipurpose rotary head, where I was hanging off the drill mast just above Trev, holding onto a hydraulic hose. Meanwhile he had his head between my legs and was screwing the end of the same hose to a hydraulic pump that actually turned the rotary head. With his hair brushing the crutch of my shorts, I couldn't resist letting go a fart that would've even made Nick Lovadina proud! Not only had I taken a couple of vitamin B tablets the night before which I'd washed down with a gallon or so of Coopers Stout, I'd also wolfed down a tin of smoked oysters to go with the scrambled eggs, salami and onions I'd eaten for breakfast. Bloody hell – but stink! I deliberately squatted down so that the bottom of the crack of my arse formed an arch over the bridge of his nose, and my fart sputtered out like a Harley Davidson pulling up at a traffic light. The beauty of it was that Trev had to stay exactly where he was, otherwise he would've got drenched with hydraulic oil, what with the hose not being screwed to the pump properly. I not only got one fart off – but two!

Even with the noise his struggling air-conditioner was making, the boss reckoned he could hear Trev swearing from his office, and that's why he came out into the yard. He told Trev to keep it down, because Noelene – his beautiful blond secretary – objected to all the vulgarity. That didn't do the boss all that much good, as Trev told him to go and fuck himself with a giant dildo with the rough end of a pineapple on the end of it. So, shaking his head somewhat forlornly, Wal retreated back to where he'd come from. I've no idea what explanation he gave Noelene when Trev continued to call me – at the top of his lungs – every filthy name his sick imagination could come up with. By then Kev had had a gutsful of his and my bullshit, and he'd gone off to have a smoke with Joe Schulz and Dave Wheeler. He must've had a fair idea that Trev and I would start swapping punches.

It was Trev that eventually threw the first punch. Like I said, he can go like a thrashing machine, and he started landing about three punches to each one of mine. Nevertheless, while he's bloody fast – there wasn't all that much weight or thought going behind his blows. Not only that, I'm a bit like a wombat when it comes to having a blue. As well as having a hard head, I put much more power and science behind my fists. I may be slow; still I hit hard! After about a couple of minutes or so I could tell that I was seriously hurting him. Blood was pouring down the front of my shirt from a burst eyebrow, mashed nose and cut lip, but Trev's eyes were literally rolling in their sockets every time I smacked him in the head. His face was also a mess because his bottom teeth had been pushed through his lower lip, and blood was dripping down from the top of his head somewhere. By then everyone in the drill yard, including the boss, were standing around yelling advice and encouragement. Out of the corner of my eye I could see Noelene, the boss' beautiful secretary, watching at the door of the office reception area! Only Kev was nowhere to be seen.

Then I started thinking of Mum! If I was to really hurt Trev, there was no way she'd understand. I eventually started to panic! I'd never seen Trev lose a blue *ever*, and I knew he'd never give up unless I knocked him out cold or did him some real damage. Also it was obvious that he'd noticed Noelene standing just outside the office's front door.

It got that way that each time I hit him, I felt like throwing up! I was easily winning, for he could hardly see through the swelling around his eyes. I searched round for Kev, but he'd simply disappeared! I looked over and saw that Noelene was still watching. I, like every bloke in the yard, have always been head over heels in love with her, and she's the main feature in a secret fantasy of mine where I save her from all kinds of evils. Even Jeff Panizza, who's married with a tribe of kids, reckons he'd eat her shit with a wooden spoon!

I put up my hands to call it quits, and a look of relief swept over Trev's face. It was obvious that those who'd been watching the blue were disappointed, but I was more interested in Noelene's reaction. She gave me the briefest shake of her head and went inside. Trev walked round to the cab of the drill truck to fetch his smokes, and the boss came up and put his hand on my shoulder. "Good on yer, Nev – mate! Trev was just about fucked. Everyone could see that. . . Righto, buddy, go and take a shower and get yourself cleaned up. Ask Ernie and he'll give you a new work shirt from the store to change into. Tonight you and Trev can camp in one of the caravans in the yard 'cause you can't go home and let your mum see you like that. Head to the Mount Lyall after, and I'll meet you there."

"It's not knock off time yet," I argued.

He just shrugged. "Who gives a fuck? Get cleaned up and I'll see you at the Mount Lyall in half an hour. You okay to drive, mate?"

"Yeah."

"Good one – see you at the Lyall."

It was the barmaid Paula at the Mount Lyall Hotel who first commented on the damage Trev had done to my face: "Fuckin' hell – Nev! You run into a black gin or something?"

I've always fancied shagging Paula, just like most of the punters who drink at the Mount Lyall. I searched her face for potential sympathy, but any impossible hopes I had were soon shattered by: "Fuckin' get round here – you useless bastard!"

It was Kev! He was sitting at the end of the bar opposite to where I was standing, and the weird green in his eyes left me with no doubt that he was horribly pissed off!

When I went round to join him, he could see that Paula and most of the pub's patrons were watching with acute interest, so he grabbed me by the arm and dragged me into the Gents shithouse.

And did he get stuck into me! Me hitting Trev was identical to hitting Dad or anyone in our family. Trev and I bluing was just cheap entertainment for the rest of the blokes in the drill yard who didn't give two fucks whether we killed each other. All Trev and I'd done was kick the Nazzari name in the guts!

Kev isn't a man of many words, so he soon cooled down. It was what he told me next that really kicked me in the balls! He reckoned he was going to marry some barmaid that he'd met at Sylvester's Nightclub, and who was working at the Piccadilly Hotel. She was a Kiwi chick and her name was *Merl Malloy!*

About a million thoughts and suggestions sprang to mind; however my brain was still aching from where Trev had tried to beat it into an omelette. I nearly asked Kev if it was Merl Malloy the nympho who Trev had nicknamed 'Jabba the Hutt', but a sixth sense told me to keep my mouth firmly shut. If there was any time I needed to talk to Trev – it was right at that moment! Kev obviously couldn't see the turmoil I was wrestling with, and I saw a faraway look in his eye when he said how he was getting on in years and wanted to settle down. He reckoned he was planning on buying a house somewhere in Kalgoorlie because Merl didn't like Boulder, and having a couple of kids!

Finally the boss pitched up and complained that his throat was as dry as a Kalahari vulture's crutch, so any further discussion about Kev marrying Merl Malloy ended immediately.

Eventually I managed to get Trev on his mobile, and we agreed to meet at the Albion Shamrock Hotel in Boulder. We must've looked a sight as we fronted up to the bar; Trev with the swelling all round his eyes and my lips puffing out like balloons. Some of the punters eyed us curiously for a second or two, and then they turned their gaze elsewhere.

"You remember that barmaid, Merl Malloy?" I quizzed Trev once we'd bought a couple of midis and found a table overlooking the street out front.

"Yeah," he agreed. "Fuckin' bush pig! You want to be careful knocking her off – you'll get a dose of the clap."

"Nah – nah," I assured him. "I haven't seen her since we were drilling on Riverina Station. You know – when she was working at the Menzies pub. It was round about last year some time."

"Fuckin slag!" he didn't soften his outlook. "She's got breath that would sit a roo dog on its arse."

"Whatever you reckon," I shrugged. "Kev told me he's gunna marry her."

Trev's smoke actually fell out of his mouth and on to the floor! "You're fuckin' kidding! Who the fuck told you that?"

"Nah – I'm not kidding," I insisted after lighting my own smoke. "Kev reckons he's been going out with her for the last couple of months. Apparently she's working at the Piccadilly Hotel. Now we know where he's been disappearing to."

Trev seemed determined to try and laugh the whole possibility off; though I pointed out that Kev wasn't the type for making up equations like that.

Merl Malloy's presence in our humble Boulder house was an insult to the whole family. Louisa and Bella plus their husbands and kids would immediately leave once she pitched up, and Dad would soon make himself scarce out in the back yard. Only Mum had any time for her, but she was caught up with the fuzzy-glow of Kev getting married and supplying her with more grand kids. It was the first time a son of hers was getting married! At first Merl talked in the house like she talked in the pubs she worked in where 'fuckin' was almost every second word, plus the odd 'cunt' or two. It was actually Dad who pulled her up on that one, and after quite a few visits she toned her language down somewhat.

"That woman stinks!" Dad confided in Trev and me when we were helping him dig out the french drain coming off the kitchen sink. "I don't know if it's her breath or her farting, but she stinks like a sceptic tank with its lid off. It looks like she never brushes her teeth."

"It's both," Trev assured him. "She must get serious bunghole 'cause the stink comes out of both her mouth and arse. You don't want to be in a car with her when she farts, Dad. You can ask just about every joker in the goldfields about that one."

"What do you mean?" Dad was caught off guard by that last remark.

I hastily intervened. "She's always dropping her guts, Dad." I didn't want the old man knowing that half the blokes in Kalgoorlie/Boulder – or perhaps the entire outback – had given Merl one.

Another thing that really incensed Dad was that Merl didn't even bother concealing the fact that she had the hots for Trev. She was all over him like a rash, and it was obvious that neither Kev nor Mum had a clue. She was forever putting her arms around him and trying to kiss him, and it ended up with Trev telling her that if she didn't leave him alone, he'd give her a backhand.

I reckon there were almost tears in Dad's eyes when he came to me for reassurance one time when he and I were alone. He's not as religious as Mum, although he accompanies her to mass most Sundays.

Out of the entire family Trev took it the hardest that Kev was hell bent on marrying Merl. To him it was as if Kev had been diagnosed with some kind of terminal illness. I wasn't that far behind him when it came to the revulsion. The whole situation was bullshit! While trying not to arouse their curiosity, I raised her name in conversations with some of the jokers in the drill yard, plus other blokes in the various pubs that I frequented. What struck me most was the contempt on the blokes' faces whenever her name came up. And yes, her eyes – forever masked by black or dark grey eye shadow – certainly did look like those of a pig in some distress!

Both my parents scarcely socialise with people who knew of Merl's reputation, so I begged Trev not to bring it up in front of Mum and Dad. When he and I tried to raise the issue with Kev, it immediately changed the colour of his eyes, and he reckoned that it was well known that Aussie blokes never have anything good or truthful to say about barmaids. Blokes are always bullshitting about how they've rooted this barmaid or that.

Eventually the worst happened and we were all kicked in the guts when Merl and Kev got married in a registry office in Perth and not one member of the family was invited! Naturally Dad was stricken and never hesitated to voice his outrage; yet Mum – though you could see the distress in her beautiful eyes – kept her feelings to herself.

Another body blow came the family's way when Kev put a deposit on a house in Dugan Street in Kalgoorlie. We got to know all about it, for the real estate agent who sold it drank at the Star and Garter Hotel where Trev and I often play pool when we're on our breaks from drilling in the bush. The house was only in Merl's name! Kev had put down his life's savings plus a guarantee on the mortgage repayments, yet his name appeared nowhere on the deeds! Like a kind of committee Dad, Trev and I fronted Kev about it, and he just told us to mind our own fuckin' business. He'd never spoken to Dad like that before!

Merl began to take on nightmarish proportions; her fat shapeless body; her bulldog cheeks; her filthy teeth and putrid breath. Being a fairly close knit community, secrets are quite hard to keep in Kalgoorlie/Boulder. Dad came home in a panic one weekend after he'd had a yarn with Julio Panizza, Jeff Panizza's uncle who was president of the Eastern Goldfields Market Gardeners Club; an establishment mostly frequented by Italians and the odd Yugoslav. Julio's a bit of a rough old bastard like his nephew Jeff, and apparently Merl Malloy had worked as a barmaid at the club. He'd had to sack her since she was also moonlighting as a prostitute and blokes from much respected Italian families were paying her big quids in the car park when they were too pissed to know any better. Old Sergio Trevella, the owner of the biggest private supermarket in the goldfields, also ended up with a dribbly dick after a brief sojourn with her, and that was a bit like an atom bomb going off because he looked like being voted in as a city councillor and had passed on the same problem to his missus who wasn't too charmed at all! As you can imagine, Dad was totally horrified when he managed to catch up with Trev and me. He suggested that he should ban Merl from our house; although both she and Kev had literally ceased coming around. She'd also managed to really hurt Mum when she told her that women who gave birth to a bunch of 'snotty-nosed sprogs' were a bunch of suckers, and how she was '*never gunna get pregnant to no bastard*'!

As my investigations into Merl's past started to bear further fruit, the more alarmed and revolted I became. According to one of the brothel madams in Hay Street, Merl had actually worked in her establishment when she first came to Kalgoorlie. Apparently it's very common for Kiwi or New Zealand women to work in the Hay Street brothels, and the bulk of the escort agency hookers in Perth are also either from Asia or New Zealand. Although I've visited various Kalgoorlie brothels quite frequently, and often used call girls on the very rare occasions that I went to Perth, I was unaware of that at the time, but I suppose it was because I have my favourite hookers in each particular brothel or escort agency, and they are without exception Aussies and white. I'm fairly suspicious of African, Asian and other dark-skinned sheilas, so tend to stay away from them. Trev also won't have bar of any women unless they're white. I understand that he's what do-gooder people call a 'racist'. He has nothing but contempt for people with darker skins, and, also similar to the boss, reckons that Australia should've hung onto its 'White Australia' policy. Not that Trev *ever needs* to pay for sex.

Unlike me, he has absolutely no trouble getting onto as much free pussy as he can handle. The only beautiful women I ever get to see with their clothes off are prostitutes and those I've hunted down via the porn sites on the internet. It was only after Nick showed me a couple of his favourite hard core porn sites on the net that I started taking any interest in Google and so on.

I further learned that Merl was banned from every brothel in Hay Street, for an undercover cop busted her for trying to sell him drugs. Between the cops and the Kalgoorlie madams – that's a *definite* no-no! Furthermore, Merl was known to have let certain clients ride her bareback or without a franger, and that's also seriously taboo when it comes to the brothels in the Eastern Goldfields. Especially when she was pocketing all the extra cash she was charging and not telling her boss about it. From what the madam told me, quite a few dozen of her regular punters picked up a dose of gonorrhoea, and the cops got to hear about it and threatened to shut her down for that one as well! That's why the brothels in Kalgoorlie have been tolerated for so many years. Picking up the clap from a Hay Street prostitute is very-very rare. Especially when the girls inspect the eye of your dick for pus or whatever before they fit a franger on. No kidding, Merl was responsible for a pox pandemic all on her own!

So what did I have on my hands back then? My elder brother was besotted with an ex or possibly current whore who pushed drugs and had given a legion of unsuspecting men a load of the clap! I've already waxed lyrical about her rotten breath and wind. If that wasn't devastating enough, Kev then went and snatched his rent from Growford Drilling, and he joined up with one of Wal's main competitors! It just didn't make sense on account of the fact that Growford Drilling's the best paying outfit in Western Australia. To join another mob had to mean that Kev would be taking a pay cut of at least twenty percent!

"You blokes going as well?" the boss demanded when Trev and I fronted up at the yard the next day and after he'd told us about it.

"Nah, fuck Kev," Trev answered for both of us. "The dickhead's just had a rush of shit to the brain."

"You reckon he's cunt struck?" Jeff Panizza was hovering around in the background and must've felt it was necessary to chip in.

"It fuckin' sounds like it," the boss chose to concur. "With Jabba the Hutt of all people!"

Him agreeing with Jeff on anything is less likely than it snowing in Kalgoorlie in the middle of summertime! Notwithstanding that, it was gut-wrenching for Trev and me listening to people talking about our elder brother like that; yet – as I mentioned before – it's bloody hard to keep secrets in the Eastern Goldfields. Kev Nazzari had married that Kiwi sheila Merl Malloy or Jabba the Hutt; no ifs and buts about it!

The conversation really went downhill after that when the boss, Jeff and Trev started discussing current affairs.

The boss started it. "Things have to be horribly fucked when you've got a female prime minister who's an atheist. Now they're talking about legalising same-sex marriages, plus the Federal Minister for Finance and Deregulation's promoting same-sex marriage 'cause it sounds like she's a lezzie and proud of it. "

"What's that about a lezzie?" Jeff Panizza's dark and perverted curiosity was aroused. "Who's a lezzie?"

"That Chinese sheila – Penny Wong or whatever," the boss replied. "She's supposed to be a senator or something. I read somewhere that they reckon she's one of Australia's most influential lesbians. Fuck me dead, it's getting that way a person has to be a poof or a lezzie in order to get anywhere nowadays. Fuckin' atheists – lezzies – the place's fucked, I tell you!"

"Yeah, but what do you reckon about that dickhead that was pulled up for sniffing some staff sheila's seat?" Trev seemed keen to add to our employer's woes.

That really had Jeff intrigued. "Which dickhead was that?"

Trev opened up a newspaper that he'd bought at the deli before coming to work. "Troy Buswell. Fuckin' Liberal leader of the opposition in West Aussie. Here – take a look."

CHAIR-SNIFFER TROY BUSWELL
'WAS IN MOCK SEXUAL ECSTASY'

THE woman at the centre of the seat-sniffing scandal involving West Australian Opposition Leader Troy Buswell says he writhed in mock sexual pleasure during the incident.

The woman, who remains unnamed, told The West Australian newspaper Mr Buswell sniffed her chair twice within 10 minutes, while groaning and making "sexually satisfying noises".

Mr Buswell has admitted sniffing the seat of the Liberal female staff member in an office at Perth's Parliament House in October 2005.

He yesterday survived a Liberal party room move to dump him in the wake of the scandal.

The woman was today reported by The West Australian as saying that Mr Buswell placed a chair on his head twice within 10 minutes, sniffing it before writhing in mock sexual ecstasy.

"We finished the meeting (with a constituent), I walked the bloke downstairs and out of parliament, and when I got back I walked into the room to pick up my notepad from the desk and Buswell started grabbing the chairs going 'aahww, which one did you sit in? I'll be able to tell'," she said.

"And then he picked them up and started sniffing them and groaning and making sexually satisfying noises. I went, 'you're sick, knock it off', and grabbed my staff and walked out, but he didn't pay attention to a word I said."

The woman said she was standing with colleagues about 10 minutes later when one of them knocked on Mr Buswell's door to ask one of his staff to lunch.

"Buswell opened the door really wide, grabbed a chair and started sniffing it, lifted it above his head sniffing it and breathing in, going 'aaww yeah'," *the woman said.*

"It was awful. My colleagues, the four men I worked with, were just stunned into silence."

Mr Buswell, who is set to lead the Liberal Party to the next election after surviving yesterday's party room meeting, says he considered resigning over the incident and its aftermath.

"I have given that consideration," he said on Fairfax Network radio.

"It's been a difficult week for me personally, but as I say that would shade into insignificance compared to the impact on the lady concerned. It would've been extremely difficult for her. It's been a difficult week for my family and my colleagues, and of course I gave that consideration."

"And you got these types of people running the fuckin' place?" the boss was visibly unimpressed.

"Hey – Wal?" Jeff was shaking with laughter.

"Yes, Jeff?" the boss was immediately apprehensive.

Jeff Panizza has never been a pretty sight! Especially if he's grinning because he's got *not one* solitary tooth in the front of his mouth! "Whatsa chances of giving us a sniff of Noelene's chair?"

That query immediately captured Trev's and my interest! Most of us employees are dead certain that the boss is doing dirty things to his secretary during his lunch hour, and he's always fairly cagey whenever anyone mentions her name.

His reply was both curt and very much to the point: "You go and get fucked – you mutant!"

That's how conversations between Jeff and our employer mostly end. Wal storming back to his office, and Jeff casually wandering off to go and traumatise someone else. Except that particular time Jeff had come up with quite a catchy tune: "I'm gunna show Senator Penny Wong my dong – doodah – doodah!"

Politics was also the main agenda in the yard some time later when Trev showed the boss another news article he'd found.

PARLIAMENT SPEAKER AND ORDAINED PRIEST
PETER SLIPPER ACCUSED OF SEXUAL HARASSMENT BY STAFFER

The Speaker in the Federal Parliament agreed to step aside because of an investigation into allegations he sexually harassed a male member of his staff and misused travel entitlements.

Peter Slipper, who stabbed his Liberal coalition colleagues in the back in November, was accused of making unwelcome sexual advances to a media adviser and rorting his taxi vouchers. The allegations were made by James Ashby, who is openly homosexual, and who has now taken out a court order for compensation after Mr Slipper made "unwelcome suggestions of a sexual nature".

Mr Ashby alleged the Speaker would send "bizarre" kisses to him by ending text messages with an X. It was further alleged that Mr Ashby, who had camped the night at Mr Slipper's residence in Canberra, was asked to shower with the bathroom door ajar and to massage his boss's neck. Apparently Mr Slipper then made moaning noises indicating "intense sexual pleasure."

Another female staffer alleged that there was a video of Slipper climbing through the window of a young male staffer; Slipper lying on a bed in only shorts and a T-shirt and hugging the staffer "in an intimate fashion"; Slipper urinating out of a window.

"Fuck me dead!" my employer was *deeply* taken aback! "Like that bloke that was leading the Libs over here – this Slipper sounds like a fuckin' moaner and groaner as well. Who's the bloke who was leading the WA Libs, Trev?"

"That Troy Buswell bloke – the chair sniffer?" my younger sibling asked him back.

"Yeah, that's the bloke," Wal agreed. "At least he's moaning over a woman and isn't a fuckin' traitor. This Slipper sounds a real slippery character to me. Typical fuckin' priest!"

"Yes, *it is* rather sordid," Dave Wheeler concurred with him. "Poofs – I mean. They seem to have a one-track mind."

"Maybe they should call him 'Vaseline'?" Jeff Panizza suggested helpfully. "This Slipper joker. I've heard them bum bandits use heaps of Vaseline to make their arses all slippery."

"I guess you'd fuckin' know about things like that," the boss refused to oblige the big fat bastard.

As it turned out, the government paid out Ashby fifty grand for all the harassment; however later on Slipper was fully exonerated by the Supreme Court or whatever. He'd done *absolutely nothing wrong*!

While the boss' relationship with Jeff could only be regarded as fairly toxic on the surface, our employer seems to get on alright with Trev. In fact they tend to agree on a lot of topics and that might be why my younger brother gets away with things that other employees certainly don't. Take for instance the time when the boss expressed his horror and total disgust at the Green Party wanting same-sex marriages to be made legal.

"Maybe you'll soon be able to leave your missus and marry Jeff," Trev suggested to Wal one morning in the drill yard.

"I'd rather have red hot needles stabbed in my eyes!" came my employer's reply.

For some extraordinary reason that seemed to offend Jeff! "Ah – come on – Wal! You can be Mummy and I can be Daddy. Trouble is – I don't fancy getting your shit up the eye of my dick or under my foreskin."

That gave Trev a further opportunity to take a poke at the boss. "Fuckin' bloody hell – Jeff! Surely you'd use a franger? After all the people who've shagged Wal – you never know what you might catch off him!"

That caused the eavesdroppers in the yard to guffaw, and Wal told Trev not to be a 'fuckwit!'

Naturally that precipitated a debate on how anal intercourse between homosexuals must involve copious amounts of shit, and how it could induce possible incontinence to whoever was on the receiving end of such intercourse. That particular discussion ended abruptly when Joe Schultz called Jeff over to help him and Nick Lovadina service Joe's drilling rig, and the conversation – as usual – then drifted on to Australian current affairs.

The boss' favourite subject! Especially since Julia Gillard was voted in as Australia's first female prime minister. "Fuckin' woylie!" is a description that he comes up with for her whenever her name's raised.

"Howzat?" Trev queried him.

Wal was more than happy to explain. "Take a look at her mouth and nose. She looks like a woylie!"

"I see her looking more like a *Cavia porcellus*," Dave Wheeler argued.

"And what the fuck's that?" Wal challenged him.

"A guinea pig," Wheeler replied. "You're right – her mouth and nose do look like a brush-tailed bettong or *Bettongia Penecillatta*, but her arse is more like a guinea pig's."

Being of a like mind, Trev fell in love with the label '*Cavia porcellus*' straightaway; although my parents were far more hesitant. It's probably the influence that the dickhead Benito Mussolini had had in their parents' lives. Mum's very nervous about Trev calling the country's prime minister a 'guinea pig'. Dad also harbours reservations; although he does admit that Julia Gillard's mouth and nose *are very similar* to that of a woylie's.

Secretly I disagreed with all of them. I found Julia Gillard both very feminine and attractive. What put her first in Joe Schultz's and my opinion is that she was responsible for setting up a *Royal Commission into Institutional Responses to Child Sexual Abuse*. She was the only one with the guts to stand up to the filthy – putrid – scabby – rotten – perverted – scum in the clergy of just about all religious denominations! Plus to expose the filthy – poxy – diseased – scummy – evil human filth that were in senior positions in those religious organisations and tried to cover everything up! She made a much better prime minister than that arrogant little prick Kevin Rudd. The boss' description of him is all

'Ps' as well: Pompous – petty – petulant – prissy – poofy – pussy! Dave Wheeler needed to go even further – pathetic – puerile – pernicious – perfidious – paltry – pillock – prat! When Nick questioned Dave as to why Rudd was so egotistical, he was told that the ex-PM was only displaying typical 'little man' syndrome, and that no one should take him the slightest bit seriously. Wheeler also reckoned that every now and then people like Rudd and Paul Keating, another ex-Labour PM, would pop up in the media like mouldy, toxic toadstools from time to time, but Nick or anyone should ignore them completely on every occasion. Dave had even more scorn for Rudd: "When Rudd was voted in as PM he carried on as if he was France's King Louis the fourteenth. *Le Roi Soleil* or the Sun King. Old Louis had an anal fistula that became famous throughout history, whereas Rudd was a pain in the Liberal Party's anus."

When I asked him what an anal fistula was, he reckoned it was common in people who suffered from anal abscesses!

Then again, if Trev had picked up a name for the current PM off Wheeler, the boss agreed wholeheartedly with my brother when he came up with a label for Tony Abbott, the federal leader of the Liberal opposition party. 'Charlie the Chimp' they agreed was an excellent name for Abbott. He was the exact replica of a 'talking monkey'.

At first the boss *just loved* the label 'talking monkey'! Especially when he practiced it on Jeff Panizza. Whenever possible he looked for an excuse to call Jeff a talking monkey, and there were a few of us drillers and offsiders who were wondering if he was trying to pick a blue with the big fat bastard? Now – that would be something to watch! Although I've been a bystander only a couple of times, Wally Growford's a serious legend when it comes to blueing! But, and by the same token, Jeff's no slouch by any stretch of the imagination. Being on the sidelines of a fracas between them would be a *really absorbing* way to pass the time!

As a matter of interest Dave Wheeler reckons that the only reason why he keeps rosary beads in the cab of his drill truck is solely for spiritual protection because Wal and Jeff are two of the 'Horsemen of the Apocalypse'! Two of the *really bad* bastards! Pestilence and Death! Dave even claims that Wal only employs Jeff on account that the two of them combined represent the darkest forces of the antichrist, and it would only be matter of time before they destroy the entire universe with their pestilence, profanity and perversity! All 'Ps' again!

There's plenty more that the boss and Jeff have in common. Both are rabidly racist. They're anti Asian or anyone with a dark skin. After the bloodshed and civil war in the Balkans, they've made up their minds that anyone who comes from Serbia and Croatia shouldn't be allowed into the country; especially after the ethnic violence demonstrated at the tennis in Melbourne, and the shots being fired at soccer clubhouses, plus cars being set on fire. Their outlook on Africans is the same after all the murder and mayhem that's been broadcasted on our televisions for decades. Then, after witnessing all the bullshit that's going on in the Middle East, they – like every driller and offsider in the yard – can't for the life of them work out why the Labour government's allowing so many people from the Middle East and Afghanistan to come illegally into Australia? If these same people carry on like they're doing in places such as Iraq, Libya, Syria, Afghanistan and Egypt, what's going to stop them doing the exact same thing in Aussie down the track?

The boss is that prejudiced and paranoid, he'll only employ blokes who were born and raised in the Eastern Goldfields. As far as he's concerned, jokers from other states such as Queensland and Victoria and so on are 'foreigners', and the same label he even attaches to people who come from Perth! The only exception to this outlook has to be Joe Schultz, and that's quite easy to understand. He inherited Joe when he purchased the company, plus Joe's a gun driller and generally drills the most metres a month. He operates the most expensive and biggest rig in the yard; a Schramm T685WS! He's fortunate that he's got Jeff Nazzari – possibly one of the most competent drillers in the universe second only to my employer – as an offsider, but having Jeff on one's crew can be a *very mixed* blessing indeed! Nonetheless, he pays the highest wages, so Wal has little difficulty in getting the best drilling expertise that the goldfields have to offer.

Another thing that Wal and Jeff share have in common is their dislike for Perth. They, Dad, Trev and I – plus just about every bloke we've known and worked with – loath the place! A fuckin' 'sand pit,' Nick Lovadina calls it.

Dave Wheeler is even more derisive of the place. "It's like a fuckin' arse with the Swan River making a crack in the middle of it!"

"Fuckin' oath!" Joe Schultz wasn't going to be left out. "You can't get a fuckin' parking spot in the cunt of a place, and a person farts and you get a power cut. They're always having fuckin' power cuts down there! Power cuts and fuckin' bushfires!"

"Yeah, and have you seen those dickheads in Perth who buy four wheel drives?" the boss jumped straight in. "Reckon they're real macho buying Land Cruiser and Nissan four-by-four station wagons and putting roo bars on and rows of spotties. They never leave the bitumen in 'em, and their wives take six goes to park the fuckin' things in the supermarket car parks!"

Trev despises Perth; especially the crowds you get there. He reckons that when you're in a crowded place, humans stink more than pigs and feral billy goats.

Most fortunately there's no reason for my family and me needing to go down to Perth that often; all the same Wal has to go to the city on drilling business from time to time. While he insists his visits are strictly to do with submitting drilling tenders and meeting with new clients, Jeff let it be known around the yard that our employer only went to the 'big smoke' in order to search for sex with transvestites in North Bridge; visit the ballet; or possibly have his septic piles or haemorrhoids attended to! Either that, or he was trying to expand his collection of nude Boy George and Camilla Parker-Bowles photos. Of course the boss was tickled pink when the same rumour made its way to him via Noelene!

Still, that wasn't quite as funny as the time when Wal went to his quack to have a prostate check up! How Dave Wheeler got wind of it, I'll never know, but he broached the subject in the yard when his drill crew, Joe Shultz's crew, plus us Nazzari brothers were having a few beers at knock off time one Friday afternoon. "I'm being fair dinkum – I doubt if you'll find a braver bastard in one life time!" Dave started out with.

That drew some mild interest from Jeff. "Who's that?"

Wheeler pointed at our employer who'd bought the couple of cartons of Emu Export cans we were busy demolishing. "The doc that poked his finger up Wal's arse!"

"What?" Jeff's eyes bugged out.

Dave seemed happy to clarify things. "Out there somewhere is a man who's actually had his finger up Wal's bum, and has lived to tell the tale! Okay, so we've got some seriously brave diggers up in Afghanistan and Iraq, but you have to. . ."

"You go and fuck your boot!" the boss cut him off. Wal's cheeks are always red like Dave Wheeler's because of the burst blood vessels from all the grog he's put away over the years; however – much to the delight of his employees present – that day his face went a deep purple!

I still couldn't believe what I'd just heard. "What you talking about – some doc shoved his finger up Wal's date? How come? What would he achieve by doing that?"

After taking a couple of steps away from our employer, Dave most likely thought it was safe to continue: "It's the way they check for prostate cancer. The doc needs to stick his finger up your arse to check if you've got any lumps on your prostate."

Nick Lovadina decided to have his presence noted: "Hey – Wal?"

The boss looked relieved that the focus was no longer on Wheeler. "What, Nick?"

"I hope you weren't having the check up done and the doc had a hand on each of your shoulders?"

Yes, I'm sure there's something going on between our employer and Noelene at lunch times when the drill yard's usually deserted. I reckon he and her get up to things that make most of us male employees' blood boil with jealousy and lust. Or so Joe Shultz says in one of his books! Still, what makes me doubly jealous is that Wal's second wife's only half his age and *a real* stunner!

There's also one other thing that's also pretty good about our employer. If you disagree with him or he gets up your nose, you're perfectly welcome to take a swing at him, and he's *more than happy* to fight you! Nevertheless, if you were ever to be so foolhardy, you have to be prepared to cop a kick in the crutch; have one or both of your eyes gouged out; or perhaps have your nose or ears bitten off! The boss never likes to lose – *ever!*

There was one time when Les Carroll, a driller on one of the RAB rigs, nearly got the upper hand after he actually king hit the boss when he was looking the other way! Not a bad strategy to come up with, I suppose, when you consider Les was taking on a real vicious, ungodly, evil and unforgiving bastard whose aptitude for street brawling has taken on almost mythical proportions throughout the outback of West Aussie!

The whole affair started off harmlessly enough when Les pulled Wal up on some metres drilled bonus that had been left out of his pay. The boss did indeed admit that there was a discrepancy and said he would put things right in Les' next pay; *however* things went rapidly downhill when our employer reckoned that Les' missus stank like an Afghan cameleer's jockstrap – was a lousy fuck – and had a head on her like a blacksmith's anvil! He even went on to say that Les' wife was so ugly; he should become a Muslim and force her to wear a niqab or full face veil! That or bring her to the yard so that the rest of us drillers and offsiders could stone her to death!

Thus the king hit!

While our boss is a lean, wiry bloke with red hair, freckles, and not an ounce of extra weight, Les is at least twice as heavy as him with large, bulky arms and legs, plus a massive beer gut.

After letting go with all he had, Les was sitting on top of the boss, throwing punches at his head as hard and fast as he could go, and we had some mildly interested spectators in the yard who thought that Wal was gone for all money!

Not Wally Growford – absolutely no way! He just grabbed Les by the ears – pulled his head down – and sank his teeth into Les' nose! He then grabbed Les by the balls and mashed his already mangled nose with a crunching head butt! The boss had the upper hand by then, and his victim was half conscious on the ground. A couple of hefty kicks in the guts followed that where Les was almost lifted into the air, and that made him throw in the towel. The holes left in his nose from Wal's false gnashers have since earned him the nickname '*Flute-snoot*'!

Those bystanders who'd watched the blue had mixed thoughts about our employer's victory over Les for the reason that the win certainly had no moral value on the surface of things. After all – it hadn't really been necessary for Wal to reckon that Les' missus was a lousy fuck and so on. Les was only after pay that had been his due. All the same Trev was good enough to point out that Wal did have his kinder moments on *very rare* occasions. Like the case when it came to Mal Castle, an offsider on one of the air core rigs. When he was out bush, Mal was always shitting himself that his missus might be playing up with some other bastard, and one evening beside the drilling camp fire at night the boss tried to put his mind at ease. He reckoned that Mal's missus was as 'ugly as a hat full of arseholes' and her breath was like a bungarra or racehorse goanna's that had just had a feed of road kill! Not only that, her armpits stank like an outback bull camel's; therefore it was very unlikely that any bloke would go sneaking around to his house while he was away. It was too dark to see if Mal received any comfort from that or not, and there were those around the camp fire who wondered how come our employer knew his wife so intimately?

Yes, Trev and the boss agree on most things when it came to politics. Both are rabidly anti the Labour Party, and they reckon that people who vote for Labour are bludgers looking for a free handout. If there's one thing they totally despise, its programmes on ABC TV, such as *Q & A* and *THE DRUM,* where you get panels of supposed experts who reckon they know everything and what's good for Australia. Those self-righteous, pompous dickheads and the tennis coverage on the TV. They reckon that blokes who play tennis are poofs; and it pays to stay out of their way when Wimbledon, the Hopman Cup and the Australian Open are on. On the other hand the boss did once confess that he'd like to have the famous Aussie tennis player Samantha Stosur's panties as a side salad to a steak sandwich. Especially after she'd just played six sets of tennis! By the same token he reckoned he didn't feel the same about Venus and Serena Williams' panties, and Jeff Panizza accused him of being a racist and threatened to report him to people he knew in Canberra.

Their next two favourite topics are the Asian invasion of Australia, and fat women. I distinctly remember one of my employer's arguments when he came into work the morning after watching the ABC's *FOUR CORNERS* programme on Chinese sex slavery: "Has Australia's drug crime risen since the fuckin' boat people have come pouring in, or is that not a politically correct question to ask nowadays? Is the place riddled with meth heads since China became our major trading partner? Can I get in the shit for simply asking for the truth? It seems that every time the cops make a drug bust, ninety percent of the crim's are friggin' Asians – Chogies, Indonesians, Singaporeans, Malaysians, Thais and Vietnamese. Far too many of these cunts have spent their lives exploiting one another in their own countries, and moving to Aussie hasn't changed that one fuckin' scrap. Nice habits some of 'em have brought with 'em – drug pushing, sweat shops, extortion, kidnapping, child prostitution, sex slaves and the Asian gangs in Perth and Sydney. You've got these people exploiting their own people – parents exploiting kids – relation robbing relation. What about all those slave Thai and Chinese hookers the cops keep busting in Sydney and Melbourne? Did you see the Four Corners programme last night? You got the Chinese enslaving the Chinese. At this rate it'll be bloody Asians enslaving disadvantaged Aussies by turning 'em into drug addicts. It's going on already and we're losing ground all the way. The Chinese are the ones responsible for all the crystal meth that you can get easier than a beer. They're fuckin' a whole generation of Aussies. I'm not bullshitting, those arseholes and do-gooders in Canberra are selling us into servitude. I'm fuckin' serious, most of us Aussies – until about fifteen or twenty years ago – were born in a land of milk and honey with opportunity practically dripping off our noses. Wide open spaces ripe for development, jobs to pick and choose, mineral wealth, tons of fish in the sea, schools and universities for our kids and our youth. Now we're giving it away to a bunch of fuckin' foreigners. You mark my fuckin' words, if they ever call for a referendum to see who wants the boat people coming in, you'd get about ninety-six percent of the white Aussies saying fuckin' bullshit they do! Still the fuckin' Greens and Labour ignore that – and want to throw the doors open to all comers . . . And another bloody thing. What about all those Muslims they've let in? They're always going crook about something or other, and you've got the government and do-gooders apologising to 'em as hard as they can go. Why doesn't someone tell 'em to get fucked, or why don't they fuck off back to where they came from if they dislike this place so much? If they were forced to do a runner from their own countries, what the fuck are they doing whinging and fuckin' grizzling over here?"

A month or so after when we were drilling not far from the nickel town of Kambalda, the boss was obliged to stay the night with us in our caravan, for it was Kev's birthday and Wal drank far too many King Brown bottles of Emu Export to be able to drive.

Once my elder brother had served up some magnificent osso buco, the boss inspected his plate minutely. "Hope you haven't bought any of that fuckin' halal bullshit?"

"What's this halal bullshit?" Kev was quite taken aback.

Trev, as usual, had to join in. "Halal's tucker that's prepared for Muslims, Kev. Otherwise they won't eat it."

"And I won't eat fuckin' halal shit, either!" My employer was adamant about that, and then he reverted to vintage Wal Growford: "I'm a Christian – not a fuckin' Muslim. Do you see the way the Muslims are pushing the fuckin' envelope over the top of us, and you've got all the fuckin' politically correct do-gooders in the Green and Labour Parties sucking on their arses? You've got dickheads that're tryin' to do away with Christmas altogether. They reckon it might offend people from other religions. When did Aussie *stop being* a Christian country? If you've got blow ins who object to our Christmas – why don't they fuck off back to where they came from? You take that Big W. They don't call Christmas trees – Christmas trees anymore. They call 'em 'Grand Pine Trees'! I'll be fucked if I'll let my missus or kids go into Big W or Woolies. . . From now on if you blokes go shopping for tucker and Growford Drilling's paying for it, you check with me first before you go buying any halal shit 'cause I won't be fuckin' paying for it!"

That became the norm for Growford Drilling's tucker arrangements. When we go bush, Wal buys all the tucker, and he's one of the most generous employers in Kalgoorlie when it come to us buying whatever we like. In fact we dine like kings when we're in the field; although we tend to stick with Coles which normally has anything we could possibly desire. There's a butcher shop in Boulder Road where the butcher proudly advertises his meat as being 'non-halal'. Wal keeps his company account there, as do quite a few other drilling and mining outfits.

When I mentioned to Dave Wheeler how the boss claimed to be a Christian, he became quite animated when I mentioned Big W's Grand Pine Tree. "That's the fuckin' Yanks for you and their fuckin' Uncle Tom president."

He had me there. "What do you mean – Uncle Tom president?"

Dave had downed quite a few beers and his language generally alters somewhat when he does that. "That fuckin Barack Obama! He's done fuck all so far as a president, and now the North Koreans and Iranians are well on their way to having nuclear weapons capability. It's the fuckin' Yanks that come up with this 'Happy Holidays' instead of 'Happy Christmas' – the politically correct, crawling cunts! They're nearly as bad as what we've got here in Aussie. . . Also, I wouldn't take any notice of Wal calling himself a 'Christian'."

"Why not?"

Dave did his best to look mysterious. "You remember me saying Wal could be working for the antichrist?"

"Yeah – I do?"

"Well, that's what you'd expect from someone working for the antichrist – claiming to be a Christian. If you're not careful and take any notice of Wal, you could end up like Jeff Panizza."

Bugger that!

Wal's opinion of fat women is no better, and Trev's his most ardent disciple. In fact Trev's outlook on fat women could be described as psychotic, or so Dave Wheeler – the company sage – reckons. Truly, according to my employer and Trev, fat women's farts are louder, gassier, and much deadlier than skinny women's – the hairs on their legs are darker and bushier – they're more likely to grow moustaches – their pussies are mantraps from which there's no possibility of escape! If you were to drive into one of them with a bull bar on your vehicle, you'd come off second best. They're to be strictly avoided at all costs, and that's regardless if you've been stuck in the bush drilling for six months!

No bullshit, both my employer and younger brother have no time for porky women whatsoever! When Dave Wheeler claimed that fat women didn't necessarily emit more 'voluminous' wind just because they were larger, he was steadfastly ignored. Trev and Wal even have a way of alerting each other whenever one of them spies a chubby female grunter coming their way. Either one yells out: "Ahoy – thar she blows!" And then: "Burratta!-Brut!-Brut!-Brut!-Burruttaaah!" At first it had everyone in the drill yard completely stuffed as to what they were carrying on about; until Trev finally explained when he was pissed in the Hannans Hotel one night. The 'Ahoy – thar she blows' came from a book that he'd read, called *"MOBY DICK"* where someone shouted out from a ship's masthead whenever a whale was sighted, and the 'Burratta!-Brut!-Brut!-Brut!-Burruttaaah' was making out that the same grunter can fart like an air compressor without a muffler on its exhaust! Seriously, it's quite nerve wracking travelling in a vehicle with the pair of them through town, as you never knew when they're going to bellow: "Ahoy – thar she blows!" And "Burratta!-Brut!-Brut!-Brut!-Burruttaaah!" at the top of their lungs!

Nothing much changed for Trev and I on the work front when Kev snatched his rent. Trev just took over as driller on our Edson 2000, and a bloke by the name of Johnny Faulkner became our extra drill offsider. When Trev and I went round to Dugan Street to query why Kev had pulled the pin on Growford Drilling, Merl met us at the front door and my elder brother was standing not far behind her. Things didn't really start off that well when Merl told us to fuck off and that we weren't welcome. When I queried Kev about that, he just shrugged and didn't say a word; nevertheless I could clearly see he was both uncomfortable and embarrassed.

"She's fuckin' got him by the short and curlies!" Trev put words to the exact same thoughts that were going through my head. It was as if Kev had died or something, the way he chose not to have a bar of us and the rest of the family.

Finally things really stuffed up! Dad called me on my mobile phone. Something was badly wrong! He *never* called me at work! When I finally got him to settle down, he said that he'd been past Merl and Kev's place and he'd seen a for sale sign out the front of it, and a sticker across the sign saying 'SOLD'! Trev and I waited for knock off time and then we headed round to Dugan Street to see for ourselves. The house was deserted! We walked around it several times and peered through some of the windows, but all the furniture was gone! One of the next door neighbours came to the fence. After asking us if we were the new owners of the house, he reckoned that Kev had told him that he and Merl were heading to New Zealand! Not only that; he'd sold his beloved Holden ute!

What the bloody hell to do? Kev had pissed off to New Zealand without telling us! Although we knew it was obviously Merl's plotting and scheming – the filthy bitch – it was impossible to believe that Kev could've gone without letting us know. We had to keep it a secret from Mum, while I could see that Dad's heart was obviously broken! Kev has always been a pillar of strength to the whole family, what with his calm and level head, and Dad started missing him dreadfully! His absence in the house has created a huge vacuum, and to the best of our knowledge we haven't done anything to him to be treated like that, so it was bloody mind boggling that such a rank slob of a woman could have such a hold on him!

I went to the boss for help due to the fact that he's most definitely one of the wisest people in my life. He's made a real poultice out of the drilling game; notwithstanding the booms and busts and the do-gooder politicians in the Labour and Green parties trying to stuff the mining and exploration game. Despite his money and somewhat abrasive demeanour, he's generally quite easy to approach and always ready to hand out the best of advice.

"I'm fucked if I know," Wal scratched the back of his neck. "Kiwiland might be a poxy little place compared to Oz, but how do you find someone over there? Kev and Jabba haven't been there all that long, so I doubt if their names and address will be on the electoral role. . . I think the population's about four million. Let me think about it. I've got a mate who used to be a Federal cop. He's retired now, but still keeps his finger on the pulse. The Aussie Federal police will be talking to the Kiwi cops all the time."

As it turned out we didn't need the boss' assistance after all. It must've been maybe six weeks later when Dad got a call from Kev on the house phone. Apparently Kev and Merl were living in a place called Queenstown, and Kev wanted Dad to tell Mum that he was okay.

It may've been the first time in his life, but Dad was truly on the ball that day! He told Kev that he was going to tell Mum that Kev was dead and that would seriously crush her. He also said that if Kev wasn't prepared to meet Trev or I in this Queenstown place, he'd never be allowed through our family door forever! That meant no Mum – no Dad – no family – period! Kev would be an outcast for the rest of his days and that his filthy, foul-mouthed, stinking, garbage wife would have to take care of his family needs from then on. Those were the *exact words* that Dad used!

It was Trev who suggested that we should have a yarn to Joe Schulz or Dave Wheeler about getting over to New Zealand. Dave, Joe, plus Nick Lovadina and Jeff Panizza, went on a trip to New Zealand some years previously, so they'd possibly know the best way of getting there. Joe's mentioned their sojourn in New Zealand in his first book.

I had mixed feelings about everything. As a holiday destination I would've much preferred Bali or perhaps Fiji or something. Although I've no reason for it, I've never had that much time for Kiwis. It could be something that I've inherited from the boss. He totally despises them!

Them, Irishmen, the British royal family and feminists. Wal really hates Irishmen! He reckons he'll never fly with Qantas again because it's run by an Irishman! Yes, while Kiwis have a reputation of being bloody good workers, my employer won't have a bar of them. He once voiced his opinion of Britain's royals. "I've got a bit of time for Queen Liz and her old man, but when it comes to their kids and their kids, you get a good idea of how interbreeding leaves you with freaks. They're the same as some of the ones you get in Tassie!"

And then, of course, there's the so-called trans-Tasman rivalry where the Aussies and the New Zealanders accuse each other of shagging sheep. That and the rugby union which the Kiwis are supposedly pretty good at. The latter's neither here nor there with me and most of my mates. Being West Aussies, Australian Rules is the only footy we ever follow. Wal reckons he'll never barrack for the Wallaby rugby union team since they're being coached by a New Zealander. He even went on further to add: "No fuckin' wonder the All Blacks are always slathering the Wallabies. What do they expect if they've got a fuckin' Kiwi coach? Must be a bunch of fuckin' queers if they can't find themselves an Aussie coach!"

What the Hay Street madam told me still left me rather curious, though. That brothels and escort agencies throughout Australia were chock-full of Kiwi women. Them and Asians.

"If the sheilas over in Kiwiland are all like Jabba the Hutt, you shouldn't have too much trouble getting onto some pussy," the boss tried to cheer me. "Let's hope they don't smell like a recently opened grave. It's got me fucked how Kev manages to throw a leg over that mangy dog. What do you reckon – does he put Vicks up his nose?"

"How come you seem to know all about it?" Jeff's queries of the boss are generally cynical. "What – you slipped her a length as well? Don't be shy, Wal. If you haven't given her one, it means that you and I are the only ones in WA who've dipped out. Mind you, I've got much more pride than you."

That prompted the boss to say that Jeff's old man or old lady should've knocked him on the head when he was first born. Or perhaps they should've drowned him in the bath as soon as Jeff's mum arrived home from the hospital?

Trev and I more or less followed the same route that Joe Schulz, Dave Wheeler and them took to New Zealand. We went on an Air New Zealand Boeing 767 from Perth to Auckland, and then we had a couple of hours wait before a connecting flight was going to take us to Queenstown. We could've done much the same by flying with Qantas, but what the boss told us about this Irish bloke running our national airline – plus him sacking Aussies and getting Asians to fix the planes – we decided to stick with Air New Zealand. Like Joe Schulz said in his first book, most of the Air New Zealand hosties were fat and quite ancient. Not only that, they were wearing stupid hats that Trev reckoned looked like a cow pat freshly dropped on their heads; nevertheless there wasn't one steward who looked to be queer. Unlike our Aussie national airline, Qantas, where it looks like quite a few of the stewards are gay.

During the flight from Aussie to New Zealand I was given a special treat! When we fronted up to the check-in counter at the Perth international airport, Trev jumped in first to make sure that he was given a window seat. As it turned out the only place available to me in the same row as him was in a seat across the aisle. Another passenger was given the seat directly next to him.

He was visibly pleased once he was ensconced in his window seat, but not for long, though! Just when he thought that he might have a vacant seat adjacent to him for the flight, up waddled a humongously fat, ginger haired woman with a patriotic All Blacks T shirt on! She was easily the same size as Kev, but just a lump of rippling jelly with no particular shape other than round! The rolls of fat around her waist and her arms literally avalanched over the armrests, and Trev found himself hard pressed against the window! From then on he seemed to be in some pain for the remainder of the flight.

Meanwhile a gorgeous little brunette, who said she was also from Boulder, came and sat next to me! What a honey! I noticed that her toenails were painted green and yellow when she curled up in her seat and fell asleep. This was a clear example of the trans-Tasman rivalry between Aussie and New Zealand that I'd heard about, and here was a cute little Aussie girl – who totally outclassed the fat slob of a Kiwi sheila overflowing all over Trev – proudly displaying the Wallabies' colours! My heart started pounding in my chest when her head gently rested on my arm! I didn't dare disturb her, so it was necessary to watch the same movie twice!

My younger brother's eyes had a haunted look about them when he told me at the Auckland Airport that the porker's breath was very reminiscent of dog shit, and her farts were on a par with Merl's and Nick's! He reckoned it needed all his powers of self control not to chunder when the plane was being kicked around by turbulence when we were flying across the Tasman Sea!

He managed to recover somewhat by the time we boarded a Virgin Airlines plane which was heading for Queenstown. That time I made sure I was given a window seat.

CHAPTER 2

Finally the plane dropped through the cloud, and the most heavenly vista rose up to greet me as I stared down through the jet's window! Massive, pointy mountains! Some even had some snow on them! It was the first time I'd ever seen snow! All the ground around the mountains was an emerald green, but what captured my attention the most was a huge, dark-sapphire-blue lake! It was beautiful!

After a couple of minutes the pilot put us down on the runway and we were surrounded by the same pointy mountains on all sides of the Queenstown Airport.

And there was Kev waiting for us!

He also had what looked to be a brand new, metallic-green Holden dual cab utility, but on the way out of the airport he reckoned it was second hand, but had done bugger all miles. We didn't actually go into Queenstown proper, but to a suburb or whatever called Kelvin Heights.

Trev certainly has never been one to stuff around. He told Kev how Dad nearly suffered a nervous breakdown when Kev literally disappeared. It was then that I saw a spark of what my elder brother had always been, for he apologised profusely for keeping everyone in the dark. He claimed that Merl wanted to embark on a new life, and that there was no way she could do that in West Aussie.

My younger brother and I were in for further surprises! Especially when Kev parked the Holden ute in front of a magnificent, two-storey mansion that had an awesome view of the sapphire-blue lake I'd seen from the aircraft. If that wasn't amazing enough, parked in the garage underneath the mansion were a Porsche Cayenne SUV and an Aston Martin sports car! "It's an Aston Martin DB9," Kev casually informed us.

Then Merl met us at the front door. After giving Trev a long, expectant and searching look, the expression on her face changed and her demeanour made no secret of the fact that he and I weren't wanted there.

"Bloody flash place!" I tried to introduce some warmth to the situation. "How come you're here?"

"We're just housewarming for some rellies of mine," Merl explained, "so fuckin' make sure you wipe your feet before you come in."

I looked over at Kev, but he quickly averted his eyes. I could see that there was something weird going on, with him not being able to look me in the eye!

Trev and I soon had our cases in upstairs bedrooms that had an even more superb outlook over the lake. Lake Wakatipu, or so Kev called it. Taking a closer look at my surroundings, I soon realised that I was in a property that was most likely worth millions! The beautiful house – the ultra expensive cars – it was like being in some kind of a dream!

When Trev and I met up with Kev and Merl in the kitchen, which had a breathtaking view of the pointy, snow covered mountains, Merl was all matter of fact. "Someone's coming round to see us in about half an hour, and I won't have you bastards sticking your noses in. He's a business associate of mine, so I don't want you giving him any wrong ideas. Just stay here in the kitchen out of sight. There's beer in the fridge over there, but don't go guzzling it."

Sure enough a silver Mercedes SUV pulled up on the concrete apron just outside the double garage that housed the Porsche and Aston Martin. It looked like Merl knew people in New Zealand with serious dollars! The door bell rang just after Trev screwed the caps off a couple of stubbies of Heineken. There was also something kind of wacky about that, as it was hard to imagine Kev ever drinking anything other than Swan or Emu Export.

"You're looking fabulous as usual Miz M," some bloke called out. "Actually it's lucky that we managed to catch up, as I might have to fly up to Wellington at any moment. It looks like things are coming together very nicely. I'd say we we're over half way there. . . Hi, Kev – how you going, cobber?"

I knew that voice from somewhere! I was dead certain of it!

I looked over at Trev, and I could see that his attention, too, was captured. So much so his head was actually cocked to one side and he was frowning.

"I've heard that voice before," I told him.

"Yeah, at the Mount Lyall back in Kal'," he was still frowning. "Greg someone. Can you remember his surname?"

I wracked my brain. "Yeah – it was Greg somebody. Give me a sec' and I'll remember his surname. He was that dodgy insurance bloke – had to do a runner. Let's see now – it was Greg. . ."

"Greg Shepherd!" the look on Trev's face turned to triumph.

"That's him!" I was more than happy to concur. Greg Shepherd! The bloke looked suspicious when I first laid eyes on him. With the Mount Lyall Hotel being a waterhole mostly frequented by blue collar workers such as drillers, mechanics and so on, Greg stuck out like a sore thumb wearing a blazer or suit, white shirt and tie. So did his fancy, upper class way of speaking and his Pommy accent. He very rarely swore, which was particularly unusual when it came to your average Mount Lyall punter. Some blokes told me that they reckoned he was rooting the female manageress and licensee of the Lyall, but the thought of shagging her was mostly uppermost in just about everyone's mind. Regardless of his collar and tie and toffee accent, Greg was a really interesting bloke to engage in conversation, even though he could talk the back leg off a brown dog. And – after a few beers – he demonstrated that he could use Aussie blue collar terminology or slang with the best of them. What actually endeared him to me the most was the way he referred to testicles. Instead of calling them 'balls' or 'nuts', which was the norm in the outback; on most occasions he used to refer to them as 'figs'!

At the Mount Lyall Trev did most of the talking to him while I mainly used to listen. It was obvious even to me that Greg was a bloke who'd been around a fair bit, and he seemed expert on a stack of subjects. He told Trev that he was born in Kenya in Africa and was brought up there. Apparently he had a uni degree of some sort from a Pommy university. He was a stocky sort of a bloke about six-foot tall, with a neatly trimmed, sandy coloured, full face beard, plus a superbly confident nature about him. His ready smile, light grey eyes and easily approachable demeanour made him quite easy to like, and the barmaids as well as the licensee of the Lyall had the hots for him. Just like Trev, I was rather taken aback when some police detectives said they were looking for him. Apparently there'd been some kind of an insurance scam, and he'd disappeared into thin air!

Trev's face was perplexed once more. "What the fuck's Shepherd doing here in New Zealand? Do you reckon Kev also met him at the Lyall back in Kal'?"

"Nah," I disagreed. "Kev stopped drinking piss in pubs by then. We first come across Greg once he and Merl got married. Do you reckon we should warn Kev that he might be dodgy? Do you reckon he's a mate of Merl's? Half the blokes in Kalgoorlie would've been through her. Especially a charmer like Greg. You saw how the barmaids at the Lyall went moist between the legs every time he showed up."

Trev just shook his head. "Let's ask Kev what's going on first before we say anything. I wonder why Merl doesn't want us to meet up with him?"

We were given the opportunity of finding out more without any input from our elder brother. Greg himself poked his head in the kitchen door while he was on his way back from the guests' shithouse. His eyes went wide. "I know you blokes – don't I? Let me see now, it was. . ."

"Back at the Mount Lyall in Kalgoorlie," Trev answered for him. "Last thing I heard about you – the cops were after you."

If that upset Greg, he certainly didn't show it. In fact he just grinned. "Yes, *that was* rather embarrassing. Let me see now – it's Trev and Nev – right? Now I remember you! Especially you, Trev, after you insisted that I was a Pom when we first met. Tell me – so what brings you to New Zealand? You on holiday or something? Is Kev a mate of yours?"

It suddenly dawned on me that the flash house, the cars and so on might belong to Greg. With his snazzy clothes and the way he always talked in millions, it was quite possible that our beautiful surroundings belonged to him. People reckoned he drove a Porsche back in Kalgoorlie, although I never managed to see it.

"We're over here visiting Kev and Merl for a couple of weeks," I told him. "Kev's our older brother. . . Is this house yours?"

That seemed to put him on the back foot. "You're Kev's brothers – you say? This house? No, this house belongs to Kev and Merl. They bought it with…"

"Fuckin' bullshit!" Trev cut him off. "How the fuck would Kev and Merl be able to afford this place?"

That really opened Greg's eyes wide with surprise. "Do you mean to say that you're his brothers and haven't heard?"

"Heard what?" I butted in.

That sat him back even further, as he wrestled with what to say next. "Ah, now I see what's going on! To tell you the truth, I don't know where to begin. Okay – to start off with – Kev won lotto. I can't remember exactly if it was twenty-three or twenty-five million. It might've been thirty million. Either way, it was one of the biggest lotto wins in New Zealand history!"

Trev glanced at me, and then concentrated further on Greg. "Yeah, but Merl reckoned that this house and the flashy cars belong to some rich rellies of hers. Why would Kev go along with bullshit like that? He would've told us if he'd won lotto. Bloody hell, but. . ."

Greg stopped him. "Look, I'm sure there's some reasonable explanation to all this. Kev's bound to tell you when the time suits him."

"Yeah, but why would he go along with a lie?" I demanded. "I've never known Kev to lie in my entire life. He wouldn't know how."

"So why you hanging around Kev?" Trev's tone became far less congenial. "You tryin' to con his lotto money off of him? You want me to tell him that the cops are after you back in Aussie?"

Greg didn't reply till after maybe half a minute because he was obviously deep in thought. "No, I wouldn't do that, if I were you. You'll only regret. . ."

"And why wouldn't we tell Kev?" I sided with Trev. "What were you up to back in Kalgoorlie, Greg? The cops reckoned you'd disappeared without trace. What happened there, mate? Why shouldn't we warn Kev?"

Greg just put his hand up and shook his head. "Look, I can explain everything that happened back in Kalgoorlie easily enough. What's got me is why Kev's not told you about his lotto win. Surely that's one of the first things he would've told you? As I said – he most likely has his reasons, but let's not precipitate anything at this juncture. For heaven's sake please don't tell him or Merl that I told you anything. . . I'd better get back to them, but there are some very important things we need to discuss urgently. Believe me, if you give me the chance to explain everything – without either Kev or Merl listening in – you'll save your brother many millions of dollars. That's a total – unadulterated fact – you blokes! Just hear me out, and then you can decide for yourselves. How's about we meet at some pub or a bar in Queenstown? I'm being bloody serious, guys – the decision you come to could make or cost Kev millions!"

"When and where are we gunna meet up with you?" Trev asked him.

Greg pointed his right index finger at him. "I always thought you were an intelligent bloke, Trev! I came to that conclusion as soon as I first met you at the Lyall. This evening and over the next couple of days you'll find me at the Speight's Ale House round about six onwards. Meet me there – without Kev and Merl present – and I might be able to save Kev, you, and the entire Nazzari tribe a whole heap of money. Meanwhile, I'd better be getting back to Kev and Merl. . . Ah yes, I'm fairly certain of what's going on here. Nevertheless, please listen to what I have to say first before you tell Kev that I mentioned his lotto win. You'd be bloody insane if you don't!"

"What do you reckon?" Trev looked over at me when Greg disappeared in the direction of the front lounge room.

I, too, was totally stuffed! "If what Greg's saying's true, it means that Kev's been putting one over Mum and Dad as well. Surely to Christ he would've told Mum if he'd won lotto?"

"It's that Merl – the fuckin' bitch!" Trev's voice became a rasp. "Kev's been keeping secrets ever since he met the dirty – stinking – slack-arsed – bush pig. I bet it's that filthy slut who's responsible for all the bullshit".

"Bugger me gently!" I still couldn't get my head around things. "What did Greg say – that Kev won over twenty million?"

Trev nodded. "Yeah, and that he and Merl bought this place. Why the fuck would Kev keep it a secret from us? He's never told a lie in his life before now."

"Merl must've told him to," I could only agree with Trev's theory. "The dirty bitch might think we're gunna try and bludge off him. . . Do you reckon we should catch up with Greg and try and find out more?"

"Bloody oath, mate! Let's find out what's going on first before we front Kev. I don't know about you, but Kev keeping things from us has given me a queasy feeling in the guts."

I nodded. "Same here, buddy. You don't reckon it's Greg who's bullshitting?"

Trev was against that notion. "What the fuck would he stand to gain? Where did he say he'd be at six?"

"At some beer hall or something."

"Nah, he called it an 'ale house' or whatever."

Getting away to meet with Greg didn't pose too many problems. Kev wasn't allowed to accompany Trev and I because Merl reckoned that she and him had an important meeting with some people in a place called Arrowtown. She also told Trev not to be a 'fuckin' idiot' when he asked if we could borrow the Aston Martin DB 9 to go into Queenstown with. She reckoned Kev's ute was more our style and that we'd better not drink too much piss in case we chundered over everything when we got back.

There were no hassles finding a place called the Speights Ale House and we found Greg in the outside part puffing on a massive cigar and quaffing from a pint glass with what looked like stout in it. "Ah – gentlemen!" he stood up to greet us. "Take a seat. Here – what can I get you?"

"Have they got any Aussie beer?" Trev asked him after taking a seat and lighting a smoke.

Greg guffawed at that. "Aussie beer? You're in the Land of the Long White Cloud, Trev. When you're in Bongoland – you drink what the bongos drink. This place belongs to the Speight's Brewery, so you'll only get brews that they make. Personally I fully recommend the Speights

Porter. They say the Brits make the best porter, but someone at the Speights Brewery has been visited by angels. Possibly another Brit?"

"Back where we work in Kalgoorlie, there's this driller who's written a couple of books," I informed him. "A blackfellah. He and some other blokes from our drilling mob came over here, and they reckoned they liked Speights Porter. The bloke who put him onto it was a Rhodesian. This Rhodesian bloke had nothing but scorn for Kiwis."

Greg arched his eyebrows at that. "A blackfellah writing books? By blackfellah – are you talking about an Aboriginal?"

"Nah, he originally come from Africa. Some ex-German colony. Next to South Africa. His name's Joe Schultz."

"Ah – you must mean Namibia! A Rhodesian bloke – you say? Does he live here?"

I could only answer in the negative. "Nah, he blew himself away with a shotgun. He also killed his brother and some sheila. It happened somewhere on the South Island."

That really sat Greg back in his seat. "Well I never! That happened four or five years ago just outside a place called Gore. The papers were full of it!"

"Yeah, according to Joe's book it would've been round about then."

"So how long have you been in NZ?" Greg turned to me after I lit a smoke.

"Just arrived this morning," I told him.

"And Kev hasn't mentioned a word about him winning lotto?"

I shook my head. "Nah, not a word."

"Well I'll be stuffed!" Greg sat back, and by the look on his face it was obvious that he was as confused as Trev and I were. "He won the Big Wednesday lotto. It was twenty-five or thirty mil', plus the Aston Martin and that Porsche Cayenne four wheel drive. There were other prizes such as free travel and an American Express card, but Kev and Merl just took the cash for those instead. . . Or should I say – Merl did?"

"How do you mean?" Trev cut in.

"How do I mean, Trev? What I mean is – Kev bought the lotto ticket, but Merl's got her hands on the cash and the cars. She also owns that beautiful house on Kelvin Heights, plus a mansion of sorts in Wellington.

What I'm saying, Trev, is that everything's in Merl's name alone. Kev hasn't got a bean. . . Okay, while you might not see anything sinister in that, let me – without bragging about my irresistibility when it comes to the fairer sex – advise you that Merl has offered to leave Kev and go with me on at least half a dozen occasions. Naturally she said she'd be taking Kev's lotto winnings with her. . . Do you get it? Merl would dump Kev and rip off his last cent in less than a heartbeat. Now that she's persuaded him to keep his lotto win a secret, it only goes to prove what I'm saying."

"Dirty – fuckin' – bitch!" Trev certainly picked up on what he was saying: "The stinking – smelly – bitch! Everyone reckoned she was a slut and a gold digger back in Kalgoorlie, and that's why she picked on a poor sucker like Kev."

"She's certainly struck the jackpot this time," Greg did little to console him. "To be perfectly frank with you, Trev – you're dead right about Kev being a total sucker. He's besotted with that rancid creature, despite her foul breath, paltry charms and putrid flatulence."

"So you've copped one of Merl's farts?" I found the expression of distaste on his face quite amusing.

Greg almost choked on his cigar's smoke. When he recovered, it was necessary to wait for a while for him to stop laughing. "Have I copped one of those smelly things Merl makes with her arse, Nev? I'll say – I have! I've always found flatulence comical. There's nothing more glorious than a good fart that's been let free at an inauspicious moment. If you want to amuse a small child – just make a farting noise. Let's face it, the sound that flatus makes *is* funny. Especially when you know where it's come from. And then there's the smell, gentlemen. It just goes to show that no matter how handsome or beautiful you are – no matter how intelligent or talented you are – your shit *still stinks*! Don't look all at once, but take for instance that gorgeous, auburn haired beauty behind you. As unlikely as this may sound – I bet that on occasions *even her* flatus is odorous. Merl's not only stinks to high heavens, she's also got a particularly putrid personality to go with it."

Trev and I took turns at taking a sly peek behind us. Maybe three or four metres away was an absolute goddess! With looks like she had, she was most likely a film star or top model. I'd read somewhere that Queenstown was often frequented by famous people from around the world. I wasn't too impressed with the brunette's male companion, though. He was either Greek, Portuguese, or a dago of some sort because his arms were covered in black hair like a chimpanzee. His ears stuck out similar to a chimpanzee's, but he sported a massive, hooked nose that jutted out of the five o'clock shadow that surrounded his mouth."

It was as if Greg could read my mind: "I wonder if that bloke with that woman can stand upright when he walks? He must have a bob or two, otherwise why would you have a beautiful girl like that being seen dead hanging around with a gorilla? The bloke's a Greek, Maltese or one of those Latin Americans. Only they can grow hair like that. The man's better off in a zoo where a lot more people can appreciate him."

"You said earlier on – that if we listened to you – we could save Kev millions?" Trev changed the subject abruptly.

Greg sat forward across the table. "Indeed I did – Trev! But we're going to have to work as a team here. Let's face it, we're certainly not going to get any immediate help from Kev himself. Unlike any living creature on this beautiful planet, Kev's oblivious to Merl's rather dubious charms – obese arse cheeks – foul breath and putrid wind. He sees her as being the same as what we see in that beautiful creature behind you. As far as Kev's concerned – Merl can walk on water, yet she'd dud him in the twinkling of an eye. Yes – Trev – you *were right* in asking me why I was hanging around Kev and Merl. And yes – Trev – my intention *was* to try and siphon off a couple of million from them if I could. . . But we need to do more than that – don't we, gents?"

"Do what?" I wanted him to explain.

"All sorts of things, Nev, but hear me out before both you and Trev go crook at me, as you Aussies say. Admittedly, *I have* shagged Merl on more than one occasion. By the same token – and by the way she was carrying on back in Kalgoorlie – you blokes have most probably rogered her as well. If you haven't, you'd be the only blokes in the entire outback of Western Australia who didn't. . . Tell me Trev – have you rumbled Merl?"

I jumped in when Trev was hesitant to answer. "Fuckin' oath – he has! And I also got a head job from her. You're dead right, Greg, most of the blokes I know back in Kal' have been through her."

"Why thanks, Nev!" he congratulated me. "Yes, while most of the blokes in Kalgoorlie were bedding Merl for reasons of perverted lust, I've been doing it here in New Zealand for the money. Seriously big money, gents. . . Righto, having got all that sordid business out of the way, let's see if we can't join forces and help Kev get his fair share of his lotto winnings? I have a plan, gentlemen."

"Oh yeah?" Trev eyed him doubtfully. "And what's that?"

I was sent to fetch more beer before Greg would continue. I decided to try the Speight's Porter and it wasn't bad! Greg saw the decision I'd made and seemed happy to compliment me. "Good choice – Nev – good choice! That's the problem with the bongos here in New Zealand. They wouldn't've. . ."

"What do you mean by 'bongos'?" Trev pulled him up.

Greg was quick to oblige. "Bongos – the personal name I have for Kiwis. . . Anyway, I'm digressing. Okay – so I think we all agree that Merl's a person with the most revolting of attributes, and you can take it from me, gentlemen, that she has no intention of sharing Kev's winnings, even though he bought the ticket in the first place. I think we also agree that Kev reckons the sun shines out of her backside, and wouldn't have a clue of what to do if she was to walk away with all the money. Furthermore, you were right, Trev, when you thought I was hanging around trying to get my filthy hands on some of the loot. . . So here's the plan. Now that Merl has millions in her name only, she's starting to actually believe that her shit *doesn't stink* – no matter how absurd and ridiculous that may sound! We've all smelt the stench from her bowels – haven't we? She's now rich beyond her wildest dreams, and now she wants to be famous. What she craves from here on is respect, gentlemen. Can you think of anything more nauseating than that? She's grabbed all of Kev's lotto money, and now she expects people to look up to her. She now thinks of herself as being a tall poppy, so to speak. . . And that's where I come in. I've got a multitude of very powerful contacts in Wellington, both in the present government, the opposition party, and in the public service. I'm a consultant to most of these people, and yes – guys – these people without exception are a collection of consummate arseholes. Mind you, that's not unusual when you're dealing with politicians and civil servants. They represent some of the lowest forms of life on earth, no matter in which country you find them. I won't go into that right now. Either way, I've managed to convince Merl that the only way she'll earn her just respect is if she's seen in the company of the high society of Wellington. Excuse me if I chunder at any sec' because the idea of Wellington having a high society has to be similar to eating a hot, steamy turd off a cracked, Chinese made, plastic plate. . . Regardless of that – that's the plan. To get Merl involved with the bongo movers and shakers in Wellington, then we'll create an organisation for her that puts her in the same echelon as these movers and shakers. That shouldn't be too hard, as we'll have birds of a feather flocking together. Turd rubbing up against turd – all congregated in a sewer – rats feasting on rat shit!"

Trev wasn't all that impressed. "Okay – so what will that achieve?"

Greg arched his fingers in front of him. "If we play our cards right, we'll achieve a lot, Trev. While ignoring what the bongos like to think of themselves, New Zealand – especially with certain individuals in the capital – is a horrible, corrupt little shithole! As crooked as any black run country in darkest Africa. They may sail their ships close to the wind in Oz, but the Aussies couldn't hold a candle to what some of the bongos are getting up to over here. The Aussies are more sophisticated – aren't they? They can usually see a public service rort when it comes along. New Zealand's a Peter Pan and Wendy land when it comes to the country's civil servants – their egos and arrogance – their contempt for the ordinary bongos in general. What's more, our bongos just love putting officials on pedestals, and thus we get the arrogance, incompetence and greed that's rampant in the New Zealand public service – be it in Wellington, Auckland or the West Coast of the South Island. . . So what do we do, gentlemen?"

He had me in his sights, so I hastily shrugged my shoulders. "Buggered if I know!"

He also shrugged. "I'll tell you then, Nev. Most of the so-called 'elite' that I've come across in Wellington are either senior public servants, politicians or politicians' advisors. You've got some who've done well in the private sector, but they're well and truly outnumbered by the trash in the public sector. So – if Merl craves respect – we'll have to travel via the public sector. I've already gone well down that track."

"You keep saying 'we'," Trev pointed out. "What have Nev and I got to do with it?"

"Bloody good question, Trev!" Greg quickly nodded. "If I'm going to line up Merl for a fall, I'll need help from people I can trust implicitly. I know you dislike the idea of me wanting to put my snout in the trough, but we find ourselves in the same boat here. By that I mean – how are we going to take back the money that Merl's stolen off Kev?"

When Trev and I offered him no reply, Greg became even more enthusiastic. "Now for heaven's sake – don't breathe a word to Kev or Merl about the lotto win. That could be the trigger for Merl when it comes to doing a runner on Kev. Not only that, she won't be too charmed that I told you about it, so it'll also leave me out in the cold and Kev will get dudded for sure. . . Look – let's face some facts here, you blokes. Merl's as slippery as a butcher's prick, and she's told me on several occasions that Kev's as thick as a brick shithouse, and how she can't wait to give him his marching orders. She's met some of my contacts in Wellington and somehow she believes that I can make Kev just disappear from the general scheme of things. Fortunately she also sees me as being her path to fame and respectability, and I've done everything in my power to encourage that. . . She's already been shagged by some of those contacts in Wellington – hasn't she? The way I heard it, she was recently sodomised by an old bloke I introduced to her barely a month ago. Can you picture it, you guys – sodomising Merl Molloy of all people? The reason why I introduced Merl to the old prick in the first place was because she said she wanted to speak to some 'legal eagle' in case she needed advice if

Kev cut up rough about her leaving him. So I introduced her to this old bastard who's a janitor at the Ministry of Maori Affairs building, and she let the randy old coot sodomise her when he told her he was a Supreme Court judge and would be on standby if Kev ever took her to court for hanging on to all the money. When I asked him why he insisted on anal sex, he reckoned he just couldn't hack her foul breath. I take it you blokes have taken a whiff of Merl's breath, Trev?"

My younger brother grimaced. "Fuckin oath – it'd make you chunder from forty yards away!"

"My bloody word!" Greg agreed wholeheartedly. Although Greg spoke like a Pom, he was expert when it came to Aussie vernacular and used it when talking to Aussies. "Look, I'm being deadly earnest, Trev – she has no intention of giving Kev a red cent. Those cars – that house you're staying in – plus a mansion in Wellington's most expensive suburb – are all *solely* in Merl's name. Even that Holden ute you've been getting around in. She hasn't allowed Kev a brass razoo!"

"So how can we help?" I asked him.

"That's my man, Nev!" he patted me on the shoulder. "How long are you intending to stay in Bongoland?"

"New Zealand – you mean?" I pushed back at him.

He grinned. "New Zealand – Kiwiland – Bongoland – all the same to me, mate. Okay, so tell me – how long are you over here for?"

I looked at Trev first. "We've come over for a couple of weeks, but the boss owes us at least a couple of months of accrued leave. We can stay even longer than that, if it'll help Kev out."

It was obvious that Greg was genuinely pleased. "Bloody good one – Nev! I've just about got all my ducks in a row. With you and Trev giving me a hand, we've got every chance of seeing Kev get a fair go."

Events fairly went at a gallop after that. When Trev and I arrived back at Kelvin Heights, Merl informed us that she wanted to make a confession. At first I thought she was going to own up about Kev's lotto win, but that wasn't the case. She actually reckoned that she'd been left a pile of money by a rich aunt of hers, and wanted to keep it a secret from everyone because she had other New Zealand relatives who'd cut up rough if they heard that she'd been the only one in her aunt's will. She sounded so plausible that I began to suspect Greg Shepherd's story; although when I went to shake Kev's hand to congratulate him, his eyes couldn't meet mine. Naturally I'd known my elder brother all my life, and if he couldn't look me in the eye – there was some *serious* bullshit going on! Fortunately Trev also picked up on Kev's queer behaviour; therefore I certainly wasn't imagining things. Kev was being forced to lie, and that was a pastime totally foreign to a bloke like him.

Merl's story became even more bizarre. She said she felt very humble to be so fortunate and wanted to give back something to the New Zealand people. That's what her aunt would've wanted, or so she claimed. And that's where Greg Shepherd came into the picture. He and several very powerful people in Wellington were setting up a brand new government department. It required a female chairperson to run everything when it was established, seeing that that it would be such a family oriented setup. She also reckoned that Greg told her that she was just the person he was looking for, and if everything worked out okay, she'd quite easily find herself on the Queen's honours list! Could Trev and I imagine it – *Dame* Merl Malloy!

We got to see Greg quite often after that. He, Trev and I entered into pact; we would work together to stuff Merl up, but Kev must be kept in the dark at all times. The latter was the real dicey part. Whenever my younger brother and I were with Greg, Kev was most times with us as well!

"So what do you think of New Zealanders?" I queried Greg during breakfast one morning.

He frowned at the question. "I don't have much time for them at all. The Kiwis – or the 'bongos' as I prefer to call them – are generally cast from the same mould. You've got the urban or city types to consider, then..."

"Why do you call 'em 'bongos'?" Kev interjected.

"It's because New Zealand's so Mickey Mouse, Kev. That's why I call it 'Bongoland' and the Kiwis 'bongos'. Some call the Kiwis 'bungongos' or 'bungungerungers', but I'm more than content using the term 'bongos'.

You certainly can't complain about the mountains, rivers and lakes, as they make this country one of the most beautiful on God's earth. It's the people themselves that tend to piss me off. Their hypocrisy – their desire to be seen as the world's most politically correct country after Aussie. Their fraudulent do-gooderism – their incessant whingeing and whining. I suppose it's the Scottish/Irish heritage of the majority of them... It's only the Poms and the Maoris, plus the Polynesians from Samoa, Tonga, Fiji and the rest of the Pacific who give the place any character or life blood. I'm not saying this to try and piss in your pocket, but at least the Aussies have some interesting British, European and convict blood in them, unlike the Kiwis who're dead boring, unsophisticated and totally mundane. No, Australia – population-wise – is made up of much superior human breeding stock. . . The bongos are also as reliable as anything. People claim the Poms whine and whinge and carry on, but they're not a patch on your ordinary Kiwi. The common bongo goes to bed at night praying that the next morning he or she'll find something to complain or be outraged about. Especially the older and middle aged types... And that's not all they're reliable for."

"So what else are they reliable for?" I pressed him to continue.

"Where the bongos' Scottish and Irish ancestries appear to merge is their petty jealousy or downright envy of other peoples' good fortune or successes. If you want a Kiwi bloke or woman to soil themselves, it's when a friend, a neighbour or even a relative looks like doing well for himself. They dislike it even more if complete strangers are having a bit of luck. They just simply can't hack it. So much so that they'll do everything in their power to prevent *anyone* from succeeding. . . Here, take a look at what it says in this newspaper."

PEOPLE ADVISED NOT TO GIVE MONEY TO BEGGARS

Government social services in Christchurch are asking people not to give money to beggars. While the number of people sleeping under bridges and in parks remains the same, the number of beggars has increased alarmingly. The request was that people should ignore beggars just in case they were making 'a jolly good living out of it!' It seems such a waste of money.

Aaron Cohen, the well known Jewish gaming entrepreneur, supported the Christchurch social services: "If you must give out your money for non profit, put it in the pokies instead. All my hotels and bars – plus those organisations such as the Royal New Zealand Returned and Service Association – have ample machines to choose from. You also have casinos if you wish to throw away your money. That is solely what they are there for. Also, I hear that beggars and homeless people are using the public barbecue at the Margaret Mahy Family Playground for cooking their meals. This facility is for those that have houses, motor cars, and can afford to come into my hotels and bars. It most definitely was not put there for the benefit of the beggars and homeless."

Mr Cohen continued: "I can understand the social services' position. Who in this country likes to see someone else making a jolly good living? That is why I am thankful that those who least can afford it still utilise my poker machines. The machines give them some glimmer of hope, whereby drugs and alcohol can't. The next time you come across a homeless person or beggar, demand that they empty their pockets. If they are in possession of more than a dollar, report them to the social services so that a forensic audit can be done on their welfare benefits."

"How miserable can you be?" Trev was first to comment.

"That's what I mean, Trev," Greg looked pleased with that comment. "You have facilities that are geared to rob those that can least afford it via poker machines and the gambling on offer in casinos, yet people are told not to waste their money by giving it to beggars. . . That's not all what's bringing the country down. You take for instance the retirees and older generation over here. A good majority of them are retired public or civil servants. If there's one thing this country's been notorious for, it has to be its bloated, overloaded public service. A legacy from its various Labour governments. . . So what do we find, gentlemen? I'll tell you. We find the country's top-heavy with a multitude of retired civil servants who've done absolutely nothing with their lives. They've done naught for their country, either, which they've plundered and raped with their incompetence, petty jealousy and greed. They've been almost successful in sucking the lifeblood out of all of those who *have tried* to achieve something. . . That you'll find, gents, happens to be a classic example of their most recent evolution."

Kev, as ever trying to see good in the world, begged to differ. "They can't be as bad as all that."

Greg regarded him doubtfully. "Who's 'they'?"

"The Kiwis – or the 'bongos' – as you call 'em."

"Listen, Kev," Greg tried to sound as understanding as possible. "You've been over here for less than three months, and Trev and Nev here barely a fortnight. Soon you're going to be bumping into some of these civil servants I'm talking about. In no time at all you'll witness first-hand the run-of-the-mill Kiwi's psyche, and then you'll remember these very words. It's been bred into the bongo to resent any success earned by others. He'll do everything in his power to prevent another bongo from getting ahead. If another bongo wants to build or develop something, the average bongo in the street will become outraged and do all in his power to stop him. If you want to plant a tree in your front yard, there'll be a neighbour across the road who'll object to it. If you want to cut down a tree in your back yard, you'll have all kinds of organisations lining up to stop you. You want to build a house, develop a farm or a business, trim your hedge, and you'll have mountains of paperwork to fill out, and legions of officials looking over your shoulder just praying that you make a mistake so that they can hinder, fine and penalise you. Then you'll have hordes of other bongos that'll gather around and clap their hands with glee when they see you fail or get punished. . . Very well then, so let's address the bongo civil service that's burgeoned out of control in Wellington? It's the Kiwi's desire to see others fail that's led to the huge number of public servants in this country. Especially under Labour governments who've tried to fiddle unemployment numbers by creating more and more civil servant positions. That's in spite of the fact that most unemployment in New Zealand's caused by bongos stopping other bongos from creating any sort of new industry. You take this current Labour Government alone. In the first few months of this year, I am not exaggerating a fraction by telling you that households and businesses have endured a tidal wave of new civil regulations. Also that in the last couple of years almost 68,000 pages of new laws and regulations were passed by Parliament. And for every page of new regulations we've seen the creation of a further public service position in order to police these new regulations. . . As you know, I come from Africa. I've also tried to do business on that continent, but have failed miserably. In sub Saharan Africa, that is. Therefore I can see no difference between New Zealand and the black African countries I've visited. Black governed countries in Africa are renowned for their multitudinous civil services, total incompetence and nepotism. Where the bongo civil service is almost identical is the total incompetence of the bulk of its public servants or employees. Or the majority of them that I've come across. Take for instance – why does a university graduated engineer work for the government or a district council? Is it that he can't find employment in the private sector where he can make a much bigger buck? Maybe it's because he's too incompetent for the private sector? So, for that matter, why does any supposed competent professional join the public sector? . . . There's another similarity that I've found between a black African civil servant and a bongo civil servant. The more incompetent and useless he or she is – the more arrogant, or the bigger ego he or she has. This's the way they've evolved, what with the self righteous, puritanical, modern day feminism and political correctness, plus Mother Grumpling do-gooderism that's taking over both New Zealand and Australia as we speak. All this is accompanied by the jealousy, the treachery and the deceit. It's in their DNA."

Kev still wasn't convinced. "I still reckon they can't *all* be like that."

"Is that a fact, Kev?" Greg could scarcely disguise the disappointment in his voice.

"Yeah, Greg. I've just been reading a book about the Kiwi blokes who served overseas in different wars. In Gallipoli and France and so on in World War One, also the blokes in World War Two. They even fought in the Boer War with the Aussies and Britain, same as in Viet Nam with the Aussies and Yanks. Thousand of Kiwis sacrificed their lives for other peoples' freedom. Some of 'em sound like a bunch of dinkum, bonzer blokes to me."

"I couldn't agree with you more," Greg was quick to consent to that. "There *was* a time not too long ago when New Zealand *could* be called 'God's Own'. It was once one of the fairest countries in the world that these old diggers fought for. The core of this country was formed by the British who first came here. They were the nation builders and the people who brought the goodwill and the pioneering spirit with them, although the Scots and Irish contributed in no small way. It was the latter who'd been programmed to endure the freezing cold weather in Southland, or the torrential rain, mud and black depressing mould on the West Coast. . . Righto, so New Zealand was once a land of milk and honey. Wool was once a pound for a pound, and an avalanche – or should I say 'tsunami' – of money was pouring in! There were opportunities for all those prepared to bend their back. The people in those days couldn't be bothered with putting up with the Maoris and all their Treaty of Waitangi nonsense. They certainly weren't into handing over fishing rights, huge forestry plantations and half the country gratis in order to settle ancient and irrelevant land title disputes. All this brown-nosing – if you'll pardon the pun – of the minorities has come about ever since the bongos have been trying to lead the planet and beat the Aussies when it comes to political correctness and bleeding-heart do-gooderism. . . It actually took some time for the politically correct and do-gooders to start eroding everything away. You have to have some sympathy for the Irish Catholics what with their sex-crazed, depraved clergy. Perhaps that's why they have their trade unionism and their inherent belief of being wronged in some way. That's why, gentlemen, the Scottish Presbyterian Church has such a foothold in Southland and Otago, plus the reason the Catholic Irish Church's so big on the West Coast."

"Yeah, but what about that child sex abuse commission that's going on in Aussie," Trev backed him. "The one Julia Gillard started up? Most of the dirty bastards that've been lumbered have Irish surnames. Those fuckin' Christian Brothers are the worst."

"You're absolutely spot on there, Trev!" Greg acquiesced. "You have to have sympathy for your ordinary Irishman and woman in the street who are in all respects innocent. Especially those in the south. All they've ever wanted is a united Ireland where they're made welcome anywhere in a land that is *rightfully* theirs. They've been some of the most faithful people to both their religion and Christendom, and too many of them have seen that loyalty cruelly betrayed. People refer to them as being paranoid, though how many Irish kids have been buggered, sodomised and molested for centuries by the Irish Catholic clergy in orphanages and State institutions? By the clergy, I'm referring to the cardinals, bishops, priests, nuns and the Christian Brothers you mentioned. The whole putrid gang of them. Let's consider one of Ireland's major exports to the remainder of the planet. You take the Aussies – they've been exporting fine wool, beef, coal and minerals throughout their brief history. You take the Kiwis – they've been exporting world class lamb, wool, dairy products and fruit for roughly the same amount of time. So what've the inhabitants of the Emerald Isle been sending out to the world? Besides the beautiful Waterford crystal, fabulous linen, plus most probably scores of books on spud recipes – what has been one of their main exports? Their pederastic, perverted, paedophile priests, nuns and Christian Brothers have been a major export. They've polluted the entire planet with their filthy practices and perversion. And now – thank Christ – the truth about their putrid, satanic ways is starting to surface at long last in both Ireland and Oz – God bless our Julia Gillard and those brave Irish souls who've decided to do something concrete about it. . . Now I'll get back to the bongos. What else are they – especially the whites – also infamous for?"

"And what's that?" I nudged him when he fell silent.

"Have you been watching the Kiwi television, Nev?" He came back at me.

"Bloody hell!" Kev jumped in. "What a load of absolute – unadulterated – crap they've got on their TV! Seriously – I thought we had to put up with a bunch of crap on Aussie TV, but it's heaps better than what the Kiwis have over here."

"Completely true – Kev – completely true!" Greg was more than satisfied with my elder brother's input. "Still, if you watch the bongos' news programmes – their current affairs shows – or their media in general – you can't help coming to various conclusions. Firstly, the pathetic inferiority complexes the bongos have when it comes to Australia and Australians. Sure you can call it 'trans-Tasman rivalry', but the bongos are forever trying to denigrate the Aussies. You just take a look at the bongo media – their TV – radio – newspapers. No kidding, guys, you'll hear them rubbishing the Aussies at least a dozen times every day, whereby the average Australian doesn't really give a rat's backside about New Zealand or New Zealanders in general. . . I'm being dinkum – Nev! Once you've been over here long enough – like me – you'll soon see how pathetic the bongo media truly is. They must think they'll charm the New Zealand public – which they most probably do – every time they try and bring Australia and Australians down. You take for instance every time Qantas or that Aussie airline, Jetstar, have any sort of a problem. The bongo media's delighted to rubbish them, or anything that might go wrong in Australia. Yes, the bongos just love clapping their hands with delight. . . Well, at least no Australian airline has flown one of its planes full of passengers smack into the side of a mountain, with the sole blame being put on one of its pilots."

"That Air New Zealand Mount Erebus fuck up – you mean?" Trev insisted.

"Too bloody right – Trev!" Greg was exultant. "What a total cock up that one was! Especially when you heard a judge saying that he'd been confronted by '*an orchestrated litany of lies*'! I must say that if you were to read the Dominion Post's article '*Erebus Crash: myths and reality*' it certainly casts Air New Zealand in a very dubious light. Qantas hasn't needed to be bailed out by the Aussie government – to the tune of eight hundred plus million – like Air New Zealand was."

"Yeah, I heard about that, too," Trev knew everything as usual. "I also saw on the internet that Air New Zealand also paid far too much for Ansett Airlines in a Dutch auction with Singapore Airlines, and then fucked Ansett right up. Apparently it was one of New Zealand's biggest corporate failures where they lost well over a billion bucks. They fucked up a bloody good airline there, and also put heaps of Aussies out of work – the dickheaded wankers!"

I couldn't help taking a jab at my younger brother. "But you were happy to fly Air New Zealand when we came over here."

His reply wasn't one you'd recommend to sensitive or decent company. "I was given no fuckin' choice – was I? You're the one who bought the tickets – ya fuckin' retarded wanker!"

"Hey – settle down!" Kev growled at Trev.

"Right you are, then," Greg hurried on. "The Australians are busy getting on with their own lives – aren't they? They're having to tackle the fuzzy-glow political correctness that's taking over Australia. They couldn't give two knobs of goat shit when it comes to a bunch of Kiwi, bleeding-heart, do-gooder – quasi-pinko-commo, south-sea nobodies. They've too many do-gooder problems of their own. . . Another thing about the Kiwi media and the people who run it – who're a prime example of the bongo populace – they rejoice when it comes to putting the boots into anyone of their own people who's made a mistake, or looks like they've failed or are about to fail. And that's whether the target of their viciousness, spite and pettiness is a multimillionaire business tycoon, or a lowly proprietor of a corner shop. You fail, or even look like failing, and the Kiwi media – with the express blessing of the Kiwi public – will be alongside in an instant to shit, piss and dance on your grave. The bongos just love watching someone come a gutser. Here lies a demonstration of their evolvement since the first whites arrived. . . By the same token, if you happen to be successful and *do make* a quid – and that's despite the efforts of just about every Kiwi in the land trying his or her damnedest to stop you – the New Zealand media and the general populace will happily go out and find a stepladder, so that they can climb up your arse. Then – if you were to somehow fail after that – they'll come sliding out again, and will happily wait in line when it comes to trying to emasculate or eviscerate you. And that – gentlemen – remains a fact to this day."

"So, if you dislike the Kiwis so much – what're you doing over here?" Kev insisted.

"It's not so much that I dislike them, Kev," Greg corrected him. "It's just the totally pathetic attitude that most of them carry around with them. The way they're prepared to turn on each other and gut each other – let alone the Aussies. I think you'll find it's because most of their women – the attractive ones – who're as scarce as rocking horse shit or moas – prefer Aussie or even Pommy blokes. And, then again, the Kiwi blokes can only get onto ugly Aussie sheilas because the Aussie blokes won't have a bar of them. The Aussie feminists and so on who're grateful for any attention they can get."

We were sitting in the outside part of the Queenstown Speights Ale House with pints of Speights Porter in front of us when Trev folded up the complimentary issue of the *OTAGO DAILY TIMES* that was supplied by the Ale House. "Looks like these Labour dickheads are gunna be given the boot."

"At long last," Greg was happy to go along with him, "but what we have right now is typical of New Zealand politics. You'll find it's the same back in Aussie. We have a Labour government in power, and the Prime Minister and all her useless, quasi-commo, politically correct, bleeding-heart, tax-wasting mob know that they're going to be kicked out in a couple of months' time. This's the same shower that's virtually bankrupted the country, and has left the bongos in the street owing billions in debt. So they want to leave a poisoned chalice for the incoming National Party – don't they? You take for instance a former female Labour PM who bought back the railways from the private sector. What could be more toxic than that? The incoming National government had to throw hundreds of millions of taxpayer dollars at a defunct transport system that was going to be run from there on by an army of equally useless public servants. From that moment on the very meagre productivity of the railways looked like never making a profit, yet the railways work force – from the general manager down to the blokes who count the railway sleepers – still have to be paid. . . Okay, so you'd think buying the railways was a big enough poisonous pill – wouldn't you, Nev?"

I shrugged. "I suppose so."

Greg grinned at that. "Not by a long shot, mate! The timing couldn't be more perfect than what we've got now. The PM and her Labour mates still have an appetite for causing more strife for the incoming National

Party. All the same, any move they make has to be even *slightly* credible, and I've come up with an idea that should really do the job."

"Yeah, and what idea's that?" Kev just had to join in again.

Greg seemed to turn the question over in his mind before he replied. "Let me give you some background first, Kev. As I've stated before – New Zealand's literally overloaded – swamped even – by an infestation of public or civil servants. And it's the capital Wellington that's the most contaminated by these types. So, in order to try and create a new branch of this already bloated civil service, it became very necessary for me to put the thinking cap on. Just about everything's already been thought of. You've got government departments that cater for nearly everything. I certainly wouldn't be pulling your legs if I told you there'd probably be about a three hundred percent overkill as far as the number of these departments goes. You've got the Department of Justice – the Defence Department – the Health Department – Maori Affairs – and so on and so on and so on. I had to come up with something novel. Naturally I needed to look at the full picture. One of the greatest money making rackets in Wellington is conducting surveys, and then setting up committees to assess and investigate the results of those surveys. Labour governments are renowned for paying megabucks for useless information. Especially medical and demographic surveys, and they're willing to pay through the nose for them. That's how I bought my first block of luxury apartments in Estepona on Spain's Costa del Sol. No kidding, it's the Labour Party and the Greens' Mother Grumplings that love to think they know which's best for your average bongo – be he or she Maori or Pakeha. What they should eat – how they should wipe their backsides after a defecating – what's best for sceptic haemorrhoids etceteras. And man – do they like conducting surveys on Maoris or their Polynesian cousins! Why do so many adult Pacific Islander women have such a few front teeth? Why do an unacceptable amount of Pacific Islander men punch or head butt their missus after drinking alcohol, or when their favourite team loses at rugby? Who have more rectal problems – Polynesian men or women? Are rectal problems more prevalent amongst Fijians as opposed to Tongans? Is the standard weight and size of Polynesian faeces greater than those of the Pakeha because the former eat more coconuts and kumaras than the latter? What's the length of the common Samoan's donger when fully erect – and so on and so forth... I'm being serious, gents, conducting ridiculous government surveys throughout NZ is a very lucrative racket for a chosen, lucky few, and there's even more to be stolen via the committees that follow them. Not only are the surveyors paid tens of thousands of dollars, the taxpayers have to fork out for the best accommodation the country has to offer to these people – the best food and drink – thousands more dollars if the people conducting the assessments use their own transport. It can cost the general public as much as a million dollars to find out what percentage of the female population has copped more than one outbreak of vaginal warts in any given year. Or it could cost more than a million bucks to find out if uncircumcised blokes pull back their foreskins all the way when they wash their dicks. I even saw where it cost the government almost two million to carry out a poll on whether the supply of two-ply shithouse paper should become the industry standard in public shithouses and tourist accommodation. Apparently there were all kinds of shock and horror when a previous half million dollar investigation revealed that too many overseas tourists were getting their fingers covered in excrement on account of the fact that New Zealand made, one-ply crap paper was too thin or inadequate to do the job! The shit really hit the fan – if you'll excuse the pun – when the government tried to make the use of two-ply shithouse paper compulsory in private dwellings. An even further ludicrously-expensive survey canvassed the outrage of those citizens who were determined that they'd use one-ply arse paper if they chose to do so, even if they *did get* shit under their fingernails. In fact – and you'll find this hard to believe – another government appraisal pointed out in no uncertain terms that there were a good many Kiwis who didn't use bog paper at all! Having such lousy wages being paid in this country, they were saving precious beer money by using their index fingers, and that obviously just had to be a health hazard! Especially when the bulk of them weren't washing their hands afterwards! When it came..."

"You're pulling our dicks!" Kev accused.

"Why do you say that?" Greg parried.

"What you reckoned about some Kiwis wiping their arses with their finger?"

Greg owned a leather briefcase that he carried everywhere with him. The case was stuffed full of files and pages from newspapers. He rapidly sorted through the files and so on, then triumphantly lifted out a newspaper cutting. "Here – take a gander at this." He held the cutting out for Kev to read.

BROADMOOR STAFF CAUGHT DIRTY HANDED BY SURVEY

More than a third of health workers fail to clean their hands every time they should, a snapshot of 17 wards at Broadmoor Hospital indicates.

Senior staff have been questioned by the Midland Counties District Health Board over an apparent fall in hand hygiene at the hospital.

The target is 100 per cent compliance.

Hand hygiene is critical to reducing the rate of hospital infections, especially those involving super-bugs resistant to currently-used antibiotics. In addition to hand-basins, soap and paper towels, pump bottles of hand gel are mounted in numerous places around Broadmoor Hospital to make it easy to comply with guidelines.

While not scientific, the snapshot found only 62 per cent of staff complied.

In line with national and international safety schemes, the board introduced a campaign communicating to staff that they must thoroughly clean their hands before and after touching a patient, before and after any healthcare procedure and after touching a patient's immediate surroundings.

Furthermore, the members of the nursing staff were encouraged to wash their hands after they had used the toilet, as this was common practice in hospitals overseas. With the staff in overseas hospitals being instructed to wash their hands after defecating, it would now become an industry norm in New Zealand where it wasn't before.

The average compliance of three wards in December 2008, before the campaign, was 72 per cent.

The clinical director of the board's quality improvement unit told board members in a memo last month that hand hygiene "was now sitting at 73 per cent, having previously been at 75 per cent".

"The latest hand hygiene compliance is 62 per cent reported on the safety boards of 10 wards out of a possible 22," says the memo, contained in board meeting papers.

"This rate is collected by the nursing staff themselves, to help them take ownership of the problem locally, and should be seen as a guide, not a statistically robust measurement."

The board papers also state that an 11-month outbreak of the super-bug ESBL in ward 33 has ended.

ESBL - extended spectrum beta lactamase-producing bacteria - is resistant to a range of antibiotics.

In affected people, ESBL is usually carried harmlessly in the bowel and doesn't need to be treated, but if it crosses into the bloodstream it can cause an infection and sometimes death.

"As you can see from that newspaper article, I'm being fair dinkum, Kev," Greg continued after scratching himself under the chin. "You go to the south of the South Island and you'll find that the use of the index finger's a very common phenomenon amongst folk of Scottish breeding. It's even worse on the West Coast were some people have never come across such an item as toilet paper. . . And it's *just that* which gave me an idea."

"Just what?" I joined in.

Greg sat back and looked me up and down. "Shit – two-ply arse paper – bongos using their fingers to wipe their bums. I'm being dead serious – turds – poos – poops – craps – bogs! In a precise nutshell – S-H-I-T – gents! . . . Hang on, Kev, and I'll explain all. As I said before, it was necessary for me to conjure up something novel in order to create a new branch of the public service. A brand new government department – if you like. Also, as I pointed out before, we already have a government organisation for just about everything. Not only that, I knew it was essential to come up with a proposal that would win the hearts of enough people in order to get government funding. So – who to target, gentlemen? The public service itself – my good fellows! Those public servants who're due to retire or have retired already. . . Let's try and get a more accurate picture of your average, career public servant. The types I've encountered are generally incompetent and overpaid, and that's why they've joined the civil service in the first place. Majority of them have spent their lives doing as little as possible – have never missed a paid sick day – have refused point blank to work on the weekend or a public holiday – know every way known to man about how to screw the system. These same animals have the utmost contempt for tax or rate payers, whereas all the while the same rate and taxpayers have funded their superannuation or pension funds to a point where it could be described as *downright larceny!* Undeserving, ineffectual creatures that've robbed and cheated their fellow citizens without the hint of a conscience all their working lives. No, I've got it wrong – not *working lives* – adult lives. . . This's the exact section of the public that I need onside. The bulk of these types are the 'Baby Boomers' – people who were born at the end of the War or in the 1950s. These Western World parasites that were born in the golden years and have raped and plundered their countries and societies ever since. 'Grey Power' or 'Golden Oldie' – retired or due to retire – public servants, who're still demanding the very best for themselves, regardless of the younger generations who have to foot the bill for decades to come. They, gentlemen, are my lottery ticket to countless millions!"

"Okay, Greg, let me try'n get my head around this," Trev was the next to speak. "What has shit gotta do with public servants and retirees?"

Greg laughed. "You've no need to get your head around it, Trev. You've put the whole equation in a nutshell. Shit and public servants! What a combination? Okay – so what does your ordinary senior public servant desire most? They crave comfort and longevity. Their ratepayer or taxpayer-funded superannuation – or their fat pensions paid for by younger generations – is keeping them in comfort, and now he and she wants to live forever. All of a sudden this country – Aussie, too, for that matter – is chock-full of retirees looking to suck the life blood out of anything that's left. . . So how do we cater for that, Kev?"

My elder brother was immediately uneasy. "Buggered if I know, Greg."

"Not to worry, Kev. It'll all become clear. Nowadays in NZ we have a huge population of senior citizens who've become very health conscience. Like I said – they want to live forever. Now they're into exercise, they're very fussy about what they eat, and they're very mindful of their bowel motions and so on. I tell you, gents, they're very conscientious about how they shit, and they try and do so as often as possible when toilet paper's being supplied free by some public facility or other. . . You take when you arrive from overseas at an airport in New Zealand. You've quaffed down a few beers on the plane, so you need to take a slash. You walk into any airport shithouse in Bongoland – be it in Auckland – Wellington – Christchurch – Queenstown – and you'll be instantly assaulted by the stench of some unwashed bongo busy taking a crap. . . You take when. . ."

"I know what you mean – Greg!" Kev was all overwhelmed. "You're not kidding, Mate! When I went for a slash when we landed in Christchurch, the Gents craphouse stank! Same as the one at the Queenstown Airport!"

"Too bloody right – I'm not kidding – buddy!" Greg beamed at him. "You get the average bongo that's on shithouse pay. The Kiwis' pay rates are way behind those of the Aussies. Even though the bloke in charge of the New Zealand Reserve Bank reckons that the Kiwis will never catch up with the Aussies, this's still rather embarrassing to the bongo government – both Labour and National. . . Okay, so this same bongo goes to visit one of NZ's international airports. He'd love to join in on all the jet-setting and so on, but he's s got bugger all money because salaries and wages in Bongoland are so pitiful. He's been robbed of his last dollar when he buys himself a beer because the prices in New Zealand airline terminals – same as in Oz – are downright theft. How can he join in when it comes to all the jet travel overseas and high adventure? The only way he can take part in things is by having a long, leisurely crap in one of the airport's shithouses. When he goes home or to work the next day, he can tell his family and work buddies how he's been the closest thing to an international Kiwi jetsetter. Naturally his family and work mates regard him with something akin to awe. He's just taken a poop in one of New Zealand's international airport shithouses – hasn't he? To them that would be like Marco Polo travelling along the Silk Road to China, or a visit to the Louvre or Tower of London. . . Mind you, it's not only the craphouses in international airports that get inundated by hordes of foul smelling bongos. You go to any public shithouse in the country – the pub – a public library – a restaurant – the cinema – a hospital – and you'll come across every cubicle full of some Kiwi grunting, groaning, sighing and heaving away. And the stink from all that crapping seeps slowly and inexorably through whichever building you're in, leaving you feeling like a good chunder. That's why we see a river of turds fouling up beaches in Auckland, the Bay of Plenty, the Marlborough Sounds and Otago. I'm not joking, guys – you take whenever a natural disaster occurs in NZ – flood – earthquake – land slip or avalanche. All we ever read about is the resultant avalanche or tsunami of turds or raw sewage sloshing over everything! I expect you could put it down to an average bongo's peasant ancestry? Who knows? Public toilets generally supply free crap paper – don't they? You take your everyday Kiwi – he or she'll go to the ends of the earth to get a free handout. . . Right you are then, bongos really know how to shit, so the behaviour of their bowel happens to be of utmost importance to them. Especially retired public servants of which this country has a chronic surplus. Therefore, with the bowel being part of one's inner body, I came up with the title for my new branch of the public service. *'THE DEPARTMENT OF INNER HEALTH!'* What better name could you have for a government agency created to serve the senior citizens of this country? Come – you have to admit it, you blokes – we're touching on a stroke of genius here!"

Kev was the kind of bloke who was always ready to hand out a compliment. "Sounds bloody good to me!"

Greg obviously knew how to take an accolade. "Why – thank you, Kev! Now, not wanting to blow my own trumpet, even I was amazed at my own brilliance. If there's another aspect about the bongo population, they're overrun by quasi-tertiary-educated idiots. New Zealand's universities have churned out thousands upon thousands of Bachelor of Arts graduates, and the majority of those I've met wouldn't be worth two lumps of lizard shit either to their country or their people. They're as numerous as human body crabs in Bongoland, as you can just about get a BA degree off the back of a Wheaties box over here. These are the same dickheads who make up a good part of the civil service. The ones that whinge constantly and are outraged at everything. The types who reckon they hate the Yanks and stick up for Muslim terrorist organisations. The ones who support black dictators in Africa. These are the swamp life that force political correctness down other Kiwis' throats, and they're almost as good at it as the Aussie do-gooders and doyens of political correctness. The bleeding-heart do-gooders who put their own agendas before their kids or grand kids. Career public servants – useless arseholes who're only an encumbrance to the working classes or anyone who actually earned *a worthwhile* degree at uni. . . These are also the suckers who'll fall for my '*Department of Inner Health*' scam. They're the ones into organic food and all that crap, and tree hugging. They're the dickheads that inspect their turds after taking a crap. They'll be the same people who'll be fighting for the government funding that you good men and I are going to plunder."

"So how much money do you reckon you'll raise?" Trev's interest was well and truly captured by then.

Greg casually stubbed out his cigarette and exhaled the last of its smoke. "Half a billion dollars."

"You have to be bloody joking!" Trev gasped. "Half a fuckin' billion?"

Greg was as cool as ever. "As you Aussies say – my bloody oath – mate! Five hundred million buckaroos! I'm on to a winner here, cobber. Bongo society guarantees my success. Take a look at the Kiwis, Trev. A bunch of quasi-socialist, bleeding-heart, politically correct do-gooders. Not as politically correct as Oz, but getting close, Trev. A bunch of arrogant dorks who know what's best for all the people in the world, yet alone themselves. You mention anything about health and saving one of them, and no bastard will dare get in your way. Not even the government auditor, or the governor of the Reserve Bank of New Zealand. Naturally my department won't only cater for retirees and wankers with BA degrees. We'll also make out that we're very concerned about the bongo kids' inner health – won't we?"

"And you reckon you're gunna get all this money just because of the way Kiwis like to shit?" Kev wanted further clarification.

"I can almost guarantee that I will, Kev – old chap. Like I said – the Kiwis not only know how to shit – they're infatuated with shit! You take the renowned – Julia Maddington. She uses shit for paint."

"Bloody crap!" I just had to challenge him.

Greg just guffawed at that. "Right terminology you're using – Nev! Look it up on the Internet under New Zealand, Julia and excrement. You take our Julia's masterpiece – *People – Prejudice – Pride – Poop*. She was wined and dined all over Aotearoa for her 'shit art'! From what I can gather, allegedly she used shit for paint in quite a few of her works. I'm not sure if she still has the post, but she was also given a top position with some famous uni' in the South Island, plus she's been awarded all sorts of grants and fellowships from a number of prestigious Kiwi institutions. Also I heard somewhere that her shit paintings are highly sought after by art galleries throughout NZ."

Trev decided to join in. "When you reckon she uses shit for her paintings – does she use her own?"

Greg frowned. "You've got me there, Trev. That's not something you'd easily purchase in any art supplies shop or supermarket, but that's not to say you can't purchase turds in tins or jars or whatever here in Bongoland. Like I said – the bongos are obsessed with human poop. One would think she'd use her own. Maybe she gets a dollop off her hubby or boyfriend, or perhaps she goes next door and borrows one of the neighbour's turds? No, I think you can be pretty certain it would be her own. It'd be easier using that than her hubby's, boyfriend's or a neighbour's crap. She'd be more comfortable with her own smell. Her hubby's or boyfriend's poops might stink too much."

"You don't reckon she used a piece of dog turd that she picked up off the front lawn?" Trev had the bit between his teeth.

"You've got me stumped again, Trev, old son," Greg admitted. "Possibly if she owned a cat – she might've used cat shit?"

Trev was really gripping the topic in both hands! "If it was her own shit she was using, how do you reckon she collected it? Do you reckon she might've squatted over her paint palette, or maybe she crapped in a cup or something? She might've even used her hand to catch it when she was sitting on the dunny, but how would she wipe her arse after that? She'd need two hands to tear the shit paper off the roll – wouldn't she?"

By then Greg, too, had been seduced by the subject. "Now that you ask, it's also got me intrigued, mate! I honestly wouldn't have a clue. You don't think her hubby or boyfriend – or even one of her kids – presented her with some crap on a saucer before breakfast? Then again – picking up a dog's turd off the front lawn would be far simpler. She'd get a much better assortment of colours that way. Have you noticed how dog turds change colour as they're drying out in the sun? I've seen some that start out black or brown, and then they go dark green and eventually end up white."

I wasn't happy being left out. "Yeah, but what happens when she's finished a painting? Does she put what shit she has left in the fridge or something?"

Greg shrugged at that. "I doubt if she'd leave it out on her paint palette overnight, Nev. What about the flies? The stink would have them buzzing around from all over. It might be unhygienic to put it in the fridge. Moreover – like I said about the dog turds – her shit would also most likely change colour if it started to dry out. I suppose the best way around that would be to keep it in an airtight jar, or perhaps finish the painting all in one go and dice whatever's left over."

I was beginning to find the conversation quite amusing. "Yeah – Greg – if she didn't use dog turds, do you reckon she might've gone on a special diet for each new painting? You know – she might've just eaten beetroot for a week, or maybe she ate yellow or green foods to change the colour of her turds? Otherwise surely her paintings would've all looked the same?"

"And what about her paintings themselves?" Trev insisted. "They'd probably stink as well?"

Greg frowned as if deep in thought. "It's very difficult to say, Trev. Maybe not if she mixed the poop with other oil paint and mineral turps, the smell might abate a bit. As for your question, Nev, I'm sure – that being an artist who's held in such high esteem by the bongo art elite – she's bound to be able to manipulate the colouring of her own turds. Why don't you phone up the uni and ask her? All the same, I doubt if she'll let you into any of her trade secrets. You'd have to be one of her students to find those sorts of things out. Either way, all the arty-farty bongos who run New Zealand's public art galleries reckon our Julia's paintings are a 'must have' in their exhibitions, despite the poop content. Possibly it's so that they can get most of the blowflies to stick to one corner of their gallery in order that those automatic, chemical fly spray gizmos don't damage other more important works of art. Who knows? ... Hang on – I know! What she should do is organise an inter-school competition in the North and South Island. Both primary and senior schools need to be included, where pupils from each class must come up with a poop and put it in a numbered jar. A raffle can be drawn to identify the next piece of crap that Julia will use in her new painting. You'll be able to kill two birds with one stone here. Firstly, can you imagine the confidence it'll give some kid when he or she can stand up in front of their classmates and tell the world that his or her turd was chosen for the latest Julia Maddington masterpiece? Secondly, Julia can keep all the jars of poop in a special, hermetically sealed building at the uni, so that she and other aspiring bongo artists will have a huge range of colours to choose from."

Even Kev found that quite funny! "Stuff me dead – if what you're saying's correct – it looks like the Kiwis *do* have an obsession with shit!"

That pleased Greg no end! "Never a truer word has been spoken, Kev. As a matter of fact – when I come to think of it – I read something in the papers on the plane the other day when I was flying down from Wellington. It could've been either Christchurch's *THE PRESS*, the *AUCKLAND HERALD* or the *DOMINION POST* from Wellington. Or possibly one of those small town rags. . . No, hang on a sec' – that's right – it was the *DIRE STRAIGHTS DAILY TIMES*! I tell you what – I've actually got the article in my briefcase!"

He opened up his trusty briefcase, and then sorted through a stack of manila files and various pamphlets and magazine brochures. "Here it is!" he gleefully held up a particular newspaper page.

My brothers and I took turns to read the article.

CHANCE TO EXPLORE BODILY FUNCTIONS

A $800,000 exhibition at a popular Otago museum, opening today, will give visitors the opportunity to get sneezed on, and smell vomit as part of a new interactive science exhibit about the human body.

It is a collaboration between the museum and the local Polytechnic.

It was hoped it would attract international interest from overseas buyers, a spokesman said.

The exhibition, set on an imaginary tropical island, is comprised of 16 interactive stations all involving aspects of the human body, such as smell, digestion, and hormones.

One interactive station entitled "Smell the Danger" encouraged people to sniff scents including apple, coconut, vomit and "poo", he said.

Another exhibit featured a clip of a woman sneezing, with added water effects.

It is expected that the exhibition will run for several months.

"Now do you see why I'm on to a winner with my Department of Inner Health?" Greg's face was a portrait of exuberance. "Like I said – the bongos live, eat and breathe poop! If not poop – chunder and snot!"

I beat Trev off the mark. "It says here that people can sniff apples, coconuts and shit and stuff. Who do you reckon supplies the 'poo', as they call it?"

"You've got me stymied once again, Nev," Greg was forced to concede. "It could be the bloke in charge of the museum. Was a name given?"

I picked up the newspaper page once more. "Nah – it just mentions a spokesman?"

"It might be him," Greg nodded. "Or it could be the museum janitor who supplies the turds. You'll most likely find that every morning when he goes for a crap, he keeps a handful of it for each day's exhibit. I suppose you'd need to keep it fresh and not let it dry out like I mentioned before about Julia Maddington's turds."

"Yeah, but what if this janitor has bunghole or gets the screaming shits?" Trev barrelled in.

Greg shut his briefcase. "That's a bloody hard one, too, Trev. He'd probably have to get one of his assistants or one of the workers at the museum to come up with a poop. Nevertheless – you've got thousands of Kiwis who'd happily volunteer for that kind of thing. Just put an advert in the *OTAGO DAILY TIMES* and you'd have legions of do-gooders pitching up with bucket loads of fresh poop. People of all ages and gender! No – I tell you what – you could get rich and famous New Zealanders to donate some of their poo. Blokes like Sir Richard Hadlee the cricketer, or Bob Jones that real estate magnate or whatever he calls himself. Or maybe that Michael Hill the jeweller or possibly Winston Peters the Maori MP who seems to have gotten into strife over dubious party fundraising and telling lots of porkies? Or people who just crave to be seen in the media. You could then run a competition where the winner gets a museum sticker or whatever. You could call it 'Whose Poo Today?' or something like that. Even if overseas visitors choose to stay away, the place's bound to be overrun with bongos. They *just love* that sort of thing! I bet you – you'll even get Kiwi turd connoisseurs coming from all over New Zealand, and they'll be sniffing the bouquet of each poop like those BA arse-bleeders who reckon they're wine experts. Don't be too astonished if you find those real professional types insisting on a taste as well. And then you could have some professor from the Otago Uni talking to a senior civil servant from Wellington? 'I say – Gerrard old chap – this poop arrived via the agency of an Iwi!' 'What makes you say that – Clifford – my good fellow?' 'It looks like a kumara – old stick. The Iwis are addicted to kumaras. Trouble is – it smells of putrid coconut. Could've come from a Samoan or Tongan of gender unknown – ho – ho – ho!'"

"Yeah – and they can do the same with the chunder!" Trev was caught up by Greg's enthusiasm. "You could get famous sports people to puke into different coloured plastic bowls, and then people can guess whose chunder it is. You know – the All Blacks or those Kiwi sheilas that play netball. Also, what about a contest where people guess what's in the chunder – carrots – peas – roast beef – mutton – salami – beer?"

"Trev! Trev! Trev!" Greg looked almost ecstatic. "With us as a team – the world *is our* oyster – my good man! Ah yes – the heavenly Silver Ferns – New Zealand's women's netball team! By the same token – what about the sneezing, cobber? Why not go the whole hog? Find some bloke or woman that's got the flu or a chest infection. Get them to cough up phlegm and spit greenies on people as they're walking past. That's bound to suck in overseas holidaymakers – being spat or sneezed on by a bongo... All the same, we have to get ourselves down to Dunedin, so that Kev can snort on some poos and chunder."

"Yeah – like fuck!" Kev didn't look too enthusiastic about that idea. "You go and sniff some Kiwi's arse, but leave me well out of it."

"Hey, Greg, what's an Iwi?" I changed the subject.

"It's what the Maoris like to call themselves – Iwis... Getting back to those bongo BA dickheads. The politically correct, arse-haemorrhaging do-gooders and arty-farty wine connoisseurs and gourmands. The ones who have a passion for pictures painted with poop. The most dramatic revolution ever to befall Bongoland cuisine was when some Yank yachtsman hurled a half-full bottle of smoky barbeque sauce overboard, and it drifted up onto one of Wellington's beaches along with all the raw sewerage and crap paper. Like I said before – the beaches of the Land of the Long White Cloud are covered in shit. You just wait..."

"It can't be all that bad," Kev stopped him.

"What can't be all that bad?" Greg thrust back at him.

"The beaches being covered in shit," Kev wasn't backing down.

Greg reached under the table and grabbed his leather briefcase once more. After ferreting around, he came up with another newspaper clipping.

RAW SEWAGE SPOILS IT FOR SURF ENTHUSIAST

Several hours after his early morning surf Jeremy Watson was still trying to rid himself of the stench he encountered in one of Wellington's Bays. Mr

Watson is one of several surfers who say they have seen sewage floating in Lyall Bay in the past two days.

"It was definitely sewage," Mr Watson said. "We all know what poo is like and it was definitely poo this morning. It was really gross."

Mr Watson, a veteran surfer, said it reminded him of what the water used to be like about 15 years ago before the Moa Pt treatment plant was opened. "There often used to be this weird sweet taste and brown froth on the surface. It was just like that again. I can still taste it now. I have had a shower and lots of food and coffee and I can still taste the gross taste. My eyes are stinging and my skin is slimy and weird."

Mr Watson said his wife, who is a teacher at a nearby school, also noticed the smell when she was driving home on Wednesday. Several other disgusted surfers also encountered it when they were out in the water on Wednesday night.

Robert Mulder said the smell was horrendous. "It was the first thing I noticed. There were large foam balls blowing across the water ... it was definitely smelly." Mr Mulder now has a rash on his face but is not sure whether it is related to the sewage.

The Environment Ministry has reported that sewage can contain disease-causing bacteria, viruses and, in some cases, parasites. It can cause infections, nausea, stomach aches, vomiting, diarrhoea, skin infections and respiratory problems. After receiving one complaint yesterday, the council sent staff to the bay but found no evidence of sewage in the water. A Council spokesman said staff would continue to monitor it. Greater Wellington Regional Council was unaware of the problem yesterday but said it would investigate.

The president of a popular Wellington board riders club said that occasionally surfers did come across sewage in the water. The council usually notified beach-goers by putting up signs, but the signs were often not prominent enough, he said. "We have been in consultation with the council about trying to organise some sort of communication with our members when we come across a problem."

"Do you see what I'm getting at?" Greg was exultant. "You go surfing in Wellington's bays and you end up with a shit paper bow tie, plus you get a rash on your face and your skin goes all slimy! And let's not forget the 'weird sweet' taste and the brown froth in your hair. Do you see how that Watson bloke reckons bongos are real experts when it comes to human turds? So they should be! New Zealand with its beautiful rivers – wonderful lakes – heavenly beaches – pristine forests and mountains – is buckling under tons of human excrement! No wonder they get so many earthquakes here. . . And the Environmental Ministry reckons that sewage contains nasty bacteria and germs and stuff, does it? How's that for revolutionary thinking? Here – take a look at this."

He opened his briefcase a further time and produced what looked to be another newspaper article of some sort.

GIARDIA IN NEW ZEALAND: OUR HIGH RATE OF GIARDIA INFECTION IS COSTING THE COUNTRY DEARLY.

'I have sometimes also seen animalcules a-moving very prettily; some of them bigger, others a bit less, than a blood globule, but all of one and the same make. Their bodies were somewhat longer than broad, and their belly was flat-like, furnished with sundry little paws."

While it's hard not to be charmed by this description of a mysterious creature with pretty movements and sundry little paws, all is not as it seems. The comment was made by 17th-century Dutch tradesman and scientist Antonie van Leeuwenhoek, who, while peering through a homemade microscope at a speck of his own faeces, recorded what's thought to be the first sighting of the intestinal parasite that causes giardia infection. Van Leeuwenhoek, now known as the father of microbiology, had no idea of the link between the creature he saw through his microscope and the illness it causes, but giardia has proved immensely successful at spreading disease.

New Zealand is much more polluted with giardia infection than other developed countries – the country's rates of infection are up to twenty-times those in similar countries. Thousands of Kiwis, and more importantly – overseas tourists – have suffered the stomach spasms, diarrhoea and vomiting that makes a giardia infection such a gruelling experience.

Giardia lives in the guts of cows, sheep, cats, dogs and other animals, but is mostly found in human faeces. Many of New Zealand's waterways have been polluted by toilet waste and rubbish. Although it's often wrongly assumed that farm animals are the main source of the gut infection in New Zealand, giardia is usually transmitted from human to human. Other ways of becoming infected include drinking untreated water or visiting children's schools, scenic tourist locations or childcare centres.

Giardia is particularly common in young children, and in people aged 30-39 – many of whom are thought to be parents of infected children, especially parents who have babies in nappies.

There is little public awareness that the water quality of the country's rivers and streams is so bad, and many people have no idea of the risk of catching gut infections such as giardia, cryptosporidium and campylobacter from New Zealand's notoriously contaminated waterways.

"So much for Bongoland's 'green and clean' image!" Greg chortled. "You blokes come from Kalgoorlie and have spent most of your years in the outback. Okay, so you don't hear the Aussies promoting the outback as being clean and green, what with the heat and the billions of flies that you get, but at least the outback *is clean*! Not like most of Bongoland where the bongos are literally up to their eyebrows in crap. . . Here, I've got more data."

Greg removed another cutting from his briefcase.

SOUTHLAND'S MOST POPULAR AND SUCCESSFUL MAYOR SPEAKS OUT TO STOP TRAIL CYCLISTS 'POOING' ALL OVER NEW ZEALAND.

Yoghurt and scroggin-eating cyclists who pedalled along thousands of kilometres of cycle trails being built in New Zealand would end up pooing all over the great outdoors, popular Invercargill City Mayor Tim Shadbolt said yesterday. Mr Shadbolt supported a remit to the Local Government New Zealand annual conference this week that called on the Government to introduce legislation, including instant fines, for freedom campers caught defecating in the countryside.

The issue has been a hot one across the South Island, with many people upset about the dirty toileting habits of many overseas travellers; especially Asians and some Israelis. Although the criticism has largely focused on people travelling in campervans without amenities, Mr Shadbolt said he believed the government's proposed 2000km of off-road cycle trails across the country would exacerbate the problem. "All these bike trails the government is building are only going to make it worse, with all those cyclists eating scroggin and yoghurt. (They will have) huge bowel motions when pedalling on bicycles all day, and there will be no toilet facilities.

An accompanying spokeswoman supported Mayor Shadbolt, and said freedom campers who defecated all over the place were a disgrace, and vehicle owners travelling the country should be fined when people who rented their vehicles were caught. She also called on the government to provide more toilet facilities at relevant spots on its state highways.

Mr Shadbolt suggested humans should adhere to rules in place for dogs. "If you take your dog for a walk you have to pick up the turd, so what about us humans?"

CHAPTER 3

"What are freedom campers?" Kev asked Greg.

"Freedom campers, Kev? They're what you call your average sightseer in his or her own back yard. A great many Kiwis just love hitching up a caravan, or climbing into a van of some sort, then they venture out to the country's most scenic spots and shit all over everything. They're also given a great deal of assistance by Israeli and Asian freedom campers. Here, take a look at this magazine article."

CAMP WASTE INFURIATES RESIDENTS

Kingston residents and visitors to the Central Otago town say they are outraged at the faecal mess left by New Zealand freedom campers at the lakeside village and want the Queenstown Lakes District Council to do something after a local put his foot on a poo found on the shore of Lake Wakatipu.

"This has caused several nervous breakdowns among residents and is fast becoming a crisis" said a Kingston Community Association spokesperson.

"We see people camping all over the place and they're leaving excrement at the lay-bys and picnic spots along the lake. It is almost impossible to walk along the lakefront reserve within the village without stepping on poo.

"If the rubbish left behind is not bad enough, the worst part is the mountain of human waste.

What is making it more outrageous is that the locals have even nicknamed one of the lakeside beaches near Kingston `poo beach' for obvious reasons."

"It appears to be a common problem around the country," the spokesman said. "On the way to Cromwell the other day, my wife had to pull off the

road beside Lake Dunstan to spend a penny, and when she returned to her car she discovered that she had human excrement on the soles of both her shoes. It is obviously getting that way that you can't step on to the side of any road in New Zealand without encountering human waste." he said.

Greg's briefcase was never far from his side. He turned to me. "You know how people collect spoons to commemorate their travels to various places in Aussie, Nev?"

I'd seen souvenir spoons in road houses and tourist outfits all over Western Australia. "Yeah, I've seen 'em."

"Good! In Europe people also collect badges from the various towns and tourist destinations that they visit. With a great many of your bongo tourists this isn't the case because they don't have enough spare cash for such luxury items on account of salaries and wages being so dismal. That sort of thing was meant for overseas tourists – wasn't it? No, for your average Kiwi it's a case of leaving a memento at a scenic location rather than taking one. That's why they like to camp under the stars at some of New Zealand's most beautiful locations, and then they must want everyone to know that they've graced these particular spots with the blessing of their presence. That's why it's almost impossible to visit these places without putting your foot on some bongo's crap! Whether it's beside a warbling brook overlooking Lake Hawea, or in the shade of native forest in the Catlins – in the alpine village of Methven with the glorious vista of the Southern Alps draped heavy with snow all before you – you'll have a Kiwi bloke or sheila squatting on his or her haunches squeezing out a pre-breakfast poop. Those who can afford it like to drape their surroundings with shit paper, and the skid marks from their turds on the same paper quite often adds to the rustic milieu or charm. Then, for those who can't afford the luxury of a bog roll, the New Zealand tourist industry itself has most generously stepped up to assist – hasn't it, Kev?"

The look on Kev's face was totally blank. "How do you mean?"

Greg squeezed his hands together. "What about the tourist brochures you find in every roadside cafe, petrol station, and tourist information centre throughout Bongoland? While overseas tourists find these handy for navigating their way around the place, your bongo freedom campers are finding the exact same brochures most useful for wiping their arses with. Okay, so some of the glossy pamphlets may not be absorbent enough to do a proper job, but it's better than having to employ the index finger – isn't it? Besides, what could be more pleasurable thin wiping your bum on the photo of some luxury hotel or lodge that's an impossible mirage because of your meagre holiday budget?"

"Fuckin' bloody hell!" Kev was severely taken aback.

Greg was literally shaking with mirth! "One of the most important words in the bongos' vernacular just has to be 'poo'. It's 'poo' this and 'poo' that – their whole culture's based on 'poo'! Look – I know! Perhaps they should call this place 'Poo Zealand' from now on? It would be far more accurate and to the point. Yes, I think I'll start calling it Poo Zealand from here onwards. . . Our wise Mayor Shadbolt turned out to be a prophet. We have a turd trail that's been put down by cyclists all along the length and breadth of Poo Zealand. You take for instance the cycle trail that follows the old abandoned railway line in Central Otago. You had two ancient and frail farmers' widows who tried to carry out their typical bongo do-gooder act by cleaning up a section of the trail just along from their cottage in the tiny ex-gold mining town of Hyde. Apparently they'd barely got a couple of hundred yards down the old railway line when they'd managed to fill the tray of their Toyota Hilux ute with human turds, bog paper, tissues, plus sheets of newspaper and glossy tourist maps and pamphlets that people employed to wipe their bums with. Not only was our Mayor Shadbolt accurate about cyclists shitting over everything, he was also spot on about the size of the turds! In fact it was the size of the turds that almost sparked bloody racial conflict here in Poo Zealand."

"How's that?" Kev demanded.

Greg waved the magazine article around in the air. "Actually it was the niece of one of the old widows who started everything. She was studying anthropology at the University of Otago. She photographed some of the larger turds and came to the conclusion that early man would've also been responsible for generating such humungous stools. It was all to do with diet – wasn't it? Early man was believed to have had a lot more seeds, berries, fruits and nuts in his diet, while modern day fitness freaks, plus greenies and environmentalists are into eating muesli bars, scroggin and all sorts of supposedly healthy crap. Therefore when it came down to...”

"What the fuck's 'scroggin'?" Trev stopped him.

Greg didn't seem to mind the interruption. "Scroggin – Trev? It's the Kiwi word for 'trail mix'. Trail mix is a mixture of nuts, grains and dried fruits that hikers, cyclists and fitness freaks like munching on when they're walking or cycling on New Zealand's tourist trails. They eat the stuff by the bucket load because it's got no real nutritional value, and the dried fruit and nuts and whatever goes streaking right through them – don't they? And just like Mayor Shadbolt suggested – this scroggin or trail mix is ejected via the agency of gigantic bowel motions – not so? You take those adverts with gorgeous sheilas in leotards chomping on muesli bars and those breakfast cereals which are full of nuts and fruits and things for breakfast. You can bet your life that later on in the day those same enchanting sheilas will be grunting out poops as long and as thick as your leg. . . Look – Nev – I know you think that's funny, but I'm being deadly earnest here."

"So how did that nearly cause racial conflict?" Kev wanted Greg to stick to the story.

"It was some shit-stirring Aussies – wasn't it, Kev?" Greg was happy to oblige. "The niece who was studying anthropology went and put a dozen or so photos of some of the largest craps on her facebook site, whereby she was asking other anthropologists worldwide what they thought of her hypothesis. Her hypothesis that the stools of early humans were identical in size and weight to modern day fitness fanatics, greenies or environmentalists. . . Okay – so to get to the point – those photos went racing around the world like lightening! Especially since she'd used her aunt's Toyota Hilux as a scale measure in order to give people some idea of the huge size of the turds! That caused some Aussie blokes who were holidaying in Queenstown to go racing to the abandoned railway line in Central Otago, and they, too, took thousands of photos of the largest turds they could find. When I say thousands of photos, I'm definitely not kidding because there were literally thousands upon thousands of turds scattered all over the countryside! They did it for a joke – didn't they? Especially when they set up a website called 'TAG THE TURD' when they got back to Adelaide. This website told the entire planet where the poops had been located, and people around the world were invited – for a small fee – to guess the length, width and weight of a turd that was displayed on the site on a daily basis. . . Well – well – well – gentlemen! The site was an instant success – wasn't it? Particularly here in Poo Zealand! I've already mentioned to you the bongos' – principally the older ones – obsession with bowel motions and so on. Nevertheless, just about every Kiwi who visited that site was as proud as punch that such huge poos were found *in their* country! It was something the Aussies couldn't claim for themselves – could they? Not only that, the NZ Minister of Tourism was also delighted because some of the photos gave people an idea of the breathtaking beauty of Central Otago. You blokes haven't seen that much of Central Otago yet, but believe me, gents, we're talking about one of the most beautiful places on God's earth!"

"Yeah, but what were you saying about all this causing racial strife?" Frustration was creeping into Kev's voice.

"Sorry, Kev," Greg acknowledged. "You've caught me wandering all over the place. . . Nonetheless, I think I need to make myself clearer on some points. The turd photos may've made certain bongos proud to be Kiwis, however the Minister of Tourism's euphoria was rather premature. Prospective tourists from around the world were staying away for fear of encountering the people who might've been responsible for those gargantuan poops. Only a giant of a person would be able to manufacture those – or so a good many potential Japanese, Chinese and other Asian tourists believed. Most of these Asians were certain that it must've been the Maoris who'd come up with the turds. After all these same potential tourists had all seen brochures on NZ that proudly displayed huge, brown men staring googly-eyed and with their tongues sticking out! Only such men as these could be accountable for such breathtaking, massive bowel motions! . . . But that didn't stop our Aussies from making a fortune out of their website – did it? Kiwis in their thousands from both the South and North Island were stumping up their five bucks Australian. With the money rolling in, our Aussies were really crafty when they started challenging people to guess where a particular turd was laid down. That cost an extra five bucks. That really sucked the bongos in, and they started sending in pictures of their own craps, and they, too, challenged other visitors to the website to identify where they'd dropped their particular poop. Not only that by a long shot, but what was the exact size and weight of the turd? . . . Don't look at me like that, Kev – I'm not bullshitting you! We saw bongos up and down the length of Poo Zealand proudly displaying their recent efforts. Not only blokes, but sheilas as well. You know – those really butch sheilas – the ones who insist on playing rugby, soccer and cricket just because they're men's games. I'm not bloody kidding, but there were these large, muscley women squatting behind gigantic stools like hunters squat behind wild animals that they've just shot. You also witnessed other lasses standing with hands on hips, staring down at their crap with a look of '*beat that if you dare*' written on their faces, plus those that stood next to their turds staring into the middle distance like those blue marlin or big game fishermen do! There were even those who'd mounted what they'd achieved on special planks of wood, or others who carried them around on special Chinese made, imitation stainless steel trays! I doubt if anyone..."

"Crap!" Trev pushed in. "You're bloody pulling our dicks!"

Greg scarcely missed a beat. "That's right – it's serious *hamuti* that we're talking about here, Trev! Especially when you consider. . ."

"What you talking about – 'hamootie?" I forced myself between them.

"*Hamuti* – Nev? It's Maori for shit. I'm not kidding, Trev, you even had some bongos sending videos to the Aussies' website – didn't you? I'll never forget this one video where there was a massive, ginger haired, freckly female marching along in a kilt. I think it was the Gordon tartan she was wearing. Yes, in fact I could swear I was told it was the green and blue with yellow stripe Gordon tartan that she was wearing. Also, wouldn't it be marvellous if it was the pipers and drummers from the Dunedin City Pipe Band that were proudly marching both in front and behind her as she ceremoniously carried a huge turd on a magnificent, genuine stainless steel tray that was a product from Sheffield, England? Not one of those Chinese stainless steel trays that rust as soon as you breathe on them. . . Seriously, guys, you should've seen the monster she was carrying on the tray – she would've had to have climbed up a stepladder to snap it off!"

When I managed to stop laughing, I took up my elder brother's cause. "Righto, Greg, but like Kev asked – what about the racial strife all this nearly caused?"

"I'm just getting to it, Nev. There *was* very nearly racial conflict, I can assure you! The Maoris have always been proud of the huge bowel motions that they can muster from a diet mainly made up of kumaras, cabbage and pigs' heads. It was a matter of '*mana*' that they could come up with bigger craps than the Pakeha or white people could. Especially Pakeha sheilas!"

"What are kumaras?" Trev tried to stay focused.

Greg turned to him. "They're a kind of sweet potato, Trev, and the Maoris just can't get enough of them. . . Anyway, despite eating as many kumaras as they could, the Maoris new that they couldn't compete with the turds that certain freckly women and girls of Scottish descent could generate from all the oatmeal porridge, muesli bars, scroggin and so forth. So they resorted to the age-old method of retaliation by complaining about how their forefathers were dudded by the Treaty of Waitangi. Furthermore, we had photographs on the Aussies' website of Pakehas having a crap in sacred places, such as on the sides of Mounts Tarawera, Tongariro and Ruapehu, and there was even one photo of quite a chubby white girl from the Southland village of Clinton taking a dump in a hot spring pool at Te Whakarewarewa in Rotorua, or well within the confines of the sacred fortress of Te Puia. From all accounts she got her rectum, fanny and lower bowel steam-cleaned by a sudden gush from the Prince of Wales '*Feathers*' geyser, although she did win the website's '*best photograph of the week*' award. . . And the Maori totally dislike losing – don't they, Trev? I imagine that's why they make such magnificent sportsmen and women. Without the Maoris in their teams, the All Blacks just wouldn't be a feature. Neither would New Zealand's national netball team – the awesome Silver Ferns. . . No, the Maoris weren't too thrilled at all when they discovered that Pakeha women could come up with larger turds than the biggest of their men folk. As I said – they started whingeing about being dudded by the Treaty of Waitangi, and they accused the whites of cheating and deliberately manipulating the size of their stools. That led to more Waitangi claims where certain Maori chiefs claimed ownership of the radio airwaves and all the fibre optic cable that had just been installed to speed up New Zealand's Third World internet communications system. If that wasn't disconcerting enough, we saw Maoris burning down other Maoris' houses in Kaitaia, Whangarei and Maungatapere, and unfortunately the white vigilantes who were sent to those towns from places such as Auckland, Gisborne and Christchurch felt compelled to bash and taser a couple of dozen or so ancient women and small kids. I think it was around that time that some big-mouthed member of the Maori Party came up with his famous jibe – *'Gee Buddy, do you believe that white man bullshit, too, do you? White motherfuckers have been raping our lands and ripping us off for centuries!'* And it didn't stop at that juncture – did it, Kev?"

Kev was caught totally unawares! "What didn't stop? What you talking about?"

Greg grinned at his discomfort. "They couldn't have Maoris burning down other Maoris' houses, and white vigilantes bashing and tasering Pacific Islander women and kids – now could they? Finally it was probably someone like Mayor Shadbolt who came up with a solution to end the violence. So they decided to call for. . ."

"You seem to have quite a lot of time for this Mayor Shadbolt," I pointed out.

"Yes, that's true, Nev," Greg was quick to admit. "He's one of the only bongos that I *actually do* hold in the highest esteem. . . Okay, so they were more or less compelled to put together another document similar to the Treaty of Waitangi that the various Maori chiefs, leaders and elders throughout Poo Zealand were encouraged to sign. I think the Maori Queen was even urged to put her name to it, but I can't guarantee that. . . Very well then, it was agreed that there'd be one final competition to see who could come up with the largest poop – a Maori or a Pakeha. And that was to be it. No more whingeing – no more burning down houses in places such as Kaitaia – no more making claims on the country's fibre optic network – no more white vigilante bashing of Polynesian women and kids. . . So the Maoris chose Rangi Hika. Some say he was related to New Zealand's most famous chief – Hongi Hika. Don't quote me on this, but I think Hongi Hika was the same bloke who kept chopping down the British flag pole in the early settlement days, thus totally pissing off the country's new masters. Or was it Hone Heke who kept chopping down the Poms' flagpole? Who gives a rat's ankle – it doesn't matter. It's only Maori stuff, anyway. . . As it turned out, the whites or Pakeha chose a freckly sheila of Scottish descent from the North Otago or South Canterbury town of Makikihi – didn't they? Her name was Fran – Simone – Crapper. She was the great..."

"Ah crap!" I stopped him.

"What do you mean 'crap', Nev?" Greg came back at me. "Crap? Like I told Trev – we're talking about serious *hamuti* here – mate."

"This Fran Crapper," I insisted. "You're making it up as you're going along. How could she have a name like that?"

Greg quickly tried to defend himself. "If you'd let me finish, Nev, I was going on to say that Fran was a great niece of Thomas Crapper the famous English plumber. While Tom didn't actually invent the flushing toilet, he came up with some magnificent improvements such as the floating ballcock. Some royal bums have sat on dunnies that Tom put together back in the UK. You take Prince Edward who later became King Edward the Seventh. When he purchased Sandringham House in Norfolk, he got good old Tom Crapper to install thirty shithouses with cedar seats and enclosures. . . Righto, and if I remember correctly, Fran was roughly in her late twenties, and – like so many Otago and Southland women – she'd let herself go a bit. That is – she was more than a little overweight. A bit like quite a few of the women you find in some of Perth's suburbs such as Ellenbrook and Joondalup. In all of Perth's suburbs, if you want me to be precise. . . As a matter of fact when the Pakeha chose a woman to take up the challenge, this decision caused quite a stir among the Maori women folk. If the Pakeha could choose a woman to represent them – why couldn't the Iwis also choose one? Heavens knows, gents, there are certainly some fairly robust Maori lasses getting around the place – aren't there? And that slapped a real dilemma on the Maori men folk – didn't it? As far as they were concerned the contest ahead of them needed to be taken care of by warriors or men. It would be bad enough having to live down being beaten by some white female, but what would happen if it could be proven that a *Wahine* could come up with a bigger poop than a *Tāne* or Maori man? That would really blow the arse out of their *mana* – wouldn't it?"

"What's this 'mana'?" Kev cut in.

Greg nodded. "It's the Maori word for inner power or self-respect. If you lose face – you lose your mana. Do you see what I'm getting at?"

"I suppose so," Kev still looked doubtful. "So do you reckon. . ?"

He fell silent when an attractive waitress came and announced that the Ale House would be doing a special on the roast lamb and veggies.

"So what happened?" I wanted Greg to carry on with the story once the waitress went back inside. "Who won the competition?'

"Righto then," Greg looked like he was still making up his mind whether to go with roast lamb or not. "First let me give you some background to the outcome of this final contest which became known as the "GREAT COMPETITION!" The PM and her political colleagues in Wellington, both Labour and National, knew that they didn't dare let the Maoris win! If the Maoris won, they'd most certainly renege on the deal, and there'd be a whole bunch of new claims that had never been thought of by their ancestors when the Treaty of Waitangi was first drawn up. So the PM called in some of the country's most cluey boffins, who – naturally enough – were Pakeha or white. The Iwis or Maoris may've been able to come up with superb rugby players, scary haka performances, and some of the bravest soldiers in the world, but the Pakeha were in the lead when it came to sufficient quantities of the required grey matter. And these boffins were instructed to take care of our Fran – weren't they? The reason why she was chosen to represent the Pakeha was because of her insatiable appetite for French fries, or 'chips' as you call them back in Aussie. Furthermore, it just so happens that her home town of Makikihi's famous for its chip factory which most probably makes the best French fries in the Universe.

Fries made from the famous *Agria* potatoes, which are a magnificent cross between the *Quarta* and *Semlo* varieties developed in Germany in 1980. Not just ordinary spuds, guys. Also, it so happened that Fran was seriously addicted to the fries from that same factory since her early teens, and every single person in the town knew how she could easily put them away by the kilo. . . Can you see the connection, Kev? The boffins knew that the Iwis would be relying on their much loved kumaras for Rangi Hika to come up with the biggest stool. He was a giant of a man even by Maori standards, so would obviously have a huge lower bowel in order to grow and bake his challenge. In fact he was so big and powerful, he could take the place of at least six paddlers on one side of a *waka taua*. I'm not kidding, but..."

"What's a 'waka – what-do-you-call-it'?" Trev decided to poke his nib in.

"A waka taua – Trev?" Greg asked him back. "It's a Maori war canoe. Depending on the tree it was carved from, a waka or war canoe can carry up to a hundred people. Rangi's waka taua wasn't quite as big as that, but it would've required at least a dozen paddlers on each side. As I said – he was so big and powerful – he could do the job of five paddlers on one side of the canoe. . . Okay, so where was I?"

"You were saying something about this Fran sheila liking chips," I reminded him.

"Good one, Nev! Bloody good to see that you've been paying attention all this time. . . The government or Pakeha boffins I mentioned, wanted to ensure that Fran was given unfettered access to the same turd building material that the Iwis had, plus they decided to add a couple of bushels a day of scroggin heavily laced with wholegrain oats and stuff. The famous Makikihi fries – made from the world famous *Agria* potatoes that were grown nearby – would duplicate the Iwi's kumaras and give Fran's turd the density and weight, while the scroggin, wholegrain and so on would give it greater size. Not only that, we had two vastly different backup support systems in place – not so? . . . Do you get the drift, Trev?"

There was a look on Trev's face as if he'd just caught a whiff of one of my farts! "How the fuck would I know what you're talking about, Greg? If you ask me – this's all bullshit! Are you trying to. . ?"

"I can assure you it's *not* bullshit, Trev," Greg quickly stopped him. "If you'll just hear me out, you'll soon change your mind. . . Yes, there were two distinctly different backup regimes once our totally different competitors started growing or developing their turds. What you have to understand is that they were each given six weeks to come with up their best effort – not a minute or second more. So obviously the longer each of them could go without taking a crap – the larger would be their product! That's just simple logic. There's no point in going for a crap after three weeks if the opposition could last out for four weeks – now was there? And this's where the difference lay. Poor Rangi found it was necessary to go it alone – didn't he? For starters, his breath became so foul that his missus packed up the kids and decamped to her mother's place. A week or two later she went on to claim that his flatulence in bed had burned all the hair off the side of her left leg! Even his work mates refused to come to work because they couldn't hack the stench! He was working in a laundry at the time and his putrid wind mixed up with that humid, steamy atmosphere was just too much for even his best mates to handle. If that wasn't disconcerting enough, poor Rangi was temporarily barred from his local RSA or Returned and Services Association club in Rotorua because one of his farts started a massive brawl amongst the various teams in the ladies' darts finals. Apparently the skipper of one team accused the captain of another team of paying Rangi to break wind just when the very last and *most crucial* dart in the competition was thrown. . . It just doesn't make sense – does it? Here we have Rangi representing the whole of New Zealand's Iwi nation, yet he still had to go to work each day in order to pay the bills. The poor bloke was just left to fight the battle on his own. The only time his fellow Maori wanted to have anything to do with him was when the *kapa haka* was on. Because he was..."

"Whatsa karper harker?" I felt I should butt in before Trev did.

Greg nodded in my direction. "I was certain someone was going to ask me that, Nev. . . Let me see now – about every two years the Maori hold a kapa haka, and this's more or less a ceremony where tribes or teams from all over NZ meet, so they can demonstrate their talents for singing, dancing, plus martial arts and so on. Then, of course, we have the hakas or war dances which the Iwi warriors invented back in the old days for scaring the shit out of their enemies. You know – Nev – the hakas or war dances that the All Blacks do at the beginning of rugby matches?"

"Yeah, I've seen 'em," Trev answered for me. "They just make dickheads out of themselves."

"Unfortunately that maybe so, Trev," Greg conceded, "but the haka and their tribal singing and dancing and so on are very important to the Iwis. Especially the hakas or war dances. Having seen a haka, Trev, you would've noticed how the Maori warriors or rugby players poke their tongues out and try to make their eyes bulge out as much as possible. That's deemed to be very effective when it comes to terrorising one's enemies. And that's where Rangi became much sought after by Bongoland's kapa haka committees. It's little wonder because he hadn't been for a shit in just over five weeks, so not only did his bunged up lower bowel cause his eyes to bug out on their own accord, he was constantly poking out his tongue and nervously licking his lips. Actually the nervous lip-licking also came naturally to him because Rangi had a fair idea of the size of the turd he was carrying around. When the time came for him to finally present it for the competition, his arsehole would be in for a rather gruelling and torrid time – wouldn't it? Apparently he'd been bunged up before, but that was only for a fortnight or so. From what I hear, on that occasion it took at least six months for his anal sphincters to return to their normal size, and he actually told a mate back then that he knew exactly the pain a woman had to endure when giving birth to an oversized baby. I suppose..."

"Hang on – what do ya mean anal 'sphincters'?" I thought I'd caught him out! "How come he's got more than one sphincter? Does it mean that he had two arseholes?"

"I'll have you know, Nev, that we've all been issued with two anal sphincter muscles – an external and internal one. These are the last line of defence when it comes to warding off incontinence. You can ask Trev here. . . Anyway, gents, Rangi was in big demand for that year's Iwi kapa kaka festival! Kapa haka recruiters from all over the North Island – from Kawakawa in the north all the way down to Wanganui in the south – all tried to poach him for their haka team. But Rangi was a born and bred native of the Whakan-Hell district – pronounced in Maori 'Fuckan-Hell', and he wasn't going to turn his back on his home town, even in the face of the fact that his missus insisted on taking out a restraining order against him visiting her and the kids at her mother's place, and that the committee of the local RSA chose to ban him from frequenting its premises until the competition was over. . . And *what a magnificent* performance, guys! Whakan-Hell won that year's kapa haka solely because of Rangi Hika's presence in those marvellous Maori festivities. Sure we witnessed excellent and scary hakas performed by teams from places such as Tauranga, Putaruru and Taupo – still the judges all voted in favour of Whakan-Hell because of Rangi. And you can easily see the reason for that, gentlemen, because there was little wonder why his eyes bugged out as if they were on stalks, and why he managed to contort his facial features in such a tortured and frightening fashion. So would you if you were scared out of your wits that the frenetic foot stamping – which is required in a haka – just might dislodge a gigantic turd that was *just busting* to find its freedom! No wonder his eyes were bugging out – his face was so scary – his tongue was poking in and out like a monitor lizard? In fact it was that very evening when the kapa haka was won by Whakan-Hell when his turd did finally escape, and his doctor saw fit to urgently sew at least seven or more stitches into his anal sphincters! . . . Can you put yourself in Rangi's shoes, Kev – going for over five weeks without having a shit?"

"He's lucky it didn't kill the poor bastard!" Kev informed him solemnly. "The longest I've gone without a shit is maybe a week, and it fuckin' near killed me when I finally did manage to get rid of it!"

"Bloody hell – as long as a week, Kev!" Greg seemed mildly startled by my elder brother's admission. "Mind you, it was a totally different story with Fran down in Makikihi. She actually went the full six weeks, but she had it much easier during the turd growing stages than poor old Rangi did. She spent her time at her parents' house and was given special paid leave by her employer on a nearby potato farm – wasn't she? Furthermore, she enjoyed the help which was coming in from all over Otago and Southland – didn't she? There were fully trained nurses travelling all the way from Invercargill,

Dunedin, Oamaru and Waimate to make sure every comfort was afforded to her. Everyone knew that Fran was serving a magnificent cause on behalf of all bongo Pakehas, and the nurses had even given her poop a name – 'Popsie'! Fran's pulse and blood pressure were checked on the hour, her temperature was taken, plus she was forbidden to be on her feet for more than ten minutes at a time. You see, carrying such a large crap around, had to be very similar to being pregnant. There was every likelihood that Fran would get burst blood vessels in her legs – which some women do when they're heavily pregnant – plus she might inadvertently let go of Popsie like a woman having a miscarriage! If she wanted to go out shopping or to church, we saw a host of volunteers just begging to have the privilege of trundling her along in a wheelchair. She was even lucky enough to have a female professor from the Lincoln University who took a six-week sabbatical in order to keep an eye on her. Lincoln University's mainly an agricultural outfit, and our professor was expert in cows calving, but you can see the similarity in the two equations – can't you, Kev? Fran taking a crap after baking it for six weeks was almost identical to a cow giving birth to a calf – wasn't it? . . . Yes, our Fran was attended to day and night. Volunteers were on hand twenty-four-seven busy massaging her ankles and neck, so that she could stay as relaxed as possible. Nobody – *and I mean nobody* – wanted Popsie to make her debut prematurely! Fran spent most of her time with her legs propped up on the sofa with a plastic bucket of delicious Makikihi fries on one side, and one of those plastic wheelie bins full of scroggin and rolled oats on the other. She was also drinking gallons of concentrated powdered milk supplements in order to add weight and binding to Popsie. As you can see – some of the country's brainiest boffins were doing their part. . . Also true – and similar to Rangi – Fran's breath *did start* to stink horribly after a week or so, and eventually her flatus became that rank even her faithful border collie, 'Chocolate Chippie', moved in with the neighbours next door. Nevertheless those who were attending to her were highly-skilled professionals and used masks which they'd carefully laced with lavender toilet deodorant spray. . . Do you think you can picture it, Nev?"

"I reckon, Greg." There was no way that I could fathom what he was saying.

Greg frowned. "Unfortunately we come across a downside to this otherwise heart warming situation. The use of toilet deodorant sprays to mask Fran's breath and odd wind breakage became addictive to some of those dedicated and loyal carers. I have it from excellent authority that the majority of those nurses that were at Fran's side are using up to two or possibly three cans of deodorant spray a day. They're not observing the practice of squirting the deodorant onto masks any more – they're actually holding the spray can nozzles directly to their nostrils and inhaling it straight into their lungs. . . Right you are then – while Rangi tried to emit flatus as loud and as long as possible, Fran was far more gentle and ladylike. She didn't deliberately try to assault people with her putrid wind, like Rangi loved doing. He deliberately sought out the highest buildings in Auckland, so that he could break wind in lifts full of people taking their lunch break. He made a point of staying away from Whakan-Hell, because the town stinks like everyone in it has just farted. Very similar to Rotorua! . . . No, it was only on very rare occasions when Fran's flatulence made any noise inside the house, plus she mostly used her ten minute breaks when she was allowed to be on her feet to go out into the garden and fluff outside. How ladylike is that? While Rangi's family and best mates gave him a wide berth, those surrounding Fran felt more and more beholden to her. Just like an ordinary woman bursts into flower when she's heavy with child, Fran too, was beginning to bloom and blossom as Popsie grew larger and larger. She exhibited the tranquillity and graces of a pregnant woman that all those around her sincerely appreciated and were drawn to, and they vowed that they'd do their utmost to emulate her as they also took on their own struggle with life. . . But, then again, in some cases Fran was much worse off than Rangi."

"How come?" Kev was totally focused once more.

Greg seemed to juggle the question in his brain. "Let me see now – how can I explain it, Kev? Okay – in a way Rangi had it far better when it came to letting go of his turd, even if his doctor needed to sew half a dozen stitches into his rectum. When Whakan-Hell won the kapa haka, the skipper of the haka team gave Rangi a bottle of tequila which he'd managed to filch out of some Pakeha sheila from Napier's BMW sports car. This happened a short while after the BMW's owner had performed fellatio on him, however let's not go there at this juncture. Let it suffice to say that although Rangi didn't like the taste of tequila – he reckoned it tasted like the castor oil his nana used to give him when he was plagued with bunghole – he drank the whole bottle on his own just before retiring to bed. Perhaps he would've enjoyed it more if he'd used salt and lemons? . . . The rest is pretty much history. I don't know if it was mind over matter, but the tequila did act exactly like castor oil! Rangi woke from his drunken stupor with a burning arsehole and cuddling up to what he at first thought was a rock or boulder of some sort!"

"You're kidding!" Kev exclaimed.

Greg was much calmer. "I've never been more dinkum, Kev! Poor Rangi passed out at least three times before he managed to get the neighbours to call for an ambulance. Luckily his next door neighbour was a respected Iwi elder because the turd might've been thrown out by the ambos or gone missing altogether! At least the old bloke kept his wits about him sufficiently to call his son-in-law. Together they managed to carry it on a wooden door into his back yard, and they stashed it behind an old fridge that was almost completely hidden by a morning glory creeper. Actually – when I refer to Rangi's poop as 'it' – perhaps I should call it 'Roger – Harawera – Winston – Piggy Muldoon', Kev?"

"And why's that?" Kev insisted.

Greg sighed with exasperation. "You had both sides spying on each other – didn't you, Kev? The Iwis knew that Fran's turd was given the name 'Popsie', so they wanted to ensure that Rangi's effort should be named after some important bongos. Seriously – they were determined to come up with a name that every bongo could personally familiarise with, and this's how they came up with the following title. A. Roger (Roger Douglas) because he almost singlehandedly rooted Poo Zealand's economy. B. Harawera (Hone Harawera) because this dynamic fellow dared to challenge the 'motherfucking' Pakehas for raping and plundering the Iwis – in an email! C. Winston after the charismatic fellow tried bullshitting his way out of an electoral funding dilemma.

D. Piggy (Robbie Muldoon) because Piggy had done his best to prove to the world how up themselves bongo MP's could be, and how bongo MPs loved looking down their noses at your average Kiwi of Scottish and Irish descent in his and her bogs and hollows."

"That's a bloody long name," Kev was puzzled. "How would they get people to remember it?"

"Now, I'm quite impressed that you brought that up, Kev!" Greg was all approval. "Yes, the Iwis picked up on that problem right away. That had them really wracking their brains. This whole turd competition was one of the most auspicious chapters in the annals of Bongoland's Iwi/Pakeha interrelationship. 'The Great Competition!' The Maoris knew that the onus was on them to make a statement that either boosted the Iwi culture and its status in the country, or they needed to make a protest that would be heard around the world. So that's why they called Rangi's turd 'O'Flaherty'."

"How come?" I prodded him.

Greg immediately looked downcast. "Because Iwi folklore has it that it was an Irishman by the name of O'Flaherty who first introduced really decent whiskey to the Land of the Long White Cloud!"

"So what happened to that Fran sheila?" I prodded Greg.

He just shook his head and looked more forlorn. "Letting Popsie have her liberty was a much more drawn out affair, Nev, and that was regardless of all the professional medical help that was there at Fran's fingertips. It was like going into labour for her – wasn't it? Especially with the pangs and cramps from all the wind and gas in her upper bowel. She'd experienced major bowel motions before, but never on this scale! They actually brought down a gun gynaecologist from Nelson whose speciality was large births, and she reckoned they'd need special forceps like you'd use on a complicated birth of a normal baby. However the forceps kept slipping off Popsie, so the professor from Lincoln University put on her extra long, green gloves – like the ones she used for cows – and she tried to wrestle the turd out! Have you heard the expression 'wrestling with a turd', Trev?"

My younger brother was certainly aware of such an expression because our boss back in Kalgoorlie frequently used the exact same term in the drill yard when someone dared to disagree with him. "Yeah, you wrestle with a turd – you get covered in shit!"

"Ah, indeed you do, Trev!" Greg concurred. "Indeed you do! All our cow birthing expert achieved was getting shit all over her special green gloves, and the other boffins were more than scared that she was making Popsie lose weight or somehow making her smaller. . . They were starting to run out of time – weren't they? The six weeks was going to be up at eight the next morning, and then they were left with only two days to get Popsie ready for presentation to an international team of judges in Wellington. Rumours were flying around like angry bees that the Iwis' competition contender was already in the capital, and that it was truly a monster! Too many reputations were at stake, Trev! Then, when they'd almost given up hope, it was actually Fran's dad who came up with a brilliant idea! Ever since she was a little girl, Fran was badly petrified of spiders. It just so happened that there was another professor of zoology from Gisborne who'd very recently returned from an all expenses, taxpayer-funded trip from Brazil because his daughter was marrying an Amazonian Indian whose tribe had only just been discovered on the banks of the Orinoco River the year before. As it happened, this zoologist had smuggled into Poo Zealand a massive female tarantula that he'd doped with cocaine and hid in the front of his jocks. Amusingly enough, the tarantula's name was 'Tamsin'. . . So a special Royal New Zealand Air Force Hercules was sent to Gisborne to fetch the Tarantula and its new owner, and then it flew on to Dunedin. From Dunedin the tarantula – which was busy suffocating in a glass jar – was driven with its master under police escort to Makikihi. Unfortunately it was dead on arrival when they got to Fran's house."

"Well I'll be buggered!" Kev was visibly taken aback.

"Yes – I know, Kev!" Greg looked equally stricken. "Sad – isn't it? If only someone could've thought of using an ordinary cardboard shoe box with holes in it? . . . Nevertheless, Tamsin never suffocated in vain, Kev.

During the afternoon when Fran was taking her siesta, the heartbroken zoologist – with tears running like swollen streams down his face – gently laid Tamsin's corpse on her chest, and. . ."

"Okay – so why've you stopped?" Trev was totally devoid of sympathy. "So what happened?"

The expression on Greg's face was still rueful. "They say that the entire populace of Makikihi – including all the workers in the chip factory – heard Fran's scream! According to the media we even had some who say they heard what sounded like a V8 Ford without a muffler starting up just after that high-pitched scream! Some said that those same explosive sounds were more like someone beating a carpet in rapid succession with a tennis racquet! . . . Either way, the exercise was a total success! Later on while having a few beers at the lawn bowls club, Fran's dad was bombarded with questions by potato farmers and townies alike. What was the size of Fran's poop – did it weigh a lot – would it beat anything that the Maoris came up with? Leaning with his back to the bar and with his chest puffed out with pride, Fran's old man came out with one stock standard answer, 'They couldn't shift it without a forklift, it, mate!'"

"You're kidding?" Trev challenged.

Greg shook his head ever so slowly. "No, I'm not, Trev. You can't blame the bloke for grabbing the opportunity of being in the spotlight with both hands. Here's a man who'd spent his entire life on the dole, and having to survive on his wife and daughter's wages. He was exaggerating, of course, still his explanation of the explosive sounds after Fran's scream were even more bizarre! No, it wasn't a Ford V8 without a muffler starting up, or someone beating a carpet with a tennis racquet! It was because the professor from Lincoln University had just lit up a cigarette at the exact same moment that Popsie was finally heaved out by Fran's petrified convulsions! To be more precise – Tamsin the Tarantula more or less frightened the living crap out of her! The explosions came from the hydrogen gas that oozed out of Popsie, and it was the Lincoln prof that ignited it with her cigarette lighter! There were even more explosions because further hydrogen from the partly digested scroggin and rolled oats was leaking out of Fran's bum, and it – too – was ignited! The poor girl suffered all her ring piece and fanny hairs being singed off, and those standing around her got most of their eyebrows blown away! The zoologist not only lost his eyebrows, but his nifty moustache as well, and Tamsin was totally cremated! They say that the explosions could be heard as far away as Oamaru, however the people from Makikihi insisted that the mayor of Oamaru and some of the councillors were just trying to be in on the whole affair because nothing exciting ever happened in that North Otago dump! Can you see the parochialism we have in Poo Zealand, Trev?"

"Poor – bloody – spider!" Kev was moved to comment. He didn't seem to have any sympathy for Fran.

"Too – bloody – true!" Greg sympathised with him. "But that wasn't the end of the story – was it?"

"How do you mean?" I asked him when both of my siblings failed to comment.

"It was Popsie – wasn't it, Nev?"

"How do you mean?" I must've sounded like a cracked record.

"Popsie turned out to be twins – didn't she, cobber? And that just had to be catastrophic – Nev! The whole competition was based solely on one turd, so there was no chance of winning what with Popsie turning out to be twins. While the one twin was a fair bit smaller than the other, there was no way that the larger one on its own would've beaten Rangi's single entrant – no way whatsoever! . . . That's why the SOS agents were patrolling Makikihi's streets the following night in their Holden panel vans. Thankfully it was a moonless night that. . ."

"What's this 'SOS'?" Kev cut in.

"SOS – Kev?" Greg turned to directly face him. "It's one of Poo Zealand's most secret organisations, mate! If you'll hold on just a moment, I'll give you a demo' as to how good they are." Greg lifted up his brief case from underneath the table and removed two folded newspaper cuttings from it.

STEPHEN WILCE INQUIRY FINDS TOTAL – ABSOLUTE – SOS FAILURE

New Zealand's Security Operation Services (SOS) staff drifted away from basic procedures when appointing a top defence official, a government inquiry has found.

Stephen Wilce bluffed his way in to the job as Chief Defence Scientist and Director of the Defence Technology Agency through a series of elaborate and sometimes extravagant lies.

He was sprung by a television sting last year, and relieved of the job, which had given him high-level security clearance.

A report by the State Services Commission into Wilce's appointment, released today, found the system for his appointment was not yet "fit for purpose".

"There were several basic lapses from expected performance," the report, by the State Services Commissioner said.

"The people of New Zealand need assurance that there were not similar failings in other Top Secret vettings carried out at around the time of Mr Wilce's vetting."

Senior officials had not checked with their counterparts in overseas agencies to see what they knew about Wilce and they had not followed up on Wilce's failure to disclose convictions once the police check had revealed that he had convictions. Officials had also failed to act on information about Wilce after he was appointed.

"The failure by SOS staff to record critical information about Mr Wilce's character, and pass it through to the vetting file, at this early juncture of Mr Wilce's employment with NZDF was significant," the report said.

The Prime Minister said: "The State Services Commissioner has said further action needs to be taken to demonstrate confidence in the vetting system, and he will report back to me in the first half of this year."

An independent, international review of the vetting system would be carried out and there would be a check on a 5 per cent sample of the Top Secret vettings undertaken at the time Wilce was employed to make sure the mistake was a one-off.

Greg had plenty more:

FANTASIST STEPHEN WILCE LEAVES NEW ZEALAND
MILITARY HIGHLY EMBARRASSED.

New Zealand's military admitted it was "seriously embarrassed" after an inquiry revealed it granted high security clearance to a scientist who lived in an elaborate fantasy world.

The head of the Defence Technology Agency Stephen Wilce spat the dummy and snatched his rent last month after it was revealed he falsely claimed to be an ex-Marine combat veteran and an Olympic bobsledder who raced against Jamaica's Cool Runnings team.

Details of an inquiry released yesterday revealed the extent of Mr Wilce's claims to incredulous colleagues, saying the Defence force's top scientist had admitted to telling porkies about himself since childhood.

It said Mr Wilce claimed to be a helicopter pilot who served with Prince Andrew, a spy with British intelligence and a Special Forces soldier who was on an IRA death list.

Among numerous other fabrications, he also said he had been a member of the Welsh rugby union team, captain of the Royal Navy swimming team and a guitarist on the British folk music circuit.

The report found Mr Wilce had embellished his resume when he was hired in 2005 and his appointment was carried out with undue haste. It called for tighter vetting procedures in Defence Force recruitment.

"Some dumb decisions were made by the Pakeha government SOS agency," Defence Force chief Lieutenant General Jerry Mateparae said.

The report found that British-born Mr Wilce had not posed a significant threat to national security.

"Mr Wilce may however present a risk to the reputation of New Zealand with its international and security partners," it concluded.

The report said concerns were raised about Mr Wilce's tendency to "bullshit" people when he was hired, but those allegations were not properly followed up.

He headed 80 staff at the agency, which provides technology support to New Zealand's military, for five years.

The Defence Force finally launched an investigation into his past last July but he resigned before it was concluded when commercial broadcaster TV3 revealed his fanciful claims.

They included being a combat veteran and a member of Britain's bobsleigh team at the 1988 Calgary Olympics, where he supposedly competed against the Jamaican team which inspired the 1993 film Cool Runnings.

"I know them all," Mr Wilce said in footage filmed by an undercover reporter. "I know all the Jamaican guys ... mad, absolute nutters."

Previous employers and colleagues told the program Mr Wilce was a "Serious bullshit artist" character who claimed he designed the guidance system for Britain's Polaris nuclear missiles, a defunct system launched 50 years ago during the Cold War.

"When you put all of the things together, when you connect all of the dots, it's bloody embarrassing," Lieutenant General Mateparae said.

He said that while screening procedures had proved inadequate, most of the failings lay with Mr Wilce's "reprehensible" conduct, and that it was all a plot by the Pakeha.

"He bullshitted about his work history, military career, achievements, academic qualifications and activities in other fields in a way that was neither honest nor complete.

"Not only have his actions damaged his reputation, they have damaged the morale of those 'rather unintelligent' dorks he led at the Defence Technology Agency, and they have damaged the reputation of the New Zealand Defence Force."

"What a bunch of dickheads!" there was a sneer on Trev's face. "I hope our ASIO blokes won't have a bar of 'em."

"My bloody oath – mate!" Greg resorted to his Aussie vernacular when it came to agreeing with him. "Anyway, these particular SOS agents in Makikihi would've liked to have gotten around in black Hummers like the Yank CIA or FBI, but all the government at the time could afford was second hand Holden panel vans. You see, the same government had just blown half the country's GDP on buying luxurious BMWs for the MPs and high up civil servants to gallivant around in. . . Nevertheless, while they may've only been getting around in Holden panel vans, the clever disguises these vehicles had – or so the SOS thought – were some of the most ingenious when it came to camouflage! For starters, each one had either a surfboard or several sets of skis mounted on their roofs. One white van had 'The Aussies cheat at cricket' emblazoned in bold red paint on one side of it, and on the other side there was a picture of Winston Peters the Maori MP with the caption "The answer is no – N-O!" I've been led to believe that was because Winnie was involved in some kind of funding nonsense at the time. Apparently he was always up to some kind of mischief or the other. Just your typical, mischievous Maori fellow. . . Then there was one van done out in green, red, and brown camouflage paint as if its owners liked to go deer stalking when they weren't surfing. We even saw one van done out in huge, bright yellow, orange, crimson and blue flowers whereby the alleged owner stated boldly in scarlet paint that he or she liked munching on pussy!... Nevertheless, all this clever subterfuge was in vain – wasn't it, Kev?

"Why's that?" Kev seemed taken aback by the description of the latter panel van.

Greg's sigh was scarcely audible. "The locals weren't fooled – were they, Kev? What do you reckon we had surrounding Makikihi, Kev?"

Kev was becoming exasperated. "How the fuck would I know – Greg?"

Greg lifted both hands up in supplication to the heavens. "Makikihi was surrounded by spud farms – wasn't it? Otherwise where would the factory get all the magnificent Agria spuds from to make their famous, best-in-the-world fries? That meant that the locals were mostly farmers, and the descendants of Irish farmers because the Paddies *are notorious* for growing spuds – aren't they, Kev? And we all know how dour and paranoid some of those of Irish stock can be. They're both jealous and suspicious of their very own shadows, and hate any neighbours plus strangers so much more. Perhaps this's because events in history have so unkindly betrayed them far too many times? . . Even though our SOS agents were getting around in dreadlocks and smoking hashish joints in the Makikihi pub itself, the locals weren't fooled for one solitary second. Even the grandchildren of the local farmers were aware that there were no decent ski slopes or surfing beaches anywhere near Makikihi, and besides – how come the vans of these mildewed, dreadlocked strangers were constantly seen parked out the front of Fran Crapper's old man's house at all hours of the night? Also, why was Fran's mum seen handing out plastic cups of steaming hot cocoa and coffee to these same strangers? It *had to have* something to do with the Great Competition – didn't it? For and after all – Fran Crapper's picture was regularly seen in both the *TIMARU HERALD* and the *OTAGO DAILY TIMES!* The townspeople of Makikihi – plus the neighbours for miles around – were bursting with pride that one of the district's daughters was chosen to represent the Pakehas in one of Poo Zealand's most prestigious and historic contests!"

"So what were these SOS people doing?" I couldn't quite understand what he was getting at.

Greg quickly looked around the place, as if checking that no one was listening in. "Perhaps I shouldn't be telling you this, Nev, because what I have to say is still top secret. Neither the Labour Government or the National Party are game to even speak of it."

"Ah – bullshit!" Trev exploded. "Now you're seriously. . ."

"Keep it down – Trev!" Greg put a finger to his lips. "Their activities had to be kept a secret – didn't they? It was only through a top bloke in the Labour Party that I found out about it. I blackmailed him – didn't I? He was using some illegal Thai over-stayers to do work on his properties, and very nearly ended up in the can for it. . . Not to worry – these SOS agents were patrolling the streets and byways of Makikihi in order to ensure there were no prying eyes or people spying on the Crapper family home. It was because of what was going on in the Crapper's house – wasn't it, Nev?"

"And what was that, Greg?" I bounced back at him.

"Like I said – Popsie turned out to be twins, Nev! I also told you that that was catastrophic for the Pakehas' cause, therefore desperate measures were necessary to rectify the situation. They decided to join the 'twins' together – didn't they? And that's why the SOS were called in to make sure that no Maoris or Maori sympathisers were spying or aware of what was going on in Makikihi on that fateful night. What you need to realise is that the Poo Zealand whites had already bowed their heads in shame for dudding the Iwis via the agency of the Treaty of Waitangi. Or at least the Labour Party and the Greens were trying their best to prove that all bongos were bleeding-heart, quasi-do-gooder apologists as to how the Maoris have been treated thus far. So – to be caught trying to doublecross the Iwis an even further time – was totally unthinkable. . . No bullshit, you blokes, the task they had on their hands was a very complex one. For starters it was essential to bring down a forensic scientist from Wellington who was an expert in ballistics. . . Why would they need a ballistics expert, Nev?"

I could see that Greg was picking on me because he wasn't game to try his luck with Kev or Trev. "I'm stuffed if I know, Greg."

"Don't lose any sleep over it, buddy," Greg was all heart. "Now we all know what a ballistics expert is – don't we? A ballistic expert can tell you if a certain gun fired a certain bullet – not so? He or she can tell by the lines on the slug that're left by the grooves in the barrel of a gun. These grooves in the gun barrel are called rifling – not so, Kev?"

"Yeah," Kev affirmed.

"Good – Kev – good! Now you won't believe this, but the grooves in a person's external anal sphincter muscle's almost identical to those grooves in a gun barrel. Thus, if they wanted to join the twins together, it was essential to ensure that the rifling from Fran's external anal sphincter lined up exactly, just in case the Maoris had a forensic expert of their own. . . Okay, so they squashed the 'twins' together end on end, and they ended up with what looked like one of those ten pin bowling skittles. Almost like a skittle, but with a point at both ends. That was the easy part, but then they had to make certain that the joins were invisible and that the rifling from Fran's anal external sphincter lined up exactly. For that they needed both an expert sculptor and artist. Now I don't know who the sculptor was, although perhaps it was Julia Maddington who painted over the joins, calling on her expertise at using shit for art?"

When Trev finally managed to stop laughing: "Bloody hell – Greg! I've never – ever – heard so much bullshit in my *entire* life!"

Greg did his best to look hurt. "So you don't believe me, Trev?"

My younger brother ignored the question. "Righto, so who won the competition?"

Greg put up a hand. "All in good time, Trev. Just let me give you an idea of the pomp and ceremony that was involved. Alright, so the bongos had been involved in other notable sporting moments such as playing World Cup rugby and competing in the Olympic and Commonwealth Games, but here we have the prestige of two different races and cultures at stake. Furthermore, it was an all-New Zealand event! As far as a contest between races, I'm not sure about the Maoris – as there's no actual full-blooded Iwis left – but it was a question of pride to those lucky souls who had *at least some* Polynesian blood coursing through their veins. . . That's where you have to hand it to the magnificent Iwis when it comes to putting on a show! They're past masters at all the pageantry and bullshit – aren't they? They're not a dour lot like the offspring of a bunch of Scots and Irish. The Iwis are also a much more attractive and exciting people than most of the whites they're burdened with! You take the Maori Women they have on the North and South Island. They're far more attractive and sensuous than those freckly fatties that exhibit the whites' recent evolution or gene pool. . . And what's dearest to a Maori warrior's heart, Trev?"

Trev could be really ignorant some times. "Fucked if I know – Greg! What do they call those stupid war dances they do?"

"Hakas – Trev – hakas!" Greg became quite animated. "Naturally they performed more than one haka at the turd presentation ceremony, but what about the *waka taua* – the mighty war canoe, mate? They selected one of the most famous of Iwi wakas – I can't remember its name – and they mounted it on the back of a low-loader truck or heavy machinery transporter – didn't they? One of the longest machinery transporters in Poo Zealand! It was a huge waka, Trev! I can't say for certain, nevertheless I'm sure it was hewn from a mighty *Tane Mahuta* – or giant kauri tree – that once stood lofty, regal, majestic and proud in the mighty Waipoua Forest! It was most probably the last one. Giant kauri – I mean. Poo

Zealand has such an atrocious conservation record. . . No – hang on just a second – Kev, old cobber. I think some North Island city council actually paid for the waka's hull to be carved, and I think they named it after some extinct bird or other. Don't write this down, but apparently some Maori tribe has been trying to scrounge it off the council for free for some years now, but the hard-arsed council's demanding a hundred and fifty grand for it. Either way, the waka was a *Taonga*, or much treasured item for all Iwi! Furthermore, the trailer of this truck was equipped with countless wheels! And this's where we're stuck with another peculiar state of affairs introduced to the folk of Poo Zealand."

"Go on," Kev urged him when he fell silent. "Stuff this stopping and starting. Finish what you were going to say."

Greg dabbed his bottom lip with the index finger of his right hand. "The most important feature of a waka taua, Kev, is the carved feature on its bow. By some extraordinary or bizarre coincidence, O' Flaherty or Rangi's turd closely resembled a tiki! You won't believe it, but. . ."

"Whatsa tiki?" I jabbed at him.

"A tiki – Nev? It's a Maori carving of a humanoid form. You've probably seen them hanging from the necks of Kiwi Pakeha women. Those white sheilas who endeavour to be more Maori than the Maori themselves. More an insult to the Iwis, if you were to ask me, . . You know those figurines – the ones with the potato-shaped heads, the big eyes and the heart-shaped mouths with tongues sticking out. They have baby-like bodies and are generally made out of greenstone or jade."

"Yeah, I know what you're talking about," Kev informed him. "You see 'em in all the tourist shops. Some of 'em are made out of green plastic."

"The ones made in China are plastic," Greg agreed with him. "Anyway, you wouldn't believe it, but Rangi's poop was very similar to a tiki – same head – same facial features – same-shaped body! So much so that the Iwi committee in charge of presenting the turd decided to fasten it on the bow of the waka taua with superglue. What you have to remember is – having been compressed for nearly six weeks – Rangi's poop was almost as solid as a rock, and it still possessed its dark-olive-green colour because it was always kept frozen in a large chest freezer. They couldn't go letting the turd dry out – could they? Not only could it shrink – it would most likely lose weight as well! Actually it was a very rare sunny day that day in Wellington, and the heat of the sun's rays altered the shape of O'Flaherty somewhat, and it became a lighter green, but in no way did they alter his size or weight. . . Righto, so the low loader truck was driven onto Lambton Quay, and O'Flaherty was the bow feature of one of the most famous waka tauas in Bongoland! We have rather a priceless incongruity here because the truck was heading north up Lambton Quay, while the rowers were rowing in the *opposite direction*! The waka was also given a complement of ferocious, ta moko-covered paddlers – all chosen because of their huge bulk and muscles. They were the finest specimens of male Maoridom to be found in the world! Now, they might've looked like a bunch of dildos as they dug their paddles into thin air because the waka was mounted on the trailer, but the crowd stopped laughing once they saw the breathtaking performance being carried out by Rangi Hika! He'd been made master of the waka and it was his job to call out the stroke or the timing for the waka's paddlers. As it happened, he'd just seen a dragon boat race on the morning TV show that day, where each dragon boat had a huge drum so that a drummer could beat a rhythm for the paddlers. Even though the Iwi turd presentation committee searched high and low in vain throughout Wellington for a dragon boat drum, Rangi wasn't going to let that spoil his finest hour, so he improvised by using an empty forty-four-gallon, BP diesel drum, the top of which was hastily wrapped in orange crepe paper. . . You should've heard the racket he made when he belted the shit out of that diesel drum with two five-pound boilermaker's hammers – bing-bong – bing-bong – bing-bong! Yes, and his voice could be heard above all that drumming – booming throughout the skyscrapers in Wellington's CBD – plus his ferocious glare made more than a few children cry with fear! They were frightened to tears either by his glare or the gruesome, green ornament that was super-glued to the bow of the almighty waka taua! . . . No, the crowd was transfixed by Rangi's performance! So much so that they failed to see the several layers of incontinence nappies that he was wearing underneath his flax skirt or *piupiu*. Identical to Fran, his bum hole still hadn't closed properly, so his turds no longer came to a point at the end in order to stop his arsehole snapping shut with a bang when he let go of them. Flipping heck – that would've made his eyes water!"

"Okay, so what did Fran do with her turd?" Kev insisted after he, too, stopped laughing.

"Her presentation was totally different, Kev," Greg's voice was almost a murmur as he seemed to be searching out a distant memory. "It was far more subtle, Kev. Fran was always passionate about horses and ponies from the time she could barely crawl. She actually saved an ancient shire horse from the knacker's yard where they were going to turn him into pet rolls. You'd never guess what his name was, Trev?"

Trev immediately took the bait! "Now *how the fuck* would I know what the fuckin' horse's name was?"

Greg was all innocence. "It was 'Dobbin' – Trev – mate! What else would you expect its name to be other than that? *All* ancient cart horses in Poo Zealand are called 'Dobbin'. . . Never mind that. Although she was never game to actually ride old Dobbin, Fran took him to every pony club event in south Canterbury and northern Otago. She'd brush him up and paint his hooves and so on, and every now and then he'd pull a special carriage which people rode around in. You'll find this quite touching, nevertheless a wealthy south Canterbury potato farmer stumped up the cash so that not only Dobbin and his carriage could be transported to Wellington, but also a dozen or so girls from the local pony club – plus their ponies – to go as an escort or guard of honour! The carriage, of course, would seat Fran, and Popsie was given pride of place wrapped in a pink satin sheet in a baby bassinette. The bassinette itself was adorned in pink velvet ribbons that almost matched Fran's grown, but not quite. Fran also wore a light pink, floral, plastic shower curtain over her head like a wedding veil, plus pink running shoes. What the veil was in aid of is anyone's guess, or perhaps she wore it to give herself an aura of mystery? Who knows? Either way it was a fairly odd sort of combination all the same. . . Now I won't go into the fact that the wealthy south Canterbury potato farmer was a paedophile who haunted children's pony clubs throughout the South Island because I don't want to sully your thoughts on what just had to be Fran Crapper's happiest day. You should've seen the spectacular cavalcade those pony club riders – plus Dobbin and his carriage – made as they proudly strutted their way up Lambton Quay! There were six pony club riders on each side of the carriage, all done out in black jodhpurs, lacy pink tops and white crash helmets! Each rider stared sternly into the distance, just like those cavalry blokes in England do whenever the Queen goes for a jaunt through London in her carriage. . . Oh damn it all – you guys – I almost forgot! I forgot the pipe band – didn't I? Nothing – *but nothing* – goes down in Poo Zealand without a pipe band! Especially when South Islanders are involved along with their Scottish and Irish heritage. I'm not exactly sure which pipe band it was, but it could've been the Dunedin P & D Band in blue and black Macrae tartan kilts, or possibly it was the Timaru Scottish Pipe Band in mostly red, Royal Stuart tartan kilts. Whichever band it was, they made a magnificent spectacle as they proudly marched in front of Dobbin and his carriage, plus the dozen or so stern-faced pony club riders. . . Are you taking all this in, Nev?"

I'd been busy watching a horribly fat woman getting stuck into her seventh chocolate éclair, so Greg's question caught me by surprise. "Yeah, I suppose so, Greg."

He nodded at that. "Good! For a second I thought you were falling asleep. . . So where was I, Kev?"

Kev was much more on the ball. "You were talking about a pipe band, and that Fran sheila riding in a carriage in Wellington."

Greg tilted his head to one side and casually nodded in agreement. "I was – wasn't I – Kev? Okay, so both contestants pulled up in front of the judges' podium. Rangi in the mighty waka taua and Fran in the carriage with her face hidden by the pink, plastic shower curtain. There was an international panel of five judges – not so? The Labour government at the time were determined that there'd be no corrupt decisions arrived at, although they'd done everything in their power to help Fran Crapper and Popsie win. They were also very wary about Indian and Paki sport cheats being involved. . . First we had a female judge from Finland, a cute little blonde, who was definitely going to vote on behalf of the Iwis because she'd had sex the night before with the Maori driver of the heavy machinery truck that was carting the waka taua. Secondly, there was a male judge from Western Australia who later on admitted that he'd voted for Fran's turd because he was from a mining background and had had a gutsful of the 'Abo' land title claims back in West Aussie. As far as he was concerned, the 'Abos', Maoris, Eskimos and whites should all be treated equally, and that suck-arsing the minority races was just sending Aussie and New Zealand down the drain. Not very politically correct. However – if it was ever put to a vote – you could more or less guarantee that your average Aussie or bongo would most likely agree with him. Perhaps not the politically correct, bleeding-heart do-gooders that've taken over Oz, though there are some blue collar workers who just might? . . . Still, disregarding that – you'd possibly never get the Johnny Mintos of this world to agree – now would you? . . . The third judge was a Nigerian bloke, who – rumour had it – was about to be elected to the FIFA voting committee, as to who would host the next soccer World Cup. Now we've all heard about Nigerians in general and how dicey FIFA's affairs are, what with that Scottish born New Zealand FIFA rep – good old Charlie Dempsey – aka Albert Steptoe – that mysteriously abstained from voting, and thus ensured that the Krauts got the tournament instead of the South Africans in 2006. Yes, there was many a cocked eyebrow when that happened, and quite a few people believed that money might've changed hands! A rather unkind thought that perhaps needs to be given *at least some* consideration? Some say that FIFA's affairs are run along lines very similar to politics in Zimbabwe and other African countries, and gents – with what we've seen on the telly lately – who could honestly blame them? Especially after that Arab bloke from Qatar – Mahomed Bin Hammam – got banned for life from having anything at all to do with international football. Then, of course, you have Sepp Blatter, the ex-President of FIFA, who some American female soccer star accused of grabbing her arse! . . . So then, and to cut a long story short, the Nigerian sold his vote to an SOS agent sent from Christchurch for the princely sum of one hundred Kiwi buckaneros, and that vote was toted up in favour of our Fran. . . Following that we had a Canadian woman from Ottawa who was a reserve player of the Canadian women's rugby league team. She was a total wild card because everyone knew she was a lesbian, and had often been reported by referees around the world for trying to smuggle a strap-on dildo onto the field. A dildo which she intended to use on other players while buried in a ruck or a collapsed scrum. Or possibly on our Fran once the judging was completed. . . Quite frightening – isn't she, Kev?"

"She sounds scary!" Kev was forced to concede. "Did she vote for Fran?"

"No – Kev! She'd mysteriously made up her mind all of a sudden to vote for O'Flaherty. . . And then finally we come across this Irish chappie from Killavullen, County Cork. No sooner had he touched down in Bongoland when he was convinced that the other judges were plotting and scheming against him, plus sniggering behind his back. This sniggering behind his back phobia had haunted him since he was a child. With good reason, though, because even his mum and dad reckoned he was a bit of a dickhead, but sadly their sniggers were more giggles of embarrassment. . . So now it was the Iwis' turn to try a little match fixing of their own. I told you that Poo Zealand was a corrupt little shithole – didn't I, Kev? When our Irish judge visited the Whakan-Hell Marae in the North Island, it took seconds flat for some very respected *kaumatua* or elders to recount how a Scottish-born, New Zealand FIFA representative abstained from voting in 2006 when it came to deciding which country should host the soccer World Cup. They also pointed out how this had caused quite a kerfuffle, and how it had made Albert Steptoe – no, Charlie Dempsey – very famous. That did the trick – didn't it? If you want to win over a dickhead – just run your little finger over his ego. Yes, our man from Killavullen wanted to be famous – didn't he? So he decided to abstain. . . You see, the Iwis were positive that they had at least three judges in the bag. For starters, they'd won the heart of the sheila from Helsinki who still winced every time she sat down for dinner or climbed onto a bar stool. No, gents, she wasn't wincing from where the truckie had inspected every one of her orifices with his old fellah, she was still recovering from the all-night session she'd enjoyed with the lezzie from Ottawa and her giant, three-speed, V12 GT dildo! The Iwis were also convinced that the Nigerian would obviously vote for a Maori because they were both dark skinned, albeit that the Nigerian was the much darker of the two. . . Are you taking this all in, Nev?"

"It all sounds pretty sleazy to me, Greg," I tried to come up with an intelligent answer.

"It does – doesn't it – Nev! But the Iwis weren't about to have their way – were they? The voting ended up a dead heat! You had the West Aussie's and the Nigerian's vote going to Fran, and the Finn's and the Canadian lezzie's going to Rangi. Our Irish judge declined to vote, and – similar to Chas Dempsey – refused to give an adequate explanation as to why. All the same *he did* – same as Dempsey – have his brief five seconds in the limelight. . . And what a dilemma this dead heat caused the Labour government at the time! Poo Zealand was nearly broke after the same Labour outfit had blown forty million of taxpayers' money only to see the bongos being thumped at the America's Cup yachting, plus they'd blown countless millions on pompous BMWs for the MPs to ride around in, plus a host of useless oxygen-stealers in the public service in Wellington. Can you see their quandary, Kev?"

"Yeah mate," Kev was tuned in. "I've seen those BMWs up in Wellington."

Greg paused to digest that reply. "The country's on the bones of its backside, yet the Labour government spends millions massaging the egos of a Pacific coconut republic's politicians and public servants. . . Nevertheless, I'm getting ahead of myself. You can't begin to understand how proud the bongos nationwide were of this turd competition! The actual competitors – Fran and Rangi and their unbelievably huge poops – were *only part* of the festivities! As usual you saw scores of bongos all trying to get ten seconds in the spotlight. For starters, the presentation of Popsie and O'Flaherty was held up in Wellington's Lambton Quay when a bunch of white men and women threw themselves in front of the truck that was carting the waka taua, O'Flaherty, Rangi and his mighty crew of Iwi paddlers. These men and women were apologising for, no – bitterly demonstrating against – the fact that they were white! Typical politically correct, do-gooder, bleeding-hearts that have evolved in Poo Zealand and Aussie over the last couple of decades – all outraged and ashamed because of the colour of their skin! Seriously – they were begging Rangi and his crew to forgive them because they were of Irish, Scottish and Welsh descent. . . Isn't that so typically Kiwi for you? No matter if you've done nothing wrong – no matter who you are – you'll always get some bongo wanting to apologise on your behalf. Same as the politically correct do-gooders you find everywhere in Oz, or on the ABC. . . No, these people weren't actually Johnny Minto and his good people, nevertheless *they were* a very similar organisation. Most of them had Bachelor of Arts degrees, and were generally a simpering, grovelling waste of space. . . Afterwards there was a demonstration by the bongo green movement. Scores of dickheads – both men and women with BAs – were marching along with banners and sandwich boards. They were protesting against the NZ farmers and agriculture in general. The chairperson of the movement, who was also a prominent supporter of the Green Party, pointed out on a loudhailer that there was no need for farmers or farming because there were ample supermarkets around New Zealand to cater for everyone. A notorious barracker of the New Zealand First Party, also desperate to capture a few seconds in the limelight, said that he agreed with the green movement wholeheartedly, and that he'd introduce a private member's bill in the House, whereby farming should be banned in its entirety altogether. . . And then we had the parade of shit trucks – didn't we?"

"Did I hear you say – *shit trucks*?" Trev's sordid imagination was once more at the surface.

"Shit trucks – Trev?" Greg's eyes were opened wide by the question. "You know what I mean, Trev. Shit trucks or septic disposal tankers are as common as grains of sand here in Bongoland. I told you the Kiwis could shit – didn't I? If you were to do your numbers on Poo Zealand's national transport infrastructure, it's not uncommon to see livestock transporters, logging trucks, tip trucks, general goods vans, plus trucks and trailers utilised on Aotearoa's highways and byways, but to each of these trucks you'll easily find two shit trucks or septic disposal tankers carting countless tons of human excrement to and fro from some destination or another. The turd festival in Wellington that day demonstrated this issue beyond all doubt! There must've been over a thousand shit trucks on display! Huge, blue Volvo tanker trucks with the words "You dump it – we pump it!" or "You shit it – we get it!" displayed on the sides of them! If I remember correctly, a truck which was driven all the way from Southland had the logo 'You muck it – we suck it!' There were other massive sewage tankers that claimed in bold writing that the same tanks were used for carting milk on the weekends! We also saw other trucks claiming "Your No2 is our No1!" and naturally there were other sewerage disposal companies calling themselves "Turd Burglars!" and we even had a truck with a sign on the back "Got poop?" . . . Truly, gents, there were literally hundreds of shit trucks of all colours and sizes – all corroborating my assertion that your average Poo Zealander shits more than any other human – no matter a person's race, culture or creed!"

"Greg!" Trev's voice could be heard all round the room.

Greg touched his lips with a finger to try and quieten him down. "What is it, Trev?"

"Who won the fuckin competition?"

Greg went all wide-eyed. "Why the Iwis – of course! The whole world was watching – wasn't it? Although senior people in the Labour Party had done their utmost to help Fran, it became obvious to them that they'd need the Green Party onside if they were to have any chance against the Nats in the polls. Furthermore, with both the Greens and Labour trying to prove to the same world what bleeding-arsed, insipid do-gooders all Kiwis are – second only to you Aussies – there was no way that they could allow a majority race to defeat a minority race in any way, shape or form whatsoever. That was regardless of the distinct possibility that the Iwi would revisit how they were dudded by the Treaty of Waitangi... As a point of fact, the Yank National Aeronautics and Space Administration was actually called in as final arbitrator. The two poops needed to be measured – didn't they? At first it was proposed that they could be measured via the Archimedes Principal, whereby each turd would be immersed in its own drum of water, and then the overflow of the drum would be measured. That was fine as far as O'Flaherty was concerned because he had the same density and durability as *pounamu* or greenstone, whereas Popsie was too fragile and what the experts referred to as 'flowery'. If Popsie was dunked into water, she'd break up in no time at all. Worse than that, she might even come apart at the join! So far the secret about Popsie being twins had escaped the attention of the Iwi faction, therefore if she was to snap in half – the consequences would've been catastrophic. You have to remember the whites had cheated the Iwis far too many times before via the Treaty of Waitangi. . . So that's where NASA came in. Apparently they had half a dozen satellites which the Yank boffins referred to as the DELTA GRID SYSTEM. These satellites followed specific orbital routes whereby they could measure an object exactly from every angle. And, gents, I'm saying *exactly!* It turned out that Fran's turd had a larger surface area of at least seven square centimetres."

"Then how come she didn't fuckin' win?" There was almost a look of dismay in Trev's eyes!

"It was the new bongo outlook on life – wasn't it, Trev?" Greg tried to console him. "It's the same as what's happening in Aussie. If you're heterosexual and white, we have those that demand that you become an apologist. The way things are going in both Oz and Bongoland, soon you'll become a pariah if your white, male and heterosexual. . . Then again, and as usual, the Iwis wanted to change the rules. Popsie may've been bigger, but O'Flaherty weighed more – didn't he? At least a kilo and a half more! The scroggin and the Makikihi fries might've given Popsie her bulk and magnificent dimensions, but it was good old Maori kumaras – that originally found their way to Aotearoa's golden shores on the mighty waka tauas of the early ancestors – that put the weight and muscle into O'Flaherty!"

CHAPTER 4

I pointed at the newspaper article that Greg still clutched in his hand. "How come you're collecting all these newspaper cuttings about Kiwis having a crap?"

"Good of you to ask, Nev. It's all part of my Department of Inner Health sting. As I said – the country's covered in shit – and it's starting to have an adverse effect on tourism. You have countless numbers of overseas tourists going home and telling people that they stepped on a bongo's turd or came down with an almost lethal dose of Poo Zealand's very own and patented brand of giardia. Something needs to be done about the bongos crapping over everything, and it can be part of my new department's charter. At long last the government's starting to realise that your average Kiwi cares little about personal hygiene or his country's image, and this's starting to have a financial impact on the country. We're just the blokes to immediately put a stop to it. . . I'm not joking, Nev. I've collected a whole heap of data that substantiates that the bongos are shitting themselves into financial oblivion, and we need to have a government agency created to put a stop to it."

"Yeah – okay – so what happened with the bottle of smoky barbeque sauce?" Trev reminded him. "The one that the Yank yachtsman threw overboard?"

"Thanks for reminding me, Trev!" Greg grinned at him. "I can think of nothing more boring than your average bongo. The way they dress – the things they do – plus their cuisine. When it comes to cuisine, they wouldn't know shit from clay – just roast and three veg – cake – sugar – and as much cream and chocolate in the females' diet as possible. No wonder there are so many morbidly obese female grunters getting around the place? You blokes are obviously of Italian descent, so are bound to know good salami when you come across it, and I've just read your drilling colleague Josef Shultz's *BASTARDS FROM THE BUSH CHRONICLE 1.* He's dead right when it comes to what some outfits are producing over here – dog shit! Smoked dog shit! With the bongos' innate desire for sugar and other sweet things, savoury foods – which are fairly common and popular in Australia and Italy – have been a stranger to the average bongo's diet. I don't know why, but the bottle of smoky barbeque sauce that our Yank yachtsman hurled overboard in the Cook Strait – and which found its way into Wellington's harbour and beached itself on the shores of Scorching Bay – sparked off the most significant culinary revolution Aotearoa or Bongoland has ever seen. Nowadays the bongos insist on smoky barbeque sauce with everything. You give them cat shit spread on mouldy toast with smoky barbeque sauce – and they'll happily accept it as some kind of exotic pizza and guzzle it down! Or at least that's how the bongos like their pizzas – the entire surface covered in smoky barbeque sauce. . . The second culinary revolution to hit the Land of the Long White Cloud was cranberry sauce. This was also introduced to Bongoland via a rather torturous route. Likewise it came via the agency of a Yank, but this time by a gigantic Negress netball player from Baltimore who was on loan to one of the local bongo women's netball teams. She was hoping to smuggle a couple of hundred grams of heroin into New Zealand by storing it in a plastic cranberry sauce bottle that she'd stashed up her fanny. She would've gotten away with it, if it hadn't of been for a professional sniffer dog that was very recently imported from Aussie. Actually it was a German short haired pointer breed of hound that was specially trained to sniff out fox holes in Tasmania. That mutt's super keen nose picked up the heroin right away – despite the fishy smell and the fact that our Negress had been surviving on a sole diet of sauerkraut, Belgian beer and smoked frankfurters. From what I was told, the customs dog handler was alerted to her because all the passengers who'd just disembarked from the same United Airways flight were all pointing in her direction. It wasn't because she was six-foot- nine and towered over everybody – it was because of the putrid flatus she'd been letting go on the plane, which was a product of her extraordinary diet. Apparently quite a few of the passengers in the economy section of the plane were violently ill, particularly small children and the elderly. One elderly bloke in the seat behind her actually fell unconscious after choking on his vomit! Yes, it was that what set alarm bells going in the customs hall at Auckland's International airport! And then – plus to cut a long story short – this bongo customs bloke did his best to emulate what he'd seen on the telly. He tasted some of the heroin – didn't he? Just like he'd seen Yank detectives doing it on American TV. Some unkind people say he also licked the outside of the cranberry sauce bottle because it had been up the Negress' fanny, but let's not go down that track because unsubstantiated rumours can put an end to the career of a man who's taken his eye off the ball for just a split second. Whichever way you look at it, he didn't have a clue of what heroin tasted like, whereas the odd drop of cranberry sauce *that did* touch his tongue precipitated the second most important culinary watershed in Bongoland's history! No one really knows why the bongos have taken to cranberry sauce, although I'm sure a Dunedin psychologist came up with the most plausible explanation. He pointed out quite rightly that the Kiwis have an incredible inferiority complex when it comes to the Yanks, just as much as they feel mediocre in the company of Australians. That's why they profess to hate Americans, even though they'll try their best to copy them – their dress – their expressions – their TV – their behaviour – their tastes in food – etceteras. You take for instance the turkey and cranberry sauce the Yanks have on Thanksgiving Day. Truly, the Americans are like gods to the bongos, even though you'll never get a Kiwi to admit it. You take your typical loud-mouthed Yankee tourists visiting the Land of the Long White Cloud. Whenever Kiwis hear their accents, they want to prostrate themselves before them and kiss their feet. Even worse – I've seen occasions where bongos have mistaken Canadians for Yanks and have gone into the same, pathetic kowtowing mode. And what's a Canadian, you blokes? A mate of mine calls them half-Yanks, which is rather unkind – don't you think? Just like the Kiwis aspire to be Aussies, the Canadians would just love people to think that they're Yanks. That's why they persist with the quasi, phoney Yank accents. They're pitifully hoping that people from elsewhere in the world will think they're from the mighty US of A. They try so hard to emulate the Yanks, but they simply don't cut the mustard – do they? No – I'm serious, Nev, the Canadians seem to have to stand in the shadow of the Yanks. They're not much good at sport – they've got nothing to contribute on the world stage – they're just pathetically grateful that they have the Yanks as neighbours. I'm certain that's what you get when you have a bunch of people who might be having difficulty piecing together a national identity, what with there being such a French and Fijian Indian influence to contend with. . . So that's why, gentlemen – unless you expressly demand otherwise – cranberry or smoky barbeque sauce will be sloshed on every dish you order in Bongoland nowadays. Yes, having cranberry and smoky barbeque sauce on everything is the nearest thing that the bongos can be to the Yanks – ever. And, while we're on the subject of bongo customs officials, tell me, Trev – were your figs given a bit of a tickle when you went through customs in Christchurch?"

That caught Trev off guard. "What you talking about?"

Greg unfolded a newspaper that Kev had purchased earlier. "It appears that when men pass through New Zealand customs, you've more than a fair chance of having your arse cheeks squeezed – your testicles groped and fondled – or your donger stroked. Here – take a look at this."

GAY CUSTOMS OFFICER KEEN TO STRIP-SEARCH, HEARING TOLD

A gay Christchurch Customs officer sought to perform more than his fair share of male passenger strip searches, say two colleagues sacked for allegedly revealing details about his behaviour.

Glenn Rankin, an assistant chief customs officer with nearly 17 years' service, and John Smith, a customs officer for eight years, were giving evidence at an Employment Relations Authority hearing this week where they are fighting to get back their jobs at Christchurch Airport.

Both men deny leaking material and said their dismissals in March were unjustified.

The hearing was told officers were concerned about a gay customs officer, described as "ostentatious", who allegedly sought more than his share of strip-search assignments and made lewd comments about male passengers.

The officer, who still works for the service and whose name is suppressed, also allegedly used recreational drugs.

Customs Service policy bars the service from asking the sexual orientation of its frontline officers because of potential charges of unlawful discrimination.

Its legal advice said passengers were not entitled to know the sexual orientation of officers conducting strip searches at airports and ports.

The customs manager, central and southern airports, told the hearing that the gay officer's search statistics could look bad, but he worked the busiest shifts and was often the only male available to search male passengers.

The service did not want Mr Rankin and Mr Smith back even if the authority decided they were unjustifiably dismissed, as managing a workplace where the three officers had to work together would be difficult, he said.

Closing submissions would be heard next week.

"Two have to go, while one's allowed to stay," Greg pushed his previous assertion further. "Two heterosexual men versus one gay fellow."

I saw a heaven-sent opportunity to take a poke at Trev! "Ah – Trev – so no wonder you had that far away look on your dial after you come out of customs? There was some bloke fondling your figs – wasn't there? No wonder you were smiling!"

"You go and root your boot!" He fired back at me. "If anyone was gunna have his donger stroked – it'd be you – you smartarse bastard! Besides, we landed in Auckland – not fuckin' Christchurch!"

"**There – there, now children**! Greg tried to calm things. "Now, Trev, do you remember me telling you about those mischievous Aussies from Adelaide who set up that *TAG THE TURD* website?"

"Yeah," Trev affirmed. "It sounded like a load of crap to me."

Strangely enough Trev's reply seemed to please Greg! "Very well then, what do you have to say about this?"

FREEDOM CAMPER EXCREMENT STILL
A DIVISIVE ISSUE IN NEW ZEALAND

LAKE HAWEA, New Zealand — Human excrement more than likely deposited by New Zealand freedom campers is still present in mountainous quantities on the south-western shore of Lake Hawea; consequently some local residents are further outraged, while others deem it to be a valuable tourist attraction.

A delegation will meet Land Information New Zealand management next Thursday to debate the pros and cons of New Zealand freedom campers using Lake Hawea's various beaches and inlets as toilets.

An inspection of the huge amount of human waste was carried out by several groups last Monday and has encouraged various arguments to come to light. There were some who condemned the practice of freedom campers defecating beside the lake for health and safety reasons, while there were those who were all for it because it could attract tourists from all over the world.

One member of the Guardians of Lake Hawea photographed the evidence, and noted that since the arrival of the Australian website TAG THE TURD, there were more and more locals obviously eager for some time in the spotlight. As a result there were far more and much larger poos being deposited by the lake, and they all can't be attributed to freedom campers alone. He also went on to say that records with regard to size, shape and weight may possibly have been broken.

He summarised by saying that tourists might find it a point of interest that Kiwis had been the orchestrators of such humongous bowel movements which were possibly the largest on the planet. It was something that all New Zealanders could justifiably be proud off.

Greg wasn't prepared to let things go at that. "Okay, Trev, did you hear about that incident between the French and Green Peace."

Trev nodded. "That happened back in 1985. If I can remember, the French made a real stuff up. What made you raise the subject?"

Greg produced another newspaper clipping which he removed from an inside jacket pocket. "It looks like France still hasn't forgiven the bongos for declaring to the world what morons their secret agents can be."

FRENCH FEMALE DOES NUMBER TWO ON DUNEDIN STREET

A recently released video has captured a French woman squatting down and doing a number two on the side of a Dunedin street. When she completed her business, she kicked her poo into the gutter.

This all happened in front of an establishment that has a security camera, and photos taken from the video are in huge demand all over New Zealand by fetishist locals prepared to pay thousands of dollars for copies.

When the women finished up, she climbed aboard a Toyota van, which was then barred from leaving by several reporters who showed her and her male companion a copy of the offending video. When she suggested that a dog had left the poo in the Dunedin street, one reporter informed her that experts had actually inspected it and ruled out any chance of it having come from an animal.

The French couple who claim to be freedom camping denied anything to do with the incident and could now face a fine of $200 if found guilty.

"What does fetish-what-you-call-it mean?" I joined the conversation.

"A fetishist, Nev? It's when someone has an unusual sexual obsession," Greg casually informed me. "In other words – a weirdo. They're quite common over here, especially on the West Coast of New Zealand. The Coast's crawling with fetishists.

Greg's words about the West Coast of New Zealand were given some credence nearly a fortnight later. My brothers and I were travelling with him to a place called Cromwell which was approximately sixty kilometres from Queenstown. "Do you remember me mentioning that the West Coast of New Zealand was inundated by fetishists?" He asked Trev who was sitting in the front passenger seat.

"Bloody oath, I do!" My younger brother answered in the affirmative.

"Yes, well," Greg nodded, "I was given undeniable proof of this over the weekend. Do you also remember me telling you how there was a huge demand for those photos of the French woman pooping on the street in Dunedin, and how the Dunedin police needed to store all existing photos in a safe because they were being used as evidence?"

Trev shook his head. "You never told me anything about cops having photos."

"Didn't I?" Greg seemed surprised at that. "I'm sure I mentioned it to someone. . . Anyway, we've had quite a scandal that's enveloped both Dunedin and the West Coast. The town of Hokitika's involved, and it's just a short distance south of Greymouth, the principal town on the West Coast. From what I can gather, someone – possibly a bent Scottish cop – was out to make a few bob on the side. Mysteriously one of the photos went missing from Dunedin's police headquarters, and it was scanned and distributed. . ."

"Yeah, I've heard of Greymouth," I leapt in. "Joe Schultz mentioned it in one of his books. He reckoned it was a real dump."

"Never a truer word spoken," Greg looked over his shoulder at me.

"Okay, so what become of the photo?" Kev queried him.

"There was hell to pay behind closed doors – not so, Kev?" Greg quickly glanced back at my elder sibling. "What you must realise is that there's always been a rather frosty relationship between France and New Zealand after the Frogs sank the *RAINBOW WARRIOR* at Auckland's Marsden Wharf. Yes, New Zealand governments – both Labour and National – have been very leery of the Frogs, and the interpretation of a French woman allegedly having taken a crap on the side of a Dunedin street has lent itself to all kinds of paranoid suppositions. Could it be another act of French sabotage aimed at lowering bongo morale? The populace of Dunedin certainly think so. They're positive that lurking in the shadows after dark are French operatives defecating in strategic places where some unsuspecting citizen might step on the result. As I speak, members of the New Zealand SOS – New Zealand's foremost anti terrorist organisation – are prowling the streets in myriad disguises. Do you remember me mentioning the SOS officers stalking Fran Crapper's parents' house in Makikihi when the Great Competition was on, Trev?"

"I bet that was also bullshit," Trev knew how to be unkind.

Greg was immune to that. "Time will tell, Trev. Let's move on. Have you any idea why the SOS is involved in this matter?"

"Nah, mate," Trev was more direct.

"I thought I might've had you stumped, Trev," Greg pursed his lips. "These agents are working hand in glove with some of the country's most capable forensic scientists and biologists, and their job is to gather up every stray stool that's been left on the streets of Dunedin, so it can be analysed. As I mentioned before, the SOS personnel are employing a host of disguises. No, *they're not* getting around in Holden panel vans any more. Do you remember me telling you how the PM blew a fortune on the America's Cup farce?"

"Yeah?"

"Good!" Greg was pleased. "Because of that and the purchase of the BMWs for government ministers and civil servants, it's been imperative to flog the Holden panel vans to Aussie car enthusiasts and replace them with Chinese made bicycles. So what we have is SOS agents pretending to be students who're enrolled at the Otago University. In order to look authentic it's compulsory to have officers seen vomiting in carefully defined locations, and they've been instructed to fall off their bicycles from time to time. While they're doing this, they have to surreptitiously gather up any vagrant turds which have been left lying around Dunedin, and store them in fake Billabong back packs. This's turned out to be a demoralising task because the City of Dunedin's usually covered in dog shit which obviously stinks to high heavens. All the same it has assisted the agents greatly with their disguise when it comes to vomiting, although it was soon discovered that this methodology mixed up the dog turds, thus interfering with the different DNA. This means that they can only allocate one turd to a single fake Billabong back pack at any one time, and the bag has to be burned after. Why they don't employ individual GLAD bags, really has me scratching my head... Do you follow, Nev?" Greg singled me out.

"It sounds bloody weird, Greg!" came my best answer.

"It does – doesn't it, Nev? Notwithstanding that, the SOS has got local government support. New council by-laws have been introduced where a person can be fined five thousand dollars if his or her dog has crapped in the street or any public places without the owner picking it up and disposing of it in a correct receptacle. This's only a temporary measure because the folk of Dunedin are proud of the mounds of dog shit in their streets, but it did at least cause what was once a frightening tsunami of smelly dog turds to actually dry up. . . You won't believe this, but barely forty-eight hours later a "Code Red" was announced. That brought the entire city to a grinding halt since rigid curfews have also been strictly enforced. . . You can understand why. One very suspicious turd was found at the foot of the Robbie Burns statue in the Octagon Plaza. This was right in Dunedin's city centre! First pass analysis revealed that it was indeed left by a human, and contained the remains of an escargot, plus some bones that had come from a frog! Now what could be more sinister than that? Two staples of the French diet! When this was also leaked to the media by one the SOS..."

"Whatsa escargot?" Kev was struggling to stay in touch.

"A snail, Kev," Greg replied. "Snails and frogs' legs are signatures of French cuisine. When it was leaked to the media that a human turd was found at the Octagon Plaza, and that it contained remnants of a snail and bones of a frog, a wave of panic washed through Dunedin, and there was almost a mass exodus north to Christchurch and across the Southern Alps to the West Coast. . . You can understand why, Kev. Firstly, it's well known that French military personnel have committed acts of sabotage in Poo Zealand before! Secondly, a French woman was seen defecating in one of the streets! Thirdly, a photograph of her doing it goes missing from one of the most secure establishments in the city, and people were convinced that French undercover agents were responsible! If that's not enough to make your blood run cold, a turd's found in Dunedin's Octagon that actually contains both *snail and frog* DNA! Much worse – at the foot of Dunedin's most hallowed personage! . . . Fortunately this wave of panic brought about answers to several conundrums. Would you care to comment on that, Nev?"

"Not really," I hastily assured him.

"Not to worry, Nev," he glanced over at me a further time. "This wave of panic I mentioned has had several issues come to light. Although it hasn't been ascertained that our French pooper's indeed an operative within the DGSE, it was eventually established that. . ."

"What's this DGSE?" Trev demanded.

Greg was quick to trot out an answer: "The DGSE or the Directorate-General for External Security. The Frogs call it the *Direction générale de la sécurité extérieure*. It's more or less the equivalent of Britain's MI6 or the Yank CIA. Or New Zealand's SOS. . . No, it couldn't be proved that agents of the DGSE are involved, however one major conundrum *was* solved. With the City of Dunedin in shutdown, and several New Zealand law enforcement agencies being in attendance, finally the dilemma of the missing photo was resolved. An envelope containing the photo was found sticking out from beneath the front door mat of Dunedin's Catholic Cathedral. Naturally the Dunedin police were pleased to get it back, and they immediately set about having it fingerprinted. . . You'll never deduce what they discovered, Nev."

"Too right, I won't," I was in complete agreement with him. "What did they discover?"

Greg pulled up in front of some massive fibreglass fruit icons – nectarine, apple, pear and apricot – items that made Cromwell famous throughout New Zealand. He turned around to face me. "There was a perfect set of fingerprints from a right hand on the front of the photo. Now, you'll never guess why these fingerprints have been so handy to the police, Nev. If you'll excuse the pun?"

I certainly didn't have a clue. "Did they manage to trace the prints to some criminal that they've booked before?"

"No, Nev!" Greg grinned at me. "The hand print had *eleven* fingers as well as *two* thumbs! What does that tell you, Nev?"

That left me truly buggered! "Stuffed if I know, Greg!"

Greg's face was a picture of glee. "It could only have been a West Coaster that stole the photograph! It's known worldwide that quite a number of West Coasters are inbred freaks. You only have to. . ."

"Hey, now I know what you're talking about," I intervened. "Joe Shultz also talks about it in one of his books, 'cept he mentions some of 'em having sixty toes."

"Absolutely, Nev! In 1974 the Kiwis tried to enter a female swimmer from the West Coast in the Commonwealth Games in Christchurch.

She had fifty toes on one foot and forty on the other, while her left hand had seventeen fingers. There was hell to pay similar to in the 1990's when Chinese female swimmers were getting around with larger figs than their male counterparts. . . Anyway, when the Dunedin police realised that it was obviously a West Coaster who'd stolen the photo, it didn't take long for him to be apprehended down in Hokitika. The police in Greymouth have whole libraries of books full of hand and foot prints with multitudinous fingers and toes. Possessing two thumbs is actually quite rare. This made it a lot easier for the West Coast cops to locate our cunning thief. . . You can imagine how pleased the Dunedin cops were to get the photo back, Nev?"

"Too right, Greg! You mentioned it before."

"It's good to see you've been keeping track, Nev. It didn't take long for our West Coast biological anomaly to be apprehended, despite the fact that it was the West Coast police that were left to track him down. He appeared more than happy to be carted over the hill to the Dunedin police headquarters. He'd never been over the hill before – had he, Nev? He was also quite prepared to answer any questions put to him, and he didn't know what a lawyer was. By *sheer coincidence* there was an international police conference taking place in the city of Dunedin. Cops from both the Americas, Europe, the UK, New Guinea, the Republic of Ireland, Israel, South Africa, Nigeria, Kenya, the Scandinavian countries, plus four state police forces from around Australia turned up for it. When the Dunedin police told their international counterparts how an individual from the West Coast of New Zealand had been apprehended, and was the chief suspect accused of stealing a photograph from Dunedin's police HQ, the various lawmen earnestly debated on how he should be interrogated. Also, I must remind you that our suspect has eleven fingers and two thumbs on his right hand. . . Naturally the Israeli police representatives tabled some recommendations first, since they were interrogating Palestinian prisoners in torture cells almost every day. They were in favour of ripping out three of the suspect's fingernails from his right hand, and at least one thumbnail. When the Aussies and Kiwis – being typical softies and very conscientious about human rights – vetoed this, the Israelis pointed out quite accurately that the prisoner would still have eight fingernails and one thumbnail left, so why should the international media take any notice? After all, the international media takes no notice of what's happening on the West Bank and Gaza. *Or at least nowadays they don't!* . . . The Israeli's then said they'd boycott the conference if their suggestion wasn't put to the vote, and only the Argentineans, Germans and the African police forces voted in favour of it... Can you tell me why, Nev?"

I struggled to come up with a useful answer. "Was it because they use the same methods?"

"Good guess – Nev! Excellent! No, it was actually because the Argentinean rep's grandad was in Himmler's Gestapo or *Geheime Staatspolizei*, and Germany's rep once used to work for the now defunct *Staatssicherhheitsdienst, Stasi* or *SSD* for short. I'll let you guys figure that one out for yourselves. The Africans also voted in favour of the Israelis' recommendation because they believed that the prisoner would be more than happy to pay a bribe after he'd had three fingernails and a thumbnail ripped out. . . There were a whole range of proposals put forward. The New Guinean reps came up with quite a novel idea. They suggested that the prisoner should be forced to watch five hours of New Guinean native dancing. You'd know the dances, Trev, where the fuzzy wuzzy men jump up and down on the spot so that their cock sheaths also bob up and down. That's when they're not tripping over each other's cock sheath. Years of experience have taught the New Guinean cops that tourists from all over the world – having watched only five minutes of native dancing – were dead keen to catch the next plane home. Fortunately that was rejected out of hand for the reason that it was regarded by the UN as a barbaric torture method. . . That's right – the Spanish *were* involved! They came across as both arrogant and flippant when they tabled their recommendations. Hadn't any of the other police forces heard of the Spanish Inquisition? Wasn't it the Catholic Church that invented several useful interrogation methods such as the *garrucha* or the *strappado*? What about the rack? As a matter of fact one of the Spanish blokes took a poke at the Yank delegation. He pointed out in all truth that

147

if it hadn't of been for the imagination of the Catholic Church inquisitors, there wouldn't be any water boarding going on at Guantanamo Bay. After being given the satisfaction of humiliating the Yanks, the Spanish then drank a toast to Tomás de Torquemada the Castilian Dominican friar who headed the Catholic Spanish Inquisition. To tell you..."

"So it was the Catholic Church that invented waterboarding?" Trev intervened. It wasn't often that he *didn't know* everything!

"They sure were – Trev!" Greg didn't dwell on my younger brother's ignorance. "As the conference progressed amongst the various police forces, both the Israelis and the Germans further suggested that electrodes should be attached to the prisoner's figs, but that was also tossed out the window. Then we had the submission from the New South Wales representatives. Just for a joke to annoy the Swedes attending, they recommended that the prisoner should be tied to a bed and have his bare feet tickled with a Cassowary or malleefowl feather. That seriously harvested howls of laughter from the Poles, Norwegians, Finns and the Danes. They were laughing hysterically because they were certain that the Swedes would cut up rough and accuse the Aussies of pirating their interrogation methodology, whereby the Swedes would've used a quill from a Skånegås or Scania goose from the towns of Vomb and Hunneberga. That's exactly what happened, and the Swedes – a female officer and a male officer who woke up one Monday morning and decided he was a woman, then every Tuesday he wanted to be a man again – were quite rude when they couldn't resist bringing up Australia's convict past. The Poms and the Canadians then stepped in and appealed to the New South Wales cops to apologise to the Swedes, and the Kiwis were given a huge boost when the Aussies did so. . . This's where you West Aussies can be proud of your police force, guys."

"Proud – why?" Kev was the first to query that.

Greg bummed a cigarette of me before replying. "It was the WA cops that came up with the final strategy that every delegate, bar the Israelis and Canadians, voted for. Don't take this as the gospel truth, but I wouldn't be the least bit surprised if the Israelis abstained because their fingernail pulling and fig shocking had been rejected. . . Tell me, gentlemen – I understand that you're not overly enamoured with Perth?"

"Bloody oath – we're not," Trev as usual was the spokesman for the Nazzaris.

"I'm inclined to have the same opinion as you," Greg murmured. "I think the most poignant memory I have of good old Perth is the long lines of Chinese crystal meth dealers, with their Bentleys, Rollers, Ferraris, and Mercedes Benzes parked all the way down the street. They were busy illegally laundering bags and bags full of cash via the Commonwealth Bank of Australia's ATM depositing gizmos – weren't they? . . . Tell me, Trev, what's your favourite recollection of Perth?"

Trev had no hesitation: "Driving east up the escarpment on my way back to Kalgoorlie."

I think Greg found his answer appealing. "Before you write off Perth altogether, let me take you on a bit of a tour of Perth's outer suburbs. Particularly two suburbs situated to the north of Perth's CBD – Balga and Joondalup. Trev, you've often mentioned that you've come across morbidly obese women in Ellenbrook and Joondalup, still I need to mention a lass who lives in Balga. She's a police constable, and her female partner – police partner – lives in Joondalup. They're both identical because they're gargantuan by any country's standards, and on a par with the Southland and West Coast grunters that you're bound to come across before too long. . . Now they say that Poo Zealand can take the honours for female fatties, though don't discount Perth's suburbs – especially those found at the foot of the Darling Scarp or Ranges that Trev just mentioned. Take for instance Balga and Joondalup. Several investigations have been embarked on as to why Perth and its suburbs have more chubby ladies than the rest of Aussie, and I found this Afghan professor's hypothesis quite fascinating. Not only did he refer to Perth and its suburbs as being mind-numbingly boring, he pointed out that the land on which most of the suburbs were situated is *dead flat* in its entirety! That means that the preponderance of Perth women aren't required to walk uphill anywhere, as there are no hills, ramps or slopes, thus they weren't getting the same exercise as women elsewhere. This was making them lazy, and causing them to binge eat all day because Perth was so flat and boring. He has a point, you know, when you take into consideration the mountains to be found in his home country. . . Now before you have a go at me, Trev, Poo Zealand's more than well endowed with mountains and hills. It's just that you'll find that the average Southland and West Coast woman's very loath to wander more than a couple of hundred metres from the local bakery. You never know when it might have a special on cream buns, or it might run out of mutton pies, chocolate éclairs, and mud cake."

"Righto, so what about these sheilas who were cops in Perth?" Kev was tired of Greg's latest detour.

"Ah – Special Constables Gerry Higgins and Rosemary Wallace – you mean, Kev?" Greg was almost savouring the names. "With the work they've been doing for the WA police force – if not police forces all over Australia – it's outrageous that they haven't been promoted to sergeant, although I won't bother boring you with details of brutal male chauvinism and misogyny that thankfully has died off in Oz for many years. . . Tell me, Nev, both these women live in the outer suburbs, yet they have to report for duty at the WA police headquarters in Perth's Northbridge. Can you possibly explain why?"

"Nah, Greg, I haven't the foggiest." Which was fair dinkum.

"It's on account of their very special talent, Nev. Similar to you – they can be relied upon for generating the foulest of wind. I was told that it began during recruit training. This was years before the Joondalup recruitment centre, when dormitories were provided for both the male and female recruits. Separate male and female dormitories, although they were barely a few metres distant from one another. That's why unisex midnight feasts were popular, plus pillow fights – the girls versus the boys. Also this was before all this silly feminism came about during these last couple of decades. Long before females insisted on taking up cricket, rugby, footy and suchlike. A sad and dark time when chauvinism and misogyny were rife. Way back when the wooden truncheon and the toe of a boot hadn't yet been replaced by tasers and pepper spray. . . Similar to countless other female recruits, back in those days our two ladies were struggling to compete against their male colleagues. I suppose this was when Rosemary and Gerry became lifelong partners. Dedicated police partners – not sexual partners, Nev – and those with the necessary rank realised that it would be criminal to separate them. . . Actually they couldn't really separate them, and I'll explain why shortly. They did everything together – bashing rowdy and drug-crazed late night revellers in that Perth nightclub cesspit Northbridge with truncheons – writing out traffic tickets – plus they were genuinely respected for fearless high speed chasing of stolen cars. . . Hold on – I'm getting ahead of myself. It was during their recruit training days that they travelled to South Korea on leave. I can't be exactly sure, though I think it was in the South Korean city of Busan where they became addicted to *kimchi*. Do you know what kimchi is Nev?"

"Yeah – I know what it is," Trev was desperate to prove *he did know everything*. "It's fermented vegetables and a staple of the Korean people."

"That it is, Trev!" Greg was happy to allow. "All sorts of vegies can be used. While Gerry simply adores Korean radishes in her kimchi, they generally give Rosemary heartburn. To make up for this the latter uses more napa cabbage or kale. Yes, gents, they both have several favourite recipes and they eat kimchi by the barrel with literally *everything*. . . Very well then, Trev mentioned fermented vegetables – not so, Kev?"

Being caught unawares, Kev sat bolt upright. "I think he might've, Greg."

Greg was content with that. "That's the whole crux of the issue, Kev – fermentation. Plus we've got napa cabbage and Korean radish. It was towards the end of the recruit training that our girls realised that they had a gift that far exceeded the various strengths of their male colleagues. It was Gerry that discovered it when her male colleagues invaded the female sleeping quarters with pillows being swung in all directions. They were holding a corner of their pillows with both hands, similar to what they'd been trained to do with riot clubs. It was a dawn raid and the element of surprise gave the young men an overwhelming advantage. Naturally Gerry was the first to grab a pillow to defend her dormitory, and in the ensuing fracas the exertion caused her to let go all the fermented gases that were compressed in her lower bowel. . . Let me quickly clarify something before I go any further.

Gerry and Rosemary had just flown in from Seoul the evening before the raid. There'd been some turbulence during the flight, but both our girls thought it was insufficient to cause all the other passengers plus the crew to employ their vomit bags – which they did! And then later on they also saw all the other recruits – both males and females – dropping their pillows and fleeing the pillow fight with their hands held over both mouths and noses, desperately trying not to vomit! Could someone have employed vomit gas or Adamsite that the Russian police frequently use on people who dare to criticise Vladimir Putin? The West Aussie recruit instructors had mentioned the use of Adamsite or *diphenylaminechlorarsine* or DM for riot control, but I very much doubt if it's employed by any of Australia's police forces. . . I won't bore you with how Rosemary and Gerry worked out that it was their rather severe flatulence – a product of their kimchi cravings – that made it almost impossible for other police personnel to work cohesively in their company. If it was in the days of Ned Kelly, they would've been sent packing immediately. Back then police women were required to be far more ladylike than they are today. Nowadays if you were to insist that female police officers have to be ladylike, you'll more than likely cop a riot baton between the legs by some feminist organisation. That's why I often wonder how gay male police officers get by without some kind of feminist body taking care of their interests? None the matter – I'm just rambling on."

"Too bloody right – you are!" Trev concurred with Greg's last statement. "What's all this got to do with French saboteurs?"

"Everything's interconnected, Trev," Greg came back at him. "It's all germane to my Department of Inner Health. Kimchi's very good for you, as fermented vegetables are excellent for your gut when it comes to creating 'good bacteria'. The downside is that the vegetables continue fermenting in your gut, and when you introduce other ingredients such as stout, you can end up with some rather disconcerting results. When vegetable yeast and hops. . ."

"I know what you're talking about!" I was given a chance to outshine Trev. "If I've had Chinese tucker with lots of vegies and a couple of bottles of Coopers Stout, I reckon I could stop a charging rhino in its tracks. You ask. .."

"Yeah – you foul-arsed bastard!" Trev became quite emotional.

"Ah – so now maybe you can understand the relevance of all this?" Greg was visibly pleased. "It didn't take our female police officers long to work out that intestinal flora could be groomed and manipulated, plus they were given a great deal of support by the assistant police commissioner. He sought the services of scientists from Canberra and Darwin, and they came up with all sorts of concoctions. Slices of Spanish chorizo sausages mixed with calf's liver and raw Norwegian herrings went so well with fermented vegetables, and the constables' good gut bacteria just loved it! Even the Australian federal police and ASIO were involved, and faxes were going to and fro to Britain's MI5 who recommended juniper and wood smoked potted pheasant and jugged hare. Naturally this was all top secret and was on a 'need to know' basis. The UN was kept strictly in the dark. . . The only major problem that cropped up was our two constables' breath. That's why you'll never see them without a handful of Fisherman's Friend lollies in their mouths, and every now and then you'll find them taking sips from plastic bottles of BRUT aftershave lotion. . . I was told by someone that crews on submarines can put up with each others' flatulence because they were always eating the same food, and thus their gas was almost identical. You might just see. . ."

"And this's all relevant to your Inner Health scam?" Trev rudely interrupted him.

"Oh – absolutely, Trev!" Greg was adamant. "The more I can learn about the behaviour of the human gut the better. I could find myself up against medical experts, so I want to be as fluent as possible. True, the medical experts over here might not be on a par with Australian experts, still one can't be too careful. I also realise that the Kiwis need to learn to bend their backs more if they're ever going to supply any meaningful competition to the Aussies. . . That's why I find the subject of Gerry and Rosemary quite stimulating. I'm sure their superior officers also share the same interest as me. Especially when it was almost impossible to get other officers to work alongside them. Like the crews of a submarine, Beth and Gerry had become inured to each other's flatulence because they both ate and drank exactly the same things, bar the Korean radishes that gave Rosemary heartburn. They both adore Carlton and United Breweries or CUB Sheaf Stout with a dash of lemonade. . . At first police headquarters thought they were being clever when they decided to transfer our girls to Wiluna. Yes, it was Wiluna – I'm sure you blokes would've heard of it?"

"Friggin' arse end of the world!" Kev beat Trev and me. "All you got are heat, dust and billions of flies."

"So I understand, Kev," Greg nodded sagely at that. "Your terminology reminds me of a labour prime minister who referred to Australia as being the 'arse end of the world'. I can't remember the man's name, but he also reminded me of an Arab I met in Cairo who was trying to sell me nude photos of his, wife, daughter and granddaughter. . . I suppose this gives me a chance to give you some idea of how lethal our two constables' flatulence is. Correct me if I've got it wrong, but apparently the Wiluna Aboriginals can get quite boisterous on occasion when they've had a few beers or a cask or two of fortified wine. This quite often leads to some individuals being accommodated in the lockup, and – in their state of intoxication – they often object to being so treated, and they voice their displeasure at the top of their lungs. That was of little consequence to either Rosemary or Gerry, since the unloading of a little body gas or flatus outside the cell doors was sufficient to render the most vociferous prisoner mute, as he or she struggled to catch their breath. It was very similar to waterboarding, or where vomit gas or *diphenylaminechlorarsine* is employed. Then, like I told you before, police forces throughout Australia are amongst the very best in the world when it comes to human rights, so when a delegation of Aboriginals from all over the Eastern Goldfields marched on WA's parliament building, our two female officers were quickly transferred to the Dumbleyung police station. They were there for barely a couple of days or less when you consider that the other police officers in their entirety promptly deserted their posts in protest. . . Perhaps one should sympathise with the police commissioner? These female police officers have never taken a sickie in their entire careers. They pass any exam or course put in front of them with flying colours. They accepted a posting to Wiluna with good cheer, and are happy to carry out any duty put before them. Furthermore, they can't be ordered to refrain from eating kimchi, for it's recognised all over as being a *genuine* health food. Nonetheless, you had police colleagues to consider, whose rights also needed to be fully protected. To cater for all these facets of the problem, they were finally transferred to the WA police headquarters in Northbridge. This course of action brought about the most suitable outcome when you..."

"Now I know your bullshitting *for real!*" Trev overrode him.

"What makes you say that, Trev?" Greg became quite ruffled.

"You're talking about the police headquarters. That's where you'd have cops by the dozen."

"Ah, I see what you mean," Greg gave ground. "I didn't say they were allowed into the headquarters complex. The office given to them was a police station wagon in the car park. An unmarked, unobtrusive, grey 1995 Ford Falcon station wagon. Plus they were given the unique working hours of between five pm and one o'clock in the morning. In the police vehicle they have a very sophisticated global positioning system and a state-of-the-art radio and recording system. . . Have you any idea of what's going on, Nev?"

I decided to answer him with a question. "Are they some kind of rapid response outfit?"

"People don't give you enough credit, Nev!" Greg assured me. "You blokes will have read about the out of control parties they have in the Perth suburbs."

"Fuckin' oath!" Trev was seriously aroused. "That's where the cops should really get stuck into those dickheaded, druggie arseholes! They don't give two stuffs about whose houses or cars they trash. Typical – fuckin' Perth – for ya!"

"Very true, Trev!" Greg was in complete agreement. "It seems that a good party in the Perth suburbs entails gallons of booze, kilos of crystal meth, fighting gate crashers and destroying every car and front window in the street. Everyone's invited – aren't they – since some brain dead dickhead advertised the party on Twitter and Facebook. Then, of course, there's the throwing of bottles and house bricks at the police who've only come to do their duty protecting the general public and the neighbourhood's property. Men and women often putting their lives on the line for only a third of the pay they justly deserve. Decent men and women trying to maintain some kind of order in one of the most boring places in Aussie, with scarcely enough resources adequate for a place half the size. . . One would presume that our revellers don't give a hoot if they injure one of the police or not. It's not the rioters fault – it's the grog and crystal meth – isn't it? As for the neighbours and the police – who gives a single rat's toenail about them? . . . This's where our two extraordinary policewomen really stand out. There's a party advertised in Wanneroo – right? Wanneroo's probably one of the most depressing suburbs in all of Perth, plus its shire council has a somewhat colourful past. It's not as violent as Armidale and Midvale, whereas I'm fairly certain grog and crystal meth are popular amongst its denizens because Wanneroo's so flat and depressing..."

"Righto, so Wanneroo's a shithouse," Trev pushed in, "what about this Rosemary and Gerry?"

"I'm glad you share the same sentiments about Wanneroo, Trev," Greg seemed quite genuine about that. "Okay, so a party's being held in Wanneroo. Our dedicated, female police officers are amongst the first to arrive at the party wearing civvies – normally black tights, tent tops and rubber thongs. Your bog standard dress mode of quite a number of women who live in Perth's suburbs. True, they might not've been invited, but you have to remember that they live in Balga and Joondalup. Therefore, and similar to a great many females that live in those suburbs, they're not petite no matter how broad your imagination is. They're gargantuan, Trev! Not as huge as the Ellenbrook heifers, but getting close, Trev – getting close! Sure – they're not as mammoth as some West Coast and Southland porkers – but they're *almost* as big! Arriving at the party early, they generally find that there's no one present that's had too much to drink or fried their brain with crystal meth. Not yet, so no one's actually game to challenge or evict such large individuals. . . Very well then, so the party picks up in pace and more and more people arrive. Gerry and Rosemary have been carefully trained to spot possible signs of trouble. . . Then again, no wonder they're so competent, seeing that the majority of Perth's suburban parties follow roughly the same pattern. The partygoers get stuck into the grog and crystal meth, so you've got a pressure cooker situation on your hands. Then the gate crashers arrive, and they're also brain dead from drugs and alcohol. Punches get thrown, and then house bricks and bottles. The riot police are called, and unfortunately some of them and the neighbours could be hurt. This never happened at any of the parties that Rosemary and Gerry attended."

"Why not?" Kev got in before Trev.

"Picture it yourself, Kev," Greg instructed him. "The Wanneroo house has filled up with partygoers. Some of them have gone outside to confront gatecrashers that have arrived by the score, and they're all packed together on the front lawn. It's just on dark and the Wanneroo Shire Council's sprinklers have just started spraying bore water in some council park or other across the road. These sprinklers have driven out further meth heads that were camping amongst the lavender bushes, and the foul bad-egg-fart stink of the Perth northern suburbs bore water can't be improving the atmosphere one iota. Rosemary casually intermingles with the invited partygoers and the trespassers out on the front lawn, while Gerry finds a position somewhere alongside the source of any music in the crowded house. When no one's watching, she turns the music up full blast. Next the people outside start screaming and running in all directions. In their entirety they're heaving out anything they might've drunk or eaten in the previous twelve hours. This's a signal for Gerry to discharge all the gas in her lower bowel, and the house is also vacated in seconds flat. All that remains are the pools of vomit and possibly beer cans and spirit mixer bottles that've been hastily discarded by the fleeing revellers. Most of the meth syringes have been dropped in the park opposite where kids might pick them up or step on them. The whole street's deserted, and peace returns to that particular neighbourhood in Wanneroo. All that remains is the acrid stench of body gas and sprinkler bore water. It's a typical humid and sultry Wanneroo night because the refreshing Fremantle Doctor breeze doesn't bother visiting that suburb anymore. A job well done and no one hurt. The police department saves a small fortune by not having to send out dozens of riot police, horses and dogs... Tell me now, Nev – doesn't that lift your spirits?"

"I reckon so, Greg."

"But what does this have to do with the cop conference in Dunedin?" Trev was still perplexed.

"By asking me that, you've allowed me to come full circle," Greg beamed at him. "If you remember, the various police organisations were working out how to interrogate the West Coast suspect. The main problem's been getting him to focus and pay attention. They tried shouting at him – threatening him – plus they tickled his feet with a feather from an endangered takahē that some Department of Conservation officer had shot some years before. All to no avail, gents. This proved to be just as fruitless, so. . ."

"What's this about someone shooting a taka-whatever?" He'd tickled my curiosity.

"It's a too long and sad story, Nev," Greg responded after a slight pause. "Don't tell anyone I told you this, nevertheless I heard it on good authority that our West Coast suspect simply didn't have a clue of what was going on. On the other hand, the Kiwi police contingent took a leaf out of the New Guineans' book, and they bombarded him with six solid hours of Southland and Otago women Scottish sword dancing. There were several CDs of this *ghastly* material – the chubby, white, hairy legs in tartan stockings, plus freckles and ginger hair, however the suspect appeared to derive pleasure from it and almost instantaneously displayed an erection. It just goes to show you that he must be short of a few roos in the top paddock, and this also has immediately become apparent to his interrogators. . . . Now you know why I insisted on telling you about Rosemary and Gerry."

"What – were they gunna have Rosemary and Gerry sit on his face and fart?" Trev's always had a debauched imagination.

"Not quite – but close – Trev! The police label for it isn't 'fart'. It's called 'Controlled Wind Breakage' or 'CWB'. Please use the term 'CWB' from now on, so that at all times we can understand one another. . . You know how religious books and texts claim to have witnessed miracles? The Bible, the Koran and even the Book of Mormon? Well, I have to say that a miracle has been witnessed very recently in Dunedin, Trev."

"A miracle – what miracle?" that had Kev wide awake.

Greg was impressed by Kev's sudden interest. "Now you'll see how things come together, Kev. The safe that was at the Dunedin police headquarters – from which the photo of a French woman taking a crap was stolen – was a walk-in job because the building used to belong to a bank. The only trouble is that the key to the safe's long lost. It was given to Dunedin's police executive superintendent when the building was handed over, and he was known to have kept it on a piece of string tied around his neck. It was eventually lost when he and a number of his officers were involved in a bloody fracas with some of the Otago University's female rugby team. . . Can you see why all this's so important, Kev?"

"No – mate."

"That's okay, Kev," Greg spared him any possible embarrassment. "The door of the walk-in safe would only stay fully closed when it was locked. So without the key, the same door was always slightly ajar. That's most likely why the photograph was stolen so quickly and easily. Sure, the Dunedin police used to keep it fully shut by putting an antique, cast iron doorstop at the bottom of the door, but I doubt that this would've fooled any career burglar. Actually, I'm not. . ."

"Ah, come on, Greg!" Trev was impatient again. "Like I asked you before – what's this got to do with French sabotage?"

"You'll find out in a minute, Trev." Greg looked at him imploringly. "As well as riot control, Gerry and Rosemary have been given additional duties. That's why they have such sophisticated transmitting and recording devices in the unmarked Ford station wagon. If there's a terror suspect – or well known criminal – who refuses to cooperate with the police, he or she might be taken for a ride round the block in our constables' vehicle.

Just before that Gerry and Rosemary usually toss a coin to see who's going to drive the station wagon and who's in charge of the CWB. . . Now I have to explain something very important, Trev. When Gerry and her trusty partner are breaking up riots in Perth's suburbs, Gerry always has to position herself as close as possible to any music that's playing, and she tries to arrange it so that the music's playing as loudly as possible. That isn't all that difficult because the organisers of Perth's suburban parties rarely give a rat's anus when it comes to upsetting any neighbours. Before you ask me, Kev – it's on account of the fact Gerry's *unable to administer* CWB quietly. While Rosemary can let flee quite incomprehensibly large pockets of CWB without a sound, Gerry can only mete out CWB in short, very loud bursts. Their body gas smells the same, but the methodology they employ when it comes to releasing it is poles apart. No matter how often they practise, the result always comes back exactly the same. As a result of that you've more or less got the same as the good cop – bad cop scenario, whereas here we have the loud cop – silent cop. And this supplies them with interesting alternatives when it comes to interrogating different suspects. They've learnt that Gerry's short loud bursts are particularly effective when it comes to the thugs, bullies and standover merchants that the payday lenders and Chinese meth dealers employ to collect money from hapless, destitute clients. The absolute scum of the earth and bottom feeders to be found in a sceptic tank. The thugs, payday lenders and the drug dealers. Also, it became very apparent how prolific and widespread Chinese crystal meth distribution was in Western Australia, and why Perth's been labelled 'Australia's Meth Capital'. . . Rosemary's most useful when terrorist or white collar fraudsters need to be given some gentle persuasion. You can understand why, Trev. Short, loud bursts of CWB can also be described as bullying tactics, while you can't say the same about silent CWB. That's why the latter's used for lowering the resolve of terrorists without some traitorous, do-gooder organisation such as Wikileaks screaming 'foul!' and insisting that terrorists' rights should be put ahead of normal Aussies. The same methodology's also helpful when it comes to corporate criminals such as Perth's Alan Bond, Laurie Connell, and let's not forget three prominent

Western Australian politicians who also spent time behind bars – Brian Burke, Ray O'Connor and David Parker. Yes, you'll always find Rosemary's CWB's the way to go with people like these, as you'll always find that white collar fraudsters and criminals always seem to have some greasy, slimy lawyer hanging out of their arses like septic haemorrhoids. . . That's why we find such sophisticated transmitting and recording technology in the Ford Falcon station wagon. Whenever there's a confession it's transmitted to police HQ, plus duly recorded within the vehicle itself."

Greg's mobile phone rang and he had to catch the next plane from Queenstown to the New Zealand capital. When he returned some days later, he invited Trev and me for lunch at the Queenstown Speights Ale House.

Trev pounced on him: "Hey Greg, what happened to that West Coast bloke with the eleven fingers?"

"Also, you reckoned something about a miracle in the Dunedin cop shop," I further reminded him. "What about those two female West Aussie cops – Rosemarie and what's her name?"

"You must be thinking of Gerry," Greg answered my query first."

"Yeah, that's the one."

Greg sipped his drink. "Actually I stopped off at Dunedin just before returning here. Yes, Nev – you've just reminded me of the miracle that was witnessed in Dunedin a short while ago. I was going to tell you about it earlier, but I had to drop everything and fly to Wellington, as you know well. During my visit in Dunedin I came across the police superintendent starting to panic. The West Coast suspect had been held without charges for far too long, and the French representatives or the *keufs* at the international police conference – both females – were getting more and more derisive. Surely to goodness a confession could be extracted from such a simpleton or *nigaude?* Keuf means 'cop' or 'rozzer' in French, and nigaude means 'booby', Nev. . . Yes, our superintendent was starting to buckle under the pressure, while he was also convinced that one of the French officers was the mystery French woman filmed taking a crap on one of Dunedin's streets. Yes, of course, although the French rep had auburn hair, while the woman in the photo was blonde, they still had facial features that were almost identical. Both were very beautiful, which happens to be typical of French women, unlike the chubby types in track pants that were so ubiquitous in the South Island of New Zealand. Perhaps the French women weren't as beautiful as some Australian women, but not doing such a bad job, either. . . In desperation the super followed up with the Canadians' suggestion. This meant showing a picture of a Canadian mounted policeman to the suspect – red jacket – corny hat – yellow stripes down the black trousers – both the officer and horse frowning sternly back at the camera. This just made the prisoner chuckle with delight because the horse's face reminded him of his Uncle Pat Murphy, the paedophile Catholic priest, while the Yank representatives were convinced the mounted officer was a fruit. To a man they were positive that any bloke who got around dressed like that – horse or no horse – simply had to have a hormonal imbalance! . . . So this's where Rosemary and Gerry came into the picture. Urgent word was sent to the police commissioner in Perth, and both our constables flew on one of those magnificent Air New Zealand Boeing 787 Dreamliners to Auckland, and they caught the very next domestic flight to Dunedin. . . They were put to work immediately – weren't they, Nev? Can you guess what instructions were given to them?"

The answer seemed obvious. "They were gunna take the West Coast bloke for a ride in a cop car and fart?"

"As I pointed out to Trev, we need to employ Western Australian police terminology, Nev. I'd appreciate it if you could kindly employ the term 'CWB'. . . You're getting warm, though Nev – but not quite. Didn't I mention that the Dunedin police headquarters had a walk-in safe?"

"You did."

"Ah, so *you have* been paying attention, Nev!" Greg was consoled by that. "The plan was that the suspect should be seated in the safe with either one or both constables. . . Gerry and Rosemary were delighted for a couple of reasons. Firstly, they were more or less being given an all expenses paid holiday in beautiful New Zealand. Better than that, they would be bound to have hundreds of Kiwi blokes lusting after them! Despite their size they'd be far more attractive than the local specimens, and there was the fact that the *greatest ambition* a Kiwi bloke had was to bed an Aussie sheila. Yes, Dunedin's a bit of a wart on the landscape, still there was the opportunity to visit Queenstown, plus the smelly mud pools and geysers and whatever have you in Rotorua and other parts of the North Island. . . Secondly, here was an excellent chance for promotion *at very long* last! . . . You'll notice that I'm employing the term 'was', Nev?"

"Why's that?" I could see that he was suddenly troubled.

Greg quickly drank more beer. "The proverbial shit has hit the fan in Dunedin, gents! Our suspect was enticed into the walk-in safe by a police officer carrying a banana, and both female constables accompanied him. . . Now this's where the miracle happened that I mentioned to you previously. With the superintendent having lost the key to the safe in a brawl, the door of the same safe remained ever so slightly ajar. While the escaping CWB forced a panicked evacuation of the entire building, plus two city blocks surrounding it, it was only then that every cop who'd attended that conference realised that a terrible accident had been *so narrowly* avoided! If Rosemary and Gerry had administered their combined CWB with the door firmly shut, both their and the prisoner's eardrums would've burst, plus their chests most likely could've collapsed. Identical to a submarine being crushed by too much outside water pressure! . . . Then what could only have been described as a nightmare swiftly followed!"

"A nightmare?" Trev was also fully focused.

"Yes, Trev, you can only call it a nightmare. When the various officers from the conference and the local police were fairly certain that the building was safe to enter again, they found the suspect bundled up in the corner of the superintendent's office! He was taking turns screaming hysterically and sobbing uncontrollably. It wasn't difficult to determine that he'd lost his faculties altogether, as well as his mind/hand coordination for he was trying to pick his left nostril simultaneously with all eleven fingers on his right hand. Poor Rosemary's and Gerry's faces were ashen as they stared vacantly at each other in horror! . . . Look, it's a good thing that Kev's not here, otherwise I would have to refuse to continue. You won't..."

"What happened?" Trev and I asked in unison.

Greg lifted his glass with shaking hands. "It wasn't the CWB treatment that reduced the suspect to a jabbering idiot. True enough, it *did indeed* make him cry, although that was only because the smell made him homesick for his mum's and twin sisters' breath. It was a photograph he was shown – wasn't it, guys?"

"What photograph?" Trev beat me to it.

Greg drank the rest of his beer. "It was a photograph that Gerry showed him. A copy of which Rosemary always keeps in her purse."

"What photograph – Greg?" Trev persisted.

Greg spoke to me instead. "Do you remember me telling you about the male chauvinism and misogyny that Rosemary and Gerry had to put up with during the early years of their careers, Nev? It's much better in all of Australia's police forces nowadays, but our two girls had endured far darker times not all that long ago. Can you guess what they've lately been using to sustain themselves with, Nev?"

I tried to sound as sympathetic as possible. "I couldn't for the life of me guess, Greg."

"I thought you mightn't, Nev," Greg sat back. "Can you help us, Trev?"

"No, Greg. What about the photo?"

With that, Greg sighed. "It was a photo of Germaine Greer – wasn't it, Trev? Rosemary carried around an identical copy in her purse. They'd used a photograph of that well known Australian feminist as a staff to lean on, and I have to confess that I've *never* seen a photograph of her to be all that enthusiastic about. Not ever! Even so, I positively *wasn't* prepared for the one I was shown by a rather shaken Queensland cop who'd also attended the conference. He was a big bloke like most Queensland cops are, but I could also see that he was well and truly shattered! . . . They say that small children and those with mental disorders can see and deduce things that grown-ups and normal people can't. Although everyone was sure that the photo had been cleverly doctored by a rather sick individual, a psychiatrist who examined our suspect was adamant that the poor creature had seen something very evil and sinister in the photo, and that he'd probably never fully recover from having done so. . . We'll leave it at that – won't we, gents?"

"Pigs arse – you bloody won't!" Trev objected strenuously. "What was wrong with the photo?"

It was necessary to buy Greg another pint of Speights Porter before he would continue: "It was a photo of your ex-PM Kevin Rudd holding hands with Germaine Greer on a beach somewhere, and they're coming straight at you! It was just as nauseating as those first videos that were taken of Bob Hawke after he'd given Hazel the flick, and was walking in his towelling robe towards the sunset holding hands with Blanche d'Apluget, who was similarly attired. . . Look – Nev – I don't know what you find so funny, as it's a rather nasty thing to fabricate about anyone. One would hardly imagine Germaine Greer wanting to have any sort of liaison with a male example such as Kevin. While in the photo Rudd closely resembled a small boy grinning and about to slurp on rather a large slice of watermelon, there was rather a contemptuous look on Germaine's face. A kind of 'What am I doing here with this misogynistic little prick?' expression. After all, wasn't he so nasty that he made an RAAF attendant cry because she wasn't serving him the right tucker? Didn't someone call him *'Kevin Rude'* after that? . . . Yes, you *heard right*, gents. For once our Kevin had swapped his normal, petulant look for a cheesy, mischievous grin. If faced with such an unbelievable scenario, he may've been turned on by the thought of holding the feminist lioness' hand, but let's be kind and put aside a little sympathy for poor Germaine. Also, don't let me forget to mention that in the photo Kevvie has a tattoo on his right shoulder – *'I come from the arse end of the world!'* I wonder if he was trying t6o copy his hero – Paul Keating. Didn't Paul say that Aussie *is* 'the arse end of the world – Trev?"

"Too bloody right – he did!" Trev acknowledged. "If you ask me – he was nearly as arrogant as Rudd."

"True – true," Greg was in agreement. "All the same I think there's also something hidden in that photo our two constables have been carrying around with them. I'm sure I can deduce something *quite extraordinary* from Germaine's facial expression in the photograph. Perhaps if reading *THE FEMALE EUNACH* to Kevvie at bedtime, he just might give up on his prissy little tantrums and behave himself like a grown up? You could liken it to potty training? She must be aware that he's only a short, little bloke – and has to bend his head right back in order to look down his nose at people – then again I must remind you that the entire equation just has to be impossible. It's amazing how perfectly innocent photos can be manipulated these days! . . . OK, our West Coaster *could* be deemed an imbecile, so let's have some compassion here as well? I don't think you have to be a small child or insane to sense the aura of malevolence the subject of this obscene photo conjures up. I have to say that I was taken aback by it. Can you think of anything more hideous? Neither Rudd or Greer are very inspiring when seen alone, nevertheless can you envisage them *both* in the *same* photo? The person who doctored it up is either insane, or truly has a diseased sense of humour. . . What I *do know* is that Rosemary's and Gerry's lives have been irrevocably changed! Returning to Aussie is the last thing on their minds."

"Why aren't they going back to Aussie?" Trev's tone was far more placatory.

"Do you remember me mentioning the Argentinean members at the conference, Trev?"

"Yeah?"

Greg's voice was still barely audible. "They were just as traumatised as Rosemary and Gerry. This has to be one of the most amazing of coincidences, all the same I think some divine influence is at play here. Nev, can you please pass me my briefcase.

I passed Greg his briefcase, and he stubbed out his cigarette before he opened it. On top of all his papers and so on there was a manila folder with DEPT OF INNER HEALTH printed on it. From this folder he pulled out a bundle of A4 pages and quite a few newspaper and magazine cuttings. He handed one cutting to me which I read and passed onto Trev.

ARGENTINE MOTHER SUPERIOR SUSPECTED OF TORTURING HER NUNS

A Carmelite mother superior in Argentina faces prosecution for alleged torture after one of her former charges told a TV show that she had gone through "hell" before managing to escape from a convent.

The 34-year-old nun, whose face was blacked out during the interview on the channel El Trece, claimed she had endured "physical and psychological" torture during her 10-year period of reclusion in the convent. This included enforced self-flagellation, the wearing of a wire garter, plus being gagged for up to a week and locked up in isolation.

"With Mother Superior Isabel I was subjected to the gag. Then she had a whip called 'the discipline' which was dipped in molten wax to make it harsher. We performed self-flagellation, beating ourselves on the buttocks, every week as a rule," the former nun from the Barefoot (or Discalced) Carmelite convent in Nogoyá, northern Argentina said.

The woman, who said she had entered the order at the age of 18, also said they were forced to wear a cilice, a "crown of wires strapped around the leg that draws blood", three times a week during Lent.

But she said the worst torture she endured was psychological, being locked up alone in a cell and hearing voices telling her that others nuns' illnesses, such as one sister's tumour, were curses wrought upon the monastery due to her sinful nature.

Two nuns have reported the mother superior, identified by the authorities only as María Isabel, claiming she kept them against their will in the gated convent grounds. In late August police raided the convent, forcing the door open after the mother superior allegedly refused to allow them to enter.

The officers seized instruments of the alleged torture, including whips, cilices and gags.

Prosecutors have recommended charges with a penalty of 15 years in prison for the mother superior, who was to face an investigating judge on Wednesday.

CHURCH LEADERS HAVE JUSTIFIED THE USE OF
SUCH INSTRUMENTS AS 'TOYS FOR PLEASURE'

"It's only a little bit of fun," said Cardinal Adolf Eichmann Junior, the Argentinean grandson of the Adolf Eichmann who was executed by Israel. These whips, cilices and gags are toys used for pleasure rather than punishment. May I remind you that monasteries and convents all have different ways of passing the time. Some Carmelite nuns not only employ whips, cilices and gags, they also wear chastity belts with built-in guillotines that guard either the back or the front orifice, and the Dominican friars have to guess which. These are very popular, and at the last Dominican monastery I visited, half the friars had to sit down to urinate, and the other half were speechless when I addressed them. The nuns themselves are making a delicious jellied brawn out of their mementos from this exercise.

"We are all human," Cardinal Eichmann continued, "and we all use different methods when it comes to amusing ourselves. The Church has the right to rule itself, and governments should enforce respect for religious freedom. Take the Republic of Ireland where the Christian Brothers enjoy physical activities with boys in their colleges and Catholic orphanages. Not only do they enjoy this leisure in Ireland, they have been dutifully engaged with boys all over the world. I have also heard that the infamous Australian Cardinal Pell once enjoyed rollicking around with small boys in Swimming pools. All this fun is perfectly normal to members of the clergy, while to others these activities may seem incomprehensible."

"What a fuckin' bunch of perverted freaks!" My younger sibling couldn't work out why Greg was so amused. "Thank Christ we've had that Julia Gillard as a PM, never mind that Rudd the Dud!"

Greg raised his glass. "I couldn't agree with you more. Let's offer a toast to Julia?"

I was more than happy to drink to Julia Gillard's health. Not only was I finding her more and more attractive every day; she got things done that needed to be done, without the poncy ego and attitude. She was the only one who'd achieved anything worthwhile when it came to dealing with the filthy scum that had used their position in the various churches to molest kids, plus the arseholes who did their best to ignore it or cover it up. I was still confused as to why Greg felt obliged to show Trev and me the newspaper cutting. "Why did you have to go to Dunedin?"

He sat back and stroked his beard. "It was important to visit someone very important to my plans. Knowing that I knew people in high places, the Dunedin superintendent was more than happy to keep me up to date re the alleged French sabotage business. I also had a brief chat with Rosemary and Gerry at the Dunedin Airport. They were booked on a flight to Buenos Aires. The poor souls were heartbroken. Not only were they devastated by the utter collapse of the West Coast suspect, their much anticipated holiday in Poo Zealand has turned out to be very disenchanting. Our constables were booked into the Southern Cross Hotel; the building of which houses the Dunedin Casino. Just as they'd imagined, there were local Otago blokes following them round in droves, yet none of these men could come up with the courage to address them in any way whatsoever. Naturally they advertised the fact that they were Aussies because everywhere they went off duty they wore either Wallaby rugby jerseys, or their 'AUSSIE – AUSSIE – AUSSIE – Oi – Oi – Oi' cricket fan shirts. They'd be walking down Princes Street, Dunedin's main drag, and there were an army of blokes of all ages and descriptions walking barely three or four metres behind them. Then, just as they turned round to speak to these guys, the same blokes would go sprinting in the opposite direction – giggling all the way! Finally – when they did manage to get a couple of farmers from a place called Ranfurly into the sack, both men wanted them to have sex standing up with their backs to them. The girls with their backs to the blokes – that is."

"How come?" I couldn't comprehend what he'd just told me.

"They were both alpaca farmers – weren't they, Nev? Apparently that's the new rage over here. Kiwi blokes – especially the rural types – have taken to alpacas rather than sheep because they don't have to get on their knees to have their way with them. Also, it's much easier on their backs. . . I'm beginning to think you've rather an odd sense of humour, Nev. If you can stop laughing and be sufficiently charitable, please find some compassion for poor Gerry. While Rosemary was drowning her sorrows with a bottle of Tasmanian whisky, Gerry managed to snare a Southland bloke in the Dunedin Casino at approximately midnight. The fellow came from a picturesque little place called Wyndham. That's approximately thirty-nine kilometres as the crow flies from Invercargill, which is more or less Southland's principal city. It seemed that he'd come looking for some rumpy pumpy in Otago's capital, for he had all the usual Southland gear."

"What gear?" Trev was on full alert!

"I knew you'd ask that," Greg chided him light-heartedly. "From what I could deduce, this fellow worked on a dairy farm just outside a place called Orepuki. He lives on the dairy farm for six days of the week, and then he spends every Sunday with his mum in Wyndham where she washes his work clothes and cooks him roast lamb for Sunday lunch."

"What's this got to do with the gear he had?" My curiosity had been grabbed similar to Trev's.

Greg cadged another smoke off me. "He works on a dairy farm – right? With all those dairy cows he was used to dealing with large ladies of the female gender – namely those cows. Yes, he was prepared to mount Gerry from behind, though what she found rather disconcerting was that he insisted on wearing rubber gumboots, a plastic raincoat and a crash helmet – all of which were stained green, and smelling of cow manure. While she could put up with that, she finally found it impossible to make motorbike noises as he pretended to steer her shoulders right and left."

It was compulsory to wait for Trev to get over his coughing fit. He'd been laughing that much, Speights Porter went down the wrong way. I was still determined to keep Greg on Track. "But why were Gerry and Rosemary catching a plane to Buenos Aires?"

"It was the reaction they'd got from the West Coast prisoner – wasn't it Nev? Not only did quite a few cops from the various police forces resign, our constables also felt obliged to do so. One of the Argentinean reps that I mentioned earlier told Gerry about the convent in Nogoyá, northern Argentina. I don't know how long they intend to be there, still it was easy to determine that they'd made up their minds that they need to be disciplined. They're just praying that Mother María Isabel has been released, so that she can tell them how to go about it. . . By the same token, we have a rather treacherous undercurrent to all this."

"What treacherous undercurrent?" Trev had regained his composure.

"It was the Canadian contingent – wasn't it, Trev?" Greg replied. "They were extremely miffed that the Yanks implied that the officer in the Canadian issue photograph was a fruit, and salt was rubbed into their wounds when they noticed that the New South Wales team and the Kiwi reps thought the Yanks were being very witty. . . You know how the various Yank police forces are notorious for shooting dead unarmed and innocent people all over the States, Trev?"

"My word!" Trev was caught unawares by that.

"Yes, they've got a shocking record of firing off the hip," Greg pursued the subject further. "When asked to come forward with a proposition, they were all for leaving the suspect in some dark alley at night. Then, when he made his way out into the street light, they would have three officers ready to open fire and use up all the ammunition in their guns during the process. That particular idea was immediately vetoed by the Dutch and Belgians. Two of the sissiest nations that fronted up at the conference. . . Oh, and I forgot – the South Africans, Kenyans and Nigerians went along with the Dutch and the Belgians, and they pointed out quite logically that how could the suspect pay a bribe to anyone if he was shot full of holes? Or maybe someone could go through his pockets? Actually, when I come..."

"What was this about the Canadians?" I wasn't going to allow him to drift off again.

"The Canadians – Nev? Having being insulted by the Yanks, and having seen the Aussies and the Kiwis laughing at the Yanks' rather unkind joke, they became quite childish and sent a complaint through to the United Nations in New York. And with the UN being overrun with sissy people such as the Belgians and the Dutch – plus questionable and corrupt states such as South Africa, Zimbabwe, Angola, Gabon, plus the Democratic Republic of Congo, Romania and Bulgaria – there were people in the UN's New York headquarters who were just itching to flex their imaginary muscles. Sure, they were delighted that no one had complained about the Israelis with their finger nail ripping and fig electrocution, for the Israelis would just turn round and tell them to jump in a lake, anyway, and the UN would be made to look like a collection of irrelevant nobodies. Which is a fair assumption when you think about it. . . The Kiwis and the Aussies were fair game – weren't they? Especially as they were competing against each to see who could be the most politically correct. As far as the Kiwis went, the UN felt that it couldn't sanction people being forced to watch fat, freckled, female sword dancers. Especially if the majority of those dancers came from New Zealand's Southland and Otago regions. . . Even more serious was the Western Australian police force's use of CWB. A female UN officer from Sweden claimed that the use of CWB was no less a crime than what Syria's Bashar Al-Assad and Saddam Hussein had committed against civilians in both Syria and Iraq. This same woman was also championing the banning of the following – 'God the Father – God the Son – etceteras – etceteras.' Actually referring to God as being a man's so chauvinistic and politically *incorrect* – isn't it? I'm quite surprised that Poo Zealand's Labour Government or Australia's Greens Party haven't thought of it first, while I hear the Aussies are working on banning the titles 'ladies and gentlemen'. Wait – hold on a minute – I need to quickly explain something."

Trev stared into his beer. "Explain what?"

"I'm glad you're giving me this opportunity, Trev," Greg looked quite relieved. "I believe that the Israeli suggestion of fingernail pulling was vetoed because police forces nowadays much prefer to employ psychological methods rather than physical ones. Out of this came quite a humorous distraction. You take the Portuguese and how similar they are to the Canadians and Kiwis. The Canadians like to think that overseas countries regard them as the Yanks' little brothers, and you have the Kiwis wanting you to think that they're the Aussies' little brothers. The Portuguese try and portray themselves as being similar with the Spanish. Younger brothers – that is. Also like the Canadians and the bongos, they're finding themselves in their neighbours' shadows. . . Nevertheless, let's put that aside for a moment. What their police delegates – or members of the *Garda Nacional*

Republicana – came up with was a three-hour video of Rafael Nadal playing six sets of tennis against Roger Federer. . . It was a farce – wasn't it, Nev?"

"If you reckon so, Greg?"

"As a matter of fact – I do, Nev. Roger Federer's Swiss, and Rafael Nadal's Spanish – not so, Nev?"

"I think so?"

"They are, Nev – they are," Greg was probably looking for exactness. "While the Swiss – who withdrew their delegates not long after the Kiwis had employed their Scottish dancer discs – thought the Portuguese were being rather childish, the Spanish cops *absolutely* spat the dummy! . . Since we're on the subject of tennis – who's that bloke who Dawn Fraser told to go back to where his parents came from? You know the one – the bloke who has hissy fits and nearly craps in his baggy tennis pants every time the crowd laughs at his childish antics?"

"I know!" Trev *always loves* a chance to show off. "Nick Kyrgios. He accused Dawn of being a racist, but he's half Greek and half Malaysian – isn't he?"

"He is indeed, Trev. I've heard his behaviour's matured somewhat, though his childish tantrums were a bit of a pain in the posterior. Most pathetic and tiresome. Maybe that's the Greek coming out in him, as by and large the Greeks are fairly insignificant when it comes to their standing in the EU. . . That's exactly how the Spanish reps behaved. Fortunately before the Swiss pulled out, one of their officers did remind everyone that the Portuguese were plucky fellows, so how's about letting them borrow Rafael for just a little while? This, of course, the Spanish refused to do, and their behaviour was very similar to that of Nick Kyrgios. They went through the ritual spitting the dummy and threatened to boycott the conference. Rafael Nadal may be one of the best tennis players that God ever put breath into, but you'd expect the Spanish attendees of the conference to have a little more generosity. Instead they were on a par with naughty Nick Kyrgios. "

"Did the Portuguese blokes show the video of Roger Federer to the West Coast bloke?" Trev quizzed Greg.

Greg's lips were puckered up with distaste. "As I informed you, Trev – the whole affair was a debacle. Our suspect watched perhaps ten minutes of the game – pretended to masturbate himself with his right hand – then fell fast asleep. One of the Norwegian cops told me that he was expecting *exactly that* reaction. After all he told me – in atrocious English – as far as a sport goes – tennis is a load of wank. He didn't actually use the word 'wank', he just jerked his fist up and down and pretended to hold his donger. Very similar to the suspect's actions."

"I'll bloody say it's a load of wank!" Trev was quite vehement about that.

"Me too – Trev!" Greg was equally as passionate. "Nonetheless, photographs depicting scary or disgusting themes were the most popular among the various police forces. You take for instance the *Garda Siochána* as a case in point. The Garda is the title of Southern Ireland's police force. Similar to the Canadians, they're great proponents of the use of photographs. Not long back they used to employ this Indian hermaphrodite with a little girl's voice singing *"DANNY BOY"* time and time again until a suspect either confessed or went totally batty. This, too, was banned by the UN and it was labelled *'perverse'*. So nowadays they're using a photograph. Try and guess what's in the photograph, Trev."

"Greg!" Trev's eyes were full of foreboding.

Greg hastily moved on. "Actually I'm quite glad the photograph *wasn't shown* to our West Coast suspect. In it there were four clergymen and what appeared to be a lawyer. More than likely a QC. It's not so much a photo of real people, though it's a very clever digital image that was designed by some outfit in Ballarat – Victoria. In the photograph they're all sitting down, bar the lawyer. Running from right to left is a Christian Brother, your run-of-the-mill senile-looking Irish priest, a bishop, and lastly a cardinal. As you would expect – they're all Catholic. I'm not sure about the lawyer. While photos of Catholic clergymen in cassocks are fairly common, the ones in the photo were *very distinct!* The Christian Brother and the priest had their cassocks pulled up to waist level and they were proudly displaying unbelievable erections. Possibly as an affront to the Israelis or all Jews, they're blatantly displaying the fact that they're uncircumcised. If that's not disturbing..."

"You really *are* insane – *aren't* you?" Trev managed to splutter.

Greg looked down his nose at my younger brother. "You'll take that back, Trev, when I've finished what I was going to say. . . Next in line we saw the bishop – didn't we? His eyes were covered with both his hands, though there was a pronounced bulge in the groin area of his cassock. . After that the cardinal can be seen passing a bag full of cash to the lawyer. . . Do I need to explain what's going on, guys?"

Somehow Greg's insane ramblings rang a bell! "I think I heard something about this bloke in Victoria who accused the Catholic Church of covering up a sexual assault by a priest or whatever? Didn't some cardinal pay a top class lawyer a hundred grand in order to shut him up?"

"Well done, Nev – well done!" Greg laughed out loud. "Later on you'll see a coincidental nexus between the Garda Siochána's photo and one that the Victorian police had. Can you illuminate your brother as to the significance of the Garda Siochána photograph?"

"Sorry, I can't mate."

"Don't let it bother you, Nev. This's where we can take our hats off to Julia Gillard. That's why the Victorian police's photo has a possible nexus to the Garda Siochána's. They have clergymen with similar ranks and poses, whereas in the Victorian police' photo the cardinal's in a swimming pool tossing a small boy into the air with one arm, and handing over a bundle of cash to what seems to be a QC. . . Now can you see the nexus, Nev?"

"Whatsa nexus?" I was confused.

"Never mind, Nev. Both photographs transmit the same message or probable warning. That a Catholic Christian brother or parish priest can sexually assault you – the local bishop will turn a blind eye to any complaint against that priest or brother – that a cardinal can get his hands on more than sufficient cash – stolen off the collection plate – to crush you in the courts, if you or the police are stupid enough to try and take the matter any further. Thanks to our Julia, it looks as though this kind of behaviour and threat may be a thing of the past."

175

"So what did the UN do about the West Aussies using that BMW – or whatever you call it?" Trev ventured back into the conversation.

"It's CWB, Trev." Greg corrected him. "Must I keep on reminding you? The use of CWB. . ."

Greg fell silent when Kev pitched up. He continued after my elder brother bought fresh pints for all of us: "The use of CWB in Australia was still in its infancy, and police forces throughout Australia were monitoring Western Australia's progress minutely. The use of CWB wasn't intended to actually cause any physical or long term harm. Take for instance the Ford Falcon station wagon that was issued to Gerry and Rosemary. It had state-of-the-art, electric window winding mechanisms. Generally when our constables were going to administer a batch of CWB, all four windows in the station wagon were wound down, for they didn't intend to mentally maim any suspects. The fact that the same windows could be wound up electronically in a split second, was only for intimidation purposes. If a suspect inhaled the CWB while the windows were down, how excruciating and unbearable would it be with the windows wound up? In most cases the windows being wound up and down was enough to get a confession if the suspect was guilty. No physical harm was caused – was it? Not unless the suspect got his fingers caught in one of the windows when it was on its way up. . . You also need to consider the therapeutic qualities of CWB. For example the gas could be deemed organic as it was made up of fermented vegetables and stimulated intestinal flora. Too much salt might've been used making the kimchi, although that's hardly likely to reveal itself in gas – is it? You just cannot beat copious amounts of hydrogen, methane and carbon dioxide to clear sinuses, tear ducts as well as removing phlegm from the back of one's throat – is there? Of course – with large quantities of hydrogen and methane involved – it's only logical that the suspects aren't allowed to smoke while they're in police property or facilities. It's just as well when you think of a catastrophe that befell Gerry. She was at home in one of those house and *miniscule* blocks of land which are all the rage in Perth nowadays. You know – where houses are built so close together, your bedroom has become an auditorium for all the next door neighbours' bowel motions and accompanying sound effects. . . I hear there was a power blackout, a phenomenon that's an everyday feature of the Perth suburbs. Gerry had just partaken of a bowl of kimchi accompanied by a tin of kippered Icelandic clams. Having enjoyed such a meal, it's little wonder we come across a little leftover CWB or flatus in the air. Especially when you discover that Rosemary had visited earlier and they'd downed perhaps half a dozen large bottles of CUB Sheaf Stout. It's dark, so Gerry uses a lighter to try and locate a candle. There's a thunderous explosion, and – very similar to Fran Crapper..."

"You've got exploding farts on the brain!" Trev looked like a cat with a mouse.

"I'll ask you only one more time, Trev – it's CWB – Controlled – Wind – Breakage," Greg punched his left palm with his right fist as he pronounced the words. "As I was about to say – the only difference between Gerry and Fran is that CWB was being worked on by experts and physicists Australia-wide under a dark cloak of secrecy. Naturally the boffins took into account the possibility of an explosion. We're talking about vast quantities of hydrogen and other flammable materials here. That's why both Rosemary and Gerry were issued with several sets of undies fabricated out of fine threads of chyrsotile asbestos, so that. . ."

"Isn't that asbestos stuff dangerous?" Kev wanted Greg to know that he knew a thing or two.

"It sure is, Kev," Greg confirmed. "The outer layer of the undies is made out of airtight material that astronauts wear inside their space suits. You remember those US astronauts on the moon, Kev?"

"My word! Bloody brave blokes – if you ask me?"

"As brave as they come, Kev!" Greg further endorsed. "That's where the expression 'As unpopular as a fart in a spacesuit' comes from. Back in those days Neil Armstrong, Buzz Aldrin and so on wore rather old fashioned spacesuits. If any one of them emitted flatus in their suits, they were required to put up with it for days on end, and sometimes they fell victim to what they call 'space sickness'. In the case of our two constables and modern day astronauts, they have a special tube that lets the flatus escape. You can see the logic in all this, Kev, as how would Gerry and Rosemary carry out CWB if the gas has no chance of escaping? . . . Another large dissimilarity between Poo Zealand's Fran Crapper and Gerry is that there's a concrete wall running past the back of Gerry's house and those of her neighbours. That's another charming feature of modern Perth housing developments. All the houses are surrounded by concrete or limestone block walls, so the atmosphere is very similar to Alcatraz or other high security prisons around the world. Rather than having criminals in cells beside your own cell, you have the neighbours. Especially with the meth heads, home invaders and car thieves getting around plundering a person's house every second night! That's probably why the Perth suburban women let themselves grow so large – it's a handy and effective way of deterring the most brazen criminal. . . You' couldn't possibly believe this, but the explosion toppled almost four hundred metres of the back wall, which consequently blocked off a major highway for at least a couple of days. It also took a couple of weeks for some of the neighbourhood's dogs to be located by the RSPCA and returned. . . Why are you looking at me like that, Nev?"

"I know what you're talking about, Greg," I found some truth in what he was saying. "I've seen some of those walls they put around those new housing developments in Perth. Some of 'em are made out of Colorbond tin."

"How observant of you, Nev!" he must've been pleased with my collaboration. "What you'll find harder to believe is that this's where the boffins were *very nearly* given the chance to test CWB on a *massive* scale! With the wall encompassing Gerry's housing development, there were a large number of people who hadn't seen a sunset for quite a few years. Some had children who'd never seen a sunset in their lives! You have to consider the lifestyle in these modern developments. The block of land your house is on is the size of a postage stamp. Your house is barely a metre away from your neighbour's and a shorter colorbond fence cuts that metre in half. You have to walk through your house if you wish to go from your front yard to your back yard. The tiny little alcove at the front of your house is not the place to have a sundowner drink because you never know when some car thief – furiously being pursued by the police – doesn't drive the stolen vehicle over the top of you. Also, with all the Chinese crystal meth-induced violence in the streets, the safest place to relax is in your back yard. Still, you've got only two metres of space between your back door to the back wall I've just mentioned. So when you're enjoying a couple of drinks outside, the only vista you have is the back wall. . . Therefore, gentlemen, when the back wall was reduced to rubble by the explosion, what do you think nearly precipitated an almost out of control uprising?"

Even Trev was sucked back in. "Those walls are to keep the traffic noise out – aren't they?"

"Yes, I suppose that's one reason," Greg allowed. "I was going to mention that the state government, who'd come up with the notion of postage stamp-sized blocks of land, might've conjured up an idea of how to dissuade people from wanting more room for their tiny houses. If you can't see it – you don't know about it – you *don't have* to have it. Take for instance a worthwhile view or anything as simple as a sunset. Now that Perth can more or less be regarded as a desert, what with the drought its being experiencing for the last couple of decades, the smog and dust are lending themselves to some slightly reasonable sunsets. Not a patch on your Kalgoorlie or Pilbara sunsets, though better than anything you get in Poo Zealand. . . So that's why both the government and the housing developers – that were making *such a poultice* out of a mere few hectares of land – were desperate to get that wall put back up as soon as possible. Can you throw any light on as to why – Trev?"

"It's obvious – isn't it?" Trev's tone was condescending. "To keep out the traffic noise."

"Mm – yes, I can grant you that, Trev," Greg compromised. "But the horse had well and truly bolted – hadn't it? Despite the housing developers and the state government's best efforts, too many of the inmates of Gerry's housing development were given some sort of a view – weren't they? It may've only been a view of the highway and possibly the back wall of another housing development, nonetheless it was much better than the vista they had before. In order to preserve – what they perceived as a miracle similar to Moses parting the Red Sea – they quickly knelt down in prayer. Following that they started hurling bits of the collapsed wall at the workers who were feverishly trying everything to hastily reconstruct it in just one day. . . Naturally the riot police became involved, and it was touch and go whether Rosemary's or Gerry's CWB capabilities should be enlisted. It would've been the first time that CWB was used *so openly* against the public – not so, gents?"

"Why stop now?" Trev was truly aroused.

Having gone quiet, Greg then examined his thumb nail. "It's hard recounting incidents where you've got police, and possibly army reservists, lined up against fellow countrymen. Australia's totally dissimilar to those Middle Eastern countries we keep hearing about on the news almost every day. That might not be so apparent to some of the multitude of Afro Australians in Victoria who're terrorising Melbourne, whereas Western Australia is far more civilised and the state's police have access – or should I say *did have* access – to CWB? . . . Most fortuitously a truce was reluctantly arrived at. If the inmates of Gerry's housing development were prepared to put down their pieces of concrete wall, the state government would hire magnificently-talented artists from Curtin University to paint each individual house's boundary wall with any landscape an occupant chose. Naturally enough some wanted African wild life vistas with Mount Kilimanjaro in the background, or Ayers Rock with the sun behind it, but the best part of the inmates wanted Indian Ocean views similar to what the very expensive houses – that much wealthier people own – at Cottesloe, City Beach and Scarborough. Suburbs that're in great demand by Chinese crystal meth dealers, or the crystal meth smugglers themselves. . . Actually this'll knock you over, nevertheless the Indian Ocean scenes were that good that quite a few people living in Cottesloe and so on sold their houses at fire sale prices. Then we find a frenetic bidding war – mostly in Cantonese to cater for the Chinese crystal meth dealers and smugglers – for houses in Gerry's housing development. I bet you're guessing as to why, Trev?"

"How the bloody hell can I guess why, Greg?" My younger brother put up a hasty defence. "Why would anyone want to live in some overcrowded slum in the Perth suburbs?"

"It was to get away from the incessant and prevailing westerlies – wasn't it Trev? How can anyone take in the sea view on the front veranda in Cottesloe or City Beach without the wind blasting the hair of your head and sending your sundowners and hors d'oeuvres flying back into your upstairs lounge room? In Gerry's housing development you don't have this problem. Additionally, with a few plastic buckets of sand – of which Perth has far more than its fair share – you can sprinkle the sand over your tiny back patio. Having done that, you can then tackle the missus side on with the back of the house, as I can think of nothing more romantic than letting the ferret out for a run, and doing an oil change on your figs while at a beach on some deserted, tropical island... What are your thoughts on this, Nev?"

I thought any suggestion like that had merit. "It'd be the way to go, Greg!"

"That's my man – Nev! The traffic thundering past within a couple of metres of your perspiring, writhing bodies can be the waves. . . Hold on, we're discussing a tropical island with calm lagoons of turquoise water – not some north Atlantic hurricane – aren't we? None the matter – we can always employ industrial grade ear plugs as usual, which is quite common in these kinds of Perth housing developments. . . You can't do that sort of thing in City Beach or Scarborough because of the wind. You're unable to even play hide the ferret at the back of your City Beach or Cottesloe house, since your neighbours will no doubt be watching and urging you on to greater efforts like boozy footy fans from an upstairs balcony. They can sit quite comfortably where they are because your house is sheltering theirs from that perpetual gale. Besides, you'll miss out on the ocean view, and it'll be much harder pretending you're on some tropical island. . . Now, gents, before I wish a happy and rewarding life to Gerry and Rosemary in Argentina, I feel I'm duty bound to highlight some of the good things about them. Do you mind, Trev?"

"I don't give a stuff what you do, Greg," Trev didn't have to be that nasty. "I lost the plot way back."

"Then maybe if I give you some gentler memories to have of Rosemary and Gerry, it might cheer you up?" Greg soothed. "Although they were handicapped

181

by having been brought up in the suburbs of Joondalup and Balga which are situated on flat swampland, like so many other unfortunate women in those suburbs they were determined to bear their crosses with dignity and no small amount of pluck. That's why they and perhaps half a dozen neighbourhood fatties loved going to the Marion Bay Falls festival in Tasmania. Plus other Falls Festivals elsewhere in Australia. Can you try to determine why, Nev?"

I just couldn't think of anything. "What's this Falls Festival?"

Greg got out one of his own smokes for a change. "They have these Falls Festival music get-togethers throughout Aussie, and they go on for several days. Literally thousands of music lovers attend these concerts and it's the most lucrative time of the year for the local Ecstasy, crystal meth and date rape drug dealers. Right at the front of the stage, where the different bands are playing, happens to be what they call the 'Mosh Pit'. That's where the crowd really bunches together and the dancing can become quite physical. It's marvellous for blokes if they want to surreptitiously let their hands wander. Grab a boob here – snatch a handful of arse there – poke a finger up a bum here – tickle a fanny with an index finger afterwards. Rub your consequent erection on the glorious thigh of the woman next to you. . . It's all part of the Falls Festival fun – isn't it, Nev? Gerry and Rosemary, plus some Balga and Joondalup buddies just loved the Falls Festival that they hold in Tasmania's Marion Bay. This happens to be a favourite venue for them because the Tassie blokes are so kinky or weird. Especially the ones from Burnie, Tarraleah and Zeehan. Especially Zeehan where you get blokes leaving the forests only once a year, and have a language totally different to all others. Very similar to the West Coast of New Zealand, you have Tasmanians living in the forests that neither the Tasmanian nor Federal governments would have a clue exist. Truly, these creatures live deep within the Savage River and Southwest National Parks, and they're just as elusive as Tasmanian tigers. These guys represent some of the most imaginative molesters out of all of Tasmania's men folk, and they're much more forward on account that they're totally unaware that what they're doing's illegal. These are the kinds of Mosh Pit blokes that our constables and their friends were after. The fact that some of the molesters had congenital oddities was neither here nor there, as long as they owned a pair of figs and a donger, and were prepared to do the deed amongst a heaving pack of sweaty, body odour-rich, dancing bodies. That meant they didn't have to wake up in the morning lying next to some bloke with an eye in the middle of his forehead, or – and even more disturbing – several sets of ears under his chin or armpits. . . You look like you want to ask me something, Kev?"

"Nah – not me, mate."

"If you require anything explained, please don't hesitate to let me know, Kev," Greg was all heart. "In the fever and bedlam of the Mosh Pit what's the point in taking an interest in who's molesting you? Better than that, Tassie blokes are only on very rare occasions choosy as to whom they molest, so women from the northern suburbs of Perth – plus the odd fatty from Southland or the West Coast – were generally catered for at the Marion Bay Falls Festival by the forest dwellers. It was satisfaction all round – not so, gents? Although these wild mountain men and foresters don't consider it consciously, some primeval instinct tells them that they need to broaden the parameters of their gene pool. Even though none of the results or products of these feverish Marion Bay Moshe Pit get-togethers ever make their way back to their sires' leafy domain. . . Furthermore, the women folk of the foresters are also happy with these goings ons, despite the fact that their men are servicing what they refer to as freakish '*outside*' women. Unfortunate women who have only ten fingers and toes. . . Would you like to try and tell me why, Nev?"

I felt I come up with a worthwhile comment to offer him. "Maybe they also reckon that the gene pool should be expanded?"

"No – not quite – Nev. These forest people eke out an existence on snails, tree slugs, birds' eggs, mushrooms, plus various edible roots that they scratch out of the earth on the forest floor. Similar to the Maoris, these progeny of early Irish and Welsh immigrants haven't t had guns or bows and arrows available to them, although I've never heard a report of them killing one of their own for the tucker bag. If they're lucky they might come across the odd Tasmanian devil's turd that can be found in the forest clearings, and this does wonders for their protein intake, what with Tasmanian devils mostly being carnivores. What I find quite surprising is that the forest folk don't eat carrion or road kill, whereas Tasmanian devils do. Perhaps they prefer to have the devils' digestive system process them first? To all intents and purposes. . ."

"Why don't the women mind the blokes shagging other women?" Trev's squalid mind obviously needed catering for.

Greg was ready for him. "It was the catering at the Marion Bay Falls Festival – wasn't it, Trev? When you've got a crowd of people busy swallowing Ecstasy pills, and injecting or smoking crystal meth, they quite often lose any connection they have with their appetites. That's why you'll find alongside the hundreds of tons of litter, human excrement and vomit, half eaten sausage rolls, hamburgers, Chiko rolls and half tubs of cold chips. These the forest men collect up in the venue's garbage bags and they take them home for the women and kids. The Falls Festivals are held around Christmas and New Year, so our tree dwellers also find this a time for much celebration, and you certainly can't begrudge them that. . . We also have the Falls Festival in Victoria – don't we, guys? Take for instance the time when a huge stampede took place in Lorne. Dozens were hurt! Thank goodness Gerry and Rosemary missed this one. I can't guarantee it, although there's some evidence that our girls' cobbers from Ellenbrook, Joondalup and Balga came up against some other stout ladies from the northern Perth suburbs of Butler and Wangara. The people in the northern suburbs of Perth are quite proud of the large number of fatties they've got, so I wouldn't be surprised if you were to discover inter-suburban parochialism almost amounting to outright militancy. With the Lorne Falls Festival not being sufficiently equipped with Tasmanian weirdos – who only really leave Tasmania's forests to attend the Marion Bay festival – the slap and tickle in the Mosh Pit must've been in short supply, so the Joondalup et al gang started making derogatory remarks about the Butler/Wangara faction who retaliated by throwing punches and emitting as much flatus as possible. That seems to be the pro forma reaction you get when some of Perth's northern suburb women are aroused or feel threatened. It's mainly a defence against heterosexual males – not so, Nev?"

"What is?" I'd completely lost track.

"Discharging large quantities of flatus as a form of protecting themselves. Quite a few women who live in Perth's northern suburbs have developed a technique for defending themselves against males who might have unsolicited intentions. The trick is for her to immediately surround herself with flatus as a first line of defence. This can be backed up with a belch that originated in the upper bowel. While other northern Perth suburbanite women don't notice anything – as well as most gay men who have to put up with their own partners' body gas during intercourse – it can be very effective when it comes to repelling any unwanted attention from straight blokes. A bit like a battleship using a smoke screen during the First World War. I think you'll find it might be the same in some of Perth's southern suburbs such as Armadale and Bibra Lake, but I refuse to guarantee it. You annoy some females who comes from north of the Perth CBD – out come the fists and the flatus. If you were a heterosexual bloke – wouldn't you try and escape the Mosh Pit at all speed if you were confronted by such a scenario? No wonder they had that stampede of all the heterosexual males at Lorne."

"Righto now, Greg – so what happened to the West Coast bloke?" I gently tried to manoeuvre him back on track

"The possibility of a miscarriage of justice is being investigated in Dunedin right at this moment, Nev. I understand two committees are being assembled, and at least one sub-committee. I've been invited to chair one of the main committees. It appears that the poor bloke was handed the same copy of the photo depicting our French crapper by someone from the North Island, and he was dead keen to use a fortnight's invalid pension money to purchase it. Nonetheless, he was tricked into handling it, and then the person from the North Island grabbed it back and ran off. In other words, gentlemen, the poor bloke was actually framed, but the Dunedin police chose to sweep the whole matter under the carpet. They still have the Scottish sword dancer business to answer for, and they're almost certain that the thief's one of their own."

"So what happened with this Rainbow Warrior in Auckland?" I changed the subject.

Greg laughed. "That's why you can fully understand why the Frogs couldn't win without British help in both World Wars. . . As Trev correctly pointed out, in 1985 French government agents blew up this Greenpeace boat in the middle of the Auckland Harbour or thereabouts, and they managed to kill a Portuguese-Dutch photographer. France, which was supposedly an ally of the bongos at the time, denied all involvement and actually joined in the condemnation of what everyone saw as a 'terrorist act'. After blowing up the Rainbow Warrior most of the Frog agents managed to make a run for it, bar a couple of them – Commander Dominique Prieur and Commander Alain Marfart. To accentuate the farce, these two were actually caught due to a Neighbourhood Watch group, and they pleaded guilty to manslaughter. The David Lange Labour government was in power at the time, and the Frog agents were sentenced to ten years in jail, but the French government threatened to cut off all supplies of French champagne to various high ranking civil servants in Wellington. These civil servants stirred up that much bother, the Frogs were asked to pay thirteen million NZ, which was about six million US at the time, and Lange agreed to back down and look the other way as long as the supplies of Frog champagne kept coming. Also the money came in mighty handy since you had a Labour government in power and the country was on the bones of its backside."

CHAPTER 5

It was necessary for Greg to urgently travel to Wellington a further time. A couple of days later he revealed what all the rush was about: "We seem to have a contagion hitting the South island, and it's doing my Department of Inner Health *the world* of good," he announced happily. "Instead of finding 'Reds under the beds', they seem to be finding the faecal calling cards of Frog saboteurs all over the provinces of Otago and Southland! Here's what the newspapers are saying about it."

FRENCH CRAPPER STILL IN CITY AND STRIKES
A FURTHER TIME IN THE SAME PLACE

A well known and respected Dunedin business owner believes that the same woman, thought to be a French agent posing as a freedom camper – who defecated in the gutter outside his business premises – is still operating in the city.

The morning after the previous incident involving a mysterious French woman, he noticed a large amount of faeces in the gutter that surpassed in size those that officers from the SOS had removed the day before. He was absolutely certain that they hadn't been generated by a dog, and he filmed them just to make sure.

The police hadn't contacted him for the footage; however a member of the SOS said that the clandestine agency was eager to have a copy, he said.

Dunedin Police said they were aware of a rumour about the incident, and that there was possibly video footage having recorded it, so their inquiries were continuing elsewhere.

"I have more!" Greg was ecstatic. "It seems that swimming pools have been the targets for quite some time now. It looks like it all started in Invercargill."

INVERCARGILL'S POOL POOPER REMAINS AT LARGE

Invercargill's mystery pool pooper remains at large, and it is now believed that French saboteurs are involved. A series of investigations carried out under the auspices of operation "Code Brown" have discovered that the serial pooper or poopers prefer to strike on Wednesday mornings, because on eight consecutive Wednesday mornings there has been contamination during the beginning of this year.

Executives from the very successful Australian website TAG THE TURD have carried out their own forensic investigation; and now the incident – which Invercargill locals have labelled 'Poo-gate' – has become famous worldwide.

Invercargill's most popular mayor ever, Tim Shadbolt, said the publicity generated by the pooing was not particularly good publicity for the city, and he believed 'Code Browns" attracted global attention because no one knew who the culprit was.

A spokeswoman, who asked to remain anonymous – and who said she would challenge Mayor Shadbolt at the next mayoral elections – said she found the whole matter thrilling. She explained this by saying that nothing exciting ever happens in the Province of Southland, yet alone Invercargill. She suggested that the visit by representatives of the Australian website TAG THE TURD had brought the province forward 'light years' when it came to world recognition.

It was easy to see that Greg was over the moon, and he passed over another news article to me. "I'd watch your step if you're thinking of going for a swim at Aqualand. It looks like Queenstown's also on the shit list – if you'll excuse the pun."

SERIAL POOPERS – BELIEVED TO BE FRENCH
SABOTEURS – SHUT DOWN POOL FOR 16TH TIME

Queenstown's Aqualand is the latest swimming centre closed week after week by a serial pooper – or poopers.

Pools at the popular centre were closed eleven out of thirteen consecutive Tuesday afternoons earlier this year. The main pool at the centre had to be closed almost a dozen times this year alone because of faecal contamination, while the learners and lap pools were similarly affected. New Zealand's top spy agency (SOS) believes that French saboteurs are more than likely involved.

The lost revenue and clean up costs are having a huge impact, a spokesperson pointed out, and we believe the culprit or culprits are the same that sabotaged Invercargill's (Southland) Splash Palace.

There were mixed reactions amongst Queenstowners to the assault on the town's swimming centre, and Australia has come up in conversations more than once. Some blame Australian skiers and disappointed Wallaby fans; however those hypothesises need to be discounted because the acts of sabotage were conducted in the summer months.

Others locals and those living nearby have expressed their optimism regarding the matter. The pool pooper or poopers – whoever they were – had put Invercargill on the world map via the Australian website TAG THE TURD. It could be Queenstown's turn any day soon.

"And do you reckon the French are behind it," I quizzed him after reading the item. "Are you sure someone's not making all this up?"

"Check out the internet under serial pooper and Invercargill's Splash Palace," Greg rejected that immediately. "It's obviously some of the locals or tourist operators who're trying to put Invercargill and Queenstown on the map. You simply need to realise that Bongoland's in the shadow of Australia. The biggest farce is up in Wellington, not on the South Island."

"Why's that?"

"We've got a Labour government in power, not so?"

"Yeah?"

"This government's made such a hash of things in the public's eye, this *apparent* French sabotage is becoming a desperately needed diversion. The trouble is that they're starting to believe all this bullshit. All of a sudden we have *no less* than four committees and double the number of sub-committees that were put together just last week in Wellington. I'm chairing the principal committee, and the whole fiasco's going to cost a poultice because all the usual consultants and public servants are involved – all with noses in the trough. These committees are *classic* Labour and cost the taxpayer millions! Millions that they're raising by shaving the funding for protecting the environment and the welfare of disabled children. That's why I'm charging the government only ten grand a day, rather than my usual twenty."

"You charge the government twenty grand a day?" I was incredulous.

He grinned at that. "And that's not counting my travel, accommodation and other sundry expenses. Most of the money's borrowed and the incoming National Party will have to find a way of paying it back... But this's not the only farce. The committee I'm chairing is actually talking about taking the fight back to the French. Did you know that the bongos bought two Australian made ANZAC class frigates – the RNZN Te MANA and the Te KAKA?"

"Nope."

I didn't think you would. Anyway, these are Poo Zealand's main fighting ships and they've been of invaluable help carrying out patrol duties up in the Gulf of Arabia and so on... Now this happens to be where the farce really starts. This committee I'm overseeing is purported to be absolutely *top secret*. It's made up of a couple of cabinet ministers and very senior public servants sworn to secrecy under the Secrets Act. Normally this kind of thing would be headed by someone similar to that Pommy bloke Stephen Wilce who the SOS so readily gave the thumbs up to. . . Never mind that, but the committee's actually talking about blockading France's naval bases with the Te MANA and the Te HAKA! That the Te MANA should be sent to the English Channel to blockade the French naval ports of Cherbourg and Brest, while the Te KAKA should be parked out the front of the Toulon naval base where the Frogs keep the fleet aircraft carrier CHARLES DE GAULLE. Also a couple of helicopter carriers, three submarines, plus maybe half a dozen destroyers, and the same number of general-purpose frigates. There might be more subs, but...”

“You’re kidding, right?” I stopped him in mid sentence.

“Kidding about what?”

I couldn’t be sure if he was pulling my dick or not. “You’re talking about *one* Kiwi frigate being up against an aircraft carrier, submarines, and half a dozen frigates and destroyers?”

“Ah, I see what you mean.” He nodded in understanding. “You need to factor in the Nelson syndrome. After being hammered by the British Navy under Nelson at the battles of the Nile and Trafalgar, the French have been very nervous about sailing any ships out of port. I mentioned that the committee I’m chairing at the Beehive’s top secret – not so?”

“True.”

Greg wound down his window in order to eject a cigarette butt. “Well then, everything that was discussed was passed by the tea lady to the bloke who cleans the PM’s toilet. This bloke’s a journo of sorts, who’s actually bribed the caretaker of the Beehive in order to get the job. He’s a paid spy for the National Party – isn’t he, Nev?”

His story was becoming more and more bizarre! “If you say so, Greg?”

“Yes, Nev, I *do* say so. I can’t tell you the bloke’s name, as he’s passing on very valuable information to me. You could call him a kind of double agent really, however he’s chasing agendas of his own, and is completely betraying the PM’s trust. The Nats want something to undermine the Labour PM – don’t they?”

“You’re telling the story,” I reminded him. “Too right – I am, Nev. Let’s call our PM’s toilet cleaner ‘Bob’? Bob’s managed to fasten a recording device under the toilet seat – hasn’t he? So now he has various recordings of the PM releasing flatus, and the toilet bowl has acted as an acoustics chamber – hasn’t it? If the recordings I’ve heard are genuine, it appears she likes singing that American gospel song *‘WHEN THE SAINTS GO*

MARCHING IN' and at the end of each verse she breaks wind. 'Oh when the saints!' – brrrt! 'Oh when the saints!' – brrrt! 'Oh when the saints go marching in!" – brrrrrt! 'Oh when the..."

"You are – *totally* – *fucking* – *insane!*" Trev had had enough.

Greg took offence to that. "We'll see, Trev. You wait till you hear one of the recordings."

"So what gives with this bloke 'Bob'?" Kev leaned forward between the front seats of the car.

Greg lit another cigarette. "To get to the point, Bob got in touch with some bongo political activist – I don't think it was Johnny Minto – and the story about the New Zealand navy blockading the ports of Brest, Cherbourg and Toulon reached French ears within an hour of it being suggested in the first place! It just shows you *how slack* security is at the Beehive in spite of SOS efforts. Mind you – they did give the thumbs up to Stephen Wilce – didn't they? Anyway, the first thing the French Defence Minister did was send a pleading fax to his British counterpart for assistance. Next the French Consul in Wellington frantically denied that agents of the *Direction générale de la sécurité extérieure* had pooped in Otago and Southland swimming pools, and if a female French national *was responsible* for crapping on a street in Dunedin, it certainly wasn't carried out under French government auspices. . . Nevertheless, the French couldn't *really* be trusted – could they? After all they'd been amongst the first to condemn the attack on the Rainbow Warrior, yet they were the perpetrators in the first place."

"So what's gunna happen now?" Trev asked after Greg had parked the Mercedes out the front of the Cromwell Brew House Bar and Bistro.

"I'm glad you brought that up, Trev," Greg congratulated him. "The Labour government's broke and they remembered how David Lange managed to squeeze the Frogs for thirteen mil'. A bloke gets killed and thirteen mil' does the trick, and *no more* problems. So the overall plan's been to try and emulate the Lange Labour government, and attempt to cadge a million US dollars off the French government. But what the PM and her merry crew have failed to realise is that the committee

I'm chairing – *alone* – is costing several million – never mind the huge cost of the three other committees and various sub-committees. . . Notwithstanding that – every cloud has a silver lining."

"How come?" I was puzzled.

There was a smirk on Greg's face when he replied: "The PM's rendition of the 'The saints' is now the principal marching music of the male homosexuals who attend the Perth Gay Mardi Gras in Northbridge. It must be very poignant to the marchers, as I doubt if all of them can emit flatus loudly anymore."

Almost a fortnight went by before Greg gave us further news about the suspected acts of French sabotage. "This business about the Frogs and sabotage has seriously got its arse on fire! When it was suggested that the New Zealand navy should blockade France's naval ports, the PM instructed her Minister of Defence to contact Australia's Chief of the Military, to ask for assistance if it was decided that the blockade should go ahead. This's left the Aussie government in quite a quandary. Although the bongos only stay in the ANZUS treaty when it suits a particular political party, New Zealand's military couldn't really approach the Yanks, what with them not allowing American naval ships into any of her harbours – could they, Trev?"

"They'd be bloody hypocritical if they did," Trev was in agreement.

"Correct, Trev," Greg affirmed. "So it would have to be Australia abiding by the ANZUS Treaty or nothing. As you know, the Kiwis aren't too popular over in OZ because the All Blacks are thrashing the Wallabies time and time again at rugby. The French aren't that popular, either, since every time France's national rugby team go onto the field against the Wallabies and other international teams, you get French players starting to bite, pinch, and testicle squash, plus they're masters at head butting and eye gouging as soon as the referee's whistle's blown. Furthermore, the Aussie government don't trust New Zealand forensic technology. Okay snail and frog DNA *has been found* in human faecal matter, but how can the New Zealand Labour government prove for certain that it was definitely *French* snail and frog DNA? . . . It was actually a member of the Australian National Party in Queensland, possibly that popular bloke Barnaby Joyce, who came up with a solution. He wanted Australian scientists – possibly the CSIRO because that organisation's the best in the world – to analyse the stool that had been found at the foot of the Robbie Burns statue in Dunedin's Octagon Plaza. . . That soon brought the NZ government crashing back to earth – didn't it, Nev?"

As usual I was uncomfortable with being set aside. "If you reckon so, Greg?"

"I do, Nev – I do! I'm not sure if it was the CSIRO or not, but Australian scientists have determined that it was a Kiwi that was responsible for desecrating the reputation of Robbie Burns. How they arrived at that conclusion is really quite ingenious. Previous research has indicated that there are two major gene pools that can be attributed to the majority of New Zealanders – that's if you discount people on the West Coast. It's all calculated by the peoples' diet. In New Zealand you have Polynesians and Pakeha. The Polynesians are infamous because of their love of coconuts, pigs' heads and kumaras, whereas the average bongo Pakeha's notorious for his or her penchant for barbecue and cranberry sauce, plus scroggin in the case of the South Islanders. Remember the Great Competition, gents. Remember Rangi Hika and Fran Crapper. Naturally sometimes the parameters between the two gene pools can be smudged, although you'll find a clear distinction that differentiates West Coasters to all other bongos. It's the warped and fractured DNA and the twinned chromosomes that're peculiar to those born on the Coast. Thus the exaggeration of finger and toe endowment, while in a particularly extreme case I heard of a man that was found with three legs in the tiny West Coast hamlet of Moana on the shores of Lake Brunner. That's roughly thirty-five kilometres east-south-east of Greymouth. Possibly a less extreme case is a woman who's living in the tiny settlement of Taylorville which you'll find beside the Grey River nearly ten Ks out of Greymouth. She has two feet coming off each ankle – two facing forward – the others facing backwards. You won't believe it, but. . ."

"Fuckin' oath – we won't believe it!" Trev's eyes were wide with exasperation. "Do you really expect us. . ?"

"Just hold on a sec', Trev," Greg put his left hand up. "Her name's Dulcie Donnelly and she comes from a family of early Irish settlers. A family famous for producing a large number of Christian Brothers from the time that Edmund Rice started the Congregation of Christian Brothers roughly around 1802. . . And we all know what Christian Brothers are notorious for – don't we, gents? We know that far too many of them have been known to rape anything that moves. Particularly children – especially young boys in Catholic Christian Brother boarding schools – placed in their care. That's where Dulcie's rather complicated genome would've come from – multiple incidences of incest. Nevertheless, we have a rather charming aspect to Dulcie's unfortunate heredity circumstances. She's much in demand in the Marlborough wine country for treading grapes. You can see why – the crafty wine makers or vintners are getting two pairs of feet stomping away for the price of one! Also here you'll find another incongruity because New Zealanders from elsewhere in the country are very hesitant to employ people from the West Coast. Especially after twins were found at Kaikoura – that's on the east coast – with four extra toes on each foot. You can fully understand people from all over the country not wanting their precious genes contaminated by West Coaster genetic aberrations. . . I'll tell you something that you've every right to disbelieve, though. A year or so ago only two others and I were privy to a conversation with the PM in her office at the Beehive. She wanted to build a fence from one end of the South Island to the other in order to stop the West Coasters from crossing the Alps and infiltrating the East Coast. Similar to the rabbit-proof fence you've got in Western Australia, or the fence the Yanks have got between the States and Mexico to keep what the Texans call 'greasers' out. Fortunately I managed to talk some sense into her, and I reminded her of all the hard work she and the Labour Party had done to advertise New Zealand as being the most politically correct country in the world. Okay – agreed – Aussie's the most politically correct country in the world, yet Poo Zealand comes a very close second. You could call the latter an ideal haven created for people like Johnny Minto and his arse-haemorrhaging and BA-toting followers. . . Later on when I discussed the PM's bizarre plan with a colleague, who was also privy to the conversation, she in turn suggested that the PM was fearful of being compared to a former female prime minister who was known to have a weird tooth configuration, and that this may've been the result of one of her ancestor's dalliances with a West Coaster. I thought that was a rather a clever hypothesis coming from a bongo who comes from the Southland town of Mataura. . . No, I take that back. I've a habit of banding Southlanders together with West Coasters, and that's terribly unfair to Southlanders. Their gene pool might be tainted by Scottish chromosomes, still they can hardly be placed in the same league as those of the West Coasters. I suppose that's like banding Kiwis together with Australians"

"You said that the Kiwi government were brought crashing down to earth," I wanted further facts.

"You're quite right, Nev – I did. Not only did the Australian scientific agency establish that the perpetrator of the blasphemy against Robbie Burns was a native of the North Island, they also managed to determine that the snail or escargot DNA came from a very rare Kiwi snail. They might've become even rarer, now that some government conservation department has killed so many of them. . . Now, Trev, you'll never guess what our Aussie scientists *also* discovered?"

"Too bloody right – I won't!" My rather abrupt sibling cast aside all doubts about that.

Greg ignored the terseness of his reply. "We know about the frog DNA – don't we? No, these weren't the remains of normal *cuisses de grenouille* or frogs' legs that the Australian scientists found in the suspicious bowel movement that was discovered in Dunedin's Octagon Plaza. Or those which the celebrated French chef, Auguste Escoffier, served up as a dish he called '*Cuisses de Nymphe a l'Aurore*', or 'Thighs of the Dawn Nymphs'. These remains were the bones of not one, but at least two and a half dozen Hochstetter's frogs which have the scientific label '*leopelma Hochstetteri*'. . . Can you see the heartbreak in all this, Nev?"

"What heartbreak, Greg?"

Greg rolled his eyes in exaggerated exasperation. "We're discussing two New Zealand animal species which are almost extinct – the giant Powelliphanta snail and the tiny Hochstetter's frog! It just shows you how pitiful New Zealand's conservation record is, despite all the greenies, bird and amoeba lovers, plus tree huggers. Not only do we discover a government conservation department decimating the Powelliphanta snail population by freezing them to death in refrigerators – plus carting them around from pillar to post – the bongos are killing scores of the endangered Hochstetter's frogs in quarrying operations near Te Puke in the North Island! . . . This gave me the opportunity to hand out some further advice to the PM. The French can be vindictive on occasion – can't they? Not only does France's national rugby team bite, eye gouge and pinch the Wallabys, they also apply the same cowardly, reprehensible sportsmanship against other countries such as the Welsh and Italians. Mind you, they tend to abstain from biting when they come up against the All Blacks. Even the most retarded French rugby supporter in the stands knows for certain that if there's one thing you should *never – ever – do*, it's *bite a Maori rugby player, regardless of whether he plays league or union!* Who can guess what dark and midnight ancestral genes might be stirred awake from the not so distant – nightmarish past – all violently ejected from their fitful slumber, and potentially evoking the most horrific and macabre of temptations? . . . Sorry – I digress. Although the information about the North Islander having shat at the foot of the Robbie Burns statue had been passed to SOS and several other privileged ears in the NZ government, we still had the PM's toilet cleaner, Bob, who now has microphones in every toilet in the Beehive. Can you understand why he went to all that trouble, Kev?"

Kev's eyes gave him away. "How the bloody hell would I know – Greg?"

"It was for Poo Zealand prestige – wasn't it, Kev? The country needs a song that they can enter in the Eurovision Song Competition with. Naturally they can't very well ask the PM herself to actually perform, still you have the possibility that someone less talented could enter the contest and mime the PM's toilet song. . . There's another reason why Bob went to so much trouble. It was the Chinese – wasn't it? Not only are they paying him fifteen dollars a month to record every conversation that takes place in the Beehive, this business about endangered species in Poo Zealand's of great interest to certain members of the Chinese Central Politburo. They're making a fortune out of illegal animal smuggling for medicinal purposes – are they not? It's a well known fact that the more endangered an animal is, the greater is its attraction to Chinese medicine dispensers. This explains why we find so many endangered animals throughout the world that haven't only been listed as extinct in the last couple of decades – even their skeletal remains have disappeared! They've been captured, killed and smuggled to China. That's where Robert Mugabe and some chosen ministers in his ZANUPF Party are making a killing – if you'll pardon the pun. They're trying to kill off all of Zimbabwe's unique native wildlife in order to create near extinct species that they can flog off to Chinese medicine dispensers, along with tons of ivory and Rhino horn from South Africa, the Sudan and Kenya. You can see what the ultimate goal of the Chinese medicine dispensers is – same as with those who collect ivory and rhino horn. If they can arrange for the African poachers to kill off all of Africa's elephants and rhinos, the value of their stocks of rhino horn and ivory will go through the roof. How's that for farsighted Sino business acumen? If you want to make a decent omelette – you need to break a couple of eggs. . . Actually, gents, that reminds me of something!"

"Reminds you of what?" Trev was testy as usual.

Greg paused to remove the cellophane wrapping from a cigar. "The PM's been taking me into her confidence more and more lately. The country's in a shambles – isn't it? Not only is the government treasury broke, revenue seems to be drying up all over the place. Tourists are staying away because they might step on some New Zealand freedom camper's turd. If that's not appalling enough, the national dairy herd is making the country one of the highest polluters per capita in the world, plus there are the fat women in Southland and the West Coast emitting flatus as lustily as the cows! She's been assured by all and sundry that she's going to be trounced at the next elections, which by all appearances looks to be the case. . . Regardless of all that, her main obsession is to try and find a way of exacting her revenge on the people of the West Coast, for she believes that they're responsible for her downfall."

"Why?" Kev asked.

Greg checked that his cigar was burning evenly. "Malicious rumours travelling throughout the Beehive claim that because she seems to have too many front teeth, she may *actually be* related to various families on the West Coast, similar to a former female Labour PM! What we have are evil rumour mongers passing around word that you'll come across dozens of people in Greymouth, Westport and Hokitika that have features very similar to hers. While I rather fancy myself as being quick off the mark, I must say that even I was astounded by my own genius!"

"And so?" Kev nudged him when he seemed more interested in the tip of his cigar.

Greg just sighed and shook his head. He sounded rather vague: "Yes – it was sheer brilliance! I knew that the PM has an attention span similar to a gold fish. That's because she's surrounded by dickheads and sycophants within her own party. Men just looking for direction from a woman. I was aware that she normally rejects all new ideas out of hand, unless they've been investigated by an expensive committee and at least two just as costly sub-committees. She's dyed-in-the-wool Labour. I was also cognisant of the fact that I had to kill several birds with one stone. I needed to address Labour's pitiful ranking in the political polls. New Zealanders – her own people – were crapping on everything. Last and worst of all – there was also the probability that she's related to various families on the West Coast."

"Get on with it, then." It wasn't like Kev to be so pushy!

I'd never seen Greg look so melancholy before! "I suggested that she cut all funding to a multitude of government welfare organisations, and invest what she saved by spending it on a zoo."

"Zoo? What do you mean by a zoo? How could that've helped?" Trev was almost as impatient as Kev.

"No ordinary zoo, Trev!" Greg perked up quite considerably. "A very special zoo. I suggested that she should have a zoo built somewhere east of the coastal settlement of Punakaiki that would securely house West Coast individuals that displayed the most striking genetic abnormalities. Not just the run-of-the-mill multi-toed and finger examples, I recommended that she should cast her net far and wide and also introduce specimens from central Tasmania and the bogs of Southern Ireland where it's not uncommon to find people with multiple heads and several sets of eyes and ears. I was also aware that the idea wouldn't only be a money spinner, but it would engender a great deal of good will. I'm sure there are countless people on the West Coast, in Tasmania and Southern Ireland that would love to be put in cages where thousands of people can be enthralled and toss them peanuts as well as pieces of carrot and bananas. Not only that, they could introduce special zoo keepers recruited on the Coast to sweep up any droppings, give them slices of honeydew melon and replenish any empty water bowls. Just like zoo keepers do in everyday animal zoos. This's were several birds can be killed with a single stone. We'd have less genetic anomalies walking the streets in the towns of the West Coast, therefore slowing down any further – much more complicated – genetic abnormalities that might just be over the horizon. Locals could be employed to look after the zoo exhibits, thus bringing down the atrocious unemployment rate to be found in those towns."

"And is the zoo gunna go ahead?" Kev pushed him further.

Greg looked mournful once more. "The PM was enchanted with the idea, and was going to ring her finance minister to organise a World Bank loan, or possibly they could cut the subsidies to pensioners buying medicines. She didn't mention setting up a single committee! . . . Nonetheless, I suddenly realised that *I had to kill* the whole scheme."

"What for?" It was my turn to query him.

Greg blew a ring of cigar smoke. "I didn't want to jeopardise funding for my Department of Inner Health. In order to build a zoo, the PM and Treasury would have to beg, steal or borrow every last cent. It was very necessary to come up with something that would change the PM's mind as fast as possible, and that's where my genius came to the fore a further time. I managed to close everything down without a minute to spare!"

"How'd you do that?" Trev was as intrigued as Kev.

Greg's normal sunny disposition returned. "I reminded her – and she readily agreed – that there was a slight chance of Labour being kicked out and the National Party taking over government. Then I asked her what was the point of building a zoo on the West Coast that was bound to win worldwide acclaim, if there was no chance of it being completed before the next elections? No matter how many workers were employed, it would take years to build. Therefore, once it *was eventually built*, there was the possibility that a National Party PM would be cutting the ribbon and either his or her name would be on the dedication stone or brass plaque. . . Naturally she canned the whole proposition in a flash!"

"Yeah, but what were you saying about so much unemployment on the West Coast?" Kev pointed out quite correctly. "They could get heaps of workers over there, and they can start off small and expand once the money starts coming in?"

"Impossible!" Greg was adamant. "Look, I may have to wander off the beaten track in order to give you an adequate explanation. First of all we have the obvious restraints that're bound to arise. First, opinion surveys will need to be carried out as to where the zoo should be erected. If that doesn't delay things for a couple of years, the greenies and conservationist groups – that'll pour out of the ground like a blocked drain – will need to be appeased. Then the results of the surveys and the promises which are made to the greenie groups will need to be investigated by several committees and sub-committees. Resource consents from the two West Coast regional councils and two district councils could possibly be sped up considerably if the PM reminds the council CEO's of how such an innovative project could earn them additional future tax and rates revenue. Though, and regardless, I'd be hesitant to bank on that. . . Now this's where I'm going to have to leave the beaten path. I can't be absolutely certain that any councils in Poo Zealand – whether regional or district – give a rat's ankle about any new development raising further revenue.

Why should they bother about bongos squabbling and objecting to the possibility of other bongos doing well out of something? Why would you trouble yourself having anything to do with an issue that could actually mean having to take risks when it comes to granting resource consent applications? Why bother complicating matters when you can just raise the rates on existing private infrastructure, plus increase the fines or penalties on infringements of the multitudinous lists of council by-laws? It's much easier to hike rates and fines than it is to *even bother* about stepping out on limb and thence having to consider a resource application's approval. . . Do you see what I'm getting at, Kev?"

It was impossible to interpret Kev's true feelings. "So far I reckon I do, Greg."

Greg sucked on his cigar, but it had gone out. After relighting it, he examined the faces of both my brothers and I. "I believe a brief history lesson could be in order. It's a commonly held belief that the New Zealand Labour Party was born in the West Coast mining town of Blackball during the miners' strike of February-June 1908. That's a load of crap! The NZ Labour Party was actually formed during the First World War. Notwithstanding that, you've got present day Labour politicians that like going on pilgrimages to Blackball, and they beat themselves on the chest and claim that it was bongo union militancy that started everything, and how it won the day for all Kiwi workers. Even more bullshit, since the whole business at Blackball was started by three Australian agitators – Pat Hickey, Paddy Webb and George Hunter. The Blackball branch of the Socialist Party, which Hickey and his mates set up, predates the famous strike by several weeks. It was *Aussies – not the Kiwis* that started everything! . . . Let's not dwell on that, and let sleeping dogs lie? All the same, the great Blackball strike was called in order that the coal miners would be given the same meal break time as other workers elsewhere in the country. That's probably where the Scots come into the picture. The Blackball miners were only allowed one fifteen-minute meal break while working their shift. What you most likely had was managers and shift bosses who were Scottish – or of Scottish descent – trying to suck up to the British mine owners and shareholders in London, by ensuring that the miners didn't waste any valuable company time underground. You'll find that a typically Scottish trait. . . However, the Blackball miners *did win,* and that's had a profound effect on New Zealand industrial relations and output today. It might be the excellent work of modern day NZ unions that have won their members two-hour lunch breaks, plus one hour each for morning and afternoon tea. That's not bad when you consider that the average bongo worker only works an eight-hour shift and too many refuse to do any overtime."

"That can't be right," Kev was obdurate about that. "That means they're working only half the time."

"I can see where you're coming from, Kev," Greg was kind enough to offer. "I'm not saying the lengths of the tea and lunch breaks are carved in stone. They vary somewhat. Let me put an equation to you. We have a factory with two assembly lines, each filling and putting plastic tops on glass jars of haemorrhoid cream. The eight-hour working day commences and the workers pitch up. First there's the cup of tea on arrival, and an in depth discussion about what happened in *COCKROACH STREET* on the telly the night before. All this has to be. . ."

"What's this Cockroach Street?" Trev just had to know.

"It's what I call that British TV programme *CORONATION STREET,*" Greg didn't bat an eyelid. "Apparently it's one of Britain's most watched television programmes and gives you a cameo of British suburban culture. If the material's accurate, it highlights in no uncertain terms that British suburbanites in the main *are indeed* cockroaches. It paints a picture whereby lower class British women will mate with a whole array of different partners, regardless of colour, gender, creed and number. And you have male stars that're convicted of multiple sexual assaults committed whilst off-camera in night clubs. The bongos just love the programme! . . . I suppose that's only reasonable if one of the main families in the show have Windass as a surname."

"Ah – bullshit!" Trev exclaimed.

"What's bullshit, Trev?" Greg went straight back at him.

"What do you mean by Windarse?"

Greg nodded in understanding. "I might've pronounced it wrong? I meant Windass – Wind-a-s-s. Perhaps if it had been an American family, you would've been justified in coming up with 'Windarse'."

"I've seen that Coronation Street," Kev admitted. "The people in it are as fucked up as some of 'em in *SHORTLAND STREET, HOME AND AWAY* and *NEIGHBOURS*. . . Still, that doesn't explain why the Kiwis are only working half a shift?"

"Yes, as I was about to explain, Kev," Greg agreed. "Like I said – first we have a discussion of the cockroaches' putrid antics on Cockroach Street, and then we take a leisurely morning crap because the employer provides free toilet paper. While doing this the daily newspaper Sudoku puzzles and crosswords need to be filled in, and that takes our worker through to morning tea time. After half an hour discussing the new All Black rugby team selection, while drinking tea and munching on banana muffins, the 'team leader' addresses her 'team members' and calls a 'team morale' or 'team bonding' meeting. Has it taken your notice how in Aussie and over here the way workers are now working in 'teams' and they refer to themselves as being 'team members'?"

"It's fuckin' pathetic bullshit, if you ask me," Kev wasn't impressed.

"What makes you say that, Kev?" Greg seemed taken aback by that; particularly with the comment having come from my usually sanguine elder brother! "You go back to when you were drilling in West Aussie. Being the driller – you would've been the 'team leader', Kev – and Trev and Nev would've been members of your 'team'. With regard to your employer, he'd be your overall team leader. It would be up to him to ensure that the other team members have the highest possible morale and can bond with him. It would be his job to give you assurance, and take every step in order to safeguard your peace of mind. It would be his task to comfort you in times of difficulty."

I had to horse laugh at that! Dave Wheeler told me that my boss was one of the Riders of the Apocalypse. The very worst bastard amongst the four of them! Also that he could be working for the antichrist! If there was any assurance to be obtained from Wal Growford, it was knowing that he was a *genuine arsehole* and *bastard* through and through, and he's never attempted to alter that in any way – *ever*! In fact he's spent years perfecting his role as an arsehole; plus he's been given only the best coaching by my younger brother and Jeff Panizza!

Though very rare, it was evident that Trev was harbouring similar thoughts to mine! "That would be the fuckin' day! The only morale boost he'd give any one of his employees, is a kick in the balls. I agree with Kev – this *'team'* bullshit is for queers!"

"It's all the rage in both Aussie and here," Greg persisted. "You look what happens when it's necessary to consult with any government department here and in Oz. They tell you that a 'team' member will attend to you or return your call. It's this new politically correct, fuzzy-glow vomit thought up by the simpering, modern day do-gooders. . . Let's put all that aside for now – shall we? The team morale therapy session lasts until lunch. After an hour of eating Marmite and boiled egg sandwiches and drinking multiple cups of coffee or tea, plus discussing how wages are much higher in Australia, the team members are about to start work when along comes the government health and safety inspector. What you must realise is that there are *thousands* of men and women who've grabbed hold of this health and safety caper with both hands – in Oz and Poo Zealand. In the government and private sectors. It's one of the biggest rackets ever dreamed up in the twenty-first century! This particular health and safety inspector has visited this same workplace plenty of times before, and has handed out countless safety pamphlets along with health and safety lectures throughout the year. Quite innocently he fronts one of the team members – a young lady from the Coromandel Peninsular town of Waihi – and he asks her where the front door to the actual workplace is? A crucial issue in the event of a fire! Okay, so the young team member takes it into her head that she's been asked a trick question and has been maliciously singled out to be laughed at by other team members, so she consequently bursts into tears. Following that, she sprints in the direction of the Ladies toilets, her female team leader barely one step behind her. Naturally this brings about a whole series of negative outcomes!

First – the distraught team member is taken aside by the team leader, while the remainder of the team fill out harassment claim forms which can only land the health and safety inspector in uncomfortably hot water. Especially since he's a heterosexual male and a Pakeha. Most fortuitously there's another government department that oversees the behaviour of public servants that go amongst the public, and that department provides highly trained councillors – who've done the two-week course at the Auckland Polytechnic – and they do their best to try and remedy the obviously warped ideology of an errant government inspector who asks workplace team members difficult questions about safety. Especially if he's heterosexual and white. While that's..."

"I don't believe I'm fuckin' hearing this!" Trev glanced over at me with hollow eyes.

"Bide with me a while longer," Greg urged him, "and you'll see this equation's actually *based on fact*. You must take the time to realise that our health and safety expert wasn't the sharpest knife in the drawer, otherwise he'd be over in Aussie earning much better money. I think it would be fair to say the same about all bongos that've stayed at home. . . Immediately the young lady from Waihi is given a six-month, fully-paid leave of absence to recover from her ordeal. Three months leave of absence is granted to two other male team members because they were traumatised by the hideous ordeal that a fellow team mate had been confronted with. It was thought that maybe an invalid pension should be given to these men, for it was widely believed that they might never fully recover. Thus much more complex morale boosting and bonding sessions in the same workplace were vital to the remaining team members, so that they can regain their nerve, and valuable discussions were held about how to recover from trick questions being raised in a working environment. Naturally all this takes place during working hours. In addition to this, it was recommended by one of the team members that the union should be asked to campaign for a shorter working week. This meant that the owner of the business needed to urgently email his customers and regretfully inform them that his firm would be late with their haemorrhoid cream orders. With the high prevalence of haemorrhoid sufferers in Poo Zealand – especially farmers riding four wheeled motorbikes with rain soaked saddles – we have a rather unnerving and dire emergency on our hands! . . . Therefore – Kev and Trev – the bongo workers don't require one-hour tea breaks and two-hour lunches – the system's giving them the time off, anyway!"

"What about the factory owner?" Kev wasn't happy to let the topic end. "Surely he'd go broke?"

"How astute of you to arrive at that, Kev!" Greg was deeply touched. "The actual truth is that I've been talking about a real haemorrhoid cream factory that was once based in Nelson. The factory's owner was a Serb, Dragan Milošević. And – before you ask me, Kev – yes, he's related to the late Slobodan Milošević. Old Slobo was his uncle via an illegitimate son of a bastard brother. He's actually a fugitive from international law agencies for crimes against humanity because he was the most junior member of Uncle Slobo's fix it team. The reason why he's walking around free as a bird is because the bongo immigration people think he's a refugee from South Sudan. How they've come to that conclusion is anyone's guess. . . Dragan managed to pay for the factory building and all the machinery with gold that he collected from his victims back in Bosnia. Like the Krauts, he collected the gold via the agency of their teeth. He managed to launder the gold – all one hundred and fifty kilos of it – with the help of a dodgy alluvial gold miner based near the West Coast town of Greenstone. When I mention one-fifty kilos of gold, it indicates that his victims were hundreds if not thousands in number. He actually bought the factory as a going concern, but almost immediately started losing money because the previous owner ran it as family business, and most of his workers were distant rellies from Greymouth and Westport. He was paying them a fraction of the award rates, and they might've been getting by with the dole and Department of Welfare rent subsidies paid into bank accounts in Greymouth, Westport and Hokitika. At least I hope that was happening. When I say..."

"Surely that's where the union *would've* stepped in?" I suggested.

"Fair point – Nev – fair point! Nonetheless, we're talking about the Nelson Region, and I'm not sure if West Coasters are allowed to live and work there.

I'm fairly certain they're banned in the Tasman and Marlborough Regions, plus there are roadblocks at all entry points stopping them from coming in. I can understand why. To put it in another perspective, look what's eventuated after dickheads introduced Australian Possums, plus Welsh stoats and Scottish weasels into Poo Zealand. A couple were introduced here and a couple there, and now we have millions decimating the local fauna and causing untold amounts of heartbreak. If West Coasters *are* also banned in the Nelson Region, one can only presume that at night the previous owner of the factory hid his West Coast rellies in garden sheds and the attics of buildings scattered all over Nelson. Nelson the town – that is. Nonetheless, I wouldn't be surprised if they were forced to live out in the open in the exotic forests which are ubiquitous in the north of the South Island. Under the stars – in winter's snow and sleet."

That must've touched a sensitive nerve with Kev. "How can a person have his rellies camping out in the open in the snow and stuff?"

"I know what you mean, Kev," Greg was sympathetic to Kev's feelings. "But, if you can live in West Coast towns like Greymouth, Westport and Hokitika, camping in the nude under the stars in a blizzard's like sleeping in a feather bed with an electric blanket. Even the Atacama Desert can be described as a much more desirable place to live in than any of those towns. . . Either way, I'm still rather puzzled."

"Puzzled about what?" Trev egged him on.

Greg fingered his gold watch band and gently shook his head. "The Nelson Region's surrounded on all sides by the Tasman and Marlborough Regions, so how were the West Coasters smuggled in, what with armed vigilantes manning roadblocks on all the access ways? They must've been smuggled in by sea on the green-lipped mussel boats, as I doubt if even the boldest and most fool hardy smuggler would dare to try and bring them in by road. It would be far too dangerous!"

"Why?" I kept my query as short as possible.

"I'll really need to take you *way off* the beaten track this time, Nev," Greg frowned as he stared into the distance. "All the way to the sovereign – or perhaps not so sovereign – Pacific Island state of Fiji. It's alleged that it was Governor Sir Arthur Hamilton-Gordon who kicked things off in 1879 when he implemented an indentured labour scheme. He wanted to help the British colonists grow sugar – didn't he? Without having to pay too much for labour? They had to look for outside workers and couldn't be bothered asking native Fijians to toil for almost nothing, since the Fijians were too busy taking it easy on the beach playing volley ball and drinking gallons of Kava or Yaqona, then snoozing-off its affects. Sure they'd catch and eat the odd wild pig or fish, and munch on a banana and coconut or two, but volunteering to plant and cut down sugar cane in the hot, tropical sun for a few pennies a day certainly didn't attract many takers. The British planters much preferred the Indian coolies – didn't they? Let me see now. . ."

"Greg, what the fuckin' hell *are* you talking about?" Trev was totally bamboozled. "What has this got to do with the factory you just mentioned, and smuggling West Coasters?"

"Okay, Trev," Greg conceded. "It's imperative that I take you to Fiji to drive home why it's so dangerous smuggling West Coasters throughout Poo Zealand. . . Tell me, Trev, have you heard the playwright Edward Bulwer-Lytton's expression 'A pen is mightier than the sword'? He came up with it in 1839?"

"Bloody oath – I've heard that before!" Kev announced proudly.

"Good on you, Kev – good on you!" Greg commended him. "Old Edward has been proved correct on the odd occasion. It was actually my Uncle Enoch – named after the famous Enoch Powell himself – who came up with the expression 'The penis is mightier than both the pen and the sword put together', and he's been proved correct on *every* occasion... Now before you come barging in, Trev, please allow me to come up with a fascinating piece of Fijian demographic history here. While Bulwer-Lytton came up with his famous expression in 1839, it wasn't that long after in January 1879 when the first thirty-one indentured Indian labourers pitched up in Fiji from New Caledonia, nevertheless they refused point blank to do any hard yakka, so the indenture contract was cancelled. Most of these Indians left while *a couple remained behind and set up house with local women!* Now do you see a nexus between those of Irish descent on the West Coast of Poo Zealand and Indian indentured workers in Fiji, Trev?"

"Greg, I haven't a clue what you're talking about!" Trev was almost pleading with him.

"All will be revealed, Trev," Greg tried to calm him. "I can't be certain if it was the labour transport ship *LEONIDAS* – named after the king of Sparta Leonidas the First – that brought in the first large batch of indentured Indian coolies. I read somewhere that she dropped off 463 Indian labourers, and within a short time a further 61,000 followed after. Most of these also went home, but *a few stayed behind!* Now do you see what I'm talking about, Nev?" Greg turned his attention to me.

"I'm like Trev," I informed him. "I can't see what this's got to do with West Coasters and a factory in Nelson."

Greg was magnanimous: "Like I told Trev – all will be revealed. I can see by the look on yours, Trev's and Kev's faces you must think I've totally lost the plot. To cut to the quick, gentlemen, that handful of indentured Indian labourers have out-bred the native Fijians by fifty-to-one, so that's why they've had an Indian prime minister and so many coups now that the Indians have taken over everything worthwhile in Fiji. I suppose one could blame it on the Kava or Yaqona. You can't really expect a man to throw his leg over his missus if he's been lying in the sun on the beach all day sipping on half coconut shells full of Kava. He'd be looking forward to having a decent kip when he goes inside – wouldn't he. The Indians aren't like that – they're into breeding huge families as soon as possible, so they can send the kids to work and earn money and breed even further. *Thus the penis is most definitely mightier than both the pen and the sword!* . . . Just take a look at India itself. They say that India has the highest incidence of lightning strikes that've hit humans. That's certainly *not difficult* to believe when you consider how many Indians can actually be found on the subcontinent. They're so numerous that I doubt that lightning can strike anywhere in India without hitting one of them. There's simply not enough room for it to miss. I'm fairly certain the same will happen in Poo Zealand and Oz when you consider how many Indians they've let in. It's the Aboriginals in Aussie and the Maoris over here that'll be disadvantaged first. Though, and notwithstanding that, we have to think of the Chinese. With all the extinct and endangered animal species they're using to keep their willies up, they might also need to be kept in perspective because they know how to breed faster than an ICBM missile can fly."

"Why's that?" Trev's interest was given a further tickle. "Why will the Maoris and Abos be disadvantaged first?"

"History explains everything in great detail," Greg latched on to my younger brother's attentiveness. "When the Dutch explorer Abel Tasman sent a party of men in a boat to meet up with some Maoris in Golden Bay – Dutch men with rotten teeth from bad gin, gonorrea and a host of other sexually transmitted diseases we find so common in the Netherlands – history records that there was an unavoidable misunderstanding because the Maoris rammed the boat with a waka and several of Tasman's men were killed. I can bet you anything you like that the Maoris wish that they'd dealt with Tasman and *all his crew*, when you consider what's happened afterwards."

"What's happened?" Kev was as attentive as Trev.

"Look into Poo Zealand's past before the Europeans arrived with copious amounts of navy rum, gonorrea, small pox and greed. The Maoris were living in Nirvana – weren't they? Perhaps not on the West Coast and Southland, but everywhere else they were. They were very environmentally conscious – weren't they? If they had too many people living off the limited resources of a particular area, they'd knock maybe a dozen or so of their number on the head and put them on the menu. This was very beneficial when it came to maintaining the protein levels in the children's diet, if fishing was not possible due to the winter cold or inclement weather, or if they couldn't catch any moas. Also you can see the simple logic of it. If they discovered that there were too many mouths to be filled, just kill a couple of people and the extra food might tide the remainder over until circumstances improved. That way they could keep the population numbers at sustainable levels, and thus their environment wasn't overtaxed. It was even much handier if you could get someone from a neighbouring tribe to eat. . . So now you can see why the Maoris survived for so long without guns, the use of metals, plus bows and arrows. All you needed was a piece of rock –preferably green stone or *pounamu* – and you can kill two birds with one stone by bumping off a nagging mother-in-law, wife or aunt, plus maybe any bloke who's not pulling his weight in the waka rowing team, or deliberately being out of step in a Kapa Haka competition. Someone who might've been in league with and Indian or Paki. Unlike on the West Coast today where they eat a lot of white bread and Macdonalds, the Iwis back in those days were very careful about the children's diet, but that seems to have been changed by the civilising influence of Europeans with their cream biscuits and buns, chocolate éclairs, mud cake and mutton pies that bongo women love to consume in such vast quantities. . . Regardless, it's not a modern diet that the Maoris need to fear most. With the current fuzzy-glow, politically correct, do-gooder government immigration policies the people here and across the Tasman have got, I doubt if too much time will pass when the whites in New Zealand and Australia – plus the Aboriginals and Maoris – find themselves in the exact same position that the native Fijians now find they're in. And they, too, will find themselves serving much harsher masters. I'll let you blokes figure out the logic of that issue yourselves."

"What's that got to do with the factory in Nelson and smuggling West Coasters?" It was a question that was still vexing me and obviously Trev.

"Why – everything, Nev!" Greg became quite animated. "Like with the Indian indentured labourers, Australian possums, Welsh stoats and Scottish weasels – the Maori rats even – what do you think might happen if a couple of West Coast breeding pairs manage to escape into the mountains or forests in other parts of Poo Zealand during a smuggling operation? The Indians were brought into hot and humid places such as Fiji, New Caledonia and Natal in South Africa because they could work in tropical conditions. But they could also breed in hot, humid tropical conditions – couldn't they? That's why the British landholders and overlords introduced Irish peasants to the West Coast of New Zealand. They couldn't get their own people to put up with the damp, boring and mouldy conditions on the Coast, whereas the Irish have thrived and bred accordingly because it's identical to the bogs and swamps they've grown so fond of in Southern Ireland, and have written so many wonderful songs about. And the Southern Irish are mostly Catholic and possibly as randy as any indentured Indian labourer – aren't they? Otherwise why do you think so many sex-crazed priests and Christian Brothers have been generated from such supercharged loins? The last thing the Labour PM wants is possible future Catholic Priests and Christian Brothers let loose in other more hospitable regions of Poo Zealand."

I didn't have a clue whether Greg was talking crap or not, so I decided to humour him before Trev went troppo. "Righto, Greg, so you've explained why the government doesn't want West Coasters moving into other parts of New Zealand, but now can you tell us. . ."

"And it sounds like it could be too late for you Aussies in some places in Australia," he pulled me up sharply. "The behaviour of the priests and other members of the clergy. According to that commission which only Julia Gillard had the gumption to set up, it looks like you've been overrun with sex-crazed clergy in all your religious denominations. I'm not sure if you've got problems with West Coasters in West Aussie, what with it being so dry, but I wouldn't be surprised if we've had mating going on with Tasmanians in the forest and mountains in central Tasmania. I'm sure you've heard the expression 'Birds of a feather flock together'?"

"Yes, I have – Greg," I admitted, "but what about that factory in Nelson? Or – even more to the point – what about that zoo you were talking about building on the West Coast?"

Greg covered his eyes with his left hand. "Fair enough, Nev, I've got some explaining to do. Where did I leave off on the Nelson factory?"

"You said that the new owner started losing money when he took over the factory," Kev was determined that Greg wouldn't stray a further time.

There was a fat chance of that! "According to the Federal Republic of Germany embassy in Wellington, Nelson has more German speaking people than anywhere else in Poo Zealand," Greg started out with. "So I wouldn't be surprised if there are more than a handful of Nazi fugitives amongst them. That could be why Dragan picked out Nelson in the first place? I doubt if your average bongo would be able to tell the difference between a Serbian war criminal and a Nazi war criminal. Especially if the Immigration Department believes Dragan's South Sudanese. . . Still, he hadn't yet taken into consideration the might of NZ unions, or the country's 'team' working practice and ethics. Back in Serbia, Bosnia and Croatia if a Muslim worker or group of workers weren't pulling their weight, Dragan would phone up various Serbian police and army mates of his, and they'd break a couple of the workers' legs, plus burn their houses down if it also took someone's fancy. Unlike in the Balkans where that sort of thing's still quite fashionable in places, the cops in New Zealand are starting to frown at that sort of behaviour, especially after all the house burning and strife in Kaitaia that we saw just before the Great Competition. . . Okay, so he couldn't arrange for chosen employees – especially the 'team leaders' of the production lines – to have their legs broken or their houses burned to the ground. Although it was possible in the harbour town of Bluff at the very bottom of the South Island – or at the very northern tip of the North Island in the Te Kao district or *just outside of* Kaitaia – it wasn't that easy finding someone to break legs or burn houses down in Nelson. Then again, if he was Croat, he might've got one of Nelson's Germans to lend a hand. The Croats and the Krauts were big buddies during the Second World War, so the Croats welcomed a bit of Nazi help to get stuck into any Serbian neighbours. Therefore, if Dragan pretended to be a Croat, and lived in Argentina, he'd have no trouble finding an ex-Nazi to do the job for him. Thanks to Eva Perón and her hubby Juan, who, with the inducement of stacks of gold stolen from Jewish teeth, welcomed with open arms whole battalions of Nazis at the end of World War Two. It sort of reminds you of old Dragan himself – doesn't it? The gold teeth – I mean? Oh yes, and don't let me forget to mention Hitler's pal in the Vatican, Bishop Alois Hudal. He supplied Vatican passports to countless Nazi war criminals and murderers! I'm not sure if Pope Pius XII had a hand it – mind you he didn't mutter a word of protest when Hitler and his murderous thugs were trying to exterminate Europe's Jews. With what they get up to in the Vatican these days, I wouldn't be surprised if nothing's changed. Especially if they currently have a Pope that was in the Hitler Youth. I presume that's why Buenos Aires most likely has droves of ex-Nazis who probably still haven't lost any talent when it comes to a bit of arson and leg breaking, even if they do find it necessary to make a getaway with wheelchairs and walkers. . . Didn't I mention, Nev, that the factory had two production lines?"

"You sure did," I was eager to keep him focused.

"Thanks for that, Nev. I wasn't sure if I had or not. In desperation Dragan harked back to the competitions he and his comrades enjoyed back in the Balkans. Who could beat up the most innocent civilians – who could rob and burn down the most civilian houses – who could stampede the largest amount of refugees into neighbouring countries, and so on and so forth. Especially in Bosnia where the UN and NATO didn't allow the Muslims to have weapons to defend themselves with. What's better than attacking and terrorising unarmed civilians who can't fight back? Especially when NATO and the UN are *making sure* they're truly unarmed? Our Dragan was also aware of the magnificent competitive spirit amongst *some of* the Kiwis. Possibly the foundation of the mighty, all-conquering All Blacks and female Polynesian shot putt throwers. What he didn't realise was that there were two different kinds of bongo that were poles apart. Similar to what you see in Australia. That's why I say *some of* the Kiwis have this fierce competitive spirit."

"Okay – carry on," Trev challenged.

Greg was unruffled by that. "I said you'll need to be patient, Trev, if you want to fully understand what I'm going to tell you next, but rest assured that it's all relevant. I think you can start off by blaming the Canadians. . . I'm sure I've got an example in one of my pockets."

Greg searched his trouser and jacket pockets, then finally found a wad of newspapers cuttings in a back trouser pocket. He sorted through them and handed one to Trev. Once opened, it was almost half a page.

I was the next to read it.

TO ENSURE EVERY CHILD 'WINS', ONTARIO ATHLETIC
ASSOCIATION REMOVES BALL FROM SOCCER

With the growing concern over the effects of competition in youth sports programs this summer, many Canadian soccer associations eliminated the concept of keeping score. The Soccer Association of Midlake, Ontario, however, has taken this idea one step further, and have completely removed the ball from all youth soccer games and practices.According to Association spokesperson, Helen Dabney-Coyle, "By removing the ball, it's absolutely impossible to say 'this team won' and 'this team lost' or 'this child is better at soccer than that child.'

We want our children to grow up learning that sport is not about competition, rather it's about using your imagination. If you imagine you're good at soccer, then you are."

A mother of one the players commented: "What a wonderful idea our children being required to use their imaginations. On the weekend we had a soccer carnival where several teams of both boys and girls attended. My daughter was in a team that was imagining they were playing for France, and the opposing team pretended that they were representing Italy. Although the Italian side held up the game quite often pretending to be injured by a foul play, which is so common with Italian teams – pretending to be hurt – the right wing on my daughter's team was magnificent when she ran off the pitch and kicked a spectator in the face. The spectator took it all in good spirit once the ambulance officers attended to him. And then, of course, there were members of the Italian team throwing themselves on the ground after they had been bitten or pinched by members of the French team. It was fortunate that it wasn't boys' teams that were playing, otherwise there could have been testicle squeezing that might not have been so much fun."

"It was the parents and spectators that made my son's game almost real," a father of one of the boys playing added. "The parents of both teams pretended that they were British and Russian soccer hooligans. I was with the Brits and managed to give one of the fathers of the opposing team a Liverpool Kiss, and I'm not sure whether it was the man's wife or the chairwoman of the carnival

who kneed me in the groin. Notwithstanding that, I recovered sufficiently to go with the mob that went into town. We smashed all the shop windows in the main street, set fire to maybe a dozen cars, and then we looted the electrical store and the supermarket. A couple of parents were injured when the Royal Canadian Mounted Police charged us on their horses, however we managed to get one of the officers onto the ground, and we – in authentic British parlance – gave him a damned good kicking! I vomited twice in the car on my way home. We're planning a riot in another town next weekend, although we wish the location to be kept a secret from the kids so that they can use their imaginations. Hopefully the RCMP on their horses will join in the fun, as several fathers have pepper sprays to squirt in the horses' eyes."

"Our imaginations were let loose almost a week before the carnival," another delighted mother joined in. "The children and some of the parents imagined that we were members of the German Football Federation's governing body, and we wrote letters to FIFA offering them bribes so that Germany could host the next soccer World Cup and not South Africa. We're not sure if we'll be successful because it doesn't look like there's someone from New Zealand, Qatar or Nigeria on FIFA's voting committee."

"My two boys' team and the opposition visualised themselves as being South American teams," one proud and happy father told our reporter. "While I was almost overcome with pride when my youngest son shirt-fronted the referee and squeezed his testicles, the best part was towards the end of the second half when both teams plus parents chased the ref' all the way to the nearest police station. I have no idea what might have happened if they had caught up with him before then."

"All in all it was a wonderful and successful get together where the parents played very important roles!" The chairwoman of the carnival finally contributed. "Unfortunately some of the ambulance crews, police and more than a few parents were quite badly hurt, nevertheless the youngsters were allowed to let their imaginations run as free as birds, thus tempting several Canadian soccer associations to ban the ball forever. Even I managed to join in when I got my knee into one of the fathers. While it might not have been planned, the highlight of the carnival was when the adults in the crowd *turned on the town's Catholic priest who had just arrived from Southern Ireland. He was noticed leaving the grounds with a small boy, so was hanged from one of the goal posts. Two of the fathers then tied a rope to his wrist and fastened it to a car so that his corpse could be dragged around the ground with everyone clapping and cheering. Unfortunately his hand came off, so we tied the rope around both his ankles. We have so much to learn, don't we? While the children took no part in any of this, it supplied fertile ground for their young imaginings. It appears that although there were 50 or more RCMP officers in attendance, not one of them saw what happened, so the coroner has chosen to ignore the matter altogether."*

"How pathetic can you be?" Trev was taken aback by what he'd read. "I've never heard of the Canadians being any good at sport."

"It seems that you Aussies are no better," Greg prodded him with.

"Bullshit – we aren't!" Trev wasn't having that.

"What about this?" Greg handed him another cutting.

SCOREBOARDS BEING REMOVED, PLUS BAN ON COMPETITION LADDERS AND MATCH RESULTS FOR JUNIOR FOOTBALLERS AS RULES ARE CHANGED BY AFL

All kids will be refused the chance to win, plus there will be no score keeping or fairest and best awards pursuant to Australia-wide changes to junior football developed by the AFL.

Countless junior footballers all over Australia will be unable to win or lose, and there will no longer be match results. Kids will also be disallowed from representative sides, and scoreboards will disappear. University research has established that it was totally unnecessary for junior footballers to even consider winning, as that was deemed the driving force of criminal regimes such as Germany's Nazis, Mussolini's Fascists, and Vladimir Putin's current dictatorial regime in Russia.

An irate Western Australian father, Chas Jackson – or 'Jacko' – who has three boys who love competitive footy, claimed that the AFL had been hijacked by 'softie' ponytailed fascists, and that women and girls should be banned from playing the game. He went on to further say: "Australia's being taken over by these bleeding-heart, do-gooders who obviously vote for the Labour Party and the Australian Greens who've become even more fascist than Hitler and Mussolini ever were, with their poncey attitude that they know what's best for all Australians. Also, if sheilas want to play footy, rugby union and rugby league, how's about letting them play against blokes' teams? Then we'll see how they go in loose or collapsed scrums, plus rucks and mauls. I'd like to smell the blokes' middle fingers afterwards."

He went on to say: "People don't come to the footy to watch players hugging and kissing each other, or ballet dancing across the field like soccer players. We couldn't be bothered with blokes carrying on like a sheila with her periods and tanking half way through tennis matches. We come to see men up against men and the punch-ups – the elbow in the throat, temple or solar plexus – the knee in the ribs or the back, and the replays of all this fun on the telly later on. You've got some people trying to eliminate all the violence, but that can't last because people won't come through the turnstiles if they succeed. With the price that tickets are costing these days, it's the biffo on the field and the bonko off the field that everybody's paying for and want. Not the soccer ponytails of some of the players. Pony tails like that British soccer poof's. We all want to watch genuine footy, not cooking shows where the judges are right up themselves and s**t all over the contestants who just roll around in it for the audience. What happened to that footy star whose girlfriend said he'd glassed her in the face?

"Then, when the season's over, we watch the Brownlow, Norm Smith and Coleman Medal awards on the telly and vote on which player's missus is showing the most of her titties. That's why we like watching best and fairest awards. A bloke might miss out on an award, but at least his wife or his girlfriend can show off her titties."

He summarised by saying: "We look for footy champions so that we can see their partner's titties when the awards are handed out. There should be a special award for the woman who shows the most titty. Because – let's face it – a lot of them try their best to impress as many people as possible, the same as their partners try to win for clubs and footy fans. Hopefully one day they'll attend medal awards wearing nothing at all. Where would footy be without that sort of thing?"

"Yeah, that's the best part of the Brownlow Medal night – the sheilas' boobs," Kev shattered what could be called a pregnant silence. "Do you see how the Aussie cricketers' wives and girlfriends do the same? One of these days one of 'em *will* show up with nothing on."

I was rather taken aback by my elder sibling's musings, for he was generally rather reserved when it came to talking about women. He'd obviously been corrupted by Merl! I could see where Chas Jackson or 'Jacko' was coming from. Australian commercial TV *does seem* to be inundated with cooking competitions where the judges or so-called celebrity chefs are carrying on as if their shit doesn't stink, and I can't understand why people would line up just to be shat on? It seems Aussie audiences like watching people lining up to be shat on by arrogant dickheads. What they do is give the audience a hint of what's going to happen in the next episode. The judges *are going to shit all over the contestant or contestants.* The audience then can't wait – can't even concentrate on anything – until the dickheaded arsehole chefs or judges *shit all over the contestants!*

Trev's rather malicious and sick sense of humour surfaced: "Do you see how they're making a big fuss about gay footy players, and now it looks like they're serious about legalising same-sex marriages?"

"You could be right!" Greg acknowledged. "I find it all rather unnerving."

That seemed to spur Trev on. "What'll happen if this same-sex marriage business goes ahead and a gay player wins a footy medal or something? Who goes along as the missus? If it's the footy player that's the mummy, surely he should be playing in a woman's footy team? Or, if the footy player's the hubby, how does his partner compete against the wives or female partners of the other straight players who're showing so much boob? Does he cut a hole in the back of his daks, so that other gay footy players or blokes in the audience can see his arse cheeks?"

"*That's what* rather unnerves me," Greg tried his best to look appalled. He had a last newspaper cutting. "I suppose this gutless approach to sport has been fostered by the same kind of human cockroaches that Cockroach Street does its best to portray. The stay at home Brits who never plucked up the courage to leave the end of the street. Certainly not the ones that built an empire."

WINNING IN INDIVIDUAL SPORTS IS BANNED AT MORE THAN HALF OF UK PRIMARY SCHOOL SPORTS DAYS:

A recent poll has revealed that 57 per cent of parents said children have 'non-competitive' sports days, although 82 per cent said that they wanted 'old school' competition to come back.

More than half of all primary schools are holding non-competitive sports days that fail to announce 'winners', according to a new survey. They host events where individual children are not singled out to compete, but instead work in teams and are recognised simply for taking part.

Fifty-three per cent of parents – the majority being fathers – said they were 'comfortable' with their child losing, believing that it wasn't 'a bad thing' because it helps build resilience and confidence.

It appears that 82 per cent, both mothers and fathers, wanted old fashioned competitive school sports days back because children must realise 'you can't always win at everything in life and sometimes you have to lose'.

Regardless, the government Director in charge of sports in state schools challenged these parents by saying that he and his board members knew what was best for all the UK's children, and that the parents who wanted competitive sports were either very ignorant, or poorly educated. Even worse – they had most likely been educated in the private school system, and were seeking to resuscitate bygone British imperial ambitions. He said that these parents' names would be put on record by the school boards for further investigation. If they were prepared to watch children humiliated on the sports field, what were they capable of in the privacy of their homes?

A spokesperson from a well known private Catholic boys' school challenged this 'cruel and evil' assumption. He pointed out correctly that the private school sector – especially Anglican and Catholic Church boys' schools – turned out far more Olympic champions than state schools. Especially in running and wrestling. This was thanks to the very 'close' attention that boys were receiving by the staff; namely the visiting clergy and members of the Congregation of Christian Brothers from Southern Ireland who loved being involved in body contact sports with young lads.

"What's the friggin' world coming to?" Kev also objected to what he'd read.

Trev was more focused elsewhere. "Greg, why are you showing us all this? What the fuck's this got to do with anything?"

"Because it's all pertinent, Trev," Greg calmly reminded him. "I've told you how Dragan Milošević was a wake up to the fierce competitive nature amongst *some of the* Kiwis. There were two production lines in his factory, so how about having a competition between them? He was fully aware that hundreds of jars of haemorrhoid cream were going missing via various employees' hand bags – particularly the team leader's on production line two. The thought of giving her the sack did cross his mind, especially since she was operating a stall at the Nelson Markets where her exclusive item for sale was *his* haemorrhoid cream. To add insult to injury she was also running an internet mail order business, and was charging only half price. That was extremely popular with dairy workers in Southland and unemployed men on the West Coast. Two of Dragan's *most important and lucrative* markets. The Southland dairy workers were all for it, when you consider they're forced to ride around on wet motorcycle saddles on very little pay, and the unemployed West Coast men had no choice but to sit around on wet public seats and benches while they plotted the downfall of a friend or perhaps a family member. . . All the same, Dragan was very hesitant to sack her."

"If she was stealing his gear, he had every right to tramp her!" Kev was incredulous.

"Oh – absolutely, Kev!" Greg immediately concurred. "All the same – his lawyer felt obliged to stop him. Most fortunately his Lebanese legal advisor. . ."

"If you're caught stealing back in Aussie, you can get the tramp," Trev was on Kev's side.

"It's becoming a grey area in this country, Trev," Greg was unconvinced. "If Dragan did sack the team leader on production line two, the first thing that would happen is he'd be hauled up by the Unfair Dismissal Tribunal or the Employment Court. He could be up against high powered community lawyers that're past masters or mistresses when it comes to wrecking capitalistic private enterprises that could be of benefit to enterprising individuals. The fact that you're paying the rent and putting food on the table for a couple of dozen employees happens to be totally irrelevant. Dragan would thus become the culprit. It would be no different to having a burglar breaking into your house. If he or she were to trip over a pair of shoes that you'd carelessly left in the passageway – and is injured in any way – you'd be liable and the burglar would be fully entitled to pursue you through the courts for damages. . . Then there's the psychological aspect. Watching *so many* jars of haemorrhoid cream going down *two production* lines might've been too tempting for the team leader of production line two, and perhaps only one or two jars might've gone missing if the business owner wasn't seen to have so many *all to himself?* Not only that – if the team leader managed to sell those jars she took for *herself,* the actual sale of those jars could become compulsory, if the team leader had begun to rely on the extra income. Conceivably she'd borrowed money and needed the additional income to pay it back? Therefore was it the business owner's fault that his employee was so tempted, and had thus become so dependent on the extra income from the missing goods? You'll notice that *I'm not* using the words 'stole or stolen'. We don't want to be accused of further traumatising the team leader of production line two. If she'd become reliant on the extra money she was getting from selling the absent haemorrhoid cream – maybe the right thing to do would be to give her a pay rise? . . . So was the working environment provided by the employer to blame? Was it necessary for the business owner to hire expensive independent councillors to see if the employee in question might be dissuaded from removing so many jars, and being a major competitor in the haemorrhoid cream industry? Either that, or there could be the hiring of government liquidation consultants who could ensure that his employees were given a satisfactory retrenchment package if the removal of the haemorrhoid cream jars eventually bankrupts him. They would be experts at finding interested parties from China to take over the business. Foreign parties being subsidised by the New Zealand Labour government. Parties that would use modern technology and not employ anyone, thus avoiding any future fuss about goods going missing."

"So what did he do?" Knowing Kev, he no doubt was hoping for a positive outcome.

Greg could only come up with the opposite: "He went ahead and offered a carton of the same haemorrhoid cream to the production line that filled, capped and packed the most jars in a week. Furthermore, he used the last of his stolen gold teeth to make necklaces for the winning team members. Possibly very unique and valuable necklaces because some of the teeth still had the previous owners' enamel and roots. . . Well never mind haemorrhoids or piles – did the shit *really hit* the fan once he'd suggested it to the team leader of production line number one! Firstly, the team members on production line number two, the one with the errant team leader, objected to competing, as they couldn't match the volumes that the opposition was capable of. It was in view of the fact that a lot of the jars on their production line weren't making it to the packaging stage. No matter how fast they filled and put tops on the jars on their line, too many by far were going astray. . . Nevertheless, gents, it was the team leader on production line one that brought the curtain down on everything."

"How did she do that?" Trev was *sort* of interested.

"The team leader of production line one was a bloke, Trev," Greg's expression wasn't a happy one. "It was very disappointing for Dragan. . . Actually you should commiserate with the man – war criminal or not. When the team leader of production line one reported that Dragan had suggested a contest, not only did the government work place environment, safety and health inspectors threaten to shut him down and fine him, the union called a strike that was given immediate permission by the chief executive of Private Industry and Employees

Rights. This consent was given seeing that the mental health or morale of the employees could be compromised. . . And this, gentlemen, is where the banning of competitive sports has influenced so much person to person interaction in both Poo Zealand and Oz today. More so in Poo Zealand. Asking the two production line team members to compete against each was driving a wedge through any bonding that the two production line team leaders had managed to instil among the various team members. This could encourage violent competitiveness, and cause disharmony amongst the workers. Also it could be an irrecoverable blow to any team member if it became apparent that he or she might've lost.
. . Please don't let that get you down. Happy endings can arise out of some of the most dismal of circumstances. Sadly Dragan was finally bankrupted and used the last of his stolen teeth to try and defend his business... Nev – did I tell you that he was in his seventies?"

"No."

"Well then, I should have. Dragan was in his mid seventies and a source of great pride was his snow-white beard. A beard that easily went half way down his chest! Even more flamboyant than Father Christmas' beard! It was his beard that saved him."

"How?" Kev sat upright. Naturally Greg's last words grabbed all of our concentration.

"It's not so hard to grasp, Kev," Greg seemed sure of himself. "In order to try and save his business, Dragan suddenly took an interest in the methodology of the factory's former owner. The previous owner had been illegally using West Coasters as workers, and they were too thick to bother about forming teams and organising themselves into any kind of group. That's why he decided to visit Greymouth and Westport, and for some reason or other he visited the tiny hamlet of Blackwater. Not Blackball – Trev – Blackwater. It could be there when suddenly a miraculous inspiration came to him."

It was my turn to give Greg a nudge. "What inspiration, Greg?"

"I must ask you to forgive me for forgetting to mention that Dragan was.
. . Let me see now – how can I explain it? Having given it some considerable

thought, the most accurate way is to describe him as being multi-sexual or pansexual. Or perhaps omni-sexual, if such a word actually exists? He'd always had problems back in Serbia trying to cater for his various sexual appetites. Having studied the West Coast natives minutely, he came to the conclusion that if he was to live in a place such as Greymouth, he could indulge in all his fantasies without those around him batting an eyelid. That's where he started wearing a very revealing miniskirt, and one of those boob tube tops. Correct, he might've looked rather incongruous with his knobbly knees, hairy legs and beard, nonetheless he was an instant hit with more than a few West Coast men and possibly the entire population of lesbians. A Swiss colleague of mine, who's actually met Dragan, has suggested that his attraction to the Coast natives is possibly because he allows his figs to dangle almost *flagrant delicto* enticingly in a crutch-less thong just below the hem of his miniskirt. Or it could be the tufts of armpit hairs which are in competition with his beard? Who cares if either's true, since he's created his very own cult which has attracted a following nationwide and internationally? A host of individuals – mostly from the gay community – are flocking to Greymouth from all over Poo Zealand – Auckland – Christchurch – Palmerston North – Blenheim – you name it! We also have people coming in from Sydney and San Francisco, Vancouver, Montreal, Ottawa – in fact from all over Canada! All prepared to donate twenty percent of their salaries or wages to the cult. So now you know why he's making a fortune. I understand the local police are battling to stop fights amongst those waiting in line to sign up and join Dragan's cult. More than a few officers are thinking of resigning because of the pressure, especially when they come up against the gangs of lesbians that can be found by the score in Greymouth, Hokitika, Westport and Hamilton. Plus those lezzies that fly in from Vancouver, Montreal and all over Canada. It appears that these ladies – if you can call them as such in Aussie – find Dragan's unusual charms irresistible. Especially his Serbian accent. . . Regardless of all that, this isn't how Dragan's making the real big quids – is it, Nev?"

I felt obliged to go along with him. "What else is he up to, Greg?"

Greg reached down and lifted his briefcase onto his lap. He went through the routine of searching through his files, and picked out one that had an orange sticker on it. "Take a look at this, gents," he passed a slip of paper to me first. "Here's some background data."

KAIKOURA TOILET CAMERA IN SPOTLIGHT AGAIN AND INFLUENCES DECISIONS WHETHER CAMERAS SHOULD BE USED IN TOILETS NEW ZEALAND-WIDE.

A camera looking into a toilet cubicle in Kaikoura has raised eyebrows, and is causing a stink. It has been suggested that the position of the camera may actually film someone sitting on the toilet. A parliamentary committee chaired by Gregory Shepherd, the principal of well known consultancy firm G. SHEPHERD and CO is looking into the pros and cons of cameras being installed in public toilets throughout New Zealand.

A submission from Gemma Frutz, the secretary of People For The Promotion Of Alternative Amusement For Tourists New Zealand (PPAATNZ), who is a Kaikoura resident, said she and her organisation were all in favour of cameras in all the cubicles in the town's public toilets. She said they offered an alternative source of tourist and local amusement other than whale watching which Kaikoura is famous for worldwide.

Ms Frutz added: "Sometimes in winter the weather can make whale watching a miserable experience, and there are occasions when the whales don't show up possibly because the Japanese have harpooned them all. What can be more enjoyable than sitting by the fire in our coffee house on a rainy day and watching the hundreds of people – both locals and tourists – who take advantage of Kaikoura's wonderful public facilities? It's quite amazing what activities some of the male gay community absorb themselves with. Cupid has been very busy with his bow and arrows, and I can see plenty of male couples lining up if same-sex marriages are legalised! Isn't it amazing how public toilets bring so many people together in his day and age?

"People would also be surprised at how many gay men and women we have in the Canterbury and Marlborough provinces. Our calculations tell us that the gays outnumber heterosexuals by about eight to one, whereas I have heard

that heterosexuals prefer not to use the facilities for fear of intruding on the gay peoples' fun. We have a giant viewing screen similar to the ones that some venues use for watching the rugby. A free cup of coffee is available for those that pay the $25 cinema fee, plus we have lower rates during the off season."

"Bugger me bloody dead!" was Trev's first and only comment.

"That's the only way to describe it, Trev!" Greg was onside. "From what I've been told, this article set Dragan well down the road to making quite a large amount of money. With his transvestite escort agency business, and his cult, he's become a prince to all those around him, and the West Coast is his principality. He's fine-tuned the art of toilet camera work, and was inspired by Gemma Frutz's comments about the antics some of the male gay community get up to. Unlike Kaikoura's camera setup, he's managed to install technology that also records the slightest sound. . . No – and you can stop laughing, Nev – it's not for recording flatus being discharged. It's to capture the groans of pain from the recipient. It turns a fair few of the male gay community on. What Dragan's tried to achieve is to film and record the mating rituals of male homosexuals. You know – very similar to David Attenborough's marvellous works? While you can hardly compare the rituals of the gays captured on film to those of a New Guinean bird of paradise, there does seem to be some unwritten protocols observed like you have with some birds of paradise. You have the tossing of a coin to determine who's going to be on the receiving end first, and then there's the gasp plus look of awe – or most likely panic and fear – when a participant sees that the other participant's so well endowed. No again, Nev – boxes of chocolates, the reading of poetry and bunches of flowers don't have a role in all this. Possibly a jab of crystal meth or P, but this's not necessarily the norm. And for the last time – no Nev – you don't have footage of the intercourse in the actual cubicles themselves. Dragan's not a pervert. He prefers to do the action filming near the hand basins, so that his subjects can spread their wings similar to the birds of paradise I just mentioned. Sure there's also coverage of the parting of the couples after their energies are spent, sometimes one with an agonised, tortured look on his face. At first it was very rare that they bid each other farewell, although when they continue coming back again and again, and are bumping into one another, future dates are organised, plus there've been more than a few discussions about betrothal if same-sex marriage is allowed by law. That's why Dragan has such sensitive recording equipment. He also keeps the names and addresses of the participants – especially those that mention future marriage prospects. I'm sure he's got something crafty up his sleeve. . . His movies have become much in demand right across the planet. I don't suppose you have to think too hard to determine the countries where they're most popular, Trev?"

"Ask him," Trev pointed at me.

"Which countries?" I jumped into the void.

"The Republic of Ireland and Canada lead the way amongst the overseas countries, Nev," Greg eyed Trev askance. "Ireland with all its Catholic clergy, and then it appears that Canada has a huge population of people who are great followers of Dragan's work, plus they're fully paid members of his cult. If you can believe his stats, it looks as if Canada has the highest number of gays per capita in the world! It's neck and neck between the Netherlands and Belgium after that, and I understand that's on account of them legalising same-sex marriage first and second respectively. . . Please take no notice of all that, anyway. Dragan's movies are most popular here – especially on the West Coast and in Canterbury. When they made those Hobbit films over here, which the local bongo actors threatened to boycott and nearly had them taken to Eastern Europe, Peter Jackson's wonderful work planted a seed in the minds of potential movie makers all over this country. All the same, it was Dragan's work that actually caused that seed to sprout. Big money was offered to him to move his headquarters from Greymouth to either Auckland or Wellington. Especially Wellington once it was proposed that that huge sign "WELLIWOOD" should be put up on Miramar Hill. . . You look like you have something to add to that, Trev?"

"I saw that Welliwood crap," Trev's features were most disdainful. "They reckoned that the sign was gunna compete against that Hollywood sign in Los Angeles. Friggin' fat chance of that!"

That caused Greg to frown. "I think it might go much deeper than that, Trev."

"How?"

"Where do you think the word 'Welli' comes into it?"

Trev gave Greg a queer look. "From the word 'Wellington'. Where else do you think it comes from?"

Greg's eyes lit up in triumph. "I don't think so, Trev! Surely you've heard of a Wellington boot? Lord knows, they're almost the Kiwi's national footwear. The rubber ones – that is. You see people wearing them all over the place, and on the South Island they're almost green from all the cow or sheep shit that the owners have just walked in. You see them everywhere – in pubs – supermarkets – doctors' surgeries – cinemas – at weddings – couples are getting married in them – all leaving deposits of cow and sheep shit everywhere. I wouldn't be surprised if you get some bongos wearing them to bed. I'm sure plenty of single blokes do, as they can be a reminder of previous dalliances. You've might've heard of putting a sheep's back legs down the front of one's wellies to stop it from escaping? Wellies is short for Wellington boots in Poo Zealand, Trev. . . Dragan would've given up half his movie business to be able to have the word "WELLIWOOD" as a label for his company, however that was not to be. He soon started making a lot of money out of another idea of his."

"What idea?" Kev was back on board.

Greg first checked his mobile phone for any messages. "Being denied the ability to use the label 'Welliwood', there was no reason for Dragan to leave the West Coast. He was still intrigued with the Kiwis love of Wellington boots, and he couldn't help noticing how the women on the Coast were turned on by men wearing them. He'd also heard from someone that it was the same in Southland and the Bay of Plenty area on the North Island. Actually, it was the same almost everywhere else – Wellington – Auckland – Dunedin – Palmerston North – just mention a place. It also came to Dragan's attention that almost every gay male he'd met had a fetish about their sexual partner being clad only in plastic raincoats and wellies. So that's now the major theme in some of his latest toilet movies. He's done so much for the gay community – hasn't he, guys? Especially for the recipients of the intercourse, plus he's made more than a few bob on the way. Take for instance the pillow that has the attached rubber clothes peg for the recipient to bite on. This protects him in case the pillow bursts. Who would enjoy having a mouthful of feathers, or the possibility of foam rubber or cotton wool going down his throat and up his nose? Another example is the rubber sheet that spares the recipient from embarrassment when his excrement gets all over the bed linen. Naturally the hi-tech pillow and rubber sheet are for use in the privacy of the bedroom or whatever, although rubber clothes pegs on their own are sometimes used in public toilets. Dragan tries to discourage this because the recipient's gasping, moaning and groaning sells his movies. . . Lastly, it was our Serb who invented the recipient sphincter whistle."

"So what the fuck's a sphincter whistle?" Trev made a big show of not believing what he'd just heard.

"I thought it would've been obvious, Trev?" Greg tried to coax him. "I've already brought up the topic of how quite a few of the gay marchers at Perth's Mardi Gas in Northbridge can't let go of flatus with the normal sound effects that heterosexual men can achieve. Those would be the blokes that've been on the receiving end of any anal intercourse in the partnership. My doctor told me that both the recipients' anal sphincters become stretched and flabby, therefore no sound is possible when intestinal gases are ejected from the bowel. Another thing that my doc brought up is how after years of stretching from intercourse, the anal sphincters become like perished elastic, and this has led to same-sex divorces in such places as Canada and the Netherlands. What Dragan's come up with is a disc with an adjustable flange that fits snugly between the recipient's internal and external anal sphincters. In the centre of the disc is a whistling mechanism that vibrates when air or flatus passes through it. This resembles the noise one gets when a heterosexual individual breaks wind. It's not quite as loud as what Nev's capable of when he first gets up in the morning, but it's better than nothing. By using an anal sphincter whistle, a gay recipient can con a new partner into believing that he's still a virgin. Being deemed as such, it makes him much more desirable. Identical to coming across a female virgin, I dare say? Mind you – he needs to ensure that he removes the whistle before any intercourse or anilingus commences, as leaving it in situ can be a dead giveaway and cause unnecessary heartbreak, mistrust and disillusionment. Actually, when you come to think about it..."

"Come on, Greg – this *has to be* bullshit?" Trev tried to reason with him.

Trev's plea was in vain. "What part don't you believe, Trev?"

"The sphincter whistles?"

"Ah – that!" Greg looked delighted. "Actually Dragan's waiting on a worldwide patent for his latest sphincter whistle. I suppose you could call it a harmonica rather than a whistle, as it's capable of quite a few notes. Do you remember Gerry and Rosemary's fetish for kimchi, Nev?"

"Yeah, I do."

"Great! The West Coast cops, who arrested the photo thief suspect, are unabashed followers of Dragan Milošević's cult. They told him about Gerry and Rosemary and how they could muster up a huge amount of intestinal gas via the agency of kimchi, Norwegian kippers and jugged hare. When Dragan sells his sphincter harmonicas, he supplies them with a pamphlet with a number of Kimchi recipes, and it's been a huge success throughout all the provinces of Poo Zealand. Especially the recipes that include smoky barbeque or cranberry sauce. With sufficient gas being passed through them, these harmonicas can play two tunes thus far. One is a fantastic imitation of a walrus farting, while the other gives a more than satisfactory rendition of *COLONEL BOGEY.* Have you heard the latter, Nev?"

I hadn't. "No!"

Greg began to recite:

"Hitler has only got one ball.

Goering has three but very small.

Himmler has something similar.
But Goebbels has no balls at all."

When Kev managed to stop laughing: "Now I know you're mad, Greg!"

"I apologise if I come across like that, Kev." Greg looked contrite. "I'm serious. Soon you can be anywhere in Poo Zealand – a shopping centre or watching the Wallabys playing the All Blacks – then you'll think the world's coming to an end when you're accosted by the sound of a walrus farting, or then you might be comforted by a fairly basic or crude rendition of Colonel Bogey. . . Apparently Dragan's working on all sorts of ideas for his sphincter whistles and harmonicas. He's writing software whereby you can have a flute, clarinet, oboe or even the relaxing notes of a violin in expert hands. With all the gay blokes that've come to the surface now that same-sex marriage has been mooted, soon there'll be entire orchestras throughout the country playing a whole range of instruments on their sphincter whistles and harmonicas. This should be cause for much celebration when you take into account that these poor souls have been unfairly shunned by society for far too long as it is. . . Look, we have the time, so perhaps we should discuss further Dragan's financial genius, Trev?"

"What financial genius?" Trev was again looking for particulars.

Greg took a purple, plastic file envelope out of his briefcase and removed a slip of paper from it. "What do you think of this, Nev?"

THAI PENIS WHITENING ALL THE RAGE

A new trend of penis whitening has captivated New Zealand, Thailand and most of Asia as men line up to have their penises whitened.

Ordinary skin whitening has been around for many decades because darker skin is often associated with being an African or Indian from the subcontinent. Lasers are now being employed to break down melanin in the skin in order to whiten penises.

A Christchurch man who, wishes to remain anonymous, was interviewed by reporters and said he had been a flasher for the last five years, and he wanted to have more impact on the women and gay men he exposed himself to in subway underpasses and on pedestrian crossings. He claimed that a whiter penis gave him much more confidence, for it contrasted very nicely with his black overcoat.

When females and some gay men passersby were given a demonstration of the man's new look penis, they said that they were more interested in its movement and size.

Blanco Zoob the chairman and owner of the Blanco-Zoob-Shine Clinic in Auckland New Zealand, which offers the service, told our reporter he had also introduced vagina whitening services three months ago. This service is for feminists who say that what is good for men, should be made available to women. "Whiter genitalia are popular among gay men, lesbians and transvestites who take good care of their private parts. They want to look good in all areas," Mr Zoob explained.

I passed the article to Trev who just shook his head. "Now I've seen everything!" he was incredulous. "But what's this got to do with this Dragon bloke?"

Greg had another article handy. "It's 'Dragan' – not Dragon, Trev. If you don't believe me – look up Thai and penis whitening on the internet. I'm only telling you what Dragan's been up to. Take this as an example. You can only refer to the man as a genius."

NEW CRAZE GIVES BACK LOST RIGHTS STOLEN FROM HETEROSEXUAL MEN IN NEW ZEALAND. WEST COAST MOVIE MOGUL INVOLVED.

Dragan Milošević the illustrious West Coast movie mogul and entrepreneur has found an innovative way of increasing his already vast fortune. Having been moved by the new fad of penis whitening that is so popular throughout New Zealand and most of Asia, his generous public spirit, that has done so much for the male gay community, is now reaching out to the male heterosexual community. With all New Zealanders being preoccupied with the possibility of same-sex marriages, heterosexual men are now regarded as second class citizens by both the media and MPs on both sides of the floor.

As an attempt to raise the morale of New Zealand's heterosexual men, Mr Milošević has come up with a secret formula that can make these men's penises a dark brown colour. This allows them the confidence to compete against gay men in society and the work force. When confronted by a member of the gay community the heterosexual man can display his new look penis, and thus find himself more acceptable to modern society.

Mr Milošević's clinic in Greymouth also provides an identical vagina service for feminists. So far the clinic has been inundated by men and feminists from the North and South Islands, plus Australia, and the video of the outcome of these new procedures has gone viral throughout the world.

"Why would anyone want a dark brown dick?" Kev was the first to find his voice.

Greg quickly looked round to see if anyone was listening. "Do you remember me showing you an article mentioning how the NZ Customs Department sacked two heterosexual officers because they were concerned about a gay officer strip searching male passengers and making lewd comments?"

Kev's reply was almost instant: "Of course – I do. What happened to 'em?"

Greg shrugged. "Apparently they were reinstated by the Employment Relations Authority or whichever, still the Customs Department has appealed... That's why it's becoming almost compulsory to have a dark brown donger nowadays. Both in Oz and Poo Zealand you've got this politically correct and do-gooder social conscience that's spreading throughout both countries. If you've got a dark brown schwanzer, it indicates that you've been sodomising a whole army of recipients, which appears to be the norm amongst many of the gay male community. They say that once you've indulged as the *male* participant – or the actual prodder – in anal sex over a period of time, your favourite body part becomes stained a dark brown. They also say that the recipient also becomes incontinent because his sphincters don't close properly. Thus the popularity with Dragan's rubber sheet to guard against any wayward excrement getting over everything. Plus there's his sphincter whistle. . . This has to be where you should take your hat off to Dragan. As a matter of fact, it's hard picturing him as an ex-war criminal. He seems to be the only one who's preparing for the onset of same-sex marriages. He's been trying his best to organise things so that the advent of same-sex marriages is received with both joy and open arms *by everybody*! For far too long we've had hatred, bias and disgust levelled at too large a percentage of our population. In Dragan's opinion now is the time to join hands as one. . . That's also why he's stayed well clear of the hospitality industry. I'm sure you know why, Kev?"

"No, I don't!"

"Isn't it obvious, Kev?" Greg couldn't keep the frustration out of his voice. "By the hospitality industry, I mean accommodation. Second only to Australia, Poo Zealand can pride itself as probably the best tourist accommodation provider in the Southern Hemisphere. You go into any hotel and motel rooms and you'll come across cleanliness, and crisp, freshly-laundered sheets, pillow cases and towels. The showers, baths and hand basins will be spotless. The cups and saucers, plates and any cutlery and glasses likewise. . . Righto, so what generally happens after a couple get married – Nev?"

I didn't see a problem with the question. "They go on a honeymoon – don't they?"

"Dead right – Nev! The majority go on a honeymoon of some sort. If either the bride or groom haven't had too much to drink – or if the groom hasn't been caught trying to shag one of the bridesmaids – it's generally the norm to consummate or re-consummate the marriage. The reason why I use the word 're-consummate' is that virgin brides and grooms are as scarce as unicorns nowadays. Most particularly in the gay communities. . . So what happens when a male gay couple want to consummate or re-consummate the marriage in someone's motel or hotel room? What happens to all those freshly-laundered pillowcases, sheets and towels? This's where you need to have some sympathy for the hotel or motel owner, plus the recipient of the consummation or re-consummation. Why – because there's more than a fair chance of shit getting over everything. . . Oh no – not again, Nev! I can't see anything funny in what I've just said."

I struggled to control myself. "Sorry – Greg."

"I'll forgive you just this once, Nev. . . It's not the same with female gay couples – is it? After all their fannies are designed to accommodate a penis – aren't they? That's just how Mother Nature intended things. It appears that a woman's vagina has also been designed to cater for child birth, and in most cases they return to roughly their original size. This's all in order when it comes to the natural scheme of things. I suppose the only difference with lesbian couples is that they might employ larger and larger dildos in order to satisfy their partners once the recipient gets on in age? . . . You could say that we've arrived at as a good a time as any to elaborate on Dragan's compassion for his fellow human beings. His heart also goes out to lesbians, not only gay men. I just mentioned lesbians employing larger and larger dildos – even if they need a mobile crane to lift them off the back of a truck. Nowadays some of the strap-on dildos are getting so large and heavy, they're becoming a danger to the wearer's back. Dragan's come up with a back brace with straps going around the wearer's shoulders and legs. This allows the dildo to be supported by both the shoulders and thighs, which helps to eliminate stress on the lower part of the spine. . . If you don't think that's innovative enough, he's also working on a winch system where pulleys are bolted on to steel girders in the ceiling. This allows the person that's wearing the dildo to raise and lower it without straining her shoulders, back or legs. Sadly, no matter the size of the dildo, the 'male' lesbian will never be able to compete with some male buck in his late teens or early twenties – will she? When you come to. . ."

"Now I've heard everything," Trev solemnly informed Kev.

"Not yet – you haven't!" Greg failed to agree. "Dragan was working on a prototype hydraulic affair, which had a Honda motor driving the hydraulic pumps. So far this's proved to be an up and down venture, which has some serious setbacks. You can't take it on honeymoon with you because most hotels object to having a Honda motor – no matter how quiet – running just outside a guest's door or window. You generally get the guests on either side strongly objecting to it. . . Anyway, enough about his good intentions towards lesbians. He's finding it much tougher catering for males, but should be commended for his efforts thus far."

"What efforts?" I pressed him.

Greg studied a signet ring on his left pinky finger. "I would venture that his biggest dilemma with assisting gay males is that they have a problem with overly-stretched anal sphincters, which quite often leads to possible talk of divorce in countries that've legalised same-sex marriage. While lesbians can employ larger and larger dildos, there's not much gay blokes can do about the size of their dongers. On porn sites you see adverts claiming to be able to extend the size of dongers, nevertheless it's all nonsense. People once deemed anal sex unnatural, since neither anal sphincter was designed to have objects thrust through them. Outwards maybe – but not inwards. It's totally unnatural in the normal scheme of things. It's rather like those Mursi, Chai and Tirma women in Africa who insert huge discs or plates in their bottom lips and earlobes. Eventually their lips and earlobes are stretched to the point of no return, and flap around if the discs are taken out. I just wouldn't know. . . Women are also more fortunate than men when it comes to their diet. The 'male' participants in a lesbian couple don't have to worry if a partner's had a meal of prunes and custard for evening dessert. Or whether she's eaten a hot curry or chilli con carne. It can't be the same for male couples – especially the so-called 'men' – if they've got foreskins. No, the males have far more pitfalls to contend with. That's where I'm sure the owners of hotels and motels would be delighted with Dragan's rubber sheets. Same as with the gay males who're on the receiving end. Not being gay, I can't verify either equation. . . You might be able to enlighten us, Trev?"

"Bullshit – I can!" Trev objected strenuously.

Greg smiled at Trev's reaction. "I'll take your word for it, Trev. Notwithstanding that, being gay is considered to be the vogue nowadays. You need to be gay if you want to get into the civil service, whereas there are some enlightened multinational organisations looking for gay men, thus turning the page on an unjust past. Perhaps Qantas may be one of those? Who knows? . . . From some of the pamphlets I've seen, your most prized possession doesn't have to be entirely dark brown. You can improvise by having a very clever, Chinese plastic doughnut that you can put your member through. It looks as if it's chocolate-coated to add to its authenticity. There are two types you can get – one that fits under the head of it, or one that's worn right at the base. I've heard of certain men that wear both at the same time, whereas I think that's rather overdoing things – don't you agree? From what I can deduce, when it comes to staining, uncircumcised men – those masquerading as gays – prefer to have from the tip of the foreskin to the base of the member stained dark brown, so that when the foreskin's pulled back, the purple-blue of the head contrasts so favourably with the darker outer skin. I believe that this procedure's also popular with the actual gay blokes themselves."

"Righto, so what's the secret formula that makes their dicks go brown?" Trev was a stickler for detail.

"Smart question, Trev! There's no great secret involved. All he uses is good, old fashioned Kiwi shoe polish, which naturally he's put in a more glamorous container. He uses the same polish for both men and women – if you're allowed to use such terms back in Oz – even so he handles all the penis staining himself. He won't go near any woman who wants a dark brown vagina."

"Why won't he?" Kev demanded an explanation.

"Dragan's a wily old fox, Kev," Greg chuckled. "As I said before, he's an omni-sexual, if such a creature exists. That means he'll roger anything that moves. Just like certain Christian Brothers. In a nutshell he likes doing the blokes because he gets to pander to the 'man side' of him. Being an omni-sexual he has a male, female and transgender personality that alternates with the different phases of the moon. He has fits of depression like women have during their periods. There are times when he falls in love and wants to roger some bloke he sees down the street. There are other occasions when he wants some bloke to roger him. It's mainly heterosexual men who come to him for penis staining so that they can compete against gay men in this new 'Compulsory Gay World' that we find ourselves in. . . Is this making sense so far, Kev?"

"I'm not sure, Greg. It all sounds fairly sick to me, mate."

"It does – doesn't it?" Greg totally understood. "Regardless, staining heterosexual men's penises appealed to his 'heterosexual side'. He's interacting with 'old fashioned men' – isn't he – and his Greymouth clinic suddenly has a 1950's or '60s 'barber shop atmosphere' about it. You know the old fashioned barber shops where blokes not only went for a haircut and a shave, but for a yarn and to hear the latest gossip and jokes. Premises where you were allowed to smoke, swear, fart, belch and tell raunchy jokes. A refuge where political correctness – if there was such an animal back then – was left out on the street. A time when butch feminists were totally unheard of. Women wore dresses and skirts – not track pants, jeans, tank tops or tights. We're talking about places that have pinups on the wall of beautiful women nude from the waist up. Women as Mother Nature intended them. You're allowed to tell the other customers what you'd like to do with those women, plus there was always that fart or belch heard in the background that seems to go on forever. It makes everyone complain – congratulate – and laugh at the exact same time. No anal sphincter whistles employed. . . Yes, gents, a sanctuary for everyday men who have absolutely no doubt when it comes to identifying their sexuality and gender. Men as Mother Nature intended them. . . My Swiss mate went along and joined in, but he pulled out just before it was his turn to be stained. He actually heard one bloke claim that he'd seen a *beautiful* woman who was *actually a West Coast local! In Greymouth of all places!* Naturally this brought about an intense debate, and most of those at the clinic accused him of cruelly pulling their legs. After arguing backwards and forwards, it was finally decided that the woman had to be either a Maori lass or some Aussie tourist. Another bloke said he'd also come across another beautiful woman in Invercargill some years before, and they determined that she must've come from Oz, or was a Maori also. . . Do you see how Kiwi men put Maori and Aussie sheilas on pedestals – Nev?"

I was battling to take it all in. "I remember those old barber shops from when I was a kid. I also remember Mum being horrified by the Playboy centrefolds that were above the mirrors."

"Then you know exactly what I'm talking about, Nev!" Greg was more than happy with my reply. "We're talking about ordinary men enjoying the company of normal men, and the main topic of their conversation is their adulation of the opposite sex. There are no fuzzy parameters here. The farts and belches are long and loud. Both intended to cause discomfort or to impress. The talk is vulgar – the worship of women is genuine and meaningful – *blokes* just being *blokes*! No wonder Dragan's clients keep coming back time and time again for treatment, thus his use of Kiwi boot polish hasn't been exposed or commented on as yet. On top of that he has every one of them secretly filmed for two reasons. Firstly, a movie of a man having his penis darkened with boot polish has enormous appeal in all the West Coast towns, as well as Wellington, Gisborne, Invercargill, Dunedin and Blenheim. The same following is found in both Southern and Northern Ireland, plus Canada and the Netherlands. On the other hand he could always blackmail his patients later on if any of them became a famous film star or a politician. . . He won't touch the women because the majority of them are feminists looking for an excuse to be outraged and to complain to the media. Female rugby union and league players who want to come across as being tough as nails like their male counterparts. Women who make out that they want to emasculate men. . . He started out doing them, but desisted when they became enraged at the fact that men had been issued with a pair of figs and a donger, while they hadn't. . . So he asks for volunteers – doesn't he, Nev? Thence you've got blokes from all up and down the Coast coming forward with their hands up. They're dead keen not only to *actually see* a fanny, there's a realistic chance that they might even come away with a smelly finger in order to savour the memory when they arrive home. . . The poor buggers are in for a shock and inescapable disillusionment – aren't they, Nev? We're talking about simple-minded blokes at this juncture. It's the tattoos that frightens them off – not so, Nev?"

"Tattoos?"

"Yes – Nev! Quite a few feminists have tattoos on their buttocks and around their shaved vaginas. While the buttock tattoos mostly depict prancing lambs, winged horses or pictures of birds flying out of their anuses – the vagina tattoos are a very different matter altogether. Quite a few of the female patients these volunteers come cross have tattoos that depict giant clams or snarling grizzly bears. Lions and saltwater crocodiles even! The artwork is done in such a way that should one consider inserting his penis in such a vagina, it would immediately be clamped by a clam or bitten off by a grizzly bear, lion or saltwater croc'! . . . Don't let that trouble you. You wait and see – there'll be people lining up to thank Dragan one of these days."

"He sounds bloody queer to me," Kev was becoming more and more like my younger brother every day! Gone were the sympathetic words he had for everything or everyone!

"Yes," Greg agreed, "but he's the only enlightened and forward thinker when it comes to the dawn of same-sex marriage. All sorts of boundaries will need to be shifted, and we'll all have to prepare ourselves for change. I've read one of his books, and must say I'm most impressed with the compassion he has for others. He's most likely trying to make up for his dastardly deeds in Serbia and Bosnia. Take for example a male couple having walked down the aisle. Consider the person who takes up the 'female' role or is on the receiving end. As time goes on, the wear and tear on his anal sphincter muscles becomes more and more pronounced. His – or should I say *her* – partner starts complaining about his penis not being able to touch the sides, and he's seen considering possible alternatives? Sure, Dragan points out that in the Netherlands and Belgium you have operations where sphincters can be tightened with the use of sutures, but even this procedure can only be employed a limited amount of times before the actual sphincters themselves can't be manipulated any further. A bit like the lips and earlobes of those African women. Naturally with that the incontinence sets in, and that further exacerbates the problem. . . So what can the 'female' partner do? Will feminist movements take him in? Or will he need to form a movement of his own where other gay men with stretched anal dilemmas can also join? You have to realise that genuine feminists will have nothing to do with males, no matter what their sexual orientation is. That's most likely on account that ordinary heterosexual men won't have anything to do with them, either. . . Let's take a look at a lesbian equation – shall we? Unlike with gay men, the receiver's the real winner here. Like I pointed out before, Dragan's mentioned how larger dildos can be employed as time inexorably goes on. . . Now I have to. . ."

"Hold on, Greg," Trev was beginning to sound exasperated. "You've already mentioned about lezzies using bigger and bigger dildos before. How's about. . ."

"No wait, Trev," it was Greg's turn to interrupt. "Like Dragan, we'll all have to adapt to enormous changes when same-sex marriages are made legal, and we have to allow the participants every chance to prosper. I'm just bringing to your attention some of the hurdles that need to be negotiated. Take for instance the paradox that awaits us. Let's look at a heterosexual relationship? As time goes by, what if the 'male' – if we'll be able to use that term in Aussie for much longer – finds it harder and harder to get an erection? Okay, we've got Viagra and so on, but that, too, has its limitations. Or perhaps his partner's breath smells like a grease trap in an abattoir? . . . Ah, now come on – Nev – that's hardly funny! . . . Where we have the paradox is that in lesbian relationships the recipient is harder to please as time goes on, while in a male gay equation the recipient finds it a much more difficult task to satisfy his partner due to anatomical wear and tear. In a lesbian setup you might have the 'male' participant injuring her back if she doesn't wear one of Dragan's special back braces. . . I was hoping that this would give you some protection against what I'm about to say next. I doubt if Kev really needs to hear this."

"Hey – hang on – what do you mean?" My elder brother was electrified. "What don't I need to hear?"

"I've always been aware of your sensibilities, Kev," Greg couldn't look him in the eye. "If you insist, then maybe I'll continue."

Kev looked beseechingly at Trev and me. "You can tell me anything that you tell Nev and Trev."

Greg still looked uncomfortable. "At least I tried to warn you, Kev. What I have to say is not only heartbreaking – it'll shock you to the core. It's a true story. . . We have a middle-aged lesbian and we'll call her Daphne – right? She has a much younger partner who's harder and harder to satisfy. Daphne's spent her savings on all kinds of dildos yet they're doing little to sustain her partner's interest. Then she comes across an advert of Dragan's, and she's immediately persuaded as to what she must do next. It's an advert describing a dildo so large, the Serb's back brace and straps *are absolutely essential!* It's Dragan's Sword of Thos – the second biggest in his range! So she orders one on the internet – doesn't she? Then, to keep everything as a surprise, she has her purchase delivered to her aunty. After smuggling the same purchase into the flat that she shares with the one she simply adores, she does all in her power to keep it a secret by hiding it in the broom cupboard. An excellent hiding place when you consider the younger woman never volunteers to help with the cleaning. . . First Daphne cooks the love of her life a splendid meal, all the while topping the same lover's glass up with Bailey's Irish Cream. There's incense burning in the background and the meal's shared under candle light, therefore the younger woman can sense that something special's just around the corner. Obligingly she heads off to the bedroom, thus giving Daphne the opportunity to strap on the giant dildo and brace etceteras. . . . Daphne then charges into the boudoir to show off her new acquisition, nevertheless tragedy strikes. Just as she races into the bedroom all trussed up with the back brace and so on – she trips over one of her lover's gym boots – the giant dildo digs into the carpet – she's pole vaulted out of the apartment window! . . . No – seriously Nev and Trev – your sense of humour's starting to alarm me. I bet you'll stop laughing when I tell you they were living on the tenth floor of their apartment building! Needless to say –Daphne was killed by the fall!"

"Oh – shit!" Typically Kev certainly found nothing humorous about what Greg had just said.

"Yes – Kev – I know!" Greg only had empathy for my elder sibling. "You can imagine what happened. Dragan's Sword of Thos dildos have a lady's personal vibrator inserted in the end of them, and it was the pointy end of the vibrator that was caught in the carpet when she tripped over. It was the sheer momentum from her charge that carried Daphne all the way to the open window. . . I'm sorry to say it, but tragedies always seem to strike in twos and threes. Are you sure you want me to continue, Kev?"

It was quite plain to see that Kev was wrestling with his emotions! "We've come this far, so you may as well finish what you were going to say."

Greg turned to me. "Do you remember me saying that there's always a woman's personal vibrator inserted in the end of a Sword of Thos, Nev?"

How could I forget anything that he'd just told me? "You reckoned there was a vibrator in the end of Daphne's, but you never said that *they all* had vibrators in the end of 'em."

"True – I omitted to say that, Nev. All Sword of Thos dildos are packaged with a woman's personal vibrator to insert in the end of it. Down the eye, so to speak. What precipitated the further tragedy is that Sword of Thos dildos are hollow. Logically this's to reduce its weight on account that the instrument itself is just under a metre long. Notwithstanding that, Dragan's brace and straps are still compulsory to protect the wearer's back. . . There were several unfortunate equations coming into play. The actual compartment that holds the personal vibrator is the unit's Achilles heel. The outer skin is made of materials that contain carbon nanotechnology. In other words the outer skin of the Sword of Thos dildo is as tough as the materials used for the wings of Boeing 787 Dreamliners. Even so Dragan's not certain that the skin will last all that long when you consider the likely wear and tear of future use. He knew his dildos would be in for a torrid time – didn't he? Subsequently when Daphne hit the deck, the dual back wheels of a cement mixer truck barrelled over her Sword of Thos, and there was suddenly very intense pressure along the length of the hollow dildo. Then, when you have the vibrator compartment being the weakest part of the structure. . . Look Kev, are you sure you need to hear this?"

"Get on with it!" Kev was far more abrupt.

Greg looked first at Trev, then at me. "You've got ten tons of weight squashing down on the middle of the dildo which is hollow. This causes the inner wall of the vibrator compartment to fail – the vibrator gets launched out of the end of the dildo like a bullet – the same vibrator goes straight through the knee of a female South Korean tourist, only *just missing* a toddler during its flight!"

"You must be kidding!" Kev was horrified.

"I'm not, Kev," Greg assured him. "Not only did the South Korean tourist lose her leg, the entire incident has gone viral across the planet. No wonder Dragan was delighted – orders for his products have started coming in from all over! Unfortunately you can't say the same for the Minister of Tourism. Overseas travellers are cancelling their holidays to Poo Zealand in their thousands. How would you like to visit some country where you have an excellent chance of a personal vibrator being shot at you from close up? People are finding the Middle East a much more plausible proposition!"

I do have something to lift your spirits, all the same, Kev."

"Oh yeah, and what's that?"

Greg was still compassionate. "There were quite a few lesbians that attended Daphne's funeral in the town of Mosgiel. That's next to the city of Dunedin. As the coffin was being driven in the hearse along the main thoroughfare of Mosgiel, Gordon Road, people could see the Sword of Thos dildo lying in state atop the coffin. It was a bit the worse for wear, if not quite flattened in the middle of it, since the back dual wheels of a cement mixer truck ran over it when Daphne landed in the street outside of the apartment building. Mercifully her body wasn't run over as well! That wasn't the most touching part of the funeral – was it, Kev?"

"What was?" Kev still hadn't fully recovered from what he'd heard.

"It was what Daphne achieved previous to her death – wasn't it, Kev?" Greg continued to be gentle with him. "She'd formed an association with other lesbians who had bad backs from utilising larger and larger strap-on dildos. When the coffin was carried out of the church on its way to the cemetery – with the Sword of Thos still riding on top of it – there were six fellow lesbians carrying it on their shoulders. . . And then we witnessed the final and most symbolic tribute – Kev! Standing four aside just outside the front door of the church was a guard of honour! Rather than holding up the customary swords or batons, they were holding aloft their partners' favourite strap-on dildo. Some could lift them up with one arm, while others had to employ both arms. Four out of the eight had Sword of Thos models! That being so, the general public were able to see Dragan's back brace in action on account of a Channel 3 film crew recording everything. You simply can't hold up a Sword of Thos for long if you don't employ a back brace and shoulder straps etceteras. . . There was perhaps one person at the funeral who didn't get *any real* joy from the occasion. It was Daphne's father, Damien. He was perfectly straight, and was aware for some time that Daphne's mother was bisexual, and that he couldn't compete with the garlic liverwurst sausage the woman across the street was utilising. I think he was. . ."

"Did I hear you right?" Kev brought him to a halt. "What do you mean – garlic sausage?"

"Perhaps I should explain?" Greg conceded. "It was a garlic liverwurst sausage. You should be able to get them in any supermarket. You know – the ones with the plastic skin. I think polony sausages are more common, and they have a red plastic skin. Some people call them 'knobs'. I think that's quite appropriate when you consider what Daphne's mother and her lesbian lover were doing with them. . . Can you tell me how Damian found out about it, Nev?"

Greg had caught me out again. "Seriously wouldn't have a clue, mate."

Greg became more businesslike. "Being a straight, heterosexual man, Damian was partial to a bit of cunnilingus from time to time. Like you Aussies put it – munching on a furburger or a bearded clam. You know what I'm talking about, Trev – that glorious taste of raw Atlantic oysters that were born and raised in the mighty Benguela Current. With the background perfume of fresh, farmed Tasmanian salmon. Bringing yourself as close as possible to Paradise while you shuffle backwards and forwards along this mortal coil. The gate to Heaven, and everything presented in the most majestic manner via the agency of God's greatest creation – a woman! The divine portal that ensures the continuation of mankind. All men have entered life via this magnificent gate and all men – or at least most of them – have spent their lives trying to re-enter it. . . Come on – Trev – you'd know what I'm talking about."

I certainly knew what Greg was talking about! While Trev had most likely indulged in cunnilingus dozens of times, I'd never been given the pleasure and was desperate to change that.

Greg swapped such a beautiful subject for a far less appetising one. "It can't be the same for gay blokes and their anilingus. For starters the smell must be nauseating in comparison to cunnilingus, then again maybe the person who's performing the anilingus can put one of Dragan Milošević's patented rubber clothes pegs on his nose to cope with the stink? . . . It's still not the same, though – is it guys? Instead of feasting on the taste of salty Atlantic oysters, you're more than likely to come across what's left of the bangers and mash from the day before, or minted peas and bacon rind. The residue from a breakfast omelette, the odd piece of partly digested pumpkin skin or carrot. Maybe even a fingernail that's completely survived the whole digestive process. I've heard grape pips are almost impossible to absorb, as well as pomegranate and guava seeds. I suppose..."

"Whatsa guava?" Kev was intrigued.

"A guava – Kev? It's similar to a pomegranate when it comes to seeds, but it has a much softer outside skin. I came across them in South Africa. You have the outside skin and a layer of flesh, and then most of the interior is comprised of seeds which are generally passed on untouched by any gastric juices. You could always tell when baboons had been raiding your guava trees because their stools were mostly made up of the seeds in pristine condition once the sun had dried them out. Tricky little seeds that can be caught up in any tooth cavities. . . Then, of course, there's the brown moustache and possible e coli bacteria to contend with. Especially if you'd just met the other bloke in a public toilet and have no idea of what he's recently been up to, or whether he's been eating pomegranates, grapes or guavas. Hardly a very pleasant scenario – don't you think, Nev? . . . Now, getting back to Damian, and how he found out about his wayward partner. Whenever he partook of cunnilingus in recent times, on every occasion his wife's fanny reeked of garlic – not farmed Tasmanian salmon. That was most strange, for she hated garlic, and accordingly it was *never* on her breath. The woman across the road always had garlic on her breath, and she was forever offering people garlic liverwurst sausage sandwiches. So it didn't take long for Damian to put two and two together. Perhaps if Damian's wife's lover had used a polony knob, it might've taken him longer to wake up to what was going on? . . In a way he was grateful for that because his wife's breath was taking on the same proportions as that of a spotted hyena somewhere in the Serengeti, and that was despite *it not* smelling of garlic. . . The sole highlights for him on the day of his daughter's funeral were the drinks and meal at the Crofters Arms Hotel. A truly magnificent pub that was just down Gordon Road from the church. Even that was somewhat marred, since only women's rugby was on the pub's big screen – the Black Ferns! He told the barman that some of the female rugby forwards must've had muscles in their shit, still I'm sure he only said that on account of being surrounded by so many women with far too much testosterone throughout the day. The barman, who played in the Taieri Eels senior team, said that more and more highly talented players were leaving the Taieri Club, seeing that they might be picked one day to play for the All Blacks. What they dreaded most was that the Black Ferns could challenge the All Blacks to see who the better team are, and that a competition just might be compulsory due to the powerful feminist movements that have taken over every sport in Auckland and Wellington, plus all over Australia. Can you imagine anything more daunting?"

"Hey – Greg?"

"Yes – Nev?"

"You reckoned that these Swords of Thos were the second biggest dildo? Which ones are the biggest?"

"So you *have* been paying attention all along, Nev!" Greg was elated. "Tell me, Nev – have you ever heard the American expression – Jesus – H – Christ?"

I had. "I've heard it a couple of times."

"Terrific – Nev! Dragan's largest model is the 'H Clarke.' Not Jesus – H – Clarke. Just H Clarke. The package for this dildo's very expensive, so only the wealthy can afford them."

"Why are they so dear?"

Greg gave my question some thought. "It's the sheer size, Nev! You can't fit one in an ordinary car or utility. It can only be transported around the place by a truck, and then you need a mobile crane to load it and unload it. That's been the problem on the West Coast where some H Clarkes are on trial. There's a pair of lesbians at a little place called Kumara who're testing one out. I'm not sure if the town's named after the Maori spud or not. The trouble is that this lesbian couple are on the move a fair bit, and they're having difficulty carting the prototype H Clarke around with them. Hiring a truck to carry it from A to B isn't too much of a hassle – it's having a mobile crane available at the destination to lift it off. It's the West Coast we're talking about which is still back in the Dark Age. The only way forward that Dragan sees, is supplying the dildo with a truck that has one of those HIAB cranes mounted on the back of it, or possibly a forklift on a trailer towed by the same truck. . . He's advertised a service where an H Clark can be hired for the night, and his company can take care of the transport logistics, but you'll be amazed at how attached some women are to their dildo – test model or not. They just can't hack the idea of it being employed to pleasure another woman, and besides that there's the chance of the spread of sexually transmitted diseases. It sounds like a dildo and truck with a mounted HIAB crane package is the cheapest way to go. I'm not sure if it'll be a success or not."

"Greg?"

"Yes, Trev?"

"What the fuck has all this *ever had* to do with a turd being found with frogs and snails in it?"

Greg's eyes lit up. "I'm quite relieved that you asked me that, Trev, as it's crucial to understand the pitfalls that my Department of Inner Health rort has to circumnavigate. Also it's nice to get away from the imponderables that might arise from same-sex marriages. Let's return to the PM? Other than her enthusiasm for placing West Coast natives in cages, plus feeding them peanuts and pieces of carrot, it's been very difficult getting anything concrete or worthwhile from her, for she's too preoccupied with the elections and being accused of having too many front teeth, which is so similar to more than a few West Coasters. She was also very much on her guard after someone told her that a previous female Labour PM had been accused of being related to someone from the Coast due to her unusual tooth configuration. . . As I've more than amply demonstrated how the work ethic of normal bongos can delay things, there's no question of considering the employment of West Coasters on account of the fact that too many of them are different to normal people. I've given you a graphic example of this when I described Dragan Milošević's rise to fame and fortune. As I also mentioned, it was only possible to dampen the PM's passion for a zoo by pointing out that a National Party PM would most likely be given the task of cutting the ribbon when it was finally opened. . . Fortunately, however, I seem to have more access to the PM's ear than most. Not as much as Bob, her toilet cleaner, but more than the brain deads in her cabinet and those sycophantic toadies hanging off her apron strings. She's taken with my idea of creating a very expensive, new government department, and that it's more than likely that the Nats will be left with no choice but to find the money to pay for it. She agrees that the word 'health' is seductive to the countless thousands of retired civil servants who're sitting back enjoying larcenous government pensions. Then, of course, she recalled how a former female Labour Party PM had purchased New Zealand Railways and how that became an albatross around the necks of the incoming National Party. . . You'll find a rather tragic footnote to all this, gents."

"And what's that?" Trev asked him

Greg's look was downcast. "A couple of evenings ago as we were leaving the Beehive in the PM's BMW limousine, she insisted that she couldn't be related to West Coasters since after all *she was* Poo Zealand's Prime Minister. Although I agreed with her instantly, it came as quite a struggle. When you consider the fact that baboons such as Paul Keating, Kevin Rudd, Robert Mugabe and

Tony Blair have all been prime ministers – and you can have people like Tony Abbott as a leader of the opposition – the choice of a West Coaster for PM in Poo Zealand could hardly be referred to as 'out of the ordinary'. Where I expect I might've cheered her up somewhat, I could've suggested that if she's *indeed related* to West Coasters, she most likely has blood ties to the British or Danish Royal families. You only have to take a look at that Prince Frederik to have sympathy for poor Mary, and you can easily detect several similarities that Prince Charles has to more than a few West Coast natives. And that's not mentioning Andrew and Edward. Poor old Andrew – does he look like he's any good at sucking toes? Perhaps that's why Fergie played away from home? . . . Let's be grateful for small mercies all the same. At least Harry looks more like James Hewitt, rather than his dad. Unfortunately you can't say the same for Prince William, though he does have a beautiful wife like his mum. . . I'm certain I stopped myself just in the nick of time!"

"Stopped yourself from what?" I wasn't happy with him leaving things there.

"Thank goodness I didn't say that the PM could be related to the British Royals. How would you like someone suggesting that you might be related to Prince Charles or either of his sons?"

"I can't take any more of this," Trev put a forefinger in each ear.

"We're just coming to the best part," Greg said loudly enough for him to hear.

"Hang on a sec', Greg." I'd also had enough. "Righto, so the Aussie scientists found Kiwi snails and frogs in the turd that was left in the Octagon at Dunedin. Then you go off in another direction talking about a zoo and putting West Coasters in it. After that you take us to Nelson where some war crim's got a haemorrhoid cream factory and is going broke. Following that you told us how the Indians have out-shagged the native Fijians, and they ended up with an Indian prime minister. You reckon the same's gunna happen in Aussie and over here. That's if the Chinese don't out-shag the Indians first. Then you show us some newspaper cuttings showing how piss weak the Canadians and Poms are. If that wasn't confusing enough, you then went on to say how Dragan

Milošević made a fortune from being a bearded transvestite, and helping queers. . . What happened when it was discovered that there were Kiwi snails and frogs in the turd?"

"Very well then, Nev," he reluctantly agreed. "I'm just trying to make certain you have all the details. . . Having the PM's confidence, I was determined to dissuade her from the idea of blackmailing the French. Word got out via ASIO that the French Admiralty was considering scuttling their fleets in Cherbourg, Brest and Toulon in order to render the New Zealand Navy's blockade pointless, however the wives, mistresses and girlfriends of all the captains and crews boarded the threatened French naval vessels, and pointed out quite rightly that the ships themselves would make unique pot plant holders that would draw visitors from far and wide. Or similar to the zoo I mentioned being built on the West Coast. That same French naval fleet had another lucrative sideline going – didn't it, Kev?"

"Oh yeah?" Kev's face was blank.

"Yes, Kev!" Greg was exuberant. "When France started rebuilding her fleet after the Second World War, there's been a fierce rivalry between the three main naval bases – Brest – Cherbourg – Toulon. You'll never guess what the competition's all about, Kev."

Kev gave me a haunted look. "Now you're really starting to pull my dick – Greg! Like Trev and Nev said – *why are you* telling us all this?"

"Oh, *I am* sorry you feel that way," Greg's face was a portrait of contrition. "What started out as a bit of fun at the naval base at Toulon, has become a fierce inter-fleet struggle. On one of the ships – I think it was a helicopter carrier – the crew possessed a Belgian dwarf as a mascot. While other ships had cats, llamas, monkeys, parrots, a Madagascan lemur – plus even a Zimbabwean night ape that looked identical to Robert Mugabe – as their mascots, this chopper carrier had a Belgian dwarf. . . So, with the French Admiralty being very hesitant about letting ships out into the open sea or international waters, the crews throughout the fleet were becoming bored. True they'd been highly trained when it came to shouting 'Down with England and *Vive La France*,' and the various coastal defences were expert at keeping an eye out for approaching British battleships, life aboard their navy vessels polishing the cannons and swabbing the decks was becoming a real drag, plus morale was as low as it was just after the Battle of Trafalgar. . . Well then, and similar to Napoleon, it was a Corsican who dreamt up the idea of how to restore self-esteem throughout the French fleet. It was his brainchild that the Belgian dwarf on his chopper carrier should be put into an empty wine barrel made of French oak. Can any of you imagine why?"

I spoke up for all of us: "No."

"I thought as much, Nev," Greg looked triumphant. "It was so that the barrel could be fired from one of the ship's depth charge launchers. Then – and this explains everything – a challenge went out to the entire fleet to see who could fire an oak wine barrel the furthest with a Belgian dwarf in it. Quite surprisingly the French Admiralty seized on this with delight. Although it meant having to find dozens of Belgian dwarfs, at long last they saw an easy, plus not too unpleasant method of keeping the ships' crews both focused and amused. The problem was that it was necessary to find a Belgian dwarf for all the ships that were equipped with depth charge launchers. Even more complicated – it was compulsory to install depth charge launchers on every navy vessel in the fleet in order to avoid a mutiny."

"And I take it that these were male dwarfs?" Trev eyed Greg with suspicion.

"Of course, Trev," Greg hastily agreed. "Nevertheless, sometimes it's quite hard to tell for certain the sex of some of them when you take into consideration this weird same-sex business. . .This brings to mind that MARRIED AT FIRST SIGHT that's so dear to you Aussies. Nev, have you. . ?"

"And what a fuckin load of shit *that has* to be!" Trev almost spat the words out. "Trust the fuckin' Danes to invent shit like that? All you get are pathetic nobodies who'll sell their arses in order to get on Channel Nine TV that's only capable of serving up puke. I wonder if these dickheads reckon they're bloody film stars or something? They're just demonstrating to the world that they've got fuck all pride! What do they do – shag like buck rats when they go on honeymoon? Does the audience get to hear if the bride likes to take it up the arse? Do they get to find out that the groom can't hack her breath and actually prefers blokes? Soon the audience will be wanting to watch 'em *actually doing it* on the TV."

"Aussie society's fucked – I tell you!" Kev was also incensed. "It makes a mockery out of dinkum marriages and vows. Trev's right – these people have got fuck all pride. Same as the sheilas you see on that programme THE BATCHELOR. Does the sheila who gives the best blow job win the competition? Does that put her first in line? Can you imagine being the fathers of these women – watching 'em behaving themselves like that in front of thousands of people? It's absolute bullshit!"

With that coming from Kev, I'm *now convinced* that he's been corrupted by Merl!

Greg was probably keen to change the subject: "Let's return to the French – shall we? They might be notorious for biting and pinching in rugby, but no one can accuse them of not being gentlemen – garlic breath or no garlic breath. Nevertheless, there've been feminist organisations all over the place objecting to male-only dwarfs being fired from depth charge launchers in oak barrels. Like in male games such as cricket, rugby and footy, the feminists are demanding that female Belgian dwarfs should be included. Now that we've sorted that, I have to point out that finding volunteer Belgian dwarfs proved to be quite difficult for the French Admiralty. Fascinatingly enough, even today a large number of them can be found living near the gay bars in the Vatican that're very popular with so many of that city's incumbent and resident clergy. Apparently the Vatican's inundated with gay Catholic priests who have a penchant for dwarfs! Not just Belgian dwarfs, but Romanian, Albanian and Bulgarian dwarfs as well. All the same – Belgian dwarfs *are* the most favoured amongst them. What I find most fascinating is that a good many of them – especially the Bulgarian dwarfs – are always found loitering outside Cardinal Pell's palace that the Aussie Catholic parishioners so kindly bought for him. I assume with all the rumours floating around back in Oz about your George, these dwarfs might think they'll come across a swimming pool somewhere in the same palace? . . . Tell me, Trev, have you heard the term 'press gang'? Also, where did it originate?"

Like Dave Wheeler back in Kalgoorlie, Trev was a mobile encyclopaedia. "It come from when the British sent gangs to round up men and force 'em into serving in the military. Mostly into the navy."

"Top marks, Trev!" Greg applauded. "You can understand the difficulties the French Admiralty came across. Not only did the dwarfs have to be Belgian, they also had to be the exact same weight, and so did the oak barrels. French issue depth charge launchers are all identical, so naturally a heavier dwarf and barrel can't be launched as far as a lighter one. While it's fairly straightforward making the barrels the same size and weight, naturally it isn't the same with the dwarfs. This's where the French press gangs not only had to clandestinely kidnap Belgian dwarfs, they were also given the task of ensuring that they were all delivered at the same weight. I won't go into the frightening details of how they fattened up some with the Foie Gras method whereby they stick pipes down their throats and force feed them with Poo Zealand mutton pies and mud cake. And I won't appal you with the sweat boxes they forced on the fatties. Let it be said that there'd be one almighty hue and a cry if the world's do-gooders get to find out about it. Let it suffice to say that a blind eye's being turned because the dwarfs being so horribly treated are to all intents and purposes Belgian. . . Can you explain that one, Trev?"

"Fucksakes – Greg!" My younger brother was *truly* flabbergasted! "How the. . ."

"No – no – don't let it worry you, Trev!" Greg urgently intervened. "It's all to do with the EU. Okay, so the EU's headquarters are in Brussels – right? The Belgians have long since realised that they've had nothing worthwhile to contribute to the organisation, so perhaps turning a blind eye to the French Navy using Belgian dwarfs for amusement might just appease the French taxpayers who have to prop up crappy little countries like Belgium, the Netherlands, Slovenia, Romania and the Republic of Ireland. I won't bother mentioning Greece. Let the French have as much fun as they like if the French and German taxpayers are prepared to keep the EU financially afloat. Especially with all this talk of Brexit. . . A huge amount of pleasure the French public are getting out of it too, Trev! To them watching Belgian dwarfs being hurled into the air creates as much amusement as the guillotining of King Louis XVI and Marie Antoinette did for their ancestors. Naturally betting on the outcomes of the competition *is involved*, and logically and unfortunately you've got Indian and Paki match fixers, plus bookmakers trying to distort the whole process. A pity don't you think, Trev?"

"Like when the Pakis rigged that no-ball caper?" I'd heard of Paki sport corruption more than once.

"Indeed – Nev – indeed! And the French Navy unwittingly assists those swindlers – doesn't it, Nev?"

"How do they do that?" I stupidly urged him on.

"It more or less goes back to the days of Nelson, Nev. That was when the British Navy ruled the waves, and when the French Navy's ships bolted in the opposite direction whenever a sail appeared on the horizon. I suppose it was very similar with Spanish contemporaries. Plus you must factor in that the French Navy spent most of its time in port being blockaded by the British Navy. That's why a fair few of France's modern naval ships still use the muzzle loader cannons and the round cannonballs. They've always had a huge surplus of them on account of the British blockades. French ships weren't given the opportunity to fire those same cannons and cannonballs at the English Navy's ships, so what's the point in installing the latest weaponry when you've got hundreds of muzzle loading cannons and thousands of round cannonballs in mint condition? . . . So what do you get when you've got unfired cannonballs rolling around all over the deck, Nev?"

I decided to adopt Trev's approach. "I'm stuffed if I know, Greg."

"It's quite easy to work out for yourself, Nev," Greg wasn't really satisfied with my reply. "First you've got the omnipresent Paki and

Indian match fixers involved. After that you have dwarfs being put in French oak barrels and fired into the air by depth charge launchers. The weight of the oak barrel and the dwarf is crucial, so what happens if some roguish fellow puts some cannonballs along with the dwarf in the same barrel?"

"It wouldn't go so far or high," Kev answered for me.

"That's it precisely, Kev!" Greg was all approval. "The French Admiralty only woke up to it once dwarfs were being drowned in all the naval bases. Previously the oak barrels were floating long enough for both them and a dwarf passenger to be retrieved, but once cannonballs were added it was a different story altogether. Sadly it's mostly Romanian dwarfs that've drowned."

"I thought you said *only* Belgian dwarfs can be used?" Trev literally pounced on Greg.

Greg was ready for him. "Agreed – Trev! Yes, of course, there was other cheating going on, similar to what you have when French rugby players run onto the field. Due to the huge demand for dwarfs amongst the clergy in the Vatican gay bars, you'd hardly get a dwarf of any nationality volunteering to be hurled into the air by a depth charge launcher. Except for maybe Romanian dwarfs. What with Romania being so backward – EU member or not – there are applications sent to Paris by dwarfs from all over the country. Especially the capital Bucharest. Sadly, gents, that's where the French Admiralty might be more than a little corrupt. They have to find a Belgian dwarf for every ship in all the fleets, otherwise – and as I've mentioned before – there could be a mutiny if some of the ships can't compete. Unlike the Canadian soccer players, the French like to compete in sport, if not in war. They're lovers more than warriors – aren't they, Trev? Little wonder there what with French women being so beautiful and desirable. Similar to your Aussie sheilas. Also, and to be truly fair, it was a visiting member from the British Admiralty that actually came up with the idea. The British have always had a low regard for the Belgians and Romanians, and see very little difference between them.

Although I'm sure that the Belgians would object to be mistaken for Romanians, and the Romanians vice versa, the British actually do have a rather valid case. . . Regardless, and to get to the point, it was suggested that Romanian dwarfs could be substituted for their Belgian counterparts, and this did actually happen on more than a few occasions with some of France's naval ships. Especially the ships that were issued with muzzle loading cannons and round cannonballs. . . It turned out a calamity, though – didn't it, Nev?"

"Because they used Romanian dwarfs rather than Belgian ones?" I asked him in return.

"You've got it in one, Nev! Actually it raises several moot points. Take for instance you Aussies. You refer to each other as 'arseholes' quite regularly, yet no one seems to take any real umbrage at that. However, when you refer to one another as being an 'Arab' – it quite often leads to fisticuffs. . . So perhaps you might have some compassion for the Belgian dwarfs? Personally I. . ."

"What about this calamity?" Trev could see that Greg was wandering off again.

"And it was truly a disaster, Trev! Once it was decided that Romanian dwarfs should covertly be substituted for Belgian dwarfs, the ships which received the former became sloughs of despond. To begin with money, jewellery and other valuables belonging to the crew began to go missing. Worse than that, human stools were being found all over the ships – in the galley pantry – the ship's laundry – the officers' mess – under the captain's bunk – even the forecastle! . . . If only the French Admiralty had taken note of what's happened after Romania joined the EU. In countries like Sweden and Denmark – and even Switzerland which isn't even a member of the EU – people have seen national crime rates in all EU countries multiply ten thousandfold. You can blame that on them allowing Romanians to come flooding in. Then, when you consider that the bulk of Romanian citizens have no idea what a toilet is – no wonder the Romanian dwarfs believed they could poop wherever it took their fancy on those French ships. Little wonder again that the French admiralty refuses to join in NATO naval exercises. You don't need sophisticated radar to find French ships – you can smell them coming from *whole oceans* away. . . Actually when you come to think of it, that's most likely why Belgian dwarfs are more popular in Vatican gay bars than Romanian ones, even though they'll have a Romanian one if pushed – the lusty fellows! I understand that in Southern Ireland the Christian Brothers and Catholic priests prefer orphans rather than dwarfs, though pigmies from the Ituri Forest have been seen in Dublin Parish from time to time."

"I don't know where to get you to start, Greg," Trev was at a total loss one evening at the Speights Ale House in Ashburton, a dairy farming town not far south of Christchurch. Greg had been up in Wellington for ten days or so, and after our last conversation there were quite a few unanswered questions. Trev battled on – all the same. "So what's happening about this supposed French sabotage business?"

Greg wasn't sure where he'd left off on that particular subject. "The French saboteurs, Trev? When it comes to that, I think you can be certain that I saved the day for both Poo Zealand's and the PM's prestige. I could only achieve that by being rather harsh with the latter. I brought to her notice that Poo Zealand was fast building a reputation of paying scant attention to its endangered wildlife. Not that long ago there was the slaughter of one of the world's rarest birds – the *takahē* – in which a government department was instrumental, and the same department could've decimated the Powelliphanta snail population which was still shrinking day by day. And what about the tiny Hochstetter's frogs, gentlemen? Plus the fact that a North Islander's DNA was found along with the snail and frog DNA? I could've gone on and insisted that she recall the fact that thousands of native eels were dying in Lake Ellesmere due to an unrestricted inflow of thousands of tons of cow shit, but that's a totally different story altogether. I use the term 'shit' reluctantly, so now you might have some notion of why the subject upsets me? I think it's about time that the UN or whoever should take the Poo Zealand government to task about their woeful conservation practices and record. If you think I'm not being serious, feast your eyes on this, my good fellows."

Out of Greg's briefcase came another newspaper article.

GUNFIGHT AT MOTUTAPU ISLAND, CONSERVATIONIST HUNTERS HIRED BY DEPARTMENT OF CONSERVATION BLOW AWAY FOUR OF NEW ZEALAND'S ENDANGERED TAKAHĒ BIRDS WITH SHOTGUNS!

Four critically endangered birds were shot and killed on Motutapu Island by conservationists after a case of mistaken identity.

300 takahē exist worldwide, while 21 can be found at Motutapu sanctuary, where the four were devastatingly shot. The department has stopped the cull and an inquiry into the matter is under way with 5% of the wild population slaughtered from the incident

The department of conservation hired a group of hunters, known as the Deerstalkers, to carry out the cull of pukeko, a non-endangered bird that poses a major threat to the rare takahē in the region.

The president of NEW ZEALAND DEERSTALKERS ASSOCIATION (NZDA), whose hunters were responsible for the killings, said he was appalled by the error. "I share with the department a concern that the deaths will affect efforts to save an endangered species," NZDA president Bill O'Leary told a reporter.

The rare takahē birds were killed by shotgun pellets when they were mistaken for the pukeko bird, a common, aggressive bird that had been slated for culling by New Zealand's Department of Conservation.

A department spokesman told local media that hunters had been carefully briefed on how to tell the difference between pukekos and takahē and were instructed to only shoot birds on the wing. Pukekos can fly while takahē cannot.

The government will now call on several committees to hold an investigation into the incident.

MISUNDERSTANDING OF BRIEFING OR
MISTAKEN IDENTITY OF SPECIES?

Comments made by Liam O'Doherty brought to light several observations with regard to the takahē slaughter on Motutapu Island. Mr O'Doherty is president of the WEST COAST MOASTALKERS ASSOCIATION *(WCMA) which has members that are positive that they have come across moas on the way back home from the pub in towns such as Haast, Dunollie, Ikamatua, and Reefton. "If you're using shotguns to shoot any bird, why shoot them on the wing, when aiming for their heads is far more humane?" Mr O'Doherty questioned the Department of Conservation's instructions. "If you shoot them only on the wing, you might just injure them because that's where they have the thickest and the strongest feathers. A head or full body shot is the better way to go about it.*

"Also, I heard that most of the birds were shot while they were flying. Why wait for them to take off, if you can get them on the ground? If it's in the tussock country it can be quite difficult finding the bodies if you haven't got a dog. Also, what's the big deal about shooting takahēs? If you go after the pukekos, you'll always get a much bigger bag, as you should find a lot more of them. Also, if you keep shooting takahēs, there won't be many of them left before long.

"The Department of Conversation should have hired WCMA to do the job. People have forgotten how we helped DoNE count the endangered keas around Arthur's Pass in the Southern Alps. They were having trouble identifying them in the forest, so their tally was compromised. That's why we shot most of the keas we could find, so that any numbers could be calculated more accurately."

A devastated member of PREVENT OUR GOVERNMENT FROM SLAUGHTERING ENDANGERED SPECIES (POGFSES) *pointed out that whenever you choose organisations which have members with Irish names, there is quite often the possibility of catastrophe or the material for some sad and unfair Irish joke. She went on to add that back in Ireland feuds between the O'Learys and the O'Dohertys were fairly common given that one of the O'Doherty patriarchs joined the side of the British and King*

William at the Battle of the Boyne while the O'Leary's were on the side of the Jacobites. She said this was typical of West Coast culture and that's why West Coasters took so much pride in their treachery towards one another.

'So what's the PM gunna do if she gets voted out?' Kev asked Greg. "If you reckon she's good at singing that song of hers, she should enter that world song contest" That was the old Kev that I was familiar with and loved. Not the one contaminated by that foul smelling, fat-arsed Merl!

"Now you'll understand why the PM confides in me," Greg, too, was touched by Kev's sympathy for the Labour PM. "That's why I went to all that trouble to tell you about Rosemary and Gerry. Being typical Aussies, they're going to take her under their wings if she's allowed to join that convent in Nogoyá, northern Argentina. A picture of her smiling has been sent to the Vatican, and she's waiting to hear back if a person with so many front teeth will be allowed to join a barefoot or discalced Carmelite convent. If the information I have is correct, having all those front teeth could come in mighty handy at the convent in Nogoyá. The same Mother Superior's still in residence, but I don't know for how long, and she thinks that if the PM's front teeth can be painted bright green with luminous paint, it would be one way of scaring away the randy Irish Christian Brothers or local Argentinean Catholic priests that can be seen hanging around her nuns like putrid mould. Especially after dark, that is. Now you can see why she kept the convent gate locked at all times. . . I tell you what, though."

"What?" Trev would've broken Mum's heart if she heard of his terrible manners.

Greg didn't seem all that put out. "I've thought of another brilliant scheme."

"And what's that, Greg?" Kev was far more polite.

"Do you remember how we were discussing that MARRIED AT FIRST SIGHT garbage?"

Kev looked like he'd been handed a shit sandwich. "Bloody puke – that's all it is."

"Yes, it is – isn't it?" Greg agreed fully. "With all this latest talk amongst the politicians of legalising same-sex marriage, it looks like it's inevitable both in Oz and Poo Zealand. . . You mentioned the other day, Trev, what may happen when male sports stars marry other men. I'm thinking of starting up an identical TV reality show where you have gay couples getting married at first sight. Where mine will be different is that the audience has to guess who the 'Mummy' figure is and who's the 'Daddy' figure? Or who's the groom and who's the blushing bride? The show can supply the audience with the odd hint or two. With the males – and I don't know if the terms 'male or 'female' will be acceptable for much longer in Oz – they can be interviewed after the honeymoon night. Close up camera shots can be taken of them when they go to sit down, so that the audience can see which one winces and which one doesn't, or which one might have a pillow feather in the corner of his mouth. Or possibly in his hair. . . This's where I'll need expert cameramen. There I go again referring to a male. . ."

"You're being serious – aren't you, Greg?" Trev couldn't contain himself any longer.

"You can bet your life – I am, Trev!" Greg powered on. "We're going to have to learn to assimilate same-sex marriage into our society. It might be harder gathering hints on the females, since one would assume that both would be the recipients in one way or another. With the *women* – and I'm not certain that that terminology will be allowed for much longer in Aussie – you don't have the rectum-stretching that you have with the males. That's unless the recipient prefers to be accommodated by her partner anally. We have so much everyone will need to take the time to consider. . . Hold on – I tell you what! How about the females being asked to raise both arms? There's the chance that you can identify the 'Daddy' figure by the amount of hair growing in armpits, or the tattoos of anchors on shoulders?"

"And you reckon you'll make a quid out of all this?" Kev sounded suspicious.

"You can be assured of that, Kev! Having spoken to the majority of the politicians around the Beehive – both Labour and Nats – they were all enthusiastic about my idea. So much so they're going to call for same-sex marriage to be legalised if the matter's put to the vote. I just fear that I might've precipitated something that we as a *supposed* civilisation might eventually regret. I can't help thinking about what happened to the Greeks and Romans."

That opened a door for me: "We gotta a driller back in Kal, Dave Wheeler, who knows a thing or two. He reckons a civilisation's fucked when you've got blokes shagging blokes and sheilas rooting sheilas. Specially if they're marrying each other."

Greg bit his lip. "He may be right – Nev – he *just may* be right!"

CHAPTER 6

My siblings and I finally managed to visit Dunedin, the South Island city that Greg had mentioned on many occasions. I wasn't all that impressed with the place; still the visit gave me much to be cheerful about. Greg's mission was to have a clandestine meeting with some mysterious individual in order to promote his Department of Inner Health, while Kev, Trev and I came along for the drive more or less as tourists. Our visit didn't start out all that propitiously. We arrived in the evening and booked into the Southern Cross Hotel which had also accommodated Rosemary and Gerry, Greg's two West Aussie constables. Our first night was comprised of Trev having a threesome with two fairly large female Dunedin natives in his hotel room. Kev being very worried because he couldn't make phone contact with Merl; me losing eighty bucks on the pokies and at roulette in the Dunedin Casino; Kev, Greg and me trying to down a drink from every bottle on the shelves in one of the local bars.

The upshot of that was Kev, Greg and me having skull-splitting hangovers, and Trev wasn't much better off because he'd drunk almost a full bottle of Captain Morgan Rum in order to be able to accommodate the 'bungarra' breath of one of the threesome participants. Also, knowing Trev, he would've drunk all that rum to finish the job on the lass with racehorse goanna breath! I've never known him to leave such a task undone!

It was Greg who suggested that we should take in some fresh sea air; so following his instructions I steered his Mercedes onto the Otago Peninsular that was roughly opposite Dunedin itself. We were some way along the peninsula when I suddenly started having cramps in my guts!

At first I was rather nervous on account that I'd consumed a gallon or so of Speights Porter, plus the score or more other drinks that we'd drunk at the bar. That was mixed up with some foul smelling, takeaway Hungarian goulash that was purchased at some Romanian fast food outlet. It was shithouse! Both the beef and the cream tasted putrid, and I was sure they were off, but I was hungry and drunk, so somehow managed to get it all down. Anyhow, it haunted me every time I belched from then on. More or less feeling guilty about my liver, I'd also taken half a dozen or more Vitamin Bs before flaking out on the bed, so I knew that should I break wind, it most surely would be accompanied by the most unpleasant of consequences!

What the heck? I knew that if I was to fart, it would upset Trev the most. Kev and Greg would just be collateral damage. It was rather chilly outside, so all the vehicle's windows were up and the heater was on low. Near perfect conditions!

Bluddie – bluddie – Hell! Just an average fart, that made not the slightest sound, caused *absolute* havoc! I was certain that the Speights Porter and the goulash had joined forces with the vitamin Bs in order to precipitate the most horrendous of outcomes! Greg was in the back seat behind me, and he was literally hanging out of the car window puking his heart out! Kev was bellowing at me to stop the car, while Trev was also spewing out of his window; all the while trying to call me the worst names his rum-befuddled brain could think of!

Fortunately I found a side street and was able to pull up. Kev was the first out, and he started to chunder on the bitumen. His huge shoulders heaved as he was wracked by spasm after spasm! That started Greg dry reaching and staggering around on shaky legs, while I found it quite difficult keeping the Mercedes between me and my younger brother. It was Kev who managed to utter the first words: "Whoever done that needs to go for a shit. Seriously you're gunna. . . "

"It was you – you fuckin' arsehole!" Trev pointed a trembling finger at me.

Like Rosemary and Gerry I was totally inured to one of my own farts, therefore I was far more composed than he was. "Don't talk fuckin' shit!" I bounced back at him. "The same smell's been on your breath all morning. What – did you kiss one of those beached whales you shagged last night?"

Finally things settled down, and for some reason or other we ended up at the Dunedin Aquarium/Portobello Marine Laboratory.

The outset of our visit to the aquarium itself caused quite a stir because the first exhibit was a massive tank that had baby sharks in it, and it was necessary to lean over the sides of the tank to see them. The tank was also full of shark shit; the odour of which – plus an additional fart on my behalf – meant Greg, Kev and Trev having to take turns at visiting the Gents shithouse. In their entirety they vacated that facility wiping their mouths and noses with toilet paper.

Eventually a guide, who claimed that she was born on the Otago Peninsula, came along and we were a group of eleven people who followed her into the main building. One of us was an absolute stunner; the most delightful redhead that was the owner of divine legs! The way her cute little arse cheeks were stashed away in the skimpiest of pink shorts did wonders for my hangover! Then there were two adult couples that were either Indians or Pakis. They were quietly chatting away in some language that I certainly had no chance of understanding. Finally there was a couple in the group that also stuck out more than the others. One of them, a middle aged woman, announced to the guide: "Hi good people – my name's Lindy and this's my husband – Jahrn. We're Canadians and we came out on the cruise ship that's docked at Port Chalmers. This's an incy wincy country you've got here, though it's quite cute all the same. Having come from Canada it seems so tiny. You could fit both the North and South Islands in just one of our provinces. Things are done much bigger in Canada, but then we have much more space, don't we. This aquarium's quite good when one considers the limited resources you have."

There was no doubting that the rather mildewed woman and her husband were Canadians; as they both had red and white caps with a maple leaf emblazoned on the front of them. There were red maple leaves on both front and back of their white T shirts, plus their bum bags and short white socks were similarly adorned. As Greg pointed out – they had *nothing* really to be that proud about.

Red maple leaves on white T shirts struck rather an uncomfortable chord with me. Possibly with Kev also. A few days before we were going for a stroll along Queenstown's lake front when we saw two blokes sitting on a bench. Not only did they have white T shirts with red maple leaves on them – they were actually kissing! They must've been enjoying themselves, for they had erections bulging out of their shorts! After witnessing that, both Kev and I needed a fair slug of Bundy Rum and an explanation from Greg: "There's nothing unusual about it, gents, what with all this same-sex marriage being legalised in the West. Soon it's going to be legal here, so you'll just have to come to terms with it. I think it'll be a while before AIDS or some equally deadly disease catches up. If the blokes were kissing and not doing you any harm, I wouldn't give it a second thought."

While I managed to put the incident out of my mind, it wasn't difficult to see that Kev was deeply disturbed by it. After seeing those Canadian tourists carrying on, and with all the talk of same-sex marriage being just around the corner in New Zealand, it was easy to deduce that he was truly troubled. So was I, and I could only put that down to the upbringing our parents gave us in a conservative place such as Boulder.

Not long after we were driving alone into Queenstown in the Holden ute, and my elder brother opened up a fraction when it came to his true feelings. He was missing Mum and Dad, plus the rest of the family dreadfully. He was even missing *the boss!* He said he wished that Merl and him could be back in their house in Dugan Street, and that she didn't have so much money. If only she could love the things that he did; the huge expanse of the outback; catching yabbies in a pastoralist's dam. The goldfields' magnificent sunsets and lime green dawns. Now that she was so rich, Merl had banished any thought of having any kids. *He was calling his lotto winnings HER money!*

Anyhow, once we got into the aquarium building itself and were walking in amongst the glass fish tanks, we were regaled by the same Canadian tourist whose husband was most likely named John, but she pronounced it 'Jahrn': "Oh Jahrn – look at the starfish! Doesn't it remind you of our first class cruise down the west coast of the States and Canada? "Oh Jahrn – is that a seahorse? Don't we have bigger ones back home in Vancouver? Yes, I'm sure Canadian ones are much bigger. Oh Jahrn – doesn't that blue and orange fish remind you of the cruise we took to the Caribbean? We were lucky to get a first class cabin on that voyage with the ship being so crowded. Jahrn and I are some of the most well known and frequent sailors with the cruise company, so they weren't going to allow the ship to sail until they'd found us a first class cabin."

Finally we were led outside again and the best part of my sojourn in Dunedin began *right then*! Parked not far from the back door was what looked to be some kind of a submarine. It was yellow and our guide claimed it was a very good replica of a deep-submergence vehicle or DSV. It had been named after some sheila by the name of Betty Batham. Either way, visitors in groups of up to fifteen people could enter the DSV and a thick steel door would be closed behind them. Following that the submersible would take the passengers on a fifteen-minute virtual dive into bottomless sea canyons in order to introduce some of the amazing animals that live in the deep sea. We'd have total darkness bar the video screen!

I realised then and there that I'd been presented with a God-given opportunity that would probably be available *only once in five life times*! It was as if the planets had been lined up! Oh holy-moly the angels in Heaven were actually smiling down at me! It was obvious that on some occasion in my life I'd done something that might've pleased the hosts in Heaven, and I was being rewarded? Or perhaps in another life? Here was an opportunity to demonstrate to the world that *I was gifted with certain* talents! I might be the middle member of three brothers – plus described as being 'mediocre' – regardless I was still unique! It was my day! Not Kev's – not Trev's – not Greg's – *it was my day!* It must be the same as winning lotto? Like an Olympian winning several gold medals? It was an opportunity that Nick Lovadina would've gladly traded his right hand for!

As I'd done previously in Greg's Mercedes, I weighed up the ramifications of letting go a fart. I knew I'd also need to be careful because when I broke wind at the shark tank, it was carrying an uncomfortable amount of moisture in it!

Furthermore, there was the noise to consider, as I didn't want the gorgeous redhead to know it was me. I fully expected Trev to go crook at me; consequently I must make sure that I accused him first. It may've worked in the car because Greg and Kev couldn't be certain if it was Trev or me who was responsible for the first outrage. Most important of all – I knew I *dare not* laugh! That would be a dead giveaway!

After we'd all entered the replica submersible and the steel door was shut behind us, we were *seriously left* in total darkness! It was vital to act fast before the video came on. I managed to let go a fair bit of wind, but it was compulsory to stop on account of the moisture content.

There was no way of anticipating the reaction I was given! Trev: For bloody Chrissakes – Ne – ev!"

The mouldy Canadian Sheila: Jahrn – Jahrn – what's that terrible smell – Jahrn? I think I'm going to be sick, Jahrn!"

I was delighted. The smell was being described as *terrible*!

Greg was equally distraught: "Can someone let us out?"

I heard a splashing sound as someone puked, and the stink from that made a useful ally to my fart!

"Jahrn – Jahrn – get me out of here – I can't breathe – Jahrn! Jahrn – Jahrn – *do something!*"

"I'm trying to find the door handle, Lindy," her hubby tried to reassure her.

Trev sounding quite alarmed: "Where the fuck's the door?"

"Jahrn – Jahrn – I'm feeling faint! I can't breathe, Jahrn!"

Greg: "Can someone *please* let us out?"

There was more coughing and splashing sounds, and that time the chunder really stank! The downside of that was that the stink of the additional spew caused my own stomach to eject the portion of Hungarian goulash that it had *simply refused* to process!

Finally the iron door was opened, and there was a stampede into the sunlight! I didn't get to see how the redhead had fared, and it wasn't necessary to accuse Trev because she went striding purposefully towards her car, and that caused her pink shorts to rise up her magnificent bum cheeks! The way her backside wobbled from side to side, and when the lower parts of her bum cheeks started to protrude from her shorts, were items *absolutely magnificent* to the beholder! It was far more appealing than the shattered look on Greg's face. There was foamy dribble in his beard and down one side of his smart tweed jacket, and Trev was staring at me like he wanted to kill me very-very slowly! More astounding – he was speechless!

With a mixture of brown, yellow and orange all over the maple leaf on the front of her T shirt, the big mouthed Canadian sheila looked as if she'd encountered the Grim Reaper himself: "Take me back to the ship – Jahrn! I don't think I can take this horrible little country anymore – the people are so uncivilised! I couldn't breathe in there – Jahrn! I'm not leaving the ship till we get to Brisbane!"

What I found most odd was the behaviour of the Indians or Pakis. The two women and one male had formed a group and they were venting their spleens on the remaining male at the top of their voices in the car park! Perhaps he'd also farted in their hire car on the way to the aquarium? I was pleased with that because just possibly Greg, Kev and Trev might think it was him and not me who'd farted? After all, there *was* a fair bit of chunder down *my own* shirt front. Most importantly – I hadn't let Nick, the Speights Porter, the vitamin Bs and the Hungarian goulash down!

Fortunately the harbour side hamlet of Portobello had a great hotel and bistro which sold icy cold Speights Summit Lager, and it was most important to down a couple of pints as a hair of the dog. We were soon laughing at Greg's: "Jahrrrn – Jahrrrn – I can't breathe Jahrrrn! I think I'm going to be sick, Jahrrrn! I can't take this place any more – Jahrrrn – the people are so uncivilised – Jahrrrn!"

He added to all the mirth when he professed to have seen a cookiecutter shark on the submarine's video that sported *less front teeth* than the NZ PM!

I most likely gave myself away, for it was imperative to make a bolt for the Gents in order to discharge the remainder of the rotten Hungarian goulash from my nether regions. When I rejoined my companions, I felt a red herring was well in order: "How you going with your Department of Inner Health?" I zeroed in on Greg.

He appeared pleased that I'd asked the question. "Splendidly – Nev – splendidly! All the same we have a committee of powerful public servants who we need to convince, then it should be plain sailing after that. There are five in this committee – a bisexual woman – a real religious bitch, plus a gay bloke who's married to a woman that's a mover and shaker in the public service on the West Coast. And then we have yours truly – Gregory Shepherd – who can't vote because it's all my idea, plus a real..."

"How come the gay bloke's married to some sheila?" Kev broke in.

"When you see his missus, you'll understand why he's gay, Kev. I wouldn't be surprised if he's the star in one of Dragan Milošević's movies. With him living on the West Coast, I'm sure the two must have met. . . He likes other men's bottoms, Kev. He gets a horn every time he goes past a Gents shithouse. . . Okay, so there are two blokes and two sheilas we must win over. The other bloke's seriously corrupt and a dickheaded, hypocritical bastard to go with it. He's the least of our worries, same with the gay bloke. It's the religious bitch and the female bisexual creature that we need to convince because the religious specimen will most likely fight us every inch of the way. Never mind, she'll immediately be pushed to one side if we have a majority vote in our favour. . . Yes, with the gay individual – we've well and truly got him by the short and curlies."

"How come?" I was still confused.

"Because of an Indian cobber of mine, Mulji Singh. This poof, Ken Mears, is a born and bred West Coaster and has a real fetish for Asian blokes. Especially young teenage Indians that're becoming fairly numerous in both Auckland and Wellington. Indians from India, not like cowboys and Indians, Nev. Yes well, it's Mulji who's setting Ken up with young Indian queers. It's quite pathetic, really, because Ken's fallen head over heels in love with this young Indian teenager, Kumar Naran. Kumar's a cunning little prick and has taken just about every last cent off of him. And, on top of that, he's been dishing out some real serious discomfort."

"How's he doing that?" Trev almost echoed me.

Greg laughed. "Ken's into young Indian blokes' bums – right? Kumar has to hand over his arse in order that he can milk the poor bastard, so he's eating the hottest Indian curries he can find. Curries which contain about eighty percent chillies! These same chillies are going straight through to his arse and then they're ending up in the eye of Ken's dick – thus burning the crap out of him."

"Bullshit!" I prodded.

"I'm being absolutely serious, Nev!" Greg eyed me sideways. "You can always tell when Ken's inserted his donger up Kumar's ring hole because he goes around with weepy, bloodshot eyes and a runny nose for days after. So would you if you had *Chocolate Bhut Jolokia* or 'ghost chillies' – all the way from Assam – up the eye of your old fellah and coated around your figs. Chillies that're easily four hundred times hotter than Tobasco! . . . My mate Mulji managed to get a photo of him chockablock up Kumar, so now you know why we don't have to worry about his vote. Okay, poofs are very trendy here in Bongoland. Under Kiwi law and in political circles throughout Wellington it's almost compulsory to be one, however Ken's wife's father is even more powerful in the bongo civil service. All in all a tangle of useless turds – all squirming around each other in the same chamber pot."

"Okay, so what about this bisexual sheila?" Just the thought of her being a pervert of some kind had obviously pricked Trev's sordid imagination.

It was as if Greg could see into his head. "I wouldn't even dream of trying to throw my leg over her. Nor would you, Trev, if you saw Helen Granite. Even Nev here wouldn't go near her with a long stick with a sharp point on the end of it. You probably think I'm. . ."

"Bloody crap!" I stopped him. "What kind of a name's that? Isn't granite a name for a kind of rock?"

Greg touched the corner of his mouth and nodded. "You've a penchant for saying 'bloody crap' – don't you, Nev? I'm not pulling your tit – her surname's Granite, and it suits her right down to the ground. She's in her late fifties and bigger than Kev, but all fat. You quite often see her at the prestigious Backbencher Pub and Cafe in Thorndon where she needs a stool for each of her arse cheeks when she sits at the bar. She's

Kiwi public service royalty born and bred, and also has a mansion in Thorndon a couple of blocks away from Merl and Kev's. I reckon, no – I know for a fact – that she's earning three-times more than any politician with the public service scams she's into. Also, she'd be more powerful than the PM herself. Trouble is, she's as cunning as a shithouse rat, so you'll need to get up real early in the morning if you're thinking of putting anything over her – let alone your leg. Nonetheless, my mate Mulji and I are working to a plan."

"What plan?" He'd really started to grab my interest.

"Like with a good few of the influential public servants in Wellington I've come across, it's her sexual needs, or perhaps perversions, that we need to take aim at. Wellington's a regular Sodom and Gomorrah, especially with the country's public servants that occupy just about every storm drain and sewer. Like I said, Helen's bisexual, so we tried to get some young, sexy hooker to suck her in, but we couldn't find a hooker in Wellington that was game enough to go anywhere near her. In Auckland neither. Regardless of the price! We then found out that Ms Granite used to be on a six-figure consultancy racket a decade or so ago with the WHO. No, not the rock band, Nev – the World Health Organisation. She was representing Poo Zealand's contribution to the organisation, so just like any senior bureaucrat who works for organisations like the WHO or the UN, she was flying all over the world first class – camping in five star hotels – chomping on the best tucker and slurping down the most expensive grog. All expenses paid by the Kiwi taxpayer. It was actually a cousin of Mulji's in Tanzania who gave us the inside oil. Apparently our good Helen, plus some old West German biddies who were also working for the WHO, had a passion for flying to Mombasa or Dar es Salaam on the east coast of Africa. You'd never guess why they liked spending so much time there?"

"Wouldn't have a clue," Trev agreed with him.

"It was because they could find local black blokes on the coral beaches with massive schlongers. You know – big dicks – zoobs – dongers – schwanzers! Penises, if you want to be socially acceptable. Yeah, big –

black – schlongers! Seriously, she went tripping backwards and forwards dozens of times, at the Kiwi taxpayers' expense, to Kenya and Tanzania, and even Zimbabwe and South Africa, in search of black puddings. She only gave it away when two of her German buddies died of AIDS. By some miracle she never caught the virus herself, although she liked the black blokes to ride her bareback at full gallop under the palm trees on the white coral sand. . . So this's where we're going to have a go at her."

"How you gunna do that?" Kev's interest was also captured.

Greg just grinned. "If it's a big, black donger she *must have* – we've decided to find her one here in Bongoland. I've got Mulji working on it right at this very minute."

Kev, Trev and I were finally able to meet Mulji Singh about a fortnight later. He was a heavyset Indian bloke with a dark blue turban, and he announced that he was a Sikh. He also claimed to be just turning forty-five, but I reckoned he was a fair bit older than that. There was a frosting of white in his black beard; he had an incredibly genuine smile and a tomahawk nose, plus he was easily a good six foot one inch tall. He was wearing what looked to be a very expensive, navy blue, pinstripe suit and a silk shirt and tie, while on his left wrist was a solid gold Rolex watch that most definitely wasn't a Bali fake. His dark red Mercedes S-Class V12 was scarcely a replica, either.

Apparently Greg had met him in Kenya when Mulji and his family were kicked out of Uganda by Idi Amin. What was most interesting about him, though, was that he showed us a photograph of a nude, skinny, lanky blackfellah that was sporting a donger that must must've been at least a foot and a half long! Or maybe more than thirty centimetres! It was easily a minimum of nine and a half centimetres thick at its base, and he owned a foreskin that dangled down probably four or more centimetres off the end of it!

"Bugger me – it can't be real!" Kev was the first to express his disbelief.

"Fuck me dead!" Trev was even more aghast. When he finally managed to settle down, he studied the picture more carefully. "His dick would weigh the same as the rest of his body! How the hell would he have enough blood in him to get it up?"

"Yeah, and I reckon if he could get it up, he'd go pale like a white bloke from all the blood draining to his donger," Kev was certain. "This sheila, Helen Granite, who you were talking about. If he got it into her – he'd split her right up the middle."

"Goodness – gracious – me!" Mulji beseeched Greg. "We do not want to hurt Helen. Kevin is right. We do not want any harm coming to her."

"I doubt if she'll come to too much harm," Greg tried to reassure him. "What's more important is that *he can* get it up. He's no bloody use to us if he can't crack a fat. Listen, Mulji, tell him he'll only receive an upfront payment if he proves that he can get an erection. Better than that – make him supply you with another photo where he's got a hard on."

"Who's this bloke?" Trev asked the Indian.

"He calls himself Richard Head," Mulji told him, "but I am sure this is just an alias. From what I have been told, he is an illegal overstayer. He has been trying to hide behind the Sudanese refugee community in Wellington, but the Sudanese people are objecting to this and are threatening to report him to the immigration authorities. Personally, I think he is a Nigerian. I have heard that the Nigerian men are infamous for having large tool kits."

"Just tools – Mulji – just tools." Trev corrected him. "You call blokes' dicks – 'tools'."

"Oh yes!" Mulji nodded with embarrassment. "The English language can be so confusing sometimes. All the same, I am not too sure if this Richard Head can get an erection."

That uncertainty was put to rest the very next weekend. It was unbelievable! Mulji came up with another photo of the blackfellah, and the bloke's dick was fully erect! It seemed to have almost doubled in size, and its head reached almost all the way to his nipples!"

Greg also produced a photo of Helen Granite. There was only one way to describe her – grossly obese and as ugly as a blown-out horse's arse! She was maybe five feet five tall, and it wasn't any sort of exaggeration to say that she was almost the same size across the middle. She was literally like a gigantic marshmallow! She was wearing a gown that reached down to her ankles, so it was impossible to see how fat her legs were. Her head was fat and round, while her cheeks hung down like a bulldog's. Like Merl's! Her face displayed a look of distaste or even an arrogant sneer on it, and her brown hair was short and only just reached the top of her shoulders. She was a big, fat, morbidly obese, obscene grunter!

"Yeah, she's bloody fat!" Kev was in total agreement with me, "but I still reckon this black bloke could do her some serious damage with his donger."

"Nah, she'll be able to handle it," Greg couldn't bring himself to agree. "Even with a schlonger like that, I doubt if he'd make any sort of an impression on the wrinkles around her knees, yet alone her fanny. Seriously, she'd be able to handle something twice as big, and even that wouldn't touch the sides. Even Dragan Milošević's Sword of Thos wouldn't make any impression on her. No, Kev, I'm not kidding you, mate. You should see the vibrator she uses. It's so massive it needs two diesel/electric locomotive engines to power it. I almost shit myself when I saw it. You should've. . ."

"Ah – bullshit!" Kev wasn't having that.

"I'm being fair dinkum, Kev," Greg stuck to his guns. "One of Helen's most lucrative public service scams is consulting to New Zealand Railways Corporation. The fitters in the railway workshops in Dunedin put together a vibrator for her made from an oxygen cylinder. You know – those oxygen cylinders that boilermakers use for oxy-acetylene torches when they're cutting steel. The diesel/electric motors themselves are actually in a shed just outside her bedroom window. She needs that amount of electricity just to kick-start it. Two-forty volts isn't nearly enough, yet alone those lithium batteries. Also, you should hear the racket the vibrator makes when it's going full bore! That's why she has to wear ear muffs and has all the neighbours' dogs barking their jacksies off for miles around! Some of the neighbours dobbed her into the council and to the cops for making such a racket, but that did them very little good. She's on the police funding committee, and a councillor for Thorndon. The neighbours have no choice but to put up with it, even though it sounds like a dozen of the Mongrel Mob going flat out through a tunnel on Harley Davidsons."

"Is this bloke for real?" Kev looked over at Mulji.

"I cannot be sure some times," the Indian looked equally doubtful. "Some of Gregory's stories can be hard to believe."

"Do you remember the power cuts they had in Auckland back in 1998, Mulji?" Greg challenged the Sikh.

"Of Course! How on earth could I forget?" Mulji answered in the affirmative. "I lost a lot of money when that happened. So did my cousins, nieces and nephews, plus my sons-in-law. It was a terrible disaster!"

Greg returned to Kev and practiced on his Aussie accent. "Yeah, you bloody should've seen it, mate! Almost all of downtown Auckland was blacked-out! The city was being powered by four main power cables. Two of these were forty-year-old, oil-filled cables that were well past their use-by date. It just so happened that these same oil-filled ones were buried in a ditch going past Helen's luxury apartment that overlooks Auckland's Waitemata Harbour. . . She's bisexual – right?"

"Yeah," Kev nodded. "So you keep saying."

"Okay then, it was one of her lezzie mates who reckoned they should plug their vibrators into these oil-filled cables. Helen thought it was a bloody bonzer idea, and, as it turned out, she was also on the board of the government's electricity watchdog at the time. I don't know how she did it, but she managed to get two sparkies from the company that actually owned the cables to wire-in their vibrators direct to the same cables in the ditch outside. . . Hey, don't look at me like that, Nev. I'm prepared to swear on a stack of bibles."

I hastily looked away. "I'm not looking at you like anything," I assured him.

"Good!" Greg focused his attention on Kev once more. "As I was saying, Helen and her lezzie mate decided that it was a brilliant idea to plug their vibrators directly into the same cables! There was no actual harm done, and everything would've been just fine if. . . Hang on a sec – let me just explain something first. Do you see how Helen's wearing a long dress or gown in the photo here?"

"Yeah?" Kev was still suspicious.

Greg was comfortable with his answer. "Alright, so you know how some women go in for body piercing?"

"Yeah, it makes 'em look like dickheads!" Kev became quite animated. "Fancy the stupid bitches putting rings through their lips and nipples. It doesn't make 'em look any better. It makes 'em look much worse, if you ask me."

"Spot on!" Greg was eager to concur with him. "You also get women who go around with silver or stainless steel studs pierced through their pissflaps. You've seen. . ."

"What do you mean by 'pissflaps'?" Mulji interrupted him.

"You know, Mulji, the vagina flaps. The Labia Majora or whatever they're called. I've just been using rather crude terminology for the benefit of the Australians amongst our number. . . Helen was also into having her labia majora pierced back in those days – wasn't she? The trouble was her fanny's that big, she decided to use three-inch bolts in order for her lezzie mates to see them! Three-inch thick ones! If that's not gruesome enough, she also had two Jesus nuts – the ones they use to hold the propeller blades onto a Chinook helicopter – screwed onto the ends of the same bolts! That's why she wears dresses all the way down to her ankles. Her labia were stretched so much by the three-inch bolts and Jesus nuts, she's needed to wear them ever since."

"So what's that got to do with the blackout in Auckland?" Trev insisted.

Greg sounded like he was dead keen to explain. "Just about everything, Trev – mate! Helen was busy reaming her fanny out with her giant, six-speed vibrator, when the wires attached to it shorted out on the three-inch bolts and the Jesus nuts! Not only was there this bloody great blue flash that could be seen all the way across the Tasman Sea to the east coast of Australia, but just about all of downtown Auckland was put in total darkness! Like Mulji said – it was an unprecedented disaster! At least twenty city blocks were without power! In the first few days the main street in the CBD – Queen Street – was practically deserted because few businesses could operate without electricity. It was necessary for the electricity companies to install mobile generators in some of the major office blocks, and it took about five weeks before an emergency overhead power cable could be put in. There must've been at least 80,000 people who were stood down at work, and a minimum of three hundred traffic lights were put out of action. The whole of Auckland was in total chaos! Apparently there were forty or more suicides!"

"And you say it was because of Helen?" Mulji looked doubtful.

"That I do, cobber!" Greg agreed with him wholeheartedly. "Having never given a second thought to the consequences of her actions, she was seen walking around after that with a blissful look on her face as if she'd seen an angel. Not just one angel – a whole squadron of them! The 200,000 volts that arced across her pissflaps, gave her one almighty orgasm! The best she'd ever had! . . . Also, do you remember the 2006 blackout that also went down in Auckland, Mulji?"

"Yes, I remember it well, but our family businesses were much more prepared for such eventualities. We had learned our lesson from the 1998 calamity."

"More or less exactly the same thing happened in 2006," Greg informed all of us. "The first thing the electricity company did after the previous blackout was remove the oil-filled cables, so there was a 110,000 volt, overhead transmission line just adjacent to Helen's apartment window. She was actually holidaying in Auckland at the time when she was overcome with an overwhelming urge to try and duplicate the orgasm she'd experienced back in 1998. The high voltage transmission line was just opposite her front door – wasn't it? She tried to get the electricity company to hook her vibrator up to it, but they wouldn't have a bar of it. And that was in spite of the fact that she was one of the most powerful civil servants in New Zealand and could make life hell even for the country's Governor General. . . She soon got by that minor impediment, nevertheless. From what I can gather, she was playing hide the rubber, strap-on donger with a female dairy farmer from the Waikato at the time, who – being a typical Kiwi farmer – was a magician with a coil of number eight fencing wire. In no time flat the two of them had Helen's six-speed vibrator connected to the transmission line out front, using fencing wire. Then, when the three inch bolts and the Jesus nuts came into play, there was another blue flash that wasn't quite as bright as the 1998 one. It had similar consequences, though. Commuter train services were suspended. Some hospitals were shut down and only emergency services were left operating. The radio transmitters in Auckland's Skytower were shut down. No one could get their mobile phones to work, and the end of semester exams being held by local universities had to be postponed. Like back in 1998, it was one almighty balls up! . . . It was soon discovered who was responsible, but there was a Labour government in at the time. It was only through Helen and some of her powerful civil servant buddies that made it possible for Labour to take over government in the first place, so big favours were owed in all directions. I don't know who it was in the Minister of Energy's office that came up with the cover-up story, but it was quiet ingenious all the same. A government news release was given to the media that the immediate cause of the blackout was determined to be a grounding cable falling across an 110,000 volt transmission line at the Otahuhu sub-station. Also that this was caused by the failure of a corroded shackle as a result of unusually high winds. This was total crap, of course, because it was Helen and her mate who threw a length of number eight wire across it."

"Goodness – me!" Mulji was shaking his head in amazement. "Helen was very lucky she did not get into serious trouble!"

Greg begged to differ. "You'll never get into strife in this country if you're a power broker in the Labour government and civil service, Mulji. Helen's come from a long line of Poo Zealand public servants that've more or less held the country by the figs for more than a century now. Her grandfather was civil service, same as her father. What makes her all the more powerful is that she's a woman, and all Kiwi men – including public servants – enjoy having their scrotums twisted slowly by a strong female leader. Surely you've noticed this, Mulji?"

"Yes, I must say that I have, Gregory. It is quite strange, really. In most cultures worldwide the men are heads of the family and most forms of government. It certainly appears that in New Zealand and also Australia men like to be led by a woman. It is most peculiar! It seems that when a marriage has lasted for more than ten years or so in this country, the New Zealand women – I am talking about the white ones – seem to grow testicles while the husbands appear to lose theirs. . . So when are we going to introduce this Mr Richard Head to Helen?"

Greg just burst out laughing. "No need to be so formal, Mulji. We must start referring to him as 'Dick' from now on. Dick being short for Richard. He'll feel much more comfortable if we do that."

"Ah – I see what you are talking about!" Mulji sounded enthusiastic. "Like people call you 'Greg' instead of 'Gregory'? Like Kev – Nev and Trev – here. So from this moment on we shall call him 'Dick Head'".

"And you reckon he's a Nigerian?" Greg's frown was directed at the Sikh.

The Indian shrugged "He is earning spare cash to supplement his dole money by selling drugs on Lambton Quay. Every Nigerian I have come across is either a drug dealer or a pimp, or at least some kind of a criminal. That is if they are not a Catholic priest in Tasmania. It has me at a loss to why countries such as New Zealand and Australia let them enter in the first place."

Greg was all agreement. "Too bloody right, Mulji! Still, we won't tell Helen he's a Nigerian. She'll be much more excited if she thinks he's a Zulu. We can say he's a direct descendant of Chaka Zulu the warrior king. We can also tell her that he's a direct cousin of South Africa's President Jacob Zuma, who's fornicating with and stealing everything that he lays his eyes on. While ignoring Johnny Minto's love of all South African black government officials, our good President Zuma's been siring bastards all over the Republic of South Africa via dozens of women. That should really have Helen's labia vibrating all by themselves!"

"Who's this Johnny Minto?" I'd heard Greg mention him before.

He gave me a wry smile. "He's one of your bongo, quasi-pinko, grand master do-gooders. He and a bunch of his politically correct, BA-toting followers had a very brief moment in the spotlight during a Springbok rugby tour back in the eighties. They reckoned that South Africa had to have a black government, and never mind the corruption, bastardry, murder, genocide, pestilence and mayhem the world has witnessed from a host of black dictators in Africa ever since the 1950s. Now perhaps you'll see what I've been telling you about how certain bongos insist that they know what's good for the rest of the world, yet alone the dickheads they've got over here? He's a real hero our Johnny – him and his merry band. He and a bunch of them decided to have a go at a lone female Israeli tennis player not so long back. You won't catch Minto and those rectum-leaking sycophants of his leaving Bongoland to carry out any protests. They wouldn't have the stomach. They know that the Kiwi cops won't lay a finger on them, and the legal system over here's also made up of a bunch of Mother Grumpling, politically correct, bleeding-heart do-gooders. No, you won't find Minto and his dickheads on the streets in Gaza or the West Bank, or protesting alongside the unemployed blacks in South Africa's slums and squatter camps who've seen their and the children's lives going down the drain after they received independence and black rule. Johnny and those heroes are nice and safe over here – aren't they?"

Apparently the coupling of Helen Granite and 'Dick Head' was a raging triumph, or was as Greg described 'a typical Wellington sex success story'! In no time at all Dick found himself ensconced in Helen's double story mansion in Thorndon, and according to Mulji he became hopelessly addicted to her chocolate mud cakes which were designed to put 'meat on him and bolster his energy'! By all accounts Dick was also a big attraction to a whole host of senior female public servants in Wellington because a photo of his massive donger had been circulated by email to every public service department surrounding the Beehive – New Zealand's parliament executive wing – plus a statement claiming that he was a 'Zulu prince' and direct descendant of Chaka Zulu himself. One of the greatest African warrior kings that had ever lived! In fact he had such an entourage of simpering females following him around, Helen got all jealous and she forbade him from leaving her house period. Whether it was Greg who'd started the rumour mill grinding or Helen, it was passed around that some of these donger-struck women left their husbands, fiancés and boyfriends in order to go chasing after Ethiopian and Sudanese male refugees in the hope that all African men were similarly equipped! I'm not kidding – there were black men from all over Africa who were pleading with the Department of Immigration to fund their tickets home. While quite a few of the Nigerians where making a very lucrative living out selling P or methyl amphetamine, plus other hard drugs to the Wellington kids and 'beautiful people' or 'trendies', they – and also according to Greg – where frantic to get visas for countries such as South Africa and Namibia where they mightn't be able to make as much money selling drugs, but at least they could live peacefully in those countries!

"How would you feel, Nev?" Greg tried to explain. "You're earning a comfy living selling drugs to the bongo kids, and you're being hounded twenty-four-seven by a horde of randy – pear-shaped – foul-breathed – hairy-legged – pale-skinned – freckly lumps of lard. . . Also, have a heart for poor Dick Head. I'd need a far bigger inducement than chocolate mud cake if you were to ask me to throw my leg over Helen. The bloke deserves a medal for bravery. Bloody hell – try and picture yourself waking up to that creature every morning? Can you imagine breathing in her flatus in bed after she's drunk several litres of Speights Porter and had a feed of takeaway Thai curry?"

"Fuck that!" Even Kev thought such a proposition was horrific.

On a lighter note, Greg removed an article from his wallet that he'd printed out that morning. "It appears that I'm not the only person to have determined that your average bongo woman has the most meagre of charms."

THE PRINCE WHO DIDN'T LOVE NZ

As New Zealand prepares for Prince William's visit, Kiwis might be able to learn a lesson or two from a royal visit 90 years ago.

Prince Edward, William's great-great-uncle who gave up being King to marry a divorcee, came to New Zealand in 1920.

He was the royal celebrity at that time, and although New Zealanders adored him, he certainly did not adore them, according to David Colquhoun of the Alexander Turnbull Library.

"(Prince Edward) was pretty close to a nervous breakdown by the time he got to Australia. He was really suffering (when he got to New Zealand)," Colquhoun says.

The Alexander Turnbull Library has several candid letters Prince Edward wrote while on his four-week tour of the country.

It turns out a dance in Nelson put the prince off New Zealand women. "We stuck it out like heroes till the supper and tried to lug those ham-faced wads of women around," a letter says.

He also described New Zealand women as "too amazingly plain and unattractive for words".

He apparently thought Kiwi men were drunks, and he clearly did not enjoy his powhiri. "I've had a terrible day of Maoris and all their comic stunts," he says in a letter.

"Too bloody right!" Trev was obviously pleased with what he'd read. "But at least you were able to call a spade a spade back in those days. Nowadays if a bloke in his position was to speak out – whether it's the truth or not – he'd be in deep shit for not being politically correct! Especially back home."

"I couldn't agree with you more," Greg was always happy with any support.

"Whatsa 'powreeree'?" I sought further clarification.

Greg obliged. "A Pōwhiri – Nev? It's a Maori welcoming ceremony where you get all the thigh and chest slapping with the hakas – the nose rubbing – the googly eyes and tongues being poked out. Like Prince Ted pointed out – horribly tedious!"

It was difficult having conversations with Greg while Kev was around because one always had to be very wary of revealing to my elder brother that there were two agendas being pursued. Not only were we all praying that Greg's Department of Inner Health would be passed by the Labour government, the same equation was going to be used to bring Merl down. The latter scheme, of course, needed to be kept well and truly secret from my older sibling.

"So what's the problem with the other sheila you need to get past? The religious bitch you mentioned?" Trev demanded.

"One of the women on the committee that we need to get the go ahead from?" Greg asked him back.

"Yeah! You've told us about Helen Granite and the queer who likes shagging Indian blokes. What about this other religious sheila?"

"Ah – now I know who you mean!" Greg nodded. "The beautiful Patrice Ramsbottom! Now what can I tell. . ?"

"Bullshit!" I butted in.

"Do you have a problem, Nev?"

"Ramsbottom! You're making things up as you're going along."

Greg touched the left side of his chest. "Cross my heart and all that, Nev. Anyway, you'll most likely get to meet her sometime in the near future. . . Yes – Patrice Ramsbottom! She's one of your classic females from the South Island – chubby – freckly – mouldy – obviously an example of white bongo evolution. Helen Granite and our Kenny Mears are way up the food chain when it comes to dear old Patrice. The only reason why she's serving on one of Bongoland's highest public service committees is because of her wealthy mother's support for the Green Party. Seriously – don't get me to comment about the Green Party. A bunch of whackers! Not only is our Ms Ramsbottom an atypical female bongo career public servant with an ego the size of the Southern Alps – she's a total dickheaded – dead useless – bleeding-arsed – do-gooder – greenie spastic! She's also one of those types who works in high security prisons and falls in love with the lowest forms of swamp life that can be found in them. She says she's found religion and can save the souls of murderers, child molesters and rapists if she gives them a blowjob. You take her latest episode when she fell in love with Haki – 'Point Two-two Bullet' to his mates – Hakaraia. This unsung hero was given life for kicking his mistress to death with his steel toe-capped, bikie boots. Previous to that, he punched his wife so hard in the head that she's now stone deaf and has no sense of taste or smell. Big man and much respected in the bikie gangs. Especially when it comes to his aptitude for administering grievous bodily harm to the female gender. . . Also, let's not mention that he's native to the Pacific Ocean. And our dear Patrice fell head over heels in love with him – didn't she?"

"Righto, so what happened?" I gave him a nudge when he stopped talking. "Why was he 'Point Two-two Bullet' to his mates?"

Greg opened a packet of smokes first. "Yes well, he wasn't called 'Point Two-two Bullet' because he was handy with firearms or whichever. It was because his dick was so small that his mates claimed it looked like a point two-two bullet. Exact same calibre and length. . . Anyhow, Patrice was on the prison parole board of Bongoland's only specialist maximum security prison – Paremoremo – when she came across Haki, and apparently she's been described as being very proud of taking the time to get to know some of the country's most dangerous and perverted criminals. Some say that she hangs around prisoners' cells like a dirty smell. As I pointed out before, she's a lass with very meagre charms. . . Nonetheless, our Patrice was besotted with Haki or 'Point Two-two Bullet' Hakaraia. He'd only served twelve years of his sentence, but I told you Patrice's mum has a huge amount of influence in party politics – didn't I? When Patrice announced that she and Haki were getting married, almost half of his sentence was commuted there and then – wasn't it? While she'd shagged and given blowjobs to most of Paremoremo's most brutal and sadistic killers – each of whom were proud owners of schlongers that would make a donkey envious – her heart was stolen completely by Haki despite the size of his tiny member. Maybe it was his tribal tattoos or Ta Moko that turned her on? Who can tell? Mind you, there were those on the staff at Paremoremo Prison who reckoned that

Haki possessed a twelve-inch tongue and could actually breathe through his ears, although...”

“Now you're *really* pulling our tits!” Trev pulled him up sharply.

Greg just shrugged at that. “I'll prove everything I've said in due course, Trev. Seriously – I kid you not. To tell you the truth – I feel quite sorry for Patrice, now that I come to think of it. . . She once possessed a black miniature poodle called ‘Strudel’ – didn't she? No, I'm not pulling your leg, Nev – she used to call it ‘Apple Strudel the Poodle’, or ‘Strudel’ for short. You might think that's pretty corny, Nev, but she thought the name was rather clever. It *is* when you come to think that a bongo civil servant with a BA degree thought it up. Yes, Strudel was clearly very dear to her because she told Haki that when they got married, Strudel would be the main witness to the happy event. She was most insistent about that. If Strudel took a shine to Haki, the marriage would've been created in Heaven. . . How could Haki disagree? He was having his sentence for murder cut in half – wasn't he? Okay, so the first time Haki and Strudel got to meet each other was at a rather inauspicious moment. It was barely half an hour before the wedding ceremony itself was supposed to take place. Haki had left the front gate of Paremoremo Prison hardly two hours before then, as that was one of the stipulations of his parole board. As soon as he left the prison, he needed to marry Patrice within three hours, otherwise he'd be violating his parole conditions. Some might say that Patrice manoeuvred all this, but we've no solid proof of it. At any rate, as soon as Haki left Paremoremo, he had to pay a visit to his old bikie gang headquarters. The reason for that was twofold. Firstly, it was necessary for him to pick up a black silk shirt and some faded blue jeans that were favourites of his, and then secondly – that was where the bridal limousine would be picking him up in order to take both him and Patrice to the registry office. When I say ‘bridal limousine’ it was actually a Ford Zephyr Mark 2 that belonged to one of his bikie gang mates. I think the bloke's name was Willie Harawira, but don't hold me to it. He was going along as Haki's best man, while a female prison officer was going to meet them all at the registry office and go as Patrice's bridesmaid. Willie was seriously proud of his car – wasn't he? The vehicle's paintwork was in mint condition, plus the seats were done out in light blue, suede leather that most likely cost Willie at least five years' profits from selling methyl amphetamine or P to school kids in Auckland. When I say 'five years' profits' I mean exactly that. The Chinese are the major methyl amphetamine and P barons in Auckland, and the commissions they pay to bikie gangs are very miserly indeed. The Chinese also control the majority of the sex trade. . . Let's not worry about that, guys. The plan was that Willie would first collect Patrice and Strudel from Patrice's mum's place, and then they'd pick up Haki at his old bikie gang's headquarters and go as a party to the registry office. What they hadn't really counted on was the pit bull/Rhodesian ridgeback/Rottweiler pig hunting dog that belonged to the bikie gang's Samoan master-at-arms! Actually it was rather big for a pit bull, so maybe its pit bull father snuck up and had his way with a female Rottweiler or a Rhodesian ridgeback when she was sleeping? Who cares a damn? It doesn't really matter. . . Can you picture it, Kev? Haki steps out of the bikie gang's fortified headquarters, all prim and proper in his black silk shirt and denim jeans, plus the steel toe-capped bikie boots that he used to kick his girlfriend to death with. You could still see the faded stain from her blood on the boots and the bottoms of his jeans, although nobody was going to let such a trivial matter spoil that joyful day – were they? The boss of the bikie gang, his Samoan master-at-arms, and several gang members shook Haki's hand warmly and insisted on getting a kiss from the blushing bride through the open back window of Willie's Ford Zephyr. There was only a mild spot of tension when the younger brother of the bikie leader pulls his donger out. He had a massive hard on – didn't he? Jokingly he points out to Patrice what she could be missing out on. Nobody knew if he was wanting her to compare his old fellah to Haki's tiny member or not because the bloke was slightly retarded from taking too much P – wasn't he? If it hadn't of been for him being a bit backward, Haki might've taken offence – not so? Especially when Patrice subconsciously licked and puckered her lips! . . . But that wasn't the case – was it? If the entire gang was to roger our Patrice, it would've meant very little skin off Haki's nose. Besides, he and every member in the gang knew that he was only going along with all this matrimonial bullshit because it was a way of getting out of Paremoremo Prison. He didn't give a single rat's toenail for Patrice – did he – the poor, pathetic creature that she is? . . . Okay, so while all that was going on, no one actually noticed that the master-at-arms' pit bull/Rottweiler pig hunting dog had just surfaced from his afternoon siesta – did they? That pig hunting dog was lord and master of all he surveyed at that bikie gang headquarters, and he didn't take too kindly to poncey, pussy poodle dogs trespassing on his home turf – did he? Sorry, guys, but what transpired after is just too awful to tell you."

"What ya talking about?" Kev sat bolt upright. "What the fuck do you mean – you can't tell us?"

"Yeah – come on – Greg!" I backed my elder sibling up. "You can't stop now."

Greg stared forlornly at our surroundings, then coughed gently into his hand. "Very well then, gents. If you insist that I must. . . According to the bikie gang's master-at-arms, his dog Hone – pronounced 'hoh-nay' – didn't have any intention of causing any *real harm* to Strudel. All he wanted to do was scare the shit out of the queer-looking stranger – not bite or savage him. And that's *precisely* what Hone did when he leaped up at Patrice's car window! His eardrum bursting barking totally frightened the living crap out of poor little Strudel! So much so that he literally rocketed around the car – a stream of dark brown liquid jetting out of his arse! There was dog shit all over Patrice's white velvet bridal gown, plus it was squirted all over the light blue suede leather seats in the back and front of Willie's Ford Zephyr! From all accounts Willie wasn't too charmed at all! What he objected to most was the stink! Strudel was a pedigree miniature poodle with all the appropriate paperwork, therefore some sort of an aristocrat in the canine world. Not some common mongrel like Hone the pig hunting dog. That's why Patrice allowed him to be fussy when it came to his tucker. He'd only eat fresh lamb's liver and raw chicken giblets – not so? And these – having fermented and putrefied in his guts – were bound to stink – weren't they? Especially when Patrice had given him half a bar of milk chocolate to calm his nerves when Willie came to pick them up at her mum's place. Because of all the excitement of the day, she'd forgotten that milk chocolate gave Strudel the squirts. . . Can you envisage what the interior of Willie's Ford Zephyr must've been like, guys? Apparently there was even a halo of shit across the ceiling of the vehicle! . . . Nonetheless, all was not lost. After swabbing out most of the dog shit from the Zephyr's rear seat and roof, Haki went with Patrice and Strudel back to her mum's place so that she could change her soiled white velvet gown for a red satin evening dress. On the way they picked up a couple of the largest bottles of Blue Stratos aftershave lotion they could find, and they sloshed the contents over the back and front seats of the car in order to try and get rid of the stink of dog crap. Willie reckoned that he might be able to get the dark brown stain out of the same leather seats if he used a stainless steel wool pot scrubber, plus a shot of crystal meth injected into his vein soon soothed his feelings somewhat. They were running late for the registry ceremony, however Patrice's mum phoned the celebrant and everything was put on hold. It was while Patrice was changing into her evening dress when her mum saw how agitated Strudel was. The poor little bastard was still shivering with fright because of that obnoxious bikie hell hound – wasn't he? Perhaps some milk chocolate might settle him down?"

"You're bloody kidding – right?" Trev became almost as worked up as Kev had just been. "And you just reckoned that milk chocolate gave him the shits?"

Greg leant forward to agree with him. "That's exactly what I said – Trev – old buddy! The stupid, dumb, half-witted, Green Party supporter gave Strudel half a bar of Cadburys milk chocolate – didn't she? The other half of the bar that Patrice gave him previously! Haki and Patrice only got to find out about it when Willie was just steering his Ford Zephyr into the car park of the registry office. Strudel spied a woman walking along the pavement with a dainty female Chihuahua on a lead – didn't he? . . . Well – but did the shit fly in all directions after that! And I mean that in every sense, Trev! Apparently Strudel was still highly strung from his meeting with Hone the pig hunting dog because he did at least another half dozen laps around Willie's Zephyr and managed to spray shit not only over Haki's black silk shirt and Patrice's red evening dress, but all over Willie's leather car seats and roof for an unbelievable *second time*! . . . Things happened in a blur after that! Possibly still under the influence of the crystal meth, Willie underwent a personality change – which comes with the drug P – and he spun round in the driver's seat of the Ford Zephyr to take a swing at Haki's head. Haki ducked, so the punch landed fair on the side of Patrice's temple – thus knocking her out cold! Haki jumped out of the vehicle clutching Strudel by the throat. He then punted the miniature poodle – a torpedo punt that would make any All Black fly-half or fullback proud – and the shitty-arsed mutt was never seen again once it landed on the roof of the registry building!"

"On the bloody roof!" Kev was instantly taken aback. "So what happened next?"

Greg seemed keen to continue. "By that time Haki had really had a total gutsful of Patrice and miniature poodles in general, so he left the scene and decided to visit his ex-wife who he'd brutally beaten up so many years before. It appears that tragedies do indeed come in threes because he bumped into his ex-mother-in-law who was a bit of a rough diamond as far as Pacific Island women go. She told him to 'fuck off and try and grow a decent-sized dick!', so he broke her lower jaw and leg in three places. . . You aren't required to be a genius, gentlemen, to figure out that he's back behind the walls of Paremoremo Prison with an extra five years tacked onto the remainder of his original sentence. He might never get out, for he's vowed to all and sundry – that should Patrice come anywhere him – he'll squeeze her head until her brains squirt out of her ears and eye sockets! And the prison wardens know he's just the bloke to do it! . . . So perhaps you now know why she's so hard to get along with, Trev?"

The smell of coffee and Greg's laughter were infectious. Snobby percolator coffee was becoming a very dear friend to me, and I was beginning to really enjoy his company.

"What's so funny?" I asked him.

"Do you remember that bleeding-heart, quasi-commo-pinko Johnny Minto that I've mentioned to you previously, Nev?"

"Was he the one who was involved in the protests against the Springboks?"

"Just the man, Nev! He's a great one for writing open letters in the newspaper. Take a gander at this."

He opened the morning's paper, and I read the article that he pointed out.

OPEN LETTER TO THE PRESIDENT OF SOUTH AFRICA

I understand a nomination has been put forward for me to receive a South African honour later this year, the Companions of O R Tambo Award, on behalf of HART and the anti-apartheid movement of New Zealand for our work campaigning to end apartheid in South Africa.

I note the particular honour is conferred by the President of South Africa and awarded to "foreign citizens who have promoted South African interests and aspirations through co-operation, solidarity and support".

We are proud of the role played by the movement here to assist the struggle against apartheid and I appreciate the sentiment behind the nomination. However after the most careful consideration I respectfully request the nomination proceed no further. Were an award to be made I would decline to accept it either personally or on behalf of the movement.

New Zealanders who campaigned against apartheid did so to bring real and meaningful change in the lives of South Africa's impoverished and disenfranchised black communities. We were appalled and angered at the callous brutality of a system based on racism and exploitation of black South Africans for the benefit of South African corporations.

However while political rights have been won and celebrated, social and economic rights have been sidelined. It is now 14 years since the first African National Congress government was elected to power but for most the situation is no better, and frequently worse, than it was under white minority rule.

The number of South Africans living on less than $1 a day more than doubled to 2.4 million in the first 10 years of ANC government. Despite strong economic growth, overall poverty levels have not improved and the gap between rich and poor has increased with many black families being driven more deeply into poverty. Unemployment remains high at around 26%.

It seems the entire economic structure which underpinned apartheid is essentially unchanged. Oppression based on race has morphed seamlessly into oppression based on economic circumstance. The faces at the top have changed from white to black but the substance of change is an illusion.

None of us expected things to change overnight but we did expect the hope for change to always burn brightly as people looked ahead for their children and grandchildren. This is now a pale gleam, dimmed by the destructive power of free-market economics.

My own country New Zealand preceded the ANC in adopting free-market economic reforms. Since 1984 we have experienced a particularly virulent dose of these vicious policies which have brought wealth to the few at the expense of the many.

Hundreds of thousands of New Zealand families have been driven out of decent employment into poverty where they struggle to raise families on part-time, poorly paid work. They are worse off now than they were 20 years ago. The same policies have brought the same outcomes to South Africa. For the majority life is tougher now than at any time since the ANC came to power.

The promises made by those who drove through the reforms in New Zealand were a lie just as they are in South Africa. Wherever these policies have been put in place anywhere in the world they have resulted in a reverse Robin Hood – a transfer of wealth from the poor to the rich.

When we protested and marched into police batons and barbed wire here in the struggle against apartheid we were not fighting for a small black elite to become millionaires. We were fighting for a better South Africa for all its citizens.

I take heart from the many community groups in South Africa fighting against privatisation of community assets; supporting settlements against forced removals; opposing police harassment and brutality; struggling for decent healthcare, water supplies and education; campaigning for decent pay, reasonable working conditions and affordable houses. These people, such as the Durban Shack dwellers, are looking for respect and dignity as human beings. Many carry the ideals of the Freedom Charter, once the bedrock document for ANC policy, close to their hearts.

Apartheid was accurately described as a "crime against humanity" by the United Nations and the ANC. I could not in all conscience attend a ceremony to receive an award conferred by your office while a similar crime is in progress.

Receiving an award would inevitably associate myself and the movement here with ANC government policies. At one time this may have been a source of pride but it would now be a source of personal embarrassment which I am not prepared to endure.

John Minto

Greg guffawed again. "What did he honestly expect? Like I also mentioned before – Africa's always been overrun with murderous dictators and thieving black governments. Since the ANC took over in South Africa, the country's heading in exactly the same direction as Zimbabwe."

"Yeah, but what's so funny?" I couldn't fathom his amusement. "It looks like the blacks over there are really getting a bum deal, and they're far worse off."

That just caused him to laugh all the more! "Same as the blacks all over Africa! The thing that's so hilarious is that the black South African government *never had any intention* of giving good old Mintie an award in the first place! Here's the ANC's response to our dear Johnny's letter."

SOUTH AFRICA DENIES AWARD OFFER FOR ANTI-APARTHEID ACTIVIST
Anti-apartheid activist John Minto is adamant he was in line to be offered a prestigious award by the South African government, despite the office of President Thabo Mbeki denying Mr Minto was ever nominated for such an order.

On Monday Mr Minto published an open letter to President Mbeki, in which he said he understood he had been nominated for a Companion of Oliver Tambo award.

The honour, named after a prominent anti-apartheid campaigner, comes in three classes and is awarded to foreign nationals for services towards and friendship to South Africa. New Zealander Trevor Richards is a past recipient of the award.

Mr Minto said he was proud of the campaigns the Halt All Racist Tours organisation he was part of staged against apartheid, but said no real progress had been made in the past 14 years to improve the lot of ordinary South Africans.

In response, President Mbeki put out a statement which said Mr Minto had not been nominated for any of South Africa's national orders.

"Don't you see what's so hilarious?" Greg's eyes were bright from laughing. "It looks like Mintie's gone public and refused to accept an award *that no one intended to give him* in the first place! If I was him, I'd feel like a real knob-licker. Even your average bongo in the street will come to think he's a bit of a dickhead after this. . . That's what's so typical of your run-of-the-mill Kiwi. You know that Susan Boyle? You know – that Scottish singer who's done so well after that British talent show?"

Of course, I'd heard of Susan Boyle! "Yeah, I know who you're talking about. She's got a bloody good singing voice. Kev bought her CD and reckons she's got another one coming out any day now. I reckon I'll buy it when it comes out."

"Too right, mate – she can seriously sing!" Greg agreed with me. "Have you heard of Dame Kiri Te Kanawa?"

I could only answer in the negative. "Nah – never heard of her."

"I thought as much, Nev. I certainly wouldn't be surprised if more people have heard of Susan Boyle than Dame Kiri Te Kanawa. Never mind – Kiri's a magnificent Kiwi opera singer or whatever and a great tribute to all bongos. Trouble is – just like most mildly successful Kiwis – she's got an ego the size of the Rock of Gibraltar. When you come to think of it – she can be downright petty."

"How come?" I queried him.

He opened a newspaper from the day before. After shuffling through the pages: "Take a look at this. Not very gracious of her – don't you think?"

DAME KIRI SLAMS SUSAN BOYLE'S OVERNIGHT SUCCESS

Dame Kiri Te Kanawa, the internationally renowned opera singer, said she is not interested in discussing the achievements of Susan Boyle and called her career a "whizz-bang" success.

The Dame is currently involved with BBC Radio 2 who are playing host to "The Kiri Prize" said that her opera singing competition was not going to produce a star like Boyle who shot to fame after her success on "Britain's Got Talent".

She said "I'm doing something classical, not whiz-bang. Whizz-bang disappears. It goes 'whizz' and then 'bang'."

When asked about the possibility of Boyle appearing in the West End version of "Les Miserables" Te Kanawa said "Let's get off that subject. Move on. You insult me by even wanting to bring it into this conversation. I'm not interested."

Te Kanawa went on to say that her competition was a step above the rest. She said "This competition is named after me and has far more stability. It's judged seriously by people with integrity who know what they're talking about."

During the conversation Te Kanawa was also questioned about the crossover appeal between different genres of music. She was asked about the great Andrea Bocelli's performance of opera.

She said "He did, once. He wants to be an opera singer, but he isn't."

"We should talk about serious classical singers if you want to stick to the subject. There's Angela Gheorghiu, Renée Fleming, Anna Netrebko performing glorious, serious, grand opera without microphones. There aren't many of us."

Even after all of that Te Kanawa does not think of herself as a diva.

"I don't think I'm a diva. I'm just a human being with an opinion that I'm not allowed, at 66 years old, to select," said the Dame.

I could only agree with Greg. Even my younger brother Trev – the uncharitable bastard – was captivated by Susan Boyle's success story. The whole world had fallen in love with a genuine battler who'd come good. "Yeah, it looks like she's really up herself. My mum likes that Andrea Bocelli. Especially when he sings that song with Sarah Brightman."

"I couldn't've described good Kiri better myself," Greg applauded me. "Our good dame must be *seriously* right up herself! Talk about the musical 'Les Misérables', Te Kanawa should be given the 'Kiri prize' for being so bloody miserable. I wouldn't be at all surprised if she's pissed off because Susan Boyle's far more famous around the world than her, and has twice as much talent. She's probably made more money than our dame, anyway. . . That's what I mean about what's so typical of your average bongo when they've enjoyed a modicum of success. You take that Michael Hill the jeweller."

"Who the fuck's he – when he's at home?"

"Are you trying to tell me that you've never heard of Michael Hill the great Kiwi jeweller?" Greg was incredulous.

"Nah – like Tinny Te Tawanaka – I've never heard of him. Has he got a jewellers shop in Auckland or something? That's like asking me who owns the pub in New Zealand. How the fuck would I know – Michael Hill the jeweller?"

He just chuckled a further time. "It's Dame Kiri Te Kanawa – not Tinny Tawanaka – Nev. No, he's not the Michael Hill who holds the Guinness Record for 'largest object removed from a human skull', even though he's obviously got an ego to match the size of Dame Kiri's. He's got jewellers shops all over Bongoland and Oz."

"So what?" I demanded.

He nodded. "He's almost as bongoish as our Dame Kiri. He makes a few bob out of selling baubles to the bongos, and then he decides he needs to write a book and tell the world to 'toughen up'! He's just the man to tell everyone – isn't he? People around the world need to read his book, so he can tell them how to 'toughen up'. I'm buggered if I know where these people get such inflated egos from. I suppose you can only blame it on the other bongos. Someone makes a couple of shekels and the rest of them want to crawl up his or her backside. What do you reckon, Nev – money must make shit rush to their brains? An old pal of mine suggested that the trouble is that most of the bongos with any get up and go are either in Aussie or elsewhere overseas. All the deadheads have been left behind. Seriously, the whole fabric of Kiwi society would collapse in a heap of bull's droppings, if the bongos have to get work visas in order to get into Oz. The Kiwis and their media like to crap all over Aussie, nevertheless without Australia's industry and dynamism, Poo Zealand would've gone down the tubes decades ago."

"The farmers over here seem to know what they're doing," I pointed out to him.

He instantly agreed. "Yes, true – Nev – I stand corrected there. I give them my most humble apologies for discounting them. Some of the New Zealand farmers *truly are* the best in the world. The only problem is they're surrounded by slackers or zombies. I expect it's the same with any Kiwi who tries to run a business over here. For every farmer or businessman you've got here in Bongoland – you'd find twenty public servants or government officials hanging off his figs like body crabs. All wanting to regulate him, plus charge him and fine him. And that's not counting every dole bludger and welfare cheat that you'll find in every road or street that comes way before any person who bends his back and tries to better himself or herself."

"Righto, you also mentioned something about another bloke in this committee?" I changed the subject.

"What committee?"

"The committee that you have to see in order to get your new department or whatever going," I reminded him.

"Ah – that committee! I've been involved in so many Labour government committees lately, it's becoming almost impossible to keep track. Okay, so I've described Helen Granite, Kenny Mears and Patrice Ramsbottom to you. Who do we have next? That's right – Allan Peacock! Putrid – corrupt – bastard! No, I won't waylay you with the fact that he likes dressing in his eldest daughter's underwear and pays prostitutes to let him clean their shower floors and shithouse bowls. No – that would take up far too much of your. . ."

"You're fuckin' joking!" Trev was all round-eyed!

"I'm not, Trev, but let's not visit that point right now. Let it suffice to say that he's got some very peculiar habits. More importantly he's a public service mandarin, and – very similar to Helen Granite – he's right at the very top of the shit heap! You could almost call him an 'untouchable' in Wellington! By that I'm not referring to an 'Untouchable' in the Indian sense – I'm actually saying that he's almost above the law here in Bongoland. . . Take for instance that you've got a tax problem. With a suitable inducement, he can have your tax file adjusted, or make the file disappear altogether. You need a resource consent whereby you want to bulldoze a road through a World Heritage park – he's just the man to see. You want to set up an investment finance company such as Hanover Finance – whereby the directors make a poultice of money and the investors lose their life savings – he's the bloke who'll organise everything and cover your back from the government if the shareholders *are ever* allowed to complain. Take me – I want to rip the bongo taxpayers off to the tune of millions of dollars – so he's just the man to have on my team. . . Look – you won't like the prick. Nor his wife Barb – the stupid – fat – revolting bitch! Especially a bloke like you, Trev, with your sensibilities about chubby women. Let me describe our Allan Peacock. Massive, bulbous nose with burst blood vessels that match his puce cheeks. Balding, but uses hair on the right side of his head to cover the bald patch. This same hair keeps falling in the opposite direction, leaving him with hair hanging to his shoulder to the right – nothing in the middle – scarcely bugger all on the left. He's got a pigeon chest – hasn't he? This's covered in grey/black hair, and is allowed to protrude outwards like the edge of a knife because he leaves the top three buttons of his shirt undone. He does that because Barb says it looks sexy – the stupid – mouldy – fat-arsed – rat-pig! His teeth are a burnt-yellow colour because he never brushes them, and like his chest – his arms are covered in grey/black hairs like a silver-backed gorilla's. There's a massive gap between his top front teeth that you could sail a Spanish galleon through. He insists on wearing short sleeved shirts because his wife Barb reckons he looks masculine, the scabby – no, I won't venture there again – dog! And, yes – he's a fucking ignorant, arrogant dickhead to go with it. . . Let's just say that this scumbag has a powerful finger in a good few government departments. He has no official title, yet he's one of the chief consultants to these same departments. He's a real mover and shaker in Wellington. Worst than that, a he's major buddy of the PM herself."

Kev and Merl's 'multi-million dollar' mansion didn't impress me all that much. Neither did New Zealand's capital Wellington; although it was pissing down rain when Trev and I first arrived. It was blowing a bloody gale, and the place wasn't enhanced that much when Greg mentioned that an earthquake would one day wipe the city off the map and kill half its residents! He also reckoned that Thorndon – the suburb where Kev and Merl's place could be found – was sitting right on a seismic fault and was bound to cop it the worst! To him that was a bonzer idea because plenty of politicians and senior civil servants had set themselves up in Thorndon, so if they were crushed to death in their 'ivory towers' Bongoland would be far better off! Fortunately he did not wish the same for Kev; nonetheless both he and Trev agreed that Merl wouldn't be that much of a loss to the human race.

To describe the 'mansion' it was a two-story, mildewed, red brick affair with a slate roof and about a half dozen or so chimneys. It was surrounded by huge trees that Greg described as being 'horse chestnuts'. About half an acre of land surrounded it, plus there was a greenhouse with several panes of glass that were either cracked or had holes in them. Kev reckoned that he was going to have a go at growing tomatoes in the greenhouse, after he'd put in a veggie patch at the back of it. All Merl was interested in was who the neighbours were and if they were 'powerful' or famous Kiwis or not. It was all pretty mouldy. It certainly wasn't a place that I'd pay three million bucks for. Even if they were only bongo dollars, as Greg liked to call them.

It so happened that the same house was just a couple of blocks away from Helen Granite's and Allan and Barb Peacock's mansions, while Patrice Ramsbottom was camping in a luxury apartment – paid for by the Kiwi taxpayers – that was just a stone's throw from Helen Granite's place. It was a 'cosy' arrangement, or so Merl described it, while Greg begged to differ when he was in the company of only me and Trev. "It's like the junction box of several sewer pipes," he began with. "A place where turds wrapped in shit paper can meet and bump heads or skid off each other. Your elder brother's excluded from that equation, of course."

"So where you gunna have this meeting with Helen Granite and so on?" I asked him.

"At Allan Peacock's place. He's the head honcho in the committee, plus he's got by far the biggest taxpayer-funded expense account. . . Now, I've already touched on the subject of your fragile sensibilities, Trev, because you won't like Barb Peacock. Neither will you take to her three kids – two girls and a boy – who should've been knocked on the head when they were born, or at least put in a sack and drowned. You won't like Barb's two miniature Jack Russell terriers, either. When I say Barb's ignorant – she's exactly that! She's a species of lower bowel bacteria, yet – like our Merl – she *actually believes* that she's sophisticated! That's what's so absolutely nauseating about her. Allan – I've already described him. He's the kind of lowlife creature that you'd liken to the crumbs of excrement found around a dog's anus. As far as Helen Granite goes – you've seen a photo of her, so you can draw your own conclusions about her outward appearance. Watch her because she's as sharp as a bloody tack! If she makes a noise like a cat trying to cough up a fur ball – or sounds like she's choking to death – she's actually laughing or amused! That's the only way you can tell because her eyes always give you the impression that she's just about to slit open your scrotum without an anaesthetic and remove your figs with a teaspoon. . . Then there's our mate, Kenny Mears. He's a fairly large and thickset creature, and likes to make out that he's a brash, rough and tough West Coaster. Trouble is – he's queer just like most of the West Coasters I've met. Like I said before – he's passionate about other men's bums. Then we have his wife Avril who's insisted on hanging on to her maiden name – Dobson. She'd be one of the most powerful public servants on the West Coast. I won't describe her now, but will leave her as a surprise. She's not actually on the voting committee, but she knows how to pull strings in high places. Naturally she isn't aware of Kenny's shortcomings, otherwise she'd cast him adrift. He'd have no chance without her. Avril's the one with the figs in the outfit – believe me. . . And lastly – Patrice Ramsbottom. Even an easygoing bloke like you will dislike her, Nev! A mouldy, boring dog like Barb Peacock – gone to fat – lank brown hair that just reaches her shoulders – freckles – glasses – also believes she's both sophisticated and a woman of the world because some dickheaded bongo institution handed her a BA. Where she'll bug you in particular, Trev, is that she makes out that she's the doyen of political correctness and likes poking shit at everything Australian. She's also a big fan of our Johnny Minto, and typical of the majority of his arse-bleeding followers."

The time finally arrived when Trev and I were going to meet the government committee members; Allan Peacock and his wife Barb; Ken Mears and his wife; Helen Granite and Patrice Ramsbottom. Kev and Merl had already met them, and there was the possibility that Patrice Ramsbottom wasn't going to pitch up. Apparently she'd opposed Greg's Department of Inner Health idea from the very outset.

Greg explained the situation: "When I started canvassing support for my scam, I felt it might be wise to wine and dine Patrice and possibly shag her for good measure. Well, I did all three, but rogering her was one of the most difficult chores I have had to embark on in my *entire life*! For starters – and like Merl – she's got breath like a dinosaur. A carrion-eating one! It's her fat, hairy, white legs that I also couldn't hack. Her obese guts, arms and arse. Worst of all – she actually believes she's irresistible to males! Okay, so I managed it the first time by insisting on doing it dog-fashion, but she kept coming back for more. When I finally couldn't stand the sight of her and ignored her phone calls, she's been on a crusade to stop me ever since."

"So who else is gunna be at this meeting?" Trev was totally unsympathetic.

"Just Mulji. Look, I know he's an Indian and would cut my throat and take my last cent, but in this particular instance I believe he's worth ten times his weight in gold. If anyone can push this deal across the line – it's him. . . Bloody hell, but dealing with bongo public servants makes me bilious. I reckon if I can pull this off, I might sell up and head for the UK or the south of France after a couple of years. New Zealand has to be one of the most beautiful countries on God's earth, but the people here are fucking it up more and more as each year goes by. You'll find times when I can feel almost sympathetic for your average bongo, although the feeling doesn't last for more than a nanosecond. The place's overrun with quasi-pinko-politically-correct-do-gooders, and – like I've told you before – for every bongo businessman in the private sector you've got twenty public servants hanging off his scrotum like infected and voracious body lice."

"So why's Mulji so important?" Trev was still unsympathetic.

Greg scratched himself under the chin. "Just wait till we get round to the Peacock's house. All will be revealed later."

"And why do we need to go along?" I questioned Greg further.

"You two are my most trusted lieutenants. Look, I can't really rely on Kev. He's salt of the earth, but let's face it – he's not the sharpest knife in the drawer. You're essential to my plans if we're going to force Merl to give him his fair share of his lotto winnings. . . Another thing – it'll be impossible to get Peacock, Granite and Co out of their ivory towers in Wellington. I'll be needing people on the ground to set things up so that we can siphon off as much money in the shortest possible time. I've already told Peacock that you and Trev are going to be part of the furniture, and he doesn't see a problem with that. Look – we're dealing with a greedy pack of arseholes here, and that suits me just fine. If I can put sufficient cash in front of them, I'll have them in the palm of my hand. Then *watch me* put the boots in."

"Yeah, but we're gunna have to get back to Aussie," Trev reminded him. "We've got maybe a couple of months of accrued leave, then we're gunna have to go back drilling."

Greg put his hands on Trev's shoulders. "Will drilling make you a millionaire in a couple of years?"

"Bullshit – it will!" I answered for my younger brother.

Greg turned to me. "I will – and that's guaranteed."

Strangely enough I had an uncanny feeling that he was genuine. I'd really grown to like him, and was starting to look up to him the same as I did with my boss back in Kalgoorlie. I admired both their styles. They'd both made a pile of money, yet they were approachable and never arrogant about such success. I believed that I could trust Wal' Growford with my life, and Greg was starting to take on the same dimensions.

CHAPTER 7

Greg's description of the committee members who were voting on whether his Department of Inner Health was going to go ahead or not couldn't have been more accurate! Allan Peacock indeed possessed a pigeon chest and a veiny, bulbous nose, but what made him all the more repulsive was his short-sleeved shirt that was unbuttoned almost to the waist, thus highlighting the silver/black hair that overflowed from under his chin, and blanketed his arms. His teeth weren't yellow – they were more of a mustardy/green. Very similar to Merl's false teeth! How he could be such a powerful and highly paid public servant left me stuffed!

His wife Barb did nothing to compliment him. She was seriously overweight and had a fat arse and legs crammed into a pair of black tights, plus she was wearing what looked to be a red, Chinese, sleeveless top that could've been made out of silk or whatever. There were pictures of Chinese pagodas and Chinamen with pigtails all over the garment. Just about every finger on her hands was adorned with a diamond ring of some sort on it, and from a thick gold chain around her neck hung also what appeared to be a massive diamond. All up she must've been wearing thousands of bucks' worth of jewellery! This jewellery, plus the orange lipstick and purple eye shadow she'd smudged around her eyes, did zero when it came to enhancing her appearance. Neither did her peroxide-blonde hair. She could be precisely described as being a frumpy slob.

I had the feeling that Allan and Barb Peacock's presence in such a magnificent house was an insult to the builder and all its previous owners.

Helen Granite was perhaps twice the size of Barb laterally; however she was a fair bit shorter. I was immediately wary of her, as her eyes seemed to be boring straight through me when I shook her hand. She also took a particular interest in Trev and she held onto his hand for at least half a minute. Her voice was dry and raspy and she communicated via a series of grunts and coughing noises. She was clad in the exact same gown that I'd seen her wearing in the photograph that Greg showed Trev and me some weeks before. It hung down off her like a sack and was totally featureless. She possessed no feminine attributes whatsoever, and Greg later claimed that she was most likely a hermaphrodite, or a person who was of neither sex. Similar to a fair few gay men or lesbians.

Ken Mears was a fairly big bloke, perhaps maybe six-foot-three, and I guessed that he weighed a hundred and fifty kilos or so. It was quite difficult picturing him as being gay, for he did come across as being a rough and tough, confident, brash type. He tried the vice grip handshake on me, but I'd spent too many years unscrewing drill rods by hand in the outback, so I soon had him trying his hardest not to show the pain.

Mears' wife Avril, who'd insisted on keeping her maiden name Dobson, was also supposed to be very powerful in the New Zealand public service, and like Greg said – it was clear that she was the one who carried the balls between them. Her voice was kind of little girlish, but firm when she told her husband to stop butting in when other people had something to say. She was a skinny and horse-faced individual with browny/green buck teeth, and she wore round, rimless spectacles. She was obviously trying to make out that she was a hippy type or whatever because she wore dark brown, bib and brace, corduroy overalls, plus a black granny print shirt. Her hands were calloused, whereas Mears' were as soft as a baby's. She possessed the greasiest and rancid-looking dreadlocks that went all the way down to her almost non-existent arse cheeks.

When Merl asked where Patrice Ramsbottom was, I was quite taken aback by Peacock's reply: "Old Ram's Arse? She's staying away in protest – the stupid fucking slag! Don't worry – her vote's not all that important."

And it was that which set the tone for the evening. Peacock's conversation was peppered with swear words, and Barb wasn't hesitant to throw in the odd 'fucking', 'wanker' or 'arsehole' here and there. Mears was equally foul-mouthed; nevertheless his skinny wife didn't seem to mind. Merl was in her element and she matched them curse word for curse word. It certainly wasn't the way I expected people so high up in a country's government to behave.

The whole evening hadn't started out all that well, anyway. Greg's flight from Auckland was running late, so Kev, Trev, Mulji and I travelled to the Peacock's Thorndon mansion in Merl's Porsche Cayenne SUV and Merl, as usual, was the driver. We'd travelled perhaps no more than a hundred metres or so when the vehicle was flooded with a throat-choking, nauseating stench! My brothers and I knew full well that Merl had farted; yet it would've been a novel and unnerving experience for Mulji. Especially when Trev, who was squashed between me and the Sikh in the back seat of the Porsche, yelled out: "Fucksakes – someone open a fuckin' window! Fuck me – bloody – dead – Merl!"

Kev, who was sitting up front next to Merl, and I had our windows down in seconds flat; still I reckon Mulji might've been temporarily paralysed by the whole affair, so both he and Merl left their windows up. Needless to say the remainder of the three minute journey was carried out in an awkward silence.

Mulji was in for a further rough time just a few minutes after! Although it was night, it was quite plain to see that the Peacock's residence was probably one of the most expensive in the suburb of Thorndon. It was a three-story affair and the garden surrounding it seemed to go out into the gloom forever. There was ample parking for dozens of cars in a special paved area designed for that purpose. Standing as a group we waited patiently in front of huge double doors that were surrounded by brightly-lit, stained glass windows, while Merl rang the door bell. The door was partially opened so that a Filipino or Indonesian woman in a kind of uniform could see who'd come calling. It was then that two black and white miniature Jack Russell terriers came streaking out, and they immediately started savaging Mulji's legs! All hell broke loose after that when Trev started yelling and booting at the vicious little bastards: "Get out – ya fuckin' mongrels!" And the yelps of pain from one dog that had copped it in the guts would've alerted the neighbours for miles around!

It took maybe a full five minutes for sanity to be restored, and it was only when we actually got inside the huge house that we saw that Mulji was quite badly bitten. The razor sharp teeth of the terriers easily penetrated his expensive suit trousers, and I saw puncture marks and lacerations all up and down his legs. In no time at all Allan Peacock told his public service chauffeur cart the Sikh down to Wellington's Wakefield Hospital in a flash government BMW 730 Ld.

Actually out in the paved car park there were two more BMW limousines! One was Helen Granite's government car complete with chauffeur, and the other was temporarily available to Avril while she was in Wellington. Her car didn't come with a chauffeur.

As you can imagine, a fairly hefty pregnant silence followed! After we'd all shook each other's hands and so on, Barb Peacock led us into a massive lounge room that would've needed both the fireplaces at each end of it to keep it warm in winter. She then distributed a champagne glass to each of us and asked which we preferred – Dom Perignon or Krug? When it became obvious that Kev, Trev, Merl and I weren't French champagne aficionados, Barb decided to give us a bit of a background on herself and her husband. "After all the years that Allan's served New Zealand's best interests, I believe we deserve nothing but the best that money has to offer, and I much prefer French to New Zealand or Australian bubbly. While the Kiwi efforts are quite commendable, the Australians only produce cat's pee. Personally I prefer Krug because it can be extremely rare and very expensive on occasions. You take for instance the 1995 vintage where little more than twelve thousand bottles were produced. It was only through Allan's contacts in the Chinese embassy that we managed to get a case. Also, I've always been nervous about getting reliable supplies of French champagne after the bloody Frog bastards sank the Rainbow Warrior."

"So it's true what Greg told us?" Trev's eyes were agape.

"Told you what?" Barb focused on him.

"Greg reckoned that France wasn't gunna allow any French champagne into New Zealand unless the two officers were released?"

"Yes, it was touch and go for quite some time," Barb agreed. "It was actually Allan who told that arrogant dork Lange to pull his head in. And now we've had this nonsense with French saboteurs pooping all over the South Island, and our brain dead PM actually suggested banning all French champagne imports into the country! . . . I've always been worried about there being a French champagne embargo. The case of Krug I mentioned is liquid gold."

At that very second Greg walked into the room. "Ah, Barb, are you referring to that little inducement that the Chinese consol handed over? Was that the case of Krug that he gave Allan for giving the go ahead for that Chinese company farm purchase just outside Hamilton? What was it – a dozen or more dairy farms? I'll take a glass of that Krug, as it was me who raised the idea with the consul in the first place."

"It wasn't as if Allan didn't deserve it, Greg," Barb tried to make out she was slightly miffed. "He worked all night to make sure that the deal went through, and was forced to do a lot of favours for those fucking wankers in the Labour Party. Also, I heard you got a jet boat out of it. That Jet boat you keep at your block of apartments at Lake Tekapo."

"How are you, Greg?" Allan Peacock was far more forthcoming. "Tell me – will you still be in Wellington on Monday? I need to help Ken and Avril raise more funding for the various DoNE branches on the West Coast. True, I know we have an army of the bastards and they're treating the Coast as a personal holiday resort and theme park, but if we don't find a way of raising more funding, unfortunately some personnel will have to get the boot. I can't say I give a rat's backside about them getting the sack, but we're talking about public service jobs being lost in Avril's bailiwick."

"Who's this DoNE?" Trev never likes to be left out of things.

"The Department of Nature and the Environment, Trev," Greg was happy to inform him. "It's Avril's brain child and she's the director on the West Coast. Like Allan says – you'll come across a huge army of DoNE personnel all over New Zealand – never mind just the West Coast. The more personnel a department has – the larger the salary for the director such as Avril. That's why Allan said there was an army of them. It's getting harder and harder to justify them all, and any revenue on the Coast's dwindling because the general populace are as poor as church mice. We're getting some money from the gold miners who want to mine on DoNE land, but we don't have that much mining going on despite the high gold price we're seeing today. Not only are DoNE putting them through a maze of red tape, we've got the Heritage Act department, plus four sets of local government councils out for what they can get – two district and two regional councils. Can you believe it – there are 35,000 people on the West Coast and you've got two regional and two district councils all trying to fine and tax them. Unlike in West Aussie where the gold miners' foremost task is the actual mining and treatment of ore, on the West Coast the major chore is navigating one's way through the obstacles put up by the various government departments. . . Mind you, the West Coast's still a bastion of the New Zealand public service. When we visit the place, you'll see that every second vehicle on the roads is a government vehicle of some sort. It's just getting very difficult to find funding for it all. Some funding was cut to DoNE when those committees were set up to investigate the possibility of French sabotage. The money had to come from somewhere to pay for all those committees. It's as if the Labour Party's trying to cut off the West Coast altogether."

"Yeah, those fucking Labour wankers and greenies in Auckland and Wellington!" Ken Mears was all in agreement. "Especially when they banned the logging of native forests."

Allan Peacock was far less vehement. "Yes, Ken, but Labour aren't going to be around for much longer. Even the countless South Auckland Pacific Islanders on the dole realise that they've almost bankrupted the place. The gravy train for some in the public service will soon come to a shuddering halt if the Nats get in. You, Avril, Helen and I should be okay, but I bet there's hundreds – if not thousands – of public servants in Wellington who must be shitting themselves. These past few months I've been inundated with phone calls from various department heads looking for comfort, but as far as I'm concerned they can paddle their own fucking canoes. It's survival of the fittest from here on in. . . That's why, Greg, your Department of Inner Health could be a lifesaver. It could be our final ticket. . ."

"Yes, but those committees that were set up over that French saboteur bullshit sucked up a lot of DoNE funding," Avril pointed out. "You, Greg, were getting ten grand a day, while you, Allan and Helen, were getting twenty grand a day via your consulting companies based in the British Virgin Islands. I had to cut right back on my consultancy company's fees to DoNE, and I only managed to make up for the shortfall when that money was deducted from the funding set aside for retarded children living on the West Coast. As you know, we have eighty percent of them out of the whole country. I was forced to take money off the flaming loony kids!"

"That's where I'm going to miss the Labour Government and all those committees of theirs," Peacock looked forlornly to Greg for comfort. "Avril, you chaired your fair share of them in Greymouth and Westport, and that snail slaughter business netted you a small fortune. It's just a pity that DoC murdered eight hundred of them. That really put a cat amongst the pigeons once the greenies and those simpering bleeding-hearts from Forest and Bird got to hear of it."

"What's this DoC outfit?" Trev just refused to be left out.

"The Department of Conservation," Greg informed him. "Another of New Zealand's myriad government departments. There's also an army of DoC personnel scattered like dandruff all over the country. . . Have a look at this." He removed a manila folder from his briefcase. "I carry this with me wherever I go because jokes of this calibre are impossibly difficult to come by.

TRAGEDY BEFALLS GIANT RARE SNAILS IN AN AVOIDABLE DEPARTMENT OF CONSERVATION STUFF UP

Up to 800 giant Powelliphanta snails were as good as murdered in Hokitika, conservationists have claimed.

"Were they trying to make Powelliphanta snail ice cream?" DoNE spokeswoman Avril Dobson challenged the government conservation department. "If it's cost Solid Energy almost $10,000,000 to relocate 6,000

snails, this could be a loss to the project of $1,333,333! And that's not counting the cost of DoC personnel and infrastructure!

The snails – which were held in ice cream containers – were supposed to be stored at 10 degrees Celsius; however it was claimed that one of the temperature-controlled cool rooms and environmental chambers had a faulty temperature probe, and the cool room was switched to zero! The snails would have died horribly by gradually being frozen to death.

Ms Dobson went on to further criticise what she insisted was an avoidable catastrophe. "The disaster occurred over Labour Weekend, and no one knew how long it took to freeze the poor snails. Naturally public service employees simply cannot be expected to work on weekends, yet alone public holidays, so the rank and file personnel are totally blameless. The responsibility for this fiasco can be squarely placed at the feet of the coal miners; although Solid Energy is a state-run enterprise."

Ms Dobson did say that something might have been done to placate distressed New Zealanders, when an Australian tourist, Bruce Simpson from Bondi Beach, offered to set up a French restaurant whereby the main dish on the menu could be snails cooked in their shells with garlic butter and parsley. While it was unknown how long Powelliphanta snails could be kept frozen before going off, sales of the snail dish might ameliorate the situation considerably.

Ms Dobson went onto say that although Bruce Simpson was an Australian and had put forward the idea of the restaurant, the Labour Government has agreed to consider it. To this end they were going to set up a committee and two sub-committees to investigate the proposal. Furthermore, the future for such a restaurant looked rosy because relocated Powelliphanta snails – collected from Solid Energy's coal mining operations – were dying like flies in the new, scientifically-chosen habitats.

In what critics claim is bureaucracy gone mad, it is estimated that these committees could cost the New Zealand taxpayers a further $25 million. Thus the cost of the snail relocation would end up at $58,333 per snail, and that did not include DoC's personnel and infrastructure costs.

A spokesman from the private sector also agreed that a French restaurant application in Hokitika might be unviable. "For starters, it's Bruce Simpson – an Australian – who'll be lodging the resource application to open a French restaurant. If the various greenie and conservation groups such as Forestry & bird and other organisations managed to delay that Aussie coal miner Bathurst Resources for so long, they'll have no trouble delaying a restaurant consent to an Australian beach bum who is believed to be growing marijuana on DoC land behind the township of Ross. Even if a Kiwi was to apply, it would take years for the consent to be granted and all those giant snails relocated by DoC will be long dead."

"There you go, Avril!" Peacock crowed. "Not only did your Panama-based company make a fortune out of those snails, you had your name in the papers New Zealand-wide. That really raised your stakes in the public service, and now you know why the greenies adore you. That Powelliphanta ice cream crack you took at DoC really touched the spot with the greenies and tree huggers everywhere!"

"These the same snails that you mentioned not long back? You know – when the Labour Government were trying to bludge off the French?" Trev's face was a portrait of disbelief.

"The very same snails!" Greg assured him. "It was a farce that awoke several comedies. Take this for instance."

Trev was handed a rectangle of newspaper.

PALMERSTON NORTH ORGANISATION EXECUTIVE WADES INTO WEST COAST GIANT SNAIL CONTROVERSY

Fifi Harmer, the general secretary of KIWIS AGAINST AUSTRALIAN HEGEMONY (KAAH), waded into the debate about whether a resource consent should be given to an Australian who has applied to set up a French restaurant in Hokitika, whereby dead Powelliphanta snails, killed on DoC land and premises, will be served up to tourists with garlic butter sauce and parsley.

"Who's to say that the snails, which are killed by DoC from relocating them, are the only snails that will end up on the menu? Has anyone in

government considered that this could encourage snail rustling? There's a rumour going round the Coast that a large percentage of the relocated snails are dying. What's to stop criminals from freezing them to death like DoC did? After all, this is the West Coast we are talking about. While I'm not accusing all West Coasters of being singular, several surveys followed by committee investigations have proved beyond all doubt that weird practices might be ubiquitous in the region. Take for instance Neville Cooper and the Cooperites at Gloriavale.

"I know they can't help it (West Coasters)," she was quick to add, "as it's a cruel penalty handed out by their inherited gene pool – the Celtic factor. Also rustling snails would obviously be a bonus to any West Coaster because wages there are so much lower than the rest of the country. Especially now that Solid Energy is not only broke, but – under state management – has managed to accrue a $389 million debt that will most likely have to be repaid by the taxpayers. We have no more money for legitimate snail collectors based in Westport, so they would obviously be tempted to illegally gather snails for the table, regardless of how rare they are."

"And besides," Ms Harmer continued, "these are New Zealand snails we are talking about, and we have an Australian wanting to cook them with garlic butter and parsley. That is a French recipe. Someone should conjure up a Kiwi recipe where we can have three vegies and lashings of barbeque or cranberry sauce."

Miss Harmer also had a suggestion to pass onto the DoC Hokitika office. "As I mentioned previously, these are Kiwi snails. As a further safeguard, I suggest that Department of Conservation staff should give each snail an All Blacks beanie to cover its shell, so it has more chance of surviving a further monitoring failure, or DoC staff forgetting to check on them. This would give them extra protection during weekends and public holidays when DoC facilities will possibly be deserted."

Greg had more information on what had to be a complete farce!

LEGACY OF FINANCIAL GREED DESTROYING RARE SNAILS

Countless rare native land snails, moved at huge expense in order to facilitate coal mining, are not surviving all that well in the new locations, conservationists are claiming. A spokeswoman, Gwendoline Portly, from BAFAM (Ban All Farming and Mining)) said she had recently visited one of these new locations, and that scores of the giant Powelliphanta snails were squashed under the tyres of her vehicle because they were obviously too weak to get out of the way.

Gwendoline did come clean on another matter: "It's true that I gathered up some of the snails that I ran over. The ones that were only slightly squashed. I gave these to that Australian, Bruce Simpson in Hokitika, and he cooked them in the shell with butter and garlic. With just a dab of barbeque sauce they were delicious! A little bit like lamb's heart, but juicier and much more subtle. They went down well with my favourite Marlborough red."

All the latest news of the tragedy has reinforced environmentalists' arguments that the snails were being murdered just for the sake of coal mining and giving West Coasters employment, or a new culinary experience. It has also been argued that the West Coast had more than its fair share of those who could be referred to as 'rather unusual' and trying to find work for them was a waste of both time and taxpayers' money, plus a danger to the environment. The Forest and Bird Society's Westport-based regional field officer, Doris Dosser, said the Mt Augustus snails were 'victims of economic desire'. The thing we're starting to see now is the worst coming out, and it could well be that this particular species of snail becomes functionally extinct in the wild," Ms Dosser said.

DESPERATE SEARCH FOR WAY OF IMPROVING
GIANT SNAILS' LIBIDO WHILE IN CAPTIVITY.

DoNE officer Walter Crumley, the department's Powelliphanta technical support officer on the Coast, said 1750 Powelliphanta snails were still living in cool stores at DOC's Hokitika office, as a "safeguard population". Those snails were declining in number because of slow reproduction and DOC was experimenting on how to improve that.

A West Coast local from the once busy coal mining town of Stillwater claimed that he might have a solution for DoC's captive Powelliphanta snails which were declining in numbers because of slow reproduction. Ray Thomas, a well known 'bushman', claimed that a large number of West Coast men needed to spend considerable time watching pornography on the internet before making sexual advances towards their wives. Perhaps if DoC were to spend time in the field filming snails mating in their native habitat, copies of the film could be shown to captive snails?

Mr Thomas' suggestion has outraged WAM (Women Against Men) president and lesbian activist Gertie Grogan. Ms Grogan is well known in political circles in Wellington for her drive to have all New Zealand women artificially inseminated rather than be debased by men. "That's so typical of men," she told our reporter. If they're not trying to pervert women, they're turning their attention to endangered snails."

"Now for my *pièce de résistance!*" Greg triumphantly brandished a last cutting. "This made you an immortal in the public's eyes, Avril."

EFFORT TO CREATE MORE EMPLOYMENT OPPORTUNITIES FOR WEST COASTERS CAUSES DIVISION AND TOURIST SCANDAL

Well known West Coast personality and director of DoNE, Avril Dobson, has come up with a ground breaking scheme to employ more West Coasters. DoC experts have managed to ascertain that the Powelliphanta snail's main diet is earthworms. Ms Dobson has suggested that since no more Powelliphanta snails were being collected for storage by DoC – due to the expense of purchasing Chinese made All Black beanies – or to be released in new localities and not to be made into ice cream (sic); perhaps those West Coasters who were employed to collect the snails should now start collecting earth worms? These worms could be deposited in the new DoC-assigned snail localities.

Though embarked on enthusiastically by West Coasters who lined up with buckets and spades, the scheme was brought to a halt three weeks after its commencement by members of NZACTOE (New Zealanders Against Cruelty To Our Earthworms). This was achieved by NZACTOE supporters lying across the road to Mount Augustus which is located north east of Westport.

It appears that NZACTOE have justification for these actions, when it was discovered that the Australian, who suggested cooking the dead Powelliphanta snails with garlic butter and parsley in Hokitika, had illegally set up a takeaway food caravan on National Highway 6 between Punakaiki and Westport. He was found illicitly selling Powelliphanta snails, that had been rustled from DoC snail resettlement locations, to Chinese tourists, plus he was doing a thriving business selling earthworm patties. Patties that he was erroneously claiming to be 'whitebait patties'.

When questioned by authorities the Australian, Bruce Simpson, defended his actions by claiming that the only Powelliphanta snails he was selling were those that were run over by various conservationists' vehicles, and that source had given him a plentiful supply. He went on to further assert that they were very popular with the Chinese tourists because they believed that endangered species were extra good for a person's libido. He also claimed that it was a clever way of stopping them from setting up their own snail smuggling rings which they were bound to do sooner or later once it was known how rare Powelliphanta snails are. Especially after the wholesale slaughter of snails at DoC's Hokitika premises. He said he was selling the earthworm patties to local West Coasters who were 'too stupid' to tell the difference between earthworms and whitebait, and there was no shortage of customers.

"You should be tapping into Dragan Milošević's antics on the West Coast?" Greg concentrated on Avril.

"Too right!" Avril agreed in her little girl voice. "He's been a one man tourist boom on his own. When's the last time you were at the Coast, Greg? It seems ages since we last saw you. Don't tell me you've grown tired of Powelliphanta snails cooked in garlic butter? They're getting harder and harder to come by. The only reliable supply is from some of the Chinese brothel owners in Auckland. The trouble is, they're making so much out of selling P to the kids, they can charge whatever they like for snails."

"Has it been that long since I last saw you and Ken?" Greg seemed troubled by that. "I've been full time on my Department of Inner Health business. Yes, I heard Dragan Milošević's keeping the Coast afloat. Apparently he's got pilgrims and cult members following him everywhere?"

"I'll say he has!" Ken Mears joined in. "Mostly poofs wanting to meet other poofs at all the public shithouses. No wonder there's so much freedom camper crap all up and down the Coast – you have to wait in line for days before you can use any of the public toilets."

"Ken's exaggerating," Avril admonished her husband. "It's not quite as bad as that, but not far off. It's mostly Canadians – both men and women. They're starting to call Greymouth 'Little Ottawa' and Westport 'Little Montreal'. Ken's right, it's mostly gays looking for dates with other gays, and they're using the Coast's public facilities as if they own them."

Knowing a bit about Ken Mears' background, I felt he was a pot calling the kettle black. I turned to Greg. "In one of those newspaper stories – what was that about Neville Cooper and Cooperites?"

Greg nodded. "Yes, Nev – his first name's spelt the same as yours. He's running a cult about sixty Ks out of Greymouth on some dairy farm called 'Gloriavale'. It's the same old – same old. It was kicked off by an Aussie by the name of Neville Cooper who now calls himself 'Hopeful Christian'. He's the father and grandfather of quite a few of his flock, and – just like any cult – he's called all the shagging 'God's work'. That's what all these cult leaders seem to do – shag everything in sight 'for God'. Same as far too many of the Christian Brothers. He overdid things back in 1995 when he sexually assaulted some woman who dobbed him in. She was backed up by Cooper's own son. The woman described old Hopeful as being '*a man of unbridled lust*'. Just like some of the Catholic clergy we're hearing about in Aussie these days. . . Yes, Hopeful was obliged to spend almost a year in the can for sexually assaulting the woman with a wooden donger, yet he's still going strong with hundreds of cult supporters. . . If I've heard right – all his female flock get around in blue, ankle-length dresses and they cover their heads with white scarves."

"Yeah, and the blokes wear blue trousers," Mears backed him up.

319

Greg ignored him and addressed Avril once more. "I hear Dragan Milošević's followers have uniforms of sorts?"

"Yes, they do!" Avril sounded almost shrill. "The women wear green T shirts and they've got a picture of a massive dildo that looks like the nuclear missiles the Yanks've got. The men wear white T shirts with pictures of chocolate doughnuts on them both back and front. . . The PM and I've been talking about shutting Milošević down, especially after that vibrator went through that woman's knee. We can't really do too much about it, as he's the only one keeping the Coast going."

"Ooh – don't go shutting him down!' Barb squawked. "Not until he's perfected his H Clarke. Allan's promised me one for my birthday."

Much to my amazement Peacock was onside with her! "Anything to make you happy, Babs! Hey Ken – Avril – surely DoNE could use a truck with a crane on it? Nobody'll notice if it goes missing. There are government vehicles disappearing all over the country."

All further conversation was impossible when the Peacock kids pitched up. Two were chubby girls who very much resembled their mother, and the boy, who was maybe ten or twelve, had the same-shaped head, nose and ears as his old man. He one of those dickheads that wore his cap back to front, and the gaps between the girls' tights and T shirts revealed rolls of fat that would most probably only grow larger and never go away.

The woman in the uniform, who Barb reckoned was her Filipina maid, had set out a whole array of snacks; pate – savouries – fresh fruit – Foveaux Strait crayfish – various cheeses and biscuits – you name it – and the kids got stuck into them without even bothering to acknowledge that anyone else was in the room. When Peacock tried to pull them up, they simultaneously grabbed two handfuls of the snacks and started heading for the door.

"Sequoia – Arapaho – Comanche – stop and introduce yourselves!" Barb was far more resolute than her hubby.

The kids just stared at us guests sullenly as they recited their names; still there was no point in trying to shake their hands because they were crammed full with a mixture of crushed snacks. Fortunately Barb let them go after that.

The kids' behaviour had been so toxic; I felt it might be helpful to lighten the atmosphere. "They're unusual your children's' names," I pointed out to Barb.

That seemed to please her no end. "Oh – yes! Like Allan and I, our kids are different to your ordinary Kiwi. They're extra special when it comes to other kids. They're far more passionate with everything that they do. That's why we were determined to give them names that were unique, so that they could outshine the mediocrity of boring Anglo Saxon, Celtic and European names in general. I've always had a passion for the North American Indians, so that's why I've named them after a particular tribe. You take the Comanche warriors. They have to be the very personification of manhood itself. I decided to call our son 'Comanche' because he's so like his father. He may still be young, but like Allan he's the very epitome of the term 'manliness'. As for Sequoia and Arapaho, those are names that're a tribute to their grace and femininity. As I'm sure you could see, they're going to grow up to be beautiful women, so Allan had better keep his shotgun loaded. It won't be long before. . ."

"Isn't 'sequoia' the name of a tree?" Trev butted in.

"Oh – no!" Barb was quite startled by that. "The Sequoia are a tribe of Indians that come from Nevada."

My younger brother could be as stubborn as a wombat sometimes. "Nah – they're not. If you take a look on the internet, you'll find sequoias are a kind of redwood that grows in California."

A black look flashed across Barb's face that demonstrated that she wasn't one who was used to being criticised. A look that clearly demonstrated that she harboured a real treacherous streak! "I'm not sure if you're aware, Trevor, that I have a fucking BA in North American natural history. You won't find anyone in the whole of fucking New Zealand who has a greater knowledge of the American Indian tribes than me. So if you would like. . ."

"Beautiful – dynamic – names!" Greg stepped into the breach.

The tension in the room dissipated somewhat when the front door bell rang, announcing that Mulji had arrived back from the Wakefield Hospital. Allan Peacock clearly knew some powerful people in Wellington because a doctor – who was also a Sikh – was waiting at the hospital to treat Mulji's injuries as soon as he arrived!

While that was quite hard to fathom, it was impossible to believe that the two Jack Russell terriers pitched up from nowhere, and they were dead keen to tackle the Sikh again! The barking that time was almost deafening in the confines of the room. It was only the lightening reflexes of the Filipina maid and Kev who grabbed hold of the dogs, which prevented another catastrophe; although the maid was given a nasty bite on the arm. I noticed that she wasn't carted off to hospital in a BMW limousine; instead she was told by Barb where to find some sticking plasters in the kitchen. She was also warned not to use too many of them.

By that time Trev was given an opportunity to whisper in my ear a further time. "How come those fuckin' mongrels keep going for Mulji? You reckon they're racially prejudiced or something? It's a wonder they don't have a go at Avril. She stinks like a corpse. Do you reckon it's all the shit that's been mopped up by those dreadlocks over the years? I wouldn't go munching on her pussy if I was you, Nev – you'll catch the Black Death."

"Let's eat!" It was Allan Peacock's turn to ease the tension in the room.

Our surroundings were amazing! If the lounge room wasn't similar to one you'd see in a royal palace, the dining room certainly was! The room's walls were done out in dark wood panelling and above it was red and gold tapestry wallpaper, while the dining room table itself and the twenty-four chairs around it where painted with gold lacquer. Two gold-plated candelabra were spaced equally along the table; both holding ten candles. We each had five knives and forks apiece, plus four spoons, and there were three glasses at the top of our place mats; two for wine and one for champagne.

I could see by the smirk on Greg's mouth that he found the seating arrangements rather amusing. Peacock sat himself down at one end of the table and there was Barb to his right and Greg to his left. Next along the table and opposite each other were Mulji and Mears, then Kev and Merl facing each other. I was at the end on the right side of Avril. Trev was wedged between Helen Granite and Mulji.

It just didn't make sense that such a beautiful house could be lived in by such cruddy people! Barb in her black tights, sleeveless top and rubber thongs or 'jandals' as the Kiwis liked to call them. Peacock himself in his skin-tight, short-sleeved shirt, wrinkled khaki trousers, and worn out running shoes. Mears in his T shirt with '*WEST COAST WILD FOODS FESTIVAL*' emblazoned on it, plus his faded denim jeans that bore a brown stain around the crutch. The latter left me wondering if it was shit from some young Indian bloke he'd rooted? Then, of course, there was Avril with her filthy dreadlocks that just had to be infested with all species of parasites. All apparently big deals in the New Zealand public service!

At least Greg and Mulji looked a million bucks in the clothes they were wearing. Mulji's charcoal, pinstripe suit, and Greg in his navy blue blazer and grey slacks. Kev, Trev and I brushed up not all that badly because we, too, were wearing blazers and slacks; Kev's and my blazer being black, and Trev's navy blue like Greg's. All three of us wore ties; an occurrence that we could never have imagined just a few weeks before.

Merl was literally *cramme*d into a white trouser suit and she had gold shoes on. That prompted Trev to comment discreetly just as we were leaving to go to the Peacock's house: "She'd better not fart in that outfit. She just might shit herself and there's no way those white daks will have any chance of hiding it!"

It became apparent that the Peacocks hadn't only one Filipina maid but two. One stood holding an empty tray in front of her while the other handed out menu cards.

Barb had an announcement to make: "Only Allan, Greg and I will be having the Krug from here on because it's so hard to find. We're down to our last half dozen bottles. The remainder of you can have Dom Perignon, and I've selected some excellent French wines to accompany the different courses. A lovely Bordeaux from Saint Emilion and a delightful desert wine from Coteaux du Layon. Sip 'em slowly 'cause they cost over four hundred bucks a bottle."

"Yeah, and the bloody steaks cost over two hundred bucks a kilo!" her hubby chimed in.

I studied my menu card more closely. We were getting paua patties as an entree. Greg explained that paua were what we called abalone back in Australia. Apparently the paua was minced up with bread crumbs, egg yolk and garlic in order to make the patties, and they were more or less considered a national Kiwi delicacy. Following that we were going to be given aged fillet steaks with genuine French truffle seasoning, and for dessert we would be served up fresh fruits steeped in hundred-year-old French cognac, accompanied by organic ice cream from somewhere in Canterbury.

"Hm, I wonder what the taxpayers are having for dinner tonight?" Ken Mears guffawed. I was certain he was half pissed. His face had gone all red and he was starting to dribble. All the same his question seemed very funny to his wife, Helen Granite and the Peacocks.

"Ah yes – where would we be without the tax and ratepayers?" Barb asked no one in particular.

Shortly after our champagne glasses were filled – Krug for the privileged three and Dom Perignon for the remainder of us peasants. Allan Peacock became all expansive. "Who shall we toast first?"

"I know!" Mears voice was becoming louder and louder. "Let's toast the patron saint of the Kiwi public service. Let's toast whoever came up with the term 'USER PAYS!'

"You're on the fucking ball tonight, Ken!" Peacock reached over to shake his hand. "Yeah, let's drink a toast to 'User pays'."

Trev was still determined to be included. "What do you mean by 'User pays'?"

Peacock just sat back in his chair and laughed. "It's a way of taxing people for everything except for the air that they breathe, but we're still working on that one. There was a time when the peoples' income taxes and council rates and so on were deemed sufficient payment for all government services. Back in those days the bulk of government and local council ancillary services were handed out free of charge. A person could get free advice, access to support and literature, plus all kinds of day to day assistance that cost nothing, but now your average tax and ratepayer has to pay for everything on top of his income taxes, goods and services taxes, vehicle licensing and council rates. 'User pays' literally means 'If you want to do anything in this country – regardless of whatever it is – you're obliged to pay some government body or another'. . . This opened up the flood gates when it came to charging your average Kiwi in the street further taxes. At first we had a fucking ball thinking up different fees and levies that we could impose on the general public. Also we concocted new laws and regulations to back up these fees and levies, and red tape was spun out by the mile. Naturally it was necessary to recruit more people into the public service to administer these new rules and regulations, and to collect the extra fees and charges, so the overall public service began to burgeon out of control. Especially under those wankers in the various Labour governments. So we were obliged to think up more fees and charges in order to pay for everyone. As time's gone on, it's been more and more difficult coming up with original and different ways of imposing additional fees and taxes, and that's why we have to rely on people like Greg here to come up with new ideas. . . As for the red tape..."

"Let's drink a toast to government red tape!" Mears cut him off.

If Peacock was annoyed at being cut off, he didn't show it. "Hear – hear! A toast to red tape!" The public service members at the table quickly raised their glasses in agreement.

When things settled down, Avril caught Peacock's eye. "Allan, tell Kev and Trev here about your love of farmers."

"Oooh – don't get him going on that!" Barb admonished her; nevertheless she started things for her husband. "Allan has never liked farmers. Especially the British. When he was barely in his teens he was forced to work for sheep farmers down in Southland because his dad left his mum penniless and went off with some Australian whore. Anyway, he worked for this one particular farmer whose wife wouldn't even let him inside the house. He had to sleep in the shearing shed and he was given his meals on the back step of the farm house. If he wanted to wash himself, there was nothing available to him except for a trough that the horses used. And that was even in the middle of winter! If that wasn't bad enough, he was sacked because he complained about the food. All they'd give him was sheep's offal and stale bread. He needed to go all the way to Blenheim before he could get another job because the same farmer passed word around Otago and Southland that Allan wasn't to be trusted."

"Yeah, but that farmer and his wife were fucking Irish – weren't they?" Ken Mears demanded clarification.

Barb just shrugged at that. "So what? They were still Southland farmers – the fucking arrogant wankers! . . . And that's why Allan was determined to get his revenge on all farmers."

"Silver fucking spooners the lot of 'em!" Peacock agreed with her. "You take most of the farmers you've got nowadays. Inherited everything from their fathers for free – didn't they? It's easy come and easy go for those arseholes!"

"Yeah, but you drew the government blueprint when it comes to fixing the bastards – didn't you, Al?" Mears was obviously a bit of a crawler. He then addressed the remainder of us. "No crap, Al wrote the bible when it came to handling resource consents. That's why he's one of New Zealand's top public servants."

"Why thank you, Ken!" Peacock seemed to relish the compliment. "Where I was most fortunate was that I joined the public service roughly at the same time that User pays was introduced back in 1986. Previous to that I was a debt collector for a hire purchase and finance company when I stumbled upon a scam that was going on between that finance company and a certain regional council that I'm not willing to name. Let it suffice to say that the fucking finance company was lending money to the council at exorbitant rates, and large sums of money weren't going where the council's ledgers said they were. The CEO of the council, plus certain chosen councillors – all farmers and extensive landowners in the area – were getting healthy kickbacks out of the whole scheme. When I threatened to reveal all, I was offered the position as Chief Resource Consent Officer for the exact same council and I was allowed to partake of some of the rewards from the *exact same* scam. Overnight I became the most powerful individual in the entire province! Not only did I have the council CEO and various councillors by the short and curlies because I could've had them jailed, I was given absolute authority over any new development that the private sector wanted to introduce to the region. If a person wanted to add a room to his house – a farmer a laneway or milking shed on his farm – a developer or a company wanting to expand – all had to apply for *my* permission. . . I then knew that if I played my cards right, I had a licence to print money. Naturally taking direct bribes wasn't the way to go. It only required one person betray you and everything would've come down around your ears like a fucking house of cards. I realised that networking was the way to go."

"What do you mean by networking?" I felt obligated to somehow contribute to the evening. The paua patties tasted crap, and Trev was proven to be dead right. Avril did smell like something that had been dead for some time! Avril's stink went further than shocking body odour because she tried to mask it with a powerful deodorant of some sort. How her husband put up with it was anyone's guess. Then suddenly I realised that if he could manage the stink of some bloke's shit on his dick, he most likely could also manage his wife's putrid dreadlocks.

"Networking, Nev?" Peacock frowned at the question. "Let me start from the beginning with a hypothetical situation. You take for instance a farmer's son who's inherited the family farm – cash that his old man's been saving for years – the whole box and dice. This farmer's son isn't the one who's ploughed the paddocks, shorn and mustered the sheep – he's contributed nothing. He has no intention of working the farm, so he sells it to some Chinese consortium and ends up with a mountain of cash in the bank. All of a sudden he thinks he's a top gun businessman and a man of the world. I'll give you an example of one particular individual who *does actually* exist. Let's call him Tom – shall we? Once he'd cashed in his father's estate, he was worth just over seven million, and back in those days seven mil' was worth about twenty today. The lucky bastard had been born with a silver spoon in his mouth – hadn't he? Tom's dad used to be a big deal in the district, plus was one of the corrupt councillors involved in the council scam. Next thing Tom wanted to build a set of self-contained tourist cabins overlooking a famous New Zealand river, and he possessed more than ample funds to do it – didn't he? But, then again, the poor bastard was left with *no choice* other than to deal with *me*! . . . The first step when it comes to following my blue print for handling resource consents is finding out how much funding the applicant has at his disposal. If he has a bundle of money, you then create an assault course of red tape whereby you can have him fleeced at every turn by your network. If the applicant isn't well funded, you just put his application at the bottom of the heap, and you ignore it for long enough that he eventually goes away. . . The second step is to point out the various pitfalls our applicant has ahead of him. You warn him that there'll have to be input from the district council, DoNE, the local Maoris, the Forest and Bird people, the New Zealand Heritage Department, the Department of Conservation and just about a dozen other entities that may object to someone who wants to build next to or near a New Zealand waterway. And that's even if you own the land freehold. The term 'freehold' in this country's all fucking bullshit! Anyone can come off the street and decide what you can or *can't do* on your land. . . Nonetheless, that's where you need to be very careful not to put your applicant off. You throw him a lifeline – don't you? You tell him that he'll come across a consultant in a nearby town that may be very expensive, but he's an expert in dealing with all the various departments and interested parties, plus knows of every method when it comes to bypassing or cutting his way through all the red tape. This consultant, of course, works for a shelf company that belongs to you, even though your name doesn't appear as a director or shareholder. That's what trusted friends and distant relatives are for. And naturally this consultant's an ex-council employee who's left the public service in order to pursue a very lucrative business that's more or less been set up via the public service itself. . . Do you understand what I've been getting at so far, Nev?"

I hastily looked around the table and saw that I was the object of everyone's attention! "Yeah – so far I do, Allan."

"Good! I've drummed it into the heads of all department chiefs – introduce as many formalities as possible, so that it's literally impossible for *anyone* in the general public to submit an application, or fill out a government form correctly without hiring a consultant. Sew confusion – move the goalposts – change the rules – shift the parameters – get the minister in charge of your department to change the laws as often as possible. In fact complicate everything so much that your minister's that confused, he or she needs your advice and guidance. And let's face it, Nev. The intelligence of your average New Zealand minister's downright pitiful. These people may be able to con and win the votes of the general public, but the bulk of them are totally incompetent. Furthermore, prove to these same idiots and dickheads that you're actually out amongst the tax and ratepayers earning your salaries. . . Fortunately the bods over at New Zealand Petroleum and Minerals have caught on very nicely because it's well nigh impossible for mineral permit holders to correctly submit compulsory annual reports on any permits. This has given rise to several agencies run by ex-Mines Department employees, and they can charge whatever fees that take their fancy. They're having a whale of a time. . . Righty-ho then – Tom was an arrogant young wanker, who came into the council offices and insisted on seeing the CEO. No, he didn't want to talk to the Chief Resource Consent Officer – he wanted to talk to the organ grinder – not the monkey. He used that exact same terminology right in front of me, so was referring to me as being a 'monkey'. The same egotistical attitude that his father was renowned for. So I was the 'monkey' – was I? It was then that I decided to take the young prick to the cleaners. Everyone in the district knew that he was worth a small fortune, so it was hardly necessary to check on his financial wherewithal. Next I pointed out the various pitfalls, and he tells me that he won't take any shit from DoNE or the Maoris because he owned the land for his tourist cabins freehold, and no bastard was going to tell him what he could or couldn't do with it. Fucking dickhead! All the same he still takes my advice and sees my local consultant – doesn't he? That's what so expensive about getting resource consents in New Zealand. I very much doubt, especially after all my effort, if any government entity will take an applicant seriously unless that applicant uses a consultant. . . Now the bulk of resource consent consultants are form-fillers. Nothing else. The majority of them that I know have no particular expertise, and have zero influence unless they're connected financially to the person or people who have the power to approve a resource consent application. And your average form-filler doesn't come cheap. Your bog-standard consultant will charge you a hundred and thirty bucks an hour, while it isn't unusual having equally incompetent people charging three to five hundred bucks an hour. My particular consultant that I recommended to people charged five hundred an hour, but he had a reputation for getting resource consents a lot faster than other consultants – not so? No mystery there as I was the Chief Resource Consent Officer. . . Let me make things perfectly clear for you, Nev. In the last three decades or so the trials and tribulations of getting a resource consent in New Zealand has become one of the country's major industries. Literally thousands of people depend on this for an income. Civil servants such as I and others have created an obstacle course, no – a minefield – of red tape for anyone wanting a resource consent or permission to do anything. The rules and regulations we've composed have been designed to squeeze every last cent possible from an applicant. . . Am I making myself perfectly clear, Nev?"

I began to wish that I'd kept my mouth shut. "Yeah, Allan – perfectly clear." My mind was totally elsewhere because Barb and Avril were feeding the fox terriers at the table! Each had a dog on her lap, and they were feeding them pieces of fillet steak that cost over two hundred bucks a kilogram!

Actually I found the whole situation mind-boggling! When the steaks first arrived, Barb offered us both smoky barbeque and cranberry sauce to go with them. At least half a dozen plastic bottles of these sauces were scattered around the table. I saw Greg wink at Trev when both the Peacocks, Avril and Helen Granite sloshed smoky barbeque sauce all over the steak. Ken Mears opted for a lake of cranberry sauce. So much for the fair dinkum French truffle sauce! Barb then went on to announce that she'd been playing a little joke on us when she said only certain people were getting the Krug champagne. In fact we were all getting Dom Perignon, but it wasn't your ordinary run-of-the-mill bubbly. It was Dom Perignon Oenotheque 1959 and she'd paid over six thousand New Zealand dollars a bottle for it! All on Allan Peacock's public service credit card! Apparently it was someone in the New Zealand diplomatic service that had smuggled the four bottles into the country, and he'd flogged them to her for a bargain! Even a fairly simple bloke like me realised her outlay for the champagne and the fillet steaks came to well over twenty-five grand! All paid for by the Kiwi taxpayers!

Another thing that also rattled me was Peacock himself. He wasn't swallowing the steak! He'd cut off a piece of steak, then put it in his mouth and chew it. After half a minute or so he spat what was left of the steak onto his fork, and then put the ball of chewed meat on the side of his plate. After a while there was a line of these soggy meat balls all round his plate. When he finally finished his meal, he put his plate on the floor and the Jack Russells literally polished it!

Greg must've seen on my face that I was taken aback by such behaviour, and he rolled his eyes in sympathy.

"Yes, the major role of a public servant in New Zealand is to raise revenue," Peacock continued. "Assisting the public comes a long way after that. Department heads now spend the majority of their waking hours trying to think up new and plausible ways of taxing the public. With the various Labour governments we've seen in power – especially this latest one – we now almost have a civil servant for every person working in the private sector. . . I know that sounds impossible to believe, but you. . . "

"Yeah!" Trev pulled him up. "I met a bloke the other day who reckoned that for every businessman in the private sector, you've got twenty public servants hanging off his balls like body crabs."

"And I bet that bloke would've been a farmer?" Barb suggested.

I glanced over at Greg, and noticed that he seemed to be having trouble swallowing his food.

"Nah," Trev disagreed with her. "It was some bloke who had a vineyard not far from Arrowtown."

I saw Greg visibly relax.

"He's still a farmer," Peacock argued. "And this's where I've spent years preaching cooperation amongst the various departments. Most of the department heads I've met are a bunch of fucking dickheads. They're jealous of their power and positions, plus they're paranoid that somebody's after the same job. This's quite understandable because they'd cut their own children's' throats to hang on to power. You take for instance the understanding I'd had with Avril and her DoNE Department when I was working for the regional council. She and I hit it off immediately, and we didn't have to say a word to know where each other was coming from. If I wanted to apply extra pressure on a resource applicant, I'd get the local DoNE department head – also a woman – to announce that one of her officers had found a skink with two arseholes on the specific land that the applicant wanted to develop. It took one phone call to this woman..."

"What about one those snails, Allan?" Mear's called out. "Or those frogs that they're wiping out on the North Island. What are those frogs called?"

"They're called '*leopelma Hochstetteri*, Ken." That time Peacock looked annoyed at being interrupted. "In most cases my friendly resource consultant would make the skink or Ken's frog problem go away for about ten grand. Four grand each for Avril and me – two grand for the DoNE department head. It was the same with the local Iwi. One of the first people I got my pet resource consultant to get in contact with was a Maori bloke who was considered to be among the local *kaumatua* or elders in the district. A grand could get him to claim that his grandfather had taken a crap under a particular tree within the applicant's land, and it would cost a further ten grand to make that problem disappear. That's what makes the paranoia about Maoris in this country such a godsend. Any Maori objection to a new development – no matter how vexatious – can hold up a resource application for years."

"Ah – yes! Let's drink to the Maoris!" It was Avril's turn to suggest a toast. It looked like she, too, was getting pissed on the champagne. The four bottles of Oenotheque 59 were quickly demolished, so we were left with ordinary Dom Perignon which only cost three hundred bucks a bottle.

"Yeah – let's drink to the fucking Maoris!" her husband's voice was literally booming!

"Hear hear!" Peacock was all agreement. "Seriously, Nev," he looked down the table at me, "the Maoris have to be the leading source of revenue for the New Zealand public service because whichever government's in power – Labour or Nats – billions of dollars are sunk into supposedly insuring that the Maoris are getting a fair deal. And I'm talking in billions! Greg here has a theory about this, and I tend to agree with him. Over the past few decades the Kiwi people – especially the so-called educated ones – seem to insist on proving to the world how New Zealand's the most politically correct nation on earth. Just behind Australia – that is. Whenever the Iwi start squawking about how they were tricked by the Treaty of Waitangi, academics around the country feel they need to shit themselves with shame! It's the same with those Canadians and the way they're crawling to the Eskimos. As an example for you. . ."

Peacock came to an abrupt halt because Barb launched herself out of her chair and gave one of the Filipina maids a resounding backhand across the face! A large bowl of fruit salad went flying in one direction, and a plastic container of ice cream emptied its contents all over the table! The hysterical barking of one of the dogs was almost deafening, yet Barb's voice still came across loud and clear. "How many fucking times do I have to fucking tell you? You serve people on the right – not on the fucking left!"

The maid just bolted for the door and Barb and the Jack Russels went hurtling after her.

"Hmm – hard to get decent help these days," Greg felt fit to announce.

"Too right!" Peacock agreed. "Barb's spent hours trying to point that girl in the right direction. A good clip around the ear should do her the world of good."

So the fresh fruit steeped in French cognac and the organic ice cream was suddenly off the menu. That didn't seem to put Barb out too much because she soon had a series of cheese cakes arrayed along the table – passionfruit – strawberry – boysenberry and caramel flavoured.

Trev probably thought it was his turn to lighten the mood. "Is it true the Maoris were cannibals and used to eat each other?"

"Oh – yes!" Barb leapt on the question. "In my BA thesis I did a comparison between the Maoris and the North American Indians. The Indians weren't cannibals, but the Maoris certainly were. If it hadn't of been for the arrival of the Pakeha, they'd still be snacking on each other to this day."

"And don't go believing that fucking bullshit about the Maoris eating enemies just so that they could poop them out again," Peacock added. "That's what the Maoris are claiming – that they ate warriors from opposing tribes and crapped them out in order to insult them."

Kev plucked up the courage to join in. "Yeah, but if they ate someone – did they eat everything? Like did they eat the hands and feet and things?"

I saw a mischievous glint in Greg's eye when he leaned across the table. "Of course they did, Kev. Especially the hands. Where do you think the expression 'finger food' come from?"

Avril thought that was so funny, champagne squirted out of her nostrils. Helen Granite looked as though she was having a coughing fit, until I realised that she, too, was pissing herself laughing.

Trev then jumped on the bandwagon. "Bloody oath, and it's the same as the Asians with their tofu – the Maoris had 'toe food'!"

That caused further giggles and guffaws around the table.

"Yes, I did a lot of research into Maori cannibalism," Barb announced proudly. "I came across the diary of a sailor off one of the whaling boats. He was actually living with Maoris somewhere in the most northern part of the North Island. He recounts how this one Maori woman gave strict instructions to her husband when he went out with war parties. Apparently he'd captured a man in one of the opposing Maori factions and he brought him home for the larder. When the prisoner was finally killed and eaten, he was deemed by the wife to have been the most delicious she'd ever tasted, so she wanted her husband to see if he could take further prisoners from the same family. Particularly family members that were teenagers because they'd have plenty of meat and would be more tender at the same time. I assume it was very similar for the Iwi back then as it is for pakeha choosing Aberdeen Angus beef, or Hereford, or Charolais today. It appears that. . ."

"You're kidding!" Kev's eyes were popping out.

"Kidding about what, Kevin?" Barb bent forward to challenge him.

"About Maoris capturing people and only killing 'em when they wanted 'em for tucker time."

"Barb's not pulling your leg," Avril dived in. "You take the east coast Maoris on the South Island when they crossed the Southern Alps to gather greenstone on the West Coast. The first thing they'd do is capture a bunch of West Coast Maoris. Not only were the prisoners forced to carry the greenstone boulders back across the Alps, they also came in handy as a source of food for the journey back. Like cattle being kept live on the hoof, so to speak. Naturally the Maoris didn't have refrigeration before the Pakeha arrived, so it was a handy way of keeping their meat from going off. It would've been terrifying for the prisoners having to wonder when they'd be next on the menu! The Maoris called human flesh '*long pig*,' and I heard the fatter victims were preferred to the leaner ones. I suppose they never used to watch their calorie intake back in those days? Same as we're seeing nowadays."

That brought about another series of guffaws from Peacock, Greg and Mears, and then there were shrieks of laughter from Barb and Merl. Trev was staring straight at me as wide-eyed as Kev, and Helen Granite was having another of her coughing laughter fits.

"So what did you end up doing to this Tom fellow, Allan?" Greg changed the subject. "The bloke who was after the resource consent?"

"Ah – Tom!" Peacock looked keen to have centre stage again. "As I said – I was determined not to grant him a resource consent, but I was still going to take as much money off him as I could. What you have to realise, Nev," he returned his attention to me, "is that the majority of resource consent officers are very nervous about granting resource consents in the first place. They don't want to set any resource consent precedents that're likely to fuck up and come back and bite them in the crutch. Consequently they'll refuse a consent at the slightest opportunity. In Tom's case he was sitting on a sea of money, and he was threatening to engage lawyers in order to speed things up. By that time I'd almost used up my entire arsenal – DoNE – the Iwi – the anal retards from Forest and Bird – a corrupt hydrologist who reported that sewage from Tom's tourist cabins would pollute the adjacent river for miles downstream – the Heritage Act people. And that's despite the fact that the bulk of New Zealand's waterways are riddled with Giardia! Giardia and the 1080 poison that they drop by the ton from choppers on the South Island. . . All in all I'd delayed the consent for five years, although I still had Tom believing that he'd be given it at any moment – the stupid prick! Call me a monkey? . . . Up till then he'd outlaid almost half a million on items such as government archaeologists who inspected his land for possible historic or heritage sites – government botanists and geologists consulting to DoNE – plus, of course, the government hydrologist that I just mentioned. That's where various DoNE agencies around New Zealand have this very lucrative arrangement that I've seen them employ quite frequently, and I must say that I take my hat off to Avril for thinking it up. Instead of sending just one officer out at a time to inspect a proposed development site – they'd send a whole platoon of them time and time again. Amongst this platoon would be a so-called experts – botanists – ornithologists – entomologists – plus experts on lizards with two arseholes etceteras. All these experts come at a price – don't they? Thousands and thousands of dollars! And don't forget my corrupt DoNE officer. She conjured up sightings of takahēs – brown kiwis with spotted balls – tuataras – and even a kakapo! I'm surprised she didn't come up with a moa sighting."

"Whatsa a 'kakapo'?" The expensive champagne had really prodded Kev out of his shell!

"It's the world's only flightless parrot," Peacock seemed mildly surprised by the query. "They're almost extinct. Same as the takahēs because incompetent DoC contractors are mistaking them for other birds and are blowing them away. As for Moas – they *are* extinct, although we get the odd sighting of one by West Coasters when they've swallowed a gutsful of booze. No, unfortunately the Maoris hunted the moas to extinction, and they almost did the same to the kakapos and takahēs. . . Do you know what's suddenly occurred to me? All these endangered birds are flightless, so no wonder that the Maoris have had such an impact on them, what with not having guns and bows and arrows. How on earth did that outfit the New Zealand Deerstalkers and DoC fuck that one up on Motutapu Island if takahēs can't fly? Some woman suggested that people with Celtic names could've been involved, and I suppose that might've been a major contributing factor? The Maoris can't be blamed for that one. . . No, if it weren't for the Pakeha, we'd have no Kakapos left, Kev."

"So what happened to poor, old Tom?" Avril wanted Peacock back on track.

"Yes – Tom – the poor dickhead!" Peacock's face was a deep red like Ken Mears'. "Called me a monkey – didn't he? Eventually I needed to watch myself because Tom was talking about employing some powerful lawyers in Auckland, so I had to make sure that I wasn't challenged via the fucking civil law courts. At that time I'd managed to delay the resource consent by a further three years. As a last resort I used a tool that's very popular with just about every government institution in New Zealand. I not only had the application file holding all the relevant documents lost once – but twice! Unfortunately a young lass in Wellington was made a scapegoat for the second loss and was dismissed, however – if you're going to make an omelette – it may be necessary to break the odd egg or two. . . Mind you, that wasn't the last arrow I had in my quiver. If there's one thing every local council in New Zealand needs – whether it's a regional or district council – it needs access to what we call 'serial objectors'. Greg here will give you a much better description of them than I can. Let it be sufficient to say that every public servant in this country owes a vast debt of gratitude to your average Kiwis in the street, and it's not just because of the taxes and rates that they pay. It's the New Zealander's fear of others doing well that's become a very powerful weapon for every government licensing agency. That's why you'd be justified in claiming that every second Kiwi was a 'serial objector' or someone who opposes any new development whether it affects him or not. . . I'm not joking. You take a property owner at the very south of the South Island back in the good old days. He wants to chop down a tree because it's blocking the view of the traffic when he wants to leave his driveway. It's a danger to him and his family. He has to put in an application with the relevant local authority to fell the tree because it might fall across a public thoroughfare. At the applicant's expense the local authority then puts a copy of the application in the local and regional newspapers and people are asked if they object or not. That's where you can have someone who lives on the North Island who can quite legally object to the tree being cut down. He can claim that he's grown to love the tree and how it's a major joy to him when he visits the area on his holidays, even though he's visited Southland only once in his lifetime. That can keep the tree standing for years to come unless the property owner takes the council to court, and that, too, can take many years and cost him a small fortune. . . Back in my day in the regional council it was mandatory to publish the final resource application parameters in the local rag, in case there were possible local objectors that hadn't been consulted. In Tom's case I published the same details in newspapers in Wellington, Christchurch and Auckland, so – and as you can imagine – there were howls of protest and outrage coming in from all over the country! Although Tom only wanted private access to about fifty metres of the river, we saw anglers, trampers, tree huggers and a host of people all objecting from far and wide. That put paid to the fucking powerful lawyers in Auckland. By then Tom was out of pocket to the tune of a couple of million. Since then I've heard the stupid bastard's got cancer or leukaemia, so he'll never live to see those cabins of his being built. All along the dickhead pleaded that he wanted to provide employment for his fellow Kiwis, but what the fuck has that got to do with the price of eggs – the pompous wanker?"

Peacock drained his champagne glass after stubbing out his cigar on a slab of fillet steak that still remained on the serving plate. The whole setup was becoming bloody weird! Everyone at the table bar Mulji smoked, but there were no ashtrays. Barb started the ball rolling by flicking the ash of her cigarette onto the remains of the cheesecake nearest her. Mears followed suit by doing the same to the cheesecake just in front of him. Perhaps two thirds of the cheesecakes were uneaten; yet they became the official ashtrays. After an hour or so cigarette butts were sticking out of them in all directions, and three remaining fillet steaks were coated with ash from Greg's and Peacock's cigars. Apparently they were Cuban cigars that Peacock had earned via facilitating another Chinese land purchase, and he reckoned that they sold retail for over a hundred American dollars each! And that was duty free in Dubai!"

Soon after that we were missing one of our party. Ken Mears was flaked out over his table mat, and his head was laying smack in the middle of a puddle of spew that he'd let go perhaps a couple of minutes before he passed out.

"Let him drown, the stupid – fucking – wanker!" Avril showed him no pity at all.

I could scarcely blame Mears for chundering because the dining room was filled with a stink that was all too familiar to those who knew Merl. I was expecting Trev to get stuck into her, but strangely enough he kept silent! There was an immediate cessation of conversation, and Mears – sitting right next to Merl – must've copped the brunt of it. Within seconds his throat and chest started convulsing as he desperately tried not to chunder. Without looking at anyone in particular, Peacock got to his feet and opened some bay windows as well as the doors at each end of the dining room, and slowly the disgusting odour dissipated. Somewhere in the distance I could hear brass band music.

"Is that din coming from that Asian circus, Allan?" Barb must've been keen to come up with any sort of a distraction.

"Yeah, Babs, they must be over at Waitangi Park."

"What about the racket they're making?" Barb further queried her husband. "Do you think we should make a complaint to the Thorndon Council?"

"But you can hardly hear 'em," Trev just had to poke his nose in.

"I know, Trevor," Barb's eyes were drilling holes in my younger brother. "Still, I don't like having so many fucking Asians parked almost on my doorstep. They're responsible for just about all the serious crime here in New Zealand – drugs – prostitution – sex slaves and extortion. It's the same in Australia, in case you haven't noticed."

Peacock tapped his glass for silence. "Righto, Greg, should we discuss business here or in the upstairs lounge room?"

Greg stood up. "The upstairs lounge room would be best because we can sit back and relax. You were saying that you've just had it swept, Allan?"

"I'll arrange a couple of decanters of port and some glasses," Barb also stood up from her chair. "I've got half a dozen bottles of beautiful thirty-year-old Colheita Port from Portugal which I managed to snap up at two thousand a bottle. I'm sure the Wellington ratepayers won't mind. It's better than anything they make in New Zealand, and much better than that cat's pee they produce in Australia."

"What's this about Allan having the lounge room 'swept'?" Kev turned to Greg as we filed out of the dining room.

"He enlisted a private security firm to come round and check the house for bugs. You know – listening devices. Being so high up in the civil service, he can't afford to have outside parties listening in to any of his public service-related conversations. It's just as well, when you hear what I've got to say."

Once we'd made ourselves comfortable in some massive leather armchairs in the upstairs lounge room, Barb came round with a decanter that was wide and flat at the bottom. "It's an Irish Waterford ship's decanter," she announced proudly. "Allan bought a couple of them and these glasses when the current Labour shower first came to power.

He was sent over to Ireland in charge of a fact-finding delegation and naturally he took me and the kids with him. There was one almighty squawk from the National Party opposition when they found out we'd travelled first class and Allan's expense account was well over fifty grand, but the PM *herself* told them where to get off. Allan simply refuses to fly overseas unless he goes first class and takes the family with him."

The last time I'd come across port, it came from a flagon of very cheap stuff that Trev and I managed to purchase from a shonky liquor store owner when we were kids. Needless to say we got horribly pissed and were crook for days after! I vowed from then on that I'd never touch port again, but the aroma coming off Barb's Portuguese gear was irresistible! As soon as the tawny coloured liquid touched my tongue, I knew I was in for a serious treat!

It was apparent that Greg wasn't the only one who collected newspaper cuttings. With a flourish Allan Peacock handed me one. "Here you go, Nev, now you can see what I've been talking about. Here's a regional council after my own heart. It reminds of the golden days."

OUTRAGED BREEDER DUMPS ALPACA
POO IN FRONT OF COUNCIL OFFICES

A battle is still raging between an Australian alpaca breeder and a regional council in the North Island of New Zealand. The breeder claims to be totally exasperated and he demonstrated this by landing the council in the poo – in every sense of the word!

The irate farmer claims that the council's water plan change 41C has "broken us apart as a family" and has caused six years of debilitating frustration and mental collapse for him and his wife.

When recently informed that the council was doing its utmost to arrive at a speedy solution, he intimated that they were talking "absolute bloody crap."

The breeder and his wife drove over 100 kilometres in order to dump a truckload of alpaca excrement in the car park of the council's offices. He claimed that it was a demonstration as to how the issue had gone beyond the pale. It was to "bring to light the family's angst and disillusionment", he said.

"*This 41 C water plan has made us unviable as alpaca breeders. I have had hundreds of meetings over the years with the council to no avail, and they refuse to allow us any surety.*"

The breeder went on to say that all his life's savings had been spent on $500 per hour consultants that were hired to prepare the resource consent application, plus to cut through the red tape, and that he was now facing financial ruin.

A spokesperson for the council said she was aware of the breeder's problems; however was not allowed to comment on them. "This is all about considering a resource consent," she explained. "It's a matter that demands very detailed investigation by several agencies such as DoNE, Iwi, independent hydrologists, and anthropologists. It has been reported that a very rare skink might have been found in the vicinity. Plus a very rare snail. After what happened to the Powelliphanta snails on the West Coast, and the takahē that were slaughtered not all that long ago, we cannot rush the issue. Also there have been public objections from concerned New Zealanders coming in from all over the country"

She went on to say: "This consent application is also in the hands of very expensive external advisors in Wellington, and we are determined that any costs accrued will be passed onto the resource consent applicant whether the consent is granted or not. All along we have been very fair and outgoing with the applicant, and hopefully all this can be resolved in the next three years or so."

After everyone had read the article, Peacock turned to Greg who was sitting in the armchair next to him. "Greg, please tell the others about this newfangled, state-of-the-art screening device that they've come up with in India." "Ah yes!" Greg nodded. "First let me give you some background. . . Let me see now – in Australia they've been busy with a bowel cancer screening programme all over the country, and so far it's cost a fortune. Labour over here would like to do the same in order to possibly win votes, but, as you know well, they've already run out of money. This's where Mulji's colleague – a certain Professor Ghandi – comes in. He's the Dean of the Taj Mahal University in Mumbai. Okay – and to cut a long explanation short – this Professor Ghandi has invented a bowel cancer screening system whereby he uses a colour chart. In a nutshell, he claims he can determine the health of a person's bowel by matching the colour of the skid marks that the person's faeces leave in a toilet bowl with his colour chart. Personally I've never seen one of these charts, but Mulji has. . . Can you tell us more about them, Mulji?"

The Sikh briefly scanned the room first. "Yes, I have seen one of these charts, Gregory, though I, too, am not exactly sure how they work. From what I understand – the lighter the colour a person's faeces are – the better the health they are in. If they are darker – they need to receive medical attention."

"And do these charts work?" Peacock queried him.

Mulji's eyes widened. "I have no idea, Allan."

"Who cares?" Greg chimed in. "If we've got a professor who's a dean of an Indian university saying they work – who's going to challenge him over here? No government agency will when you've got all the department heads busily watching their few remaining pennies. Besides, Allan, those bean counters from the Department of Health have begged both you and I to come up with ways of raising them extra funding, so they're hardly going to allow anyone from their outfit to make any waves. Especially after all those committees and sub-committees we chaired in order to investigate possible French espionage. Millions were taken from almost every department. . . As I've said all along – Labour must realise they're going to be kicked out in this upcoming election, and they're desperately looking around for a poisoned challis that they can leave the Nats with. If they can pass a bill installing my Department of Inner Health through the House in the next couple of months, we can lock in five-year contracts with the new department heads that we choose to run the show. Sure, the Nat's are going to take a sharp knife to public service numbers, but I doubt if they'll do anything drastic in the first twelve months. They'll be too busy putting out fires that previous Labour governments have lit years ago. Take the railways for starters. The horse will have well and truly bolted by then because we should've set up offices in every region, and recruited an army of staff to occupy them."

"So how much funding will you need to set all this up, plus what's in it for us?" That seemed to be the first time that Helen Granite contributed to any conversation.

"Ah – I'm glad you asked that, Helen!" Greg beamed at her. "About sixty-five million to start the ball rolling, then I've budgeted for a hundred million per calendar year after that. As I've pointed out before – we're looking at half a billion dollars over the next five years. . . The pay will be the same for any department board member – say $250,000 to $300,000 per annum. Naturally you'll get all the lurks and perks – car – superannuation package – expense account – travel allowance – private medical insurance. Plus, of course, you should get at least three trips overseas per year – all your expenses paid with a thirty percent premium. . . But that's not where you'll really clean up. Next we'll establish the necessary consultancy agencies, and I can see you picking up an extra $300,000 to $400,000 per annum there. . . I've calculated it out that you and Avril should make $600,000 to $700,000 and Allan and I should pick up maybe $800,000 to $1,000,000 a year. Being department head, Merl should pick up roughly the same. Professor Gandhi has agreed to oversee the technical and medical side of things, and Mulji is still negotiating with him. I can see Mulji and the Prof picking up $450,000 per annum each."

"And why are you and Allan getting more than Avril and me?" Helen didn't seem happy with that. "You take the CEO of the Invercargill museum. You can see all the exhibits in twenty minutes flat, and they're paying him $300,000 a year. What makes you and Allan so special?"

"Because Greg thought all this up in the first place, and it's me who'll be putting my fucking balls on the line, Helen," Peacock moved back into the conversation. "We'll be having to put up with some monumental changes if the Nats get in. I'll have half a dozen National Party MPs – all of whom will be on the front bench after the next elections – gunning for me as it is because I've backed those dickheaded pricks in Labour more than I should have. I should've been like you, Helen – I should've jumped off Labour's sinking ship a couple of years ago like any professional public servant. I fucking should've remained politically impartial."

"Don't worry, Helen," Greg picked up the baton. "As the department grows, so will the perks. There'll be kickbacks when we rent offices – buy department vehicles and uniforms – and the consultancy fees will increase as the whole setup becomes more entrenched. This could amount to several million for each of us per year. The figures I gave you previously are just the beginning."

Helen still looked glum. "I was expecting a lot more."

Thank goodness Trev knew all the right questions to ask, as it gave the Nazzari contingent the only avenue to supply something intelligent. "Let me get this right, Greg. You're talking about the government coming up with half a billion over five years because you've got a colour chart that some professor reckons can tell if you've got bowel cancer or not? Also you reckon you don't care if it works or not?"

"You've got it in one, Trev!" Greg gave him a bow. "We'll call it the *'THE GREAT NEW ZEALAND SKID MARK CONSPIRACY'!* With the political situation facing the country at this very juncture, I couldn't think of a better time to strike. With people like Allan and his faithful wife, Barb – plus with the able assistance of Avril and Helen here – I'm pretty certain we can pull this off."

"Yeah, and I reckon we can, too," Peacock held up his glass for more port. "There are those in the halls of power who owe me more than a few favours, and I'll start calling them in on Monday. Let's drink a toast to the Department of Inner Health and the 'Great New Zealand Skid Mark Conspiracy'."

"Hear – hear!" Greg agreed, and even Mulji looked delighted.

"To the 'Great New Zealand Skid Mark Conspiracy'!" Avril also raised her glass.

"So how's young Richard?" Greg abruptly changed the topic while he was filling Helen Granite's glass with port.

"Richard who?" Helen coughed back at him.

"Young Richard Head the Zulu that Mulji and I introduced to you?"

"Dick Head – you mean?" Helen's voice was still a dry rasp. "I caught him stealing cash and jewellery, so I had him deported back to Nigeria.

Zulu – my fucking arse! Where the fuck did you get the idea he was a Zulu? He's like all Nigerians I've come across, a fucking – lowlife – conman – drug pusher and thief! Unlike Trevor here. Tell me, Trev – what're you doing tomorrow night?"

The look on Trev's face was almost identical to when I told him that Kev was intending to marry Merl, and he nearly dropped the Cuban cigar that Peacock had just lit for him. As I've said before – he could be seriously quick off the mark when situations demanded it: "Tomorrow night – Helen? I won't be here. I have to be back in Queenstown to pick up Professor Ghandi off the plane."

"You know, Greg – this Department of Inner Health of yours could be more fun than what we were given during the Great Competition," Peacock went to Trev's rescue.

Kev was the first to jump on that statement. "So there *was a* turd competition? I thought Greg was just pulling our legs."

"Oh yes – the Great Competition!" Peacock's eyes widened. Then he suddenly frowned. "Along with all the corruption that came with it?"

"What corruption are you talking about?" Trev was obviously relieved to be rescued from Helen Granite.

Peacock pointed to his wife. "If Barb was picked instead of Fran Crapper, the Pakeha would've bolted in, and we would've had no need to get the SOS involved. Not only would Barb *not deliver* twins – she would've come up with a turd twice the size of Rangi Hika's. . . Not so – Babs?"

Quite incredibly there was an even fiercer look on Barb's face! "Yes – those corrupt fucking arseholes!"

Peacock sat back in his chair and puffed on his cigar before elaborating. He first pointed a finger at the ceiling. "You take the upstairs shithouse – the one in our ensuite. Barb's clogged that one solid at least half a dozen times, plus the three we've got downstairs. Costs a bloody fortune to get them cleared! That's why she goes across to the Karori Library. She's blocked up the toilets on every floor, plus – what with Labour being in – she's jammed most of the facilities at the Beehive. I'm forever having to wipe some public service department head's arse, so Barb spends a lot of her time up in the Beehive.

Over the space of a month she knocked out the public gallery shithouse, the one in the foyer for the MPs, plus the PM's very own personal boghouse just across from her office. She blew the crap out of that microphone that was under the seat when the toilet overflowed. You should've seen the turd she left in the PM's toilet – it was the size of a Zeppelin! Seriously, I'm not talking out of my arse. . . I kid you not, Kev – if Babs was picked instead of Fran Crapper – the fucking Maoris wouldn't've stood a chance!"

"Too – fucking – right – Al!" Barb's eyes were like broken glass.

"How come Fran Crapper was chosen, Al?" Avril further authenticated Greg's story.

"It was because Fran's father's related to an enthusiastic and financial supporter of the fucking Green Party. The PM needed all the help she could get from the Greens, so that's how Crapper got picked."

"Yes, and I beat her by two turds to one when we had the best out of three preliminary trials," Barb's eyes were now like bullets! "Fran could eat as many Canterbury spuds as she liked, but she wasn't a patch on me with my pumpernickel bread rolls, authentic Swiss Gruyere cheese and genuine French pâté de foie gras. I could put more weight and size on my turds in a fortnight than what she could do in a month. She only beat me the once when I picked up diarrhoea from some green-lipped muscles that were served up to me at the Beehive's banquet hall. I still say to this day that it was because of a Samoan waitress who hadn't washed her hands. Why they keep letting these Pacific Island losers in, is totally beyond me."

"Listen, Trev, old son," Greg patted my younger brother's arm. "I might have to get you to stoke our Helen Granite's boilers. If you give her a good rogering, perhaps she won't be so greedy?"

"Like fuckin' hell – you will!" Trev was dead set against the idea. "You ask Nev. He's desperate for a free root. Fuck me dead – I swear she fondled my balls a couple of times."

"Is that why you were staring over at me?" I revelled in his discomfort. "You looked like you'd seen a ghost."

"Yeah, I'm not kidding – she put her fuckin' hand on my crutch a couple of times!"

We were travelling in Greg's Aegean Blue Bentley, that he kept in Wellington, to the Grand Mercure Hotel. Trev and Greg were up front, and Mulji and I were in the back seat. Kev and Merl had stayed behind at the Peacock mansion, and we'd left Merl discussing with Barb the best way to get hold of decent house servants.

That was the next subject that was raised by me in the Bentley. "Did you see that smack Barb gave that Filipina maid in the mouth?" I called out to Greg. "Fuck me – you wouldn't get away with something like that back in Aussie."

"Barb hasn't a worry in the world," Greg eyed me in the rear view mirror. "Those two Filipina girl's came here on a phony student's visa, so now they're overstayers – aren't they? Barb's pretending that she'll be getting them residency permits, and that's why they're working at the Peacocks for nothing. She's got them sleeping on mattresses in the downstairs laundry. They're toiling away for her twenty-four-seven, and all they're getting paid is food leftovers from the table. If they whinge about it, she'll see that they're deported like Helen did to our Dick Head. I suppose you could justifiably call it 'slave labour'."

"Yes, that is quite common over here, as it is in India," Mulji backed him up. "There are hundreds of Thai and Filipina girls working as domestic labour in Wellington, and they are being paid nothing. The Chinese have some of them working as sex slaves in the brothels in Auckland and Wellington, and no one seems to be doing anything about it. That Barbara – her heart is as cold as ice."

"Yeah – what a fuckin' dog!" Trev took things a step further. "Hey, Greg, was it right about what she said about the champagne? You know – that Dom Perignon costing six grand a bottle?"

"Oh yes!" Greg never hesitated. "She did well to get Oenotheque 1959 for only six thousand bongo dollars a bottle. I've seen later vintages retailed over here for eight thousand. What you need to realise is – Barb didn't pay for it – the bongo taxpayer did."

"The waste of all that food was terrible!" Mulji steered the conversation elsewhere. "I wonder why Barb did not give you proper ashtrays, Gregory? You had the use of ashtrays in the main reception room and upstairs."

"It was because of the Filipina maids, Mulji," Greg replied.

"Howzat?" Trev pushed in.

Greg stopped the Bentley in order to give way to a taxi. "Like I said before, the maids get the scraps from the Peacock's table. They're going to have to pick out the cigarette butts from those cheese cakes and scrape the ash of what was left of the steak. I suggest that you could put it down to Barb just being a nasty, malicious bitch. Apparently the Belgian colonists used to do the same when Belgium governed the Congo. That's the Democratic Republic of Congo nowadays. The only other time I've seen it was with a Scottish family back in Kenya. These people know they're obliged to feed their servants because they're paying them nothing or a pittance, but they're loathe to see them having any sort of a special time of it. The food we were given tonight was very expensive, so Barb was determined that the maids aren't going to enjoy it as much as we did. What we're dealing with here are petty, consummate scumbags, Mulji."

"I see!" The Sikh seemed happy with that explanation, although he was equally baffled about another item. "But what was that terrible smell? You know – that smell that made Kenneth Mears vomit? I was very lucky that the smell did not make me vomit as well. . . Actually – when I come to think of it – there was the same smell in the car when we were travelling to the Peacock's house. It was terrible!"

"That was just Merl farting," Trev casually informed him. "That Mears might be a dickhead, but you can't blame him for chundering. He was sitting right next to Merl when she dropped her guts."

Mulji was none the wiser after that explanation. "Dropped her guts? What are you saying – she dropped her guts? Are you trying to tell me that Merl was responsible for that horrible smell?"

"Too bloody right – mate!" Trev assured him. "Merl farted both in the car and at the Peacock's place. The more you have to do with her – the more you'll get to know the stink."

"Now do you believe me about the Great Competition? Greg poked at Trev. "Never mind the stink of Merle's flatus – you should've been around Barb when she was practising for the finals against Fran Crapper. You won't believe this, but I'm positive Allan was turned on by the stench! You should've seen the way..."

Trev sounded almost overwhelmed. "Yeah, but did you see the look of pride on Barb's face when Peacock reckoned she'd blocked up all those shithouses? He seemed just as proud as her! "

Greg was equally enthused. "I know – Trev – I know!"

"So you and Allan were not joking with us?" Mulji insisted.

"Never a more honest word," Greg assured him.

"I see," the Sikh sounded doubtful. "Hey, Gregory. . . Tell me – do you think they liked the idea of Professor Ghandi's screening contraption?"

Greg chuckled and lit a cigarette with the vehicle's lighter. "Peacock liked it, and that's the main thing. He's crapping himself with the prospect of the National Party winning the next elections. By backing the Labour PM, he's certainly put his shirt on the wrong horse. Either way, he sees my Department of Inner Health as being his ultimate salvation. . . I tell you what, Trev – you nearly gave me a heart attack. "

"How come?"

"When you informed Peacock that someone told you that for every Kiwi businessman you have twenty public servants hanging off his figs like body crabs."

"Bloody oath!" I agreed with Greg. "I thought you were gunna fuck things right up!"

Trev turned round to face me. "Nah, Nev – just keeping Greg on his toes. Fuck me – did ya see that fuckin' Barb? She reckoned that a Sequoia was some Indian from Nevada. A Sequoia's a fuckin' tree – for fucksakes!"

Greg laughed out loud. "I know, Trev – an absolute bottom feeder – our Barb Peacock. Do you see how much store she put on her BA degree? That should give you the measure of that fat, revolting slob."

The following day Kev, Trev and I went for a tour of Wellington with Greg in his beautiful Bentley. I was getting used to being driven around in flash cars. Merl's Porsche Cayenne – Greg's Mercedes and Bentley – and I'd also been given a ride into Queenstown in Merl's Aston Martin DB9. The latter thrill was somewhat marred because Merl's breath was awfully foul that day. There was almost an aura about her that Dad had described the most precisely; she smelled like a septic tank with its lid off.

Greg escorted us throughout the Beehive or the executive wing of New Zealand's parliament buildings. Everyone seemed to know him – most of the MPs both Labour and National – the chief of the Defence Department – the head of the Police Department – the Minister of Maori Affairs. All seemed keen to see him, plus found time for a chat.

We then stopped off at the famous Backbencher Pub and Cafe for lunch, one of Helen Granite's favourite watering holes. Even more people at that establishment seemed anxious to be included in Greg's conversations. Apparently some of them were the country's most senior public servants and leading business people! And that's not to mention the gorgeous women! I'm not kidding – I came across exotic blondes, brunettes and redheads all hanging off his every word! Women that I could only dream about! Delightful women like the news readers we that were on TV back in Aussie. Even more surprising, they seemed quite interested *in me* when Greg said I was one of his advisors! It wasn't necessary to do that, yet he did! I was living another life on different planet! Beautiful women being interested in me!

I could see that Kev was mostly uncomfortable and way out of his depth, and I, too, felt very much the same; however Trev took everything in his stride. He was right in amongst everything, chatting and joking away with everyone that Greg introduced to us. He looked both smart and comfortable in a new suit and tie. It was also very noticeable that Greg had won my younger brother over totally. All memories of him having to do a runner from Kalgoorlie had long since disappeared. He was obviously very wealthy, and some of the most powerful people in New Zealand appeared eager to share his company.

It was also abundantly clear that Greg was a gun manipulator. He chuckled quietly to himself and turned to me when we were alone outside the Beehive complex. "It looks like things have settled down after my little French saboteur caper."

"What do you mean – *your* saboteur caper?"

He was even more amused. "Yes, I think I received help from on high. I was responsible for the turd placed at the foot of Robbie Burns statue, but the contamination at Invercargill's Splash Palace and Queenstown's Aqualand was just bongos behaving like typical bongos. A few words here and there in all the right ears and I had Dunedin in shut down, and the government of Poo Zealand contemplating declaring war on France."

I was still taken aback. "How did you get frog and snail DNA into that crap that was put near the statue?"

"You'd remember our ex-Serb war criminal Dragan Milošević?"

I could hardly have forgotten such a character. "Yeah?"

"He needed a favour, so I got him to organise someone from the North Island to purchase a couple of dozen Hochstetter frogs and a couple of Powelliphanta snails on the Chinese black market up in Auckland. The Hochstetter frogs and Powelliphanta snails are big ticket items back in China, seeing as they're becoming fewer and fewer in number. I'm not sure if the Chinese black market traders have DoC to thank for that, especially now that takahēs are much sought after by Chinese traditional medicine dispensers. Either way, Dragan's agent – an ex-female jockey from Matamata – ate the frogs and one of the snails, and she was also responsible for our West Coast suspect handling the photograph of some French woman allegedly having a crap on the side of a Dunedin street. She's the person I had to see when we went to Dunedin, and you singlehandedly tried to suffocate your brothers, me and other innocents in that yellow submarine. She found out about the police safe not being locked after getting a constable from Invercargill drunk, and she managed to steal the photo once she'd drugged the police station's normal tea lady. . . With that Stephen Wilce farce still in the back of SOS minds, there's nothing like a small amount of intrigue that includes possible French skulduggery. . . And that's not the end of it – is it, Nev?"

"The end of what?"

"The Dunedin dog shit saga. If you were to venture into the back yard of SOS' headquarters in Wellington, you'd come across whole ship's container loads of fake Billabong backpacks all carrying specimens collected by the SOS in Dunedin. A cat's been put among the pigeons after *human* DNA was found in a dog stool that was actually *placed in Robbie Burns' lap* in the Octagon Plaza! I bet you'll never guess what happened there?"

"I bloody doubt it!"

"You should have more faith in yourself, Nev," Greg reproached me. "It was a parting favour from Dragan – wasn't it? One of his cult followers is in charge of the incinerator at the Dunedin Hospital. He managed to waylay a spleen, plus a portion of lower bowel and a couple of appendixes before they went into the furnace. He fed these to his cocker spaniel, and left the proceeds in Robbie Burns' lap."

"How come this Dragan bloke owes you so many favours?"

Greg led the way to a place sufficiently distant from the Beehive complex so that we could smoke.

After lighting a cigarette, he turned to me. "I've been promoting his rubber poop cover sheets and sphincter whistles. I've also been in various politicians' ears with regard to something that would be a boon for hotel and motel owners on both the North and South Islands."

"And what's that?"

Greg looked at his watch before replying: "I very much doubt if it'll be long before same-sex marriages are made legal here. At long last thousands of couples will be able to come forward into the light as equals. As I brought to your attention not long back, Dragan has done a great deal to enable gay couples to emerge from the darkness of bigotry and unjust humiliation. The latest idea he's come up with is honeymoon suites for male couples. I've seen a booklet on one, and at first glance you can't help feeling it has sadomasochistic connotations. That's because the bed and furniture are all made of stainless steel, and the TV plus all the electrical appliances are stored in waterproof glass containers. The mattress on the bed has a rubber outer lining, plus the pillows. Dragan's rubber sheets also made up the bed linen. There are only white tiles on the floor, and no mats or carpets of any description. The walls and ceiling are also tiled, and the curtains in the room are identical to the one in the shower. A very powerful fire hose is positioned just outside the door to the motel or hotel room. All this is so that when the cleaners come to service the honeymoon suites, all they have to do is stand in the doorway and turn the fire hose on at full blast. A skilful fire hose operator can strip the rubber sheets from the bed, plus the pillowcases, and these are hosed into a special drain that passes them through to a heavy duty washing machine. . . Do you know how some motel and hotel rooms come with a shower cap, plus soaps and shampoo?"

I knew what he was talking about. "Most of 'em also have tea bags, and sugar and coffee sachets."

"They do all of that," Greg agreed. "Dragan's honeymoon suite brochure also advertises disposable, plastic spittoons, plus plastic mouth guards that protect teeth both in the upper and lower jaw."

"What are the spittoons and mouth guards for?"

That seemed to catch Greg off guard. "If I can remember correctly, they're there to facilitate any anilingus that might take place. The spittoons are provided to accommodate any grape, pomegranate or guava pips. And I understand the mouth guards are to stop any gooseberry, guava or strawberry seeds from getting into tooth cavities. . . Do you remember me telling you that I've read one of Dragan's books?"

"I think you said you were impressed?"

Greg suddenly looked serious. "Yes, I was! The advice that Dragan gives out to those that are contemplating a same-sex marriage comes from his own hard earned experience. He fell in love with some young bloke who came from the gold mining town of Reefton. His name was Brent. Like a good many West Coasters this young bloke had never been 'over the hill'. This's how the locals call it when someone ventures out of the dark, dank, crappy confines of the Coast. So Dragan decided to take Brent on a trial honeymoon. I suppose it's the same as what the couples in Married at First Sight do. Yes, you can believe it, and – using your Aussie blue collar worker vernacular – Dragan had every intention of shagging the arse of Brent! First they travelled down to Haast in Dragan's BMW, and then they took the highway leading over the Haast Pass through the tiny hamlet of Makarora to the beautiful lakeside town of Wanaka. They didn't stop there, but travelled onto Cromwell. . . We were there not long back – the place where they have those huge fruit icons – apple – pear – apricot – nectarine. . . There's another wonderful fruit they grow in Cromwell – not so, Nev?"

"And what would those be?"

"Cherries – Nev – cherries! Dragan simply adored Cromwell's cherries. The best cherries in the world just behind Aussie cherries. It was the cherry season and he just couldn't wait for Brent to try Cromwell's marvellous cherries. Naturally Brent also fell in love with them and managed to consume at least a couple of kilos. . . This was to haunt Dragan early the following morning – wasn't it?"

There was no way I could answer his question. "What happened?"

Greg sympathised with me. "Tough question – I know, Nev. While eating the cherries Brent swallowed the stones as well. Unlike Dragan – who spat the stones out of the car window as they drove down to Alexandra – Brent swallowed all of his. It nearly proved to be fatal!"

That certainly grabbed my attention. "What – did the stones get stuck in the bloke's guts or something?"

"No – Nev! Just as the sun was coming up, Dragan decided to practice a bit of anilingus on Brent because the young bloke had suffered a fairly torrid time from all the sodomy and so on. Within seconds of getting started, Dragan nearly choked on a cherry stone that almost made its way into his lungs! He wasn't expecting to come across a cherry stone – was he, Nev? It's a miracle that the emergency staff at Invercargill's Kew Hospital managed to remove the stone after he was flown there as fast as possible by helicopter. . . That's why his book's so popular with his gay male audience. It has a whole chapter on what the gay recipient should eat and what foods to avoid. Take for example what very hot curries are doing to Kenny Mears! . . . The next chapter covers safety equipment. I've already told you about the mouth guards, nonetheless there's a paragraph on safety goggles."

"Safety goggles? What would anyone need safety goggles for?"

Greg acknowledged a passerby. "I don't mean goggles are required *by all* male gay couples. It was another lesson he learnt via the agency of Brent. Brent was a virgin when he went with Dragan on the trial honeymoon. That is – he'd never been buggered before. Not only that, coming from the Coast, he'd also acquired a taste for Monteith's Black Beer – and who can blame him? It's nearly as acceptable as Speights Porter. That's why Dragan brought along a couple of cartons of it when they first set out. Being a typical male he was going to get Brent a little tipsy so that he could have his wicked way with him – the dastardly old fox! . . . It was shortly after he was discharged from Kew Hospital when he carried out another attempt at performing anilingus on Brent. I think this was in a Deluxe King room at Invercargill's Ascot Park Hotel. Brent had just partaken of four or five stubbies of Monteith's Black Beer that he used to chase down some smoked sausage-wrapped Scotch eggs that they'd purchased at a Vietnamese noodle outlet, and this almost led to another catastrophe – didn't it, Nev."

"You're kidding!"

I'd never seen Greg more serious! "I'm not kidding – Nev! Brent still had a remaining cherry stone on board, and he nearly took Dragan's eye out when his lower bowel gas – generated by the Black Beer and the smoked sausage-wrapped Scotch eggs – ejected the last stone. It hit him right in the corner of his left eye! . . . I mentioned that Brent had just recently been a virgin – didn't I, Nev?"

"Yes – you did."

Greg's face relaxed. "That meant that his anal sphincters hadn't been stretched too much, thus the velocity with which the cherry stone was discharged. So, that's why I mentioned that safety goggles are only recommended to *some* gay couples. The recommendation is only made to those couples where the recipient has only recently experienced being sodomised. Once a relationship has stood the vagaries of time, goggles are no longer required since the recipient's anal sphincters are too flaccid to engineer any velocity. That means that the only way a person – who is practising the anilingus – can get hurt is, by choking on a cherry stone that he might've inadvertently swallowed. . . I have to admit that working in with Dragan has been very worthwhile indeed! You should see what he's got planned if same-sex marriage *does* come in."

I found the possibility revolting. "It doesn't sound right, if you ask me."

"I feel obliged to agree with you, Nev," Greg put his shoe on his cigarette butt. "Nevertheless, people like Dragan are preparing for what looks like the inevitable, and so *we all* must. Especially with all the talk that's being going on in the Beehive about a 'conscience' vote. Not only that – you've got the political correctness that's taking over OZ. I wonder what happened to all the infamous Aussie ANZAC and Eureka Stockade spirit?... Never mind, it's people like Dragan who're preparing for same-sex marriage, and he looks like making a fair quid out of it. As I told you before, he's kept in touch with quite a few male gay couples who he's captured on camera. Especially those who've raised the question of marriage. Being the leader of a worldwide cult, he believes he has the powers to go as a celebrant for male gay ceremonies, though you'll come across those in the Beehive and upper echelons of the public service who wish to prevent that. Avril's one of them. I don't know if she suspects that something might be going on between Ken Mears and Dragan. The latter has visions of setting up special wedding and honeymoon packages for male gay couples, whereby he presides over the ceremony in the public toilet were they first met. The toilet will become like a chapel, so to speak. You can see where he's coming from since quite a few couples cherish dearly the moment and the place where they first met. He's also thought of employing mobile beds that can be wheeled into the same public toilet, and for an additional sum he'll be prepared to film them when they re-consummate the marriage. . . How's that for lateral thinking? It has to be on a par with '*Married at First Sight*' or '*The Bachelor*' – don't you think? Except his equation will have far more dignity than the other two programmes. No doubt you'll have the same amount of bonking, fellatio, and anilingus rather than cunnilingus, as the other programmes have during the honeymoon period, but at least Dragan's couples aren't going to be interviewed and asked about it in front of millions of viewers afterwards. . . While we have those who're trying to stop his plans, I've agreed to help him find a way round them. He scratches my back and I scratch his."

I was still confused. "What's it all in aid of? What's in it for you?"

"Do you remember me mentioning the huge fees to be obtained by sitting on the various committees the Labour Party's so infamous for?"

I sure did! "You reckoned that you usually charge twenty grand a day, but you cut it back to ten."

"True – I did, Nev. When that ape Peacock told you about networking, he certainly upped his game after meeting me. Five other personnel who're generally selected to attend committees are only present on account of yours truly. They give half their fees to me, thus I usually pick up forty grand or more per day. It's the same with Peacock and Helen. That's why these committees cost the taxpayers a fortune. My frog and snail caper was designed to initiate further committees, plus it allowed me to get closer to the PM. With the government being so broke, it was necessary to come up with something that harboured international ramifications. God knows where the PM and Treasury found the money?"

"How did you get on to all this?" I asked Greg as we were heading down to the Cook Strait ferry terminal the next day.

"Get on to what?"

"What you're doing here in New Zealand," I sought to clarify my query. "You're obviously making a poultice, and all the big knobs reckon the sun shines out of your arse."

"Why thank you, Nev!" he'd obviously been flattered by my last remark. "Let me see now – which is the best way to explain? I don't want to sound arrogant, but like your younger brother Trev – I've been very fortunate when it comes to having some appeal to the fairer sex.

. . When I last arrived here some years ago, I was hopelessly low on funds, nevertheless I still had the smart clothes you saw me wearing back in Kalgoorlie. Then again, the reason why I chose Poo Zealand as a temporary place of refuge – that bit of insurance bother back in West Aussie's sorted now – is because Mulji had set up shop over here. He supplied me with suitable accommodation and appropriate transport, while I scoured Wellington for opportunities. . . Tell me – what comes to mind when you think of the Beehive?"

I thought quickly. "The Beehive? That's where the politicians and government people meet."

"Very true, Nev, but for me the word 'Beehive' also conjured up delicious thoughts of honey and honey pots. . . At first it was my intention to seduce and move in with some female cabinet minister or a powerful civil servant, nevertheless – identical to what you'll find in most Western World countries – I was confronted by a horde of obese, ugly mangy dogs with breath only slightly better than your sister-in-law's. Party politics and the civil service in this place have attracted some of the mangiest, mouldiest specimens of female humanity that you wouldn't encounter even in your worst of nightmares. . . So the thought of rogering some of them obviously had bile burning the back of my throat – didn't it? You've met Helen Granite and Avril Dobson as a case in point. . . So I set up my HQ at the Domino and Spoon Tavern, which is just as popular with politicians and civil servants as the Backbencher Pub and Cafe which we visited yesterday in Thorndon. From that moment on I lay in wait for some hairy-legged bag of blubber to come along. You know, you could always tell which person had a high up job in the civil service because the more senior they were – the louder their mouths were. Also they were the ones who just loved flashing their department credit cards around for all to see. Especially from Friday lunch time onwards. The majority of them would be fairly pissed come three in the afternoon, and, if you listened carefully, you'd soon find out who was up whom and who was having to pay for it. I'm not kidding you – department expenses and perks – defence budget cuts

– and various government fundraising methodologies were discussed loud enough for anyone to hear. As it happened, Avril Dobson gave me my first real break. The reason for this was twofold. The day before I met her, I heard a couple of MPs from Auckland plotting and scheming against her. Apparently Ken Mears was siphoning off funds from one of the West Coast's largest charities. He most probably needed the money for paying the Indian bum boys that Mulji was supplying him with. Our Ken was also the second reason for why Avril should be looking over her shoulder. You saw how he can't handle his booze round at the Peacocks' place. Once he gets a gutful of grog, he can't help running off at the mouth about the scams he, Avril and Allan Peacock are into. . . Ye gods – it makes me nauseous when I think about it!"

"What does?"

His smile was wry. "You were sitting next to Avril. Didn't you notice something rather peculiar?"

An immediate answer came to mind. "She smelled like a dead roo that's been run over and left in the sun for a week back in Kal'!"

That caused him to grin. "That's putting it mildly – Nev! What with her having married a total dickhead, there was no problem getting her to follow me around to the Thorndon apartment that Mulji lent me. . . Look, I don't expect you to believe me, but after a brief sojourn with our Avril in the sack, I found at least five different types of vermin on my pillows and sheets afterwards! These varied from your run of the mill body lice, hairy maggots that were just about to sprout wings, plus the egg capsules of a *Blatella Asahinai*! Much to my absolute horror, I was confronted by..."

"The egg capsules of what?" I stopped him.

Greg's grin returned. "The egg capsules of an Asian cockroach. I immediately thought she might've bedded some Paki or a Sri Lankan, so you can imagine my further dilemma, even though I was reassured by the fact that a man from either of those countries would be far choosier. Not like some Tasmanian mountain men and foresters. . . Yes, I'm sure Avril showers and keeps her body reasonably clean – still those fecund, fetid, rotting dreadlocks make prime real estate for a host of creepy crawlies – don't they? Then, of course – and as you pointed out – we had the stench of dead bodies. . . So how do you roger a creature such as that? Normally I adopt the dog-fashion method with public servant women in order to avoid them trying to kiss me, plus the rancid breath, but with Avril that was impossible because I didn't want those dreadlocks anywhere near my most treasured asset. Then I thought of the missionary position where I could shove the dreadlocks well to one side, but then it would've been compulsory to cop her kisses, putrid breath and to see her green teeth. I was surely horribly drunk at the time because I allowed her to sit astride me, and the first item to swipe across my face were those dreaded – dreadlocks! How I didn't lose what I had for dinner – I *do not* know!"

"Bloody hell – Greg – you must've been fairly pissed!" I sympathised with him in order to get him to continue. "So did Avril introduce you to Allan Peacock?"

Greg had exchanged the Bentley for his Mercedes SUV, and he had no choice but to suddenly brake the latter in order avoid some bloke on a pushbike who was holding up an entire lane of the early morning traffic. One of those dickheads with all the bike racing gear on – helmet – skin tight outfit – special shoes – sunglasses.

"Yes, her introduction to Peacock was one of my biggest breaks," Greg continued, "although by then I'd managed to stitch up consultancy contracts with a number of politicians and senior public servants – both male and female. Actually it's amazing how some of your common folk put politicians on pedestals. So *what is* a politician, but an egotist and a yapper who *actually expects people to believe that* he or she has something to offer his or her electorate? From my experience both politicians and public servants are a self-serving bunch of liars and con merchants all out to pamper mammoth egos, and stuff their pockets and hand bags. They're not an overly intelligent lot, other than their rat cunning when it comes to trying to climb to the top of the shit heap. That's why there are very lucrative equations for those who possess only half a brain."

"How's that?"

"It's fairly straightforward, Nev. From what I've seen so far in this country, the primary aim of politicians over here is to last long enough to secure a full pension and all the travel perks etceteras that come with retirement. It's the same with the public servants, and the sole focus of these parasites is on outrageous salaries, luxury perks, expense accounts, plus superannuation and pension packages. . . And, of course, all these perks and pensions require an ocean of money – don't they? Money that has to be stolen off the rate and tax payers. You heard what that lower bowel bacteria Peacock said – the primary purpose of the public service is to think up more ways of taxing and fining the public. And we're not dealing with the brightest of specimens here – are we? You're not required to be all that intelligent to be a public servant, and that's regardless of your position or rank. That's why so much of the tax payer's money's blown on consultants such as myself. The first chore I was given here in Wellington was to work out novel ways of fining people, and I have to say I was an unprecedented success. . . When we stop, I'll show you proof of this."

About five minutes later we'd reached the Cook Strait ferry car park, and then Greg took some time sorting through his briefcase. Finally he produced a newspaper cutting.

WARDENS TOLD TO HIT 100 A DAY

The capital's parking wardens are encouraged to write 100 tickets a day, a former warden has revealed.

One senior warden told junior staff he ticketed his own mother $200 for no registration to raise his daily quota, while another was nicknamed The Terminator because he was quiet and quick, former parking warden Adrian Lubbe said.

The allegations come after The Dominion Post revealed this month that Wellington motorists had been stung with almost $10 million in parking fines in the past year, and some wardens had faced so much abuse that they quit.

The council said the allegation of a 100-a-day benchmark was "total nonsense" and issuing 100 tickets in one shift was difficult and very rare.

But Mr Lubbe said there was a handful of senior wardens who consistently issued 100 a day.

A warden in Christchurch said yesterday that anyone who issued more than 100 tickets daily had their names etched on a "high scorers" cricket bat. That was confirmed by Christchurch City Council, which said the bat featured the names of wardens who excelled in meeting "performance objectives".

The warden, who quit because he disagreed with the service's ethos, revealed there were monitors in the staffroom ranking the performance of each warden and who had issued the most tickets. "There's a culture of the more tickets you give out, the better warden you are."

The same warden, aged, 36, who worked for Parkwise for six months, said wardens were discouraged from issuing warnings – "the logic behind this is that if there is a problem let the `customer' – for want of a better word – write in.

"I don't believe that the job should be about [ticket] numbers. There's a good place for parking wardens, but ... they are not benefiting the public," he said. "As individuals they're really nice, but they really do train wardens to be cold and heartless."

Parkwise referred questions to the council. The council has consistently denied wardens were given quotas and says parking tickets are "not about generating revenue".

Wardens in Wellington issued 272,000 tickets worth $9.9m in the year to last June, $700,000 more than the year before. That is a daily average of 745 tickets worth $27,000.

The council contracts parking services to Parkwise, a subsidiary of Armourguard, which is owned by Tyco International, a firm registered in Luxembourg. The council refused to say what proportion of each ticket went to Parkwise because of commercial sensitivity.

A council infrastructure director said there was no "strict directive" about how many tickets must be issued and wardens were given some discretion.

But it was known how many tickets were likely to be issued in any part of the city any given day; wardens issuing consistently fewer tickets were scrutinised. "The wardens are not employed to come to work and sit around and do nothing."

PARKING WARDENS' SECRETS

* The best place to send the fastest wardens is to the streets around Wellington District Court because hearings regularly go overtime, so even those who have fed the metre can be caught unawares.

*Parking areas near or adjacent to hospital emergency departments are also very lucrative because people are more likely to be disorientated if they have family or friends needing emergency care.

* During university exams, two parking wardens should be sent to the Kelburn campus to ticket students parking in two-hour spots for three-hour exams.

* Rather than just writing tickets as necessary and appropriate, a target should be set in each category of ticket. Many more $40 dollar tickets should be issued rather than $12 tickets in any month. We need more $40 tickets.

I was a bit suspicious of Greg's yarns when it came to scorning the Kiwis, but the article certainly didn't do them any favours. "Fuckin' hell – what kind of prick would fine his own mother just to keep up with his quota?"

Greg laughed at that. "That just describes your average bongo in a nutshell. I couldn't've done better myself."

"And you reckon you thought up all these different ways of fining people?"

"Yup! It wasn't all that hard. My favourite one was the District Court setup. You get some poor joker being fined *inside* the court house by a magistrate, and then you get a traffic warden fining him on the *outside* of the same court house. Like I said – you only need half a brain and you can be a much sought after consultant here in Wellington, and you'll have plenty of politicians and public servants deed keen to pay you for your services."

"So how's your new Department of Inner Health going?"

"Swimmingly – Nev – swimmingly! We have a great deal to discuss with Trev."

HERE ENDS THE FIRST OF THE TRANS TASMAN SCROLLS.

www.ingramcontent.com/pod-product-compliance
Lightning Source LLC
Chambersburg PA
CBHW030550180626
46816CB00005B/1481